Praise for
The Thing About Home

"In this zippy outing from McKnight (*All She Dreamed*), a humiliated social media influencer rediscovers her roots . . . McKnight lays out some vivid low country history, and her fully realized characters—especially Casey and her sometimes superficial, sometimes serious trials—ring true. This is perfect for fans of Natasha D. Frazier and Pat Simmons."

—PUBLISHERS WEEKLY

"*The Thing About Home* is a beautifully written story about family, self-discovery, secrets, and forgiveness. It is a truly wonderful and most enjoyable read!"

—KIMBERLA LAWSON ROBY,
NEW YORK TIMES BESTSELLING AUTHOR

"Rhonda McKnight has written a gorgeously vivid, heartfelt novel that stirred my emotions from the first page. I loved getting to know the characters and wanted to stay in their lives forever. Through a dual timeline, parallels in the women's stories were expertly delivered in contemporary and historical voices that will have readers exploring their own lives and legacies. I tried to slow down as I came closer to the last page because I didn't want this book to end."

—VICTORIA CHRISTOPHER MURRAY, NEW YORK TIMES
BESTSELLING AUTHOR OF THE PERSONAL LIBRARIAN AND
NAACP AWARD-WINNING AUTHOR OF STAND YOUR GROUND

"Southern writing at its best, *The Thing About Home* is a warm, atmospheric reminder that *home* is more than just a physical place—it's family and friends and safety and unconditional love."

—EMILY MARCH, NEW YORK TIMES BESTSELLING AUTHOR

"In *The Thing About Home*, Casey Black's shiny world of New York fashion and always-on social media implodes. Finding her roots allows Casey to heal and calm the chaos that has consumed her life. In *The Thing About Home*, Rhonda McKnight pens a safe place, a Lowcountry boil that's soup for the soul. Expertly weaving a dual storyline of a rich matriarchal past with the tumultuous present, McKnight builds upon her women's fiction repertoire with a fresh perspective on grief, forgiveness, and finding oneself in the midst of the storm."

—VANESSA RILEY, AWARD-WINNING AUTHOR OF
ISLAND QUEEN AND *QUEEN OF EXILES*

"In *The Thing About Home*, Casey Black's perfect life has just crashed and burned, forcing her to seek refuge in South Carolina. Ms. McKnight does an excellent job exploring not only what coming home can represent, but also the importance of family history and legacy. The reader is not only given a captivating story but also a lesson in life. A well-written exploration of love and acceptance."

—JACQUELIN THOMAS, AWARD-WINNING AUTHOR

"Rhonda McKnight has written a story chock-full of Southern comfort. It reads like a Lowcountry recipe that's seasoned with just the right amount of family, love, history, culture, and self-discovery. As her characters become deeply rooted in culture, you'll find yourself longing for the same connection to home."

—TIA MCCOLLORS CROSS, BESTSELLING AUTHOR
OF THE *DAYS OF GRACE* SERIES

"You will get lost in this book. Every moment, every step that Casey takes to finding herself is magical. Rhonda McKnight is a masterful storyteller. Hands down, *The Thing About Home* is the best book I've read in a long time."

—VANESSA MILLER, AUTHOR OF *THE LIGHT ON HALSEY STREET*

The Thing About Home

the Thing About Home

A NOVEL

RHONDA McKNIGHT

THOMAS NELSON
Since 1798

The Thing About Home

Published in Nashville, Tennessee, by Thomas Nelson. Thomas Nelson is a registered trademark of HarperCollins Christian Publishing, Inc.

Thomas Nelson titles may be purchased in bulk for educational, business, fundraising, or sales promotional use. For information, please email SpecialMarkets@ThomasNelson.com.

Library of Congress Cataloging-in-Publication Data

Names: McKnight, Rhonda, author.
Title: The thing about home : a novel / Rhonda McKnight.
Description: Nashville, Tennessee : Thomas Nelson, [2023] | Summary: "A disgraced social media star flees to South Carolina's Lowcountry in search of refuge and connection to the family she's never known"-- Provided by publisher.
Identifiers: LCCN 2022048668 (print) | LCCN 2022048669 (ebook) | ISBN 9780840706324 (paperback) | ISBN 9780840706324 (epub) | ISBN 9780840706324
Classification: LCC PS3613.C56817 T55 2023 (print) | LCC PS3613.C56817 (ebook) | DDC 813/.6--dc23
LC record available at https://lccn.loc.gov/2022048668
LC ebook record available at https://lccn.loc.gov/2022048669

Printed in the United States of America
23 24 25 26 27 LBC 5 4 3 2 1

For my ancestors:
Elijah McKnight/Louisa Thames McKnight
and Anthony Gibson/unknown
Eddie McKnight/Francis Gibson McKnight
Jimmie L. McKnight
&
Bessie Kennedy McKnight
John Kennedy/Laura Wilson Kennedy
Downing Kennedy/Katie Kennedy and
George Wilson/Francis Wilson

Black Family Tree

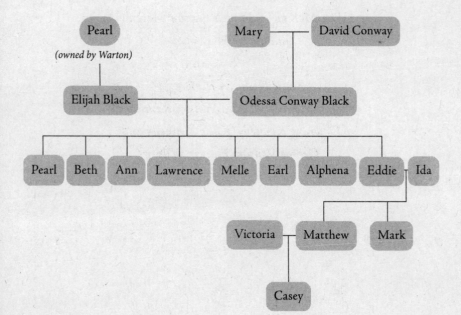

Conway Family Tree

Bishop Conway was set free by his father Hugh Conway at age 13. He purchased his mother Sara and his half-siblings (Isaiah, Ruth, and Luke) and owned their families.

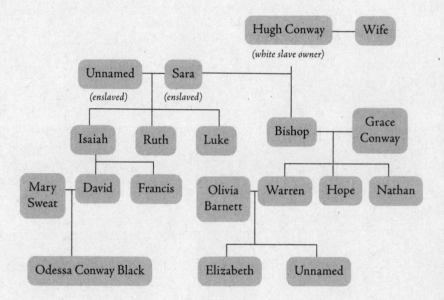

1

I STEPPED INTO MY LIMOUSINE AND PRESSED THE BOTTOM of my wedding dress flat. The scent of coconut and lemongrass filled the interior of the cabin. I imagined if cream and sunshine had a scent, this would be it. Today, I needed aromatherapy to do what it was supposed to do—relax me.

"Congratulations on your wedding." The driver offered me a genuine smile.

"Thank you. It's a vow renewal ceremony." I hunched my shoulders like an excited teenager. "Seven years."

"That's a lot to be proud of. He's a lucky man."

Drew and I were both lucky. That's what I'd told myself just this morning, but still an uneasiness rose in my belly and formed a knot dead center. Something was bothering me, and I couldn't put my finger on what.

A lingering shiver died in the heat of the warm vehicle. I dropped into the plush leather seat and pushed the niggling thought of worry from my mind.

Heaven.

I closed my eyes and moaned like I'd taken shoes off after waiting tables for twelve hours. This car was everything.

The door opened again. "I have your bag." My assistant, Swella Avery, was gifted in assisting.

I opened my eyes and squinted against the sunlight gleaming over Swella's shoulder. "As soon as I get back from my honeymoon, you are getting a huge bonus."

Swella's green eyes bugged like glassy volcanic rock. Her luminous, spiked red hair shot out like lava from a recent eruption. "Please let it be enough for the new Valentino jeans."

I laughed. "Done. Now, don't text me. Don't call me. Don't anything me. I need a few minutes of peace."

"Peace is yours." Swella poked her head in and inhaled demonstratively. "I didn't overdo it with the spray, did I?" Not waiting for my answer, she snatched her head out. "We'd better get going." She waggled her shoulders and reminded me, "It's almost over." With a shove of the door, she disappeared. I was sure she was just glad to get this day ticked off her to-do list. It was seven months in the making, and I'd been running her all over the city.

Guilt rushed in. I could have let her ride with me. That's what she'd wanted. That's what the whole "I have your bag" intrusion was about, but I didn't owe her a piece of my space. Not today. I wanted quiet. I wanted to be alone with my thoughts.

The car rolled forward, moving effortlessly through my Park Slope neighborhood, past Prospect Park on the left. I watched the tops of bare trees fly by. A light coat of ice from the sprinkling of snow we'd had the day before decorated the limbs. I was hopeful they would have leaves soon. A month ago, the groundhog forecast an early spring, but he was unreliable. New York winters submitted to no authority, certainly not one steeped in superstition and regulated by a rodent.

My phone buzzed. Expecting it to be Drew, I warmed a little around my heart. He hadn't texted or called me since early this morning. We weren't in "new" love, but I expected a little excitement and romance.

The text was from my mother: Don't be late.

"As if," I whispered, deleting it. I was thirty-six years old, and I'd never been late to any meeting or event in my life. My mother's lectures on timeliness were repetitive and exhausting, yet effective, so I was grateful for her consistency.

I swiped until I located my husband's number and tapped to dial. After two rings, it went to voicemail. *He's busy.*

That's what I told myself, but a strange tension hovered in our home, one that I summarily dismissed as prerenewal stress. But try as I might to ignore it, my intuition kept nagging in a familiar female voice—my own—that something was wrong, or maybe it was that something was worse. Things had been off between Drew and me for a long time. But in forty-five minutes, we'd declare our love, celebrate it, and then fix whatever might be broken under the warm Hawaiian sun.

I raised the phone, twisted my face into that dumb duck-lip, and captured my image. Humming to lyrics playing in my mind, I typed the caption: *I'm at the chapel and I'm going to get married.*

Minutes later, with the help of the driver, I eased out of the limo and joined my part of the wedding party, which included my maid of honor / cousin / bestie, Leslie Parker, and my former supermodel friends, Alexis and Reese. All but Swella, who I'd treated to a black and crystal-beaded Carolina Herrera suit, were wearing form-fitting, off-the-shoulder, silk sage dresses under faux fur shawls that matched the fur wrap keeping me warm.

"Let's get a pic," Swella suggested, and the women I loved flanked me and posed with enthusiasm and bright smiles.

Waving us toward the building, Swella led our small party through the packed parking lot. The cars were all empty. Everyone was inside. It hadn't snowed or rained as predicted.

I silenced the annoying little voice *again*. It was a liar. Today was going to be perfect.

～

Twenty minutes later, the annoying little voice could no longer be ignored. This wasn't a wedding, but I'd told Drew I didn't want him to see me until the ceremony, so when he knocked on the door of my bridal suite and insisted I join him across the hall in the pastor's study, the hairs stood up on the back of my neck.

The heavy door closed with a *thud* that echoed in the corridor behind us. I waited a beat and then another as Drew stood there in his luxurious Giorgio Armani tuxedo—the tuxedo I picked out for him.

Discomfort reddened his face. He looked away from me. When he returned his eyes, his expression was odd, so I steeled myself for what he had to say.

"I can't go through with the ceremony."

Drew's brittle words floated above me. They wouldn't land in my brain, but I registered fear. It slammed into my back. Splitting me in two: Casey ninety seconds ago and Casey now. Those were two different people. Both were residing . . . fighting . . . attempting to survive this hack job.

I didn't know what else to say, so I said words that forced him to repeat himself.

"You heard me, Casey. I can't go through with the ceremony."

In my choice of two-and-a-half-inch heels, I had to look up at Drew. I usually wore higher heels, but I'd wanted him to tower over me a bit. His height would play into my viewers' fantasies. A tall, dark, and handsome man never got old, so his looks were a part of the fairy tale I was delivering today. The one he was . . .

Canceling?

No!

The heat kicked on with a knock, sending a flood of warm air from the vent above. Drew's earthy cedar cologne mixed with the damp scent reeking from the air vent, offering the odor of sweet, wet wood. It made me nauseous.

In this small pastor's study, there wasn't much space between us, but I stepped closer to him, laughed uncomfortably, and said, "Of course you can."

My words were solid, but my footing was not. The plush, spongy carpet in this room made me bounce. Between the flooring and Drew's statement, I was shook. We were hashtag relationship goals.

"No. I can't, and there's no point in you making me say it over and over again."

Wishing and hoping I'd heard him wrong was over. His *can't* whirled around in front of me like a swarm of gnats. This was all convoluted. This was all wrong. I sputtered, stating the obvious, "I've planned this for months."

I was Casey B, a successful beauty influencer—makeup, hair, and fashion. This wasn't an ordinary ceremony. It was a public one. As in nearly-a-million-views-just-this-week kind of public.

Drew and I had originally eloped. When I shared our sweet story in a video, it was comments from a few of my followers that sparked the idea to have a vow renewal ceremony so I could have an actual wedding with a dress and pictures and all the fanfare that came with weddings. This event was personal, but it was also a part of my business. We'd both lived, breathed, and eaten it for . . . "Seven months, Drew."

He clenched his jaw, ticking his mouth slightly to the right. "Is that what you're most upset about? Your time?"

I tried to tell myself I was shocked, but I wasn't sure it was true. The voice in my head had been warning me for weeks. I cupped my hands together in front of my waist. "At what point did you decide . . ." I paused, taking a deep breath to push the nausea that crept up my throat back into my belly.

Drew sighed dramatically, bothered before meeting my eyes with cold, detached ones. "I'm not renewing our vows." My heart skipped a few beats before he added, "I want a divorce."

The room spun. If I had a crank in my belly, my stomach couldn't churn more. Discomfort rose in my torso to my chest and spread from the center to my shoulder blades.

My eyes burned, but I fought crying. I couldn't let tears ruin my makeup.

A rattling series of knocks on the old wooden door caused me to jump. Drew and I broke eye contact. Seconds later, Swella stuck her head around the doorjamb before easing her body through the small slit she'd allowed herself to have.

"Mr. Carter." She smiled. Why she always called him that when he was simply Drew, I didn't understand. She continued, "I guess it's not a bad thing for the groom to see the bride at a vow renewal." She giggled. At twenty-two, if you weren't giggling, you were living life all wrong. But I had nothing to laugh about, so Swella had to go.

I returned my gaze to Drew. With my eyes, I asked the question weighing down my tongue: *Are you really going to do this?*

Drew's lips thinned. His Adam's apple rose and fell. A wordless tilt of his head was his answer.

He's doing this.

"Swella"—I slid my eyes in her direction—"we need more time."

Swella's smile dropped. She was intuitive. Her job included anticipating my needs and reading my moods. She'd spent enough time in our home, heard enough arguments, survived enough his-and-her bouts of the silent treatment to know the energy in the room was off. She backed out. "The camera crew is on the clock." I could hear her clicking heels fade as she disappeared down the hall.

The cameras.

The ceremony was being livestreamed on my platforms. The team I was working with for a documentary about social media influencers was gathering photos and video. So were various beauty magazines and a producer from Born TV network. The producer was hunting footage for a potential reality television series about my life as a former model turned influencer. This had to happen. I wouldn't recover from the humiliation of a canceled ceremony.

I raised one hand to my pounding heart and pointed toward the door with the other. "Did you hear that, Drew? There are cameras out there."

Drew stuck his hands in his pants pockets. He looked up at me with the saddest eyes I think I'd ever seen. "There are always cameras. That's the problem."

Dismissively, he turned his back. I grabbed him by the arm. "You're not going anywhere."

Drew did a half turn in my direction, his eyebrows knit together, and he pulled his elbow from my grasp.

I didn't perspire easily, so when the long trickle of sweat traveled down my spine, I knew my subconscious was fully aware of what my conscious mind was fighting. The man standing before me had been checked out for months. But when exactly had he stopped appreciating what I did? When did the cameras become too much? We both knew his work as a civil rights attorney was more important than mine, but we also knew my work paid the bills. My business afforded him the luxury of following his passion. He couldn't resent all that I'd built. Could he?

"We are *not* getting a divorce. Come on, Drew. Seven

years . . ." My attempt at levity failed with the fear that caused my voice to crack. "We *are* renewing our vows."

Deep grooves furrowed his forehead. He squared his shoulders. He didn't answer me.

I continued, "Let's say for the sake of argument, you want to separate while we figure some things out. You know this event is bigger than whatever is wrong with our marriage." I raised a hand to my forehead. "Please, we can go to counseling. We can fix this, but not if you do this today. Not if you destroy me like this."

"I thought if I got dressed, I could go through with it, but I can't make myself stand at that altar and say, 'I do.' Not to you. Not again." He paused for a moment and took a few steps back—strategically distancing himself from my pain. "I'm tired. I can't live in front of the cameras anymore."

I inhaled and exhaled before doing a slow count to five. Something in me thought I could change his mind. My husband was reasonable. He *could* be reasoned with. "Drew, I've been in this business since we got married. You encouraged me to do it."

"I encouraged you because I didn't know how toxic it would be. I didn't sign up for life on social media."

I raised a hand to my chest. "You signed up for me."

"Not like this." He had the nerve to be losing patience. I could hear it in his voice. "I told you that."

I bit back the impulse to scream. My mind went back to the conversation we'd had a year ago. Drew expressed bother about the number of hours I worked. My response—I was still building, trending upward in my numbers past my competition. I'd had offers for a sunglass line and a makeup line. Per my mother, the contracts weren't good, but it was just a matter of time before the right offer would happen.

We'd talked about my work, so this made no sense. I pushed his voice out of my head. I tried to pace in a tight little circle like I always did when I was stressed. I learned to move in a small space when I modeled because small spaces were all I had in the dressing rooms. But my train wouldn't permit me to move freely. It was long and heavy like the anger rolling through me. "How could you tell me you want a divorce like this—on this day?"

Silence hung between us for a few moments. I had no idea what he was thinking. He wasn't readable, but he had to realize I was right, and he was wrong—right? He had to know he couldn't blame this all on me.

"You work constantly. And when you're not on your phone, you're putting on makeup or changing your clothes to get in front of the camera." Drew took a few more steps away from me toward the window he likely wanted to escape through.

"So you couldn't have interrupted me and said, 'Hey, wife, I'm unhappy. I'm having second thoughts'?"

He responded as if he hadn't even heard my question. Like he had no responsibility to ring the alarm. He turned and looked at me again. "When you're not doing all that, you're talking about it. Planning it. Staging it." Drew pulled his tie loose. "This makes me a jerk. I know that."

"'There are more than two hundred people in the sanctuary,'" I howled like a hurt animal. I had three million followers across my platforms. This event belonged to them just as much as it belonged to us. Hot tears burned my eyes. There was no coming back from this. I'd hate him forever.

Drew stepped to me. He placed his hands on my shoulders. "I thought if I just got here, I could go through with it. I thought I could look at you and say, 'I do,'" he said, still defending his betrayal, "but I can't."

I opened my mouth to say one more please, but I knew in the millisecond before I moved my tongue not to bother. There was nothing in his eyes.

The heater buzzed and another *whoosh* of air carried his cologne to my nostrils. It faded quickly, just like his image as he turned and backed from the room, dragging every bit of who I was with him.

2

I DIDN'T MOVE FOR A LONG TIME—FIVE MINUTES, TWENTY minutes, or maybe an hour—I wasn't sure. When you get blindsided, you just don't know.

The door opened without a knock, and even though my back was to it, I knew only one person in this spot who would take entry, and that was my mother. "What are you doing in here? Why aren't you with your girls?"

My girls. I'd forgotten about them. Gripping the sides of my dress, I turned in my mother's direction. "Drew left."

My mother shifted her weight from the left to the right as if fighting to keep her balance. I'd done the same thing to her that Drew did to me—sucker punched her. She grimaced and pulled her head back. "What do you mean he left?"

Suddenly, I was tired. Seven-months-of-planning-and-shopping-and-sharing-on-social-media tired. "He's gone. He's not going to marry me."

"What am I missing here? He's already married to you!"

Finally, I moved. I moved from my position in the center of the room to the nearby desk. I leaned against it at first and then resigned myself to sitting. I needed to get off my feet. I was tired of bouncing on the carpet. "Mom, those are semantics. He's not going to do the ceremony. He wants a divorce."

My mother's eyes bugged. The last time I'd seen her look like that, I was sixteen years old, doing a photo shoot in Paris. An older model pulled my blouse, exposing my bra. My mother's eyes had nearly come out of their sockets. She'd leapt on the stage and snatched the model so hard, the woman's shoe shot like a missile across the room. I hadn't seen that look in twenty years. "When did he leave?"

She always had to have the details. If she didn't have the deets, she couldn't assign blame. "Fifteen or twenty minutes ago. I don't know. A long time ago."

"Why didn't you tell me so I could stop him?"

This time I was the one grimacing. "Stop him from what?"

"From humiliating you." My mother's disappointment was palpable. "Do you have any idea where he would go?"

I stood, reached for the clips at my hip and unhooked the train. I rolled it into a ball and tossed it onto a chair. I dropped back against the desk. "Maybe home. I don't know."

"He wouldn't dare go back to the house." She took out her phone.

I blinked. "Who are you calling?"

"Drew. He can't be far."

Drew wasn't going to answer the phone. In this heated moment of hurt, my mother was the last person my husband was going to want to talk to. As expected, she got his voice mail.

She left a tempered message. "Drew, you need to come back. Whatever you two have going on, you can either try to work it out with some counseling or something like that." She paused, raised her eyes to mine, and continued, this time offering a concession. "Or if you feel like you just can't work it out, you can ask for a divorce tomorrow, but you cannot do this to her. This is unfair. Call me. Let me know that you're on the way." She sat in the pastor's chair.

A few minutes passed. My mother released a long sigh. She knew what I knew. Drew wasn't coming back to this church.

More minutes passed with my mother back on her feet, pacing. I busied myself, scrolling through the comments on my social media. There were thousands of them.

> @YourGirlCaseyB You're a late bride. I thought you said you
>   weren't going to be late.
> @YourGirlCaseyB Can't wait to see you.
> @YourGirlCaseyB We're waiting. I know you're going to be
>   beautiful.

I pushed the button to close the screen.

My mother stopped. She raised an index finger. "We need to flip this."

My mother could give a master class in management. She'd more than successfully managed my career from the time I was two years old—from the first disposable training pants commercial and the hundred that followed, to my second career as a plus-sized model. I wasn't really a big girl. I was just too big for a size six, and at five-eleven, size eight was on the chunky side for modeling.

"We'll say you called it off." Reading my mother's expression, I could see she thought it was a good idea. It was not. She must have read my face, because the next words rolled out of her mouth in a pensive tone. "Let him look like the one who was left."

It was me who sighed this time. The ridiculousness of the suggestion was unlike her. Like me, Drew had her shook. "I can't do that."

"Why not?"

"Because for one, no one will believe it. I've been doing videos all day."

My mother's frown implied stupidity on my part. "You can explain that away."

"And for two"—the heat in my voice shut her mouth— "people will find out it's not true."

"How? This was a conversation between you and Drew. You told him you didn't want to marry him, and he left. You thought recommitting would save your marriage, but you realized once you put the dress on it would not."

Hot tears threatened to burn my eyes as Drew's words came back to me.

"I thought if I got dressed, I could go through with it."

I suppressed irritation. She hadn't stopped talking. I caught the tail end of "You convince the world that you want the divorce, not him."

I pushed off the desk. "That's insane. I can't lie about something like this. Our friends and family are out there."

My mother rolled her eyes. "No one has that many friends. We couldn't find fifty people related to us if we won the Mega Millions lottery."

The words *whose fault is that* rolled around in my head, but this wasn't the time to discuss how we didn't fool with our folk. There were other relatives on my mother's father's side, but she stopped talking to her father when he left her mother when she was a teenager—or maybe the real story was he stopped talking to her. In any event, he died when I was a teen. My mother had a weird relationship with family period, and she wanted me to have the same. She'd spent the last seven years dismissing the Carters as my family. It annoyed me to no end because they'd always been sweet to me. I hadn't seen as much of them in recent years, big

14

holidays being the only time I could spare, but still, marriage connected us. "Drew's family is my family."

"We'll see what that looks like after today." My mother rolled her eyes so hard, if she wasn't careful, she would need to see an ophthalmologist soon.

"You. Can. Blame. Him, Casey." Each word came off her mouth like individual little sentences. She was insistent, but she was wrong.

"Drew will tell his side of the story. Who knows who else he's already told?"

My mother stomped a foot, which meant she was ready to fight me on this. "It's your word against his. He's not the one with the followers." She reached into the pocket of her Chanel dress and removed a cigarette case and lighter. I thought she'd quit last year. She turned her back to me while she lit and inhaled. It was like she didn't want me to witness the first hit of her addiction.

"You're not supposed to smoke in here."

She inhaled and blew a long, uncaring plume away from me.

She paced and smoked, all the while banging her fist against her thigh. "This is so typical of Drew," she said. She meant: *This is typical of you.*

I took it as she intended—personally.

"*Casey, don't marry beneath yourself. That's a mistake a lot of beautiful, intelligent Black women make.*"

Why did she have to be right? More importantly, why did I have to be wrong?

My mother took another drag off her cigarette and blew the smoke out. She stopped moving. I saw disappointed realization in her eyes. "We can't say you want the divorce. His prenup is written on a paper napkin from the Diamond Parrot Hotel."

My wedding was unplanned. Drew and I flew to Key West.

We eloped in front of an internet-certified officiant on a Blue Marlin fishing boat. If I'd ever done anything cliché in my life, it was that. Once we got back to New York, my mother insisted he sign a postnup. I had money, and he swore he had no interest in it, but he was only going to let my mother instigate so much. The terms were loose.

My mother was on the move again. How she walked so steadily on the carpet, I had no idea, but she seemed to move in concert with it, like a trapeze artist on a tight rope. "We're going to sue. You'll have every dime he'll ever earn by the time we get finished with him."

I was still processing the idea of divorce. "Sue for what?"

My mother cocked her head and sputtered, "Oh, my dear daughter, what won't you sue for? A good lawyer will calculate and manufacture losses that occurred today. Drew is going to wish he'd stayed." She stuck the cigarette back in her mouth, looking at me as if she dared me to protest a lawsuit.

The wedding itself cost a fortune. Most of it was sponsored, but I was still out of nearly $70,000. Then the TV show money came to mind. Surely, Drew considered the losses there—or had he been acting purely from a place of hurt and disappointment?

My mother's next question sliced through my sorrow. "Are you sure he's not cheating?"

My first thought was no, but then, "I don't think so. How would I know?"

"How would you know?" My mother guffawed. "You're supposed to be paying attention to your marriage. That's what married people do."

"And what would you know about paying attention to a marriage?" Like a child expecting to get hit, I closed my eyes. I could feel her making steps toward me. I opened my eyes to her pissed-offedness. I was sorry for that statement, but I was under a lot of pressure—more than she was.

"I know what I've learned in books and on *Oprah*. You chose to marry him, so you should have been keeping up."

I wanted to match her snark, but all I had was the pitiful insistence that I had not failed. "Contrary to what's happening right now, I think I've done a decent job of keeping up with Drew." I wrung my hands and then twisted my wedding ring on my finger.

My mother walked to a nearby table and dropped the cigarette in a cup of water on a side table that appeared to long have been abandoned. "We need a plan."

Before we could come up with one, there was a knock on the door. My mother rushed to snatch it open. Swella, flanked on the left and right by the wedding planner and the wedding coordinator, stood there. I glanced at the clock on the wall. We were more than a half hour past the time I was scheduled to come down the aisle.

"Drew is sick," my mother offered before they could ask. "We're waiting on him to get himself together."

Swella's eyes met mine. Before, she'd suspected something was wrong. Now she knew for sure. She said something to the women, and they went back down the hall. My mother held the doorknob so tightly Swella had to push a little and slide through the small opening to get to me. "Is there anything I can do for you?"

I raised a hand to my temple and rubbed. "I could use some water," I said. "And my bag."

She left the room and was back in less than a minute with both. She cracked the lid and, with a trembling hand, placed it into my sweating palm.

Swella's lip quivered on whispered, knowing words. "What do you want me to do?"

How I wished I had a task I could assign her, but there was

nothing to do here. A choice needed to be made. Either I was going to walk into the sanctuary and tell those people my husband had abandoned me, or I was going to punk out and let my mother handle it. I slid my eyes in my mother's direction. She managed me, my life, my money. And she would manage this. "Nothing." I smiled tightly, reached for her hand, and squeezed it. "We just need a few more minutes."

"Do you want Leslie? She's been keeping the other girls occupied."

I shook my head. "I'm texting her."

Swella blinked nervously, backed to the door, and left the room.

I sent Leslie a text: Drew is gone. I need you to keep everyone in that room until I leave.

Minutes ticked by. My mother sighed. "There's no point delaying this. I'll announce the wedding is off. I'm not going to offer an explanation until you figure out what you want to say."

I nodded. We were finally in agreement.

"It'll be okay eventually." My mother's smile did not reach her eyes. "Most women have had their hearts broken. They'll empathize with you."

I bounced back a few feet, picked up my bag, and walked out the door behind my mother. There came a fork in the corridor— one led to the sanctuary, the other to the lobby. We paused briefly, our eyes locking in the way they always did when we had a problem my mother had to fix. Over the years there were many— business and personal problems. She was my fixer.

Her mouth twitched. I wasn't sure if she was going to smile or frown, but then she did neither. Wordlessly, we went our separate ways.

The limo was where I'd left it. I pulled the door handle before the driver could exit, threw my bag inside, then after gathering my skirt, I slid across the smooth leather seat.

"Where can I take you?" I hadn't noticed it before, but now that I needed comfort, I noticed his voice. It was soothing and warm.

I caught his eye in the rearview mirror. He knew the wedding was off. I didn't want to see pity. He was kind enough not to express any. Where do you go when there's no place you want to be—in a wedding dress with no groom? My phone vibrated. I didn't have a great signal in the church, so for the most part it had been quiet. It vibrated again and again. I removed it from my bag. I had sixteen text messages. Already.

I opened one from Leslie: Where are you? Let me help.

Leslie texting meant my mother's speech was finished, which meant my nightmare was beginning. I sighed and looked toward the entrance of the church. The doors opened on both sides. With military precision, two ushers assumed their posts and the first of the guests spilled out of the building.

I returned my attention to the man in the rearview mirror and forced myself to speak loudly enough for him to hear so I wouldn't have to repeat myself.

"Take me home."

3

I BOLTED UPRIGHT. PANIC COURSED THROUGH MY NERVES. MY heart was pounding double the normal number of beats per minute. The alarm on my phone squawked at ten decibels. I reached for it and silenced the reminder to change my meal plan order for this week. Pausing deliveries was on Swella's to-do list because I was supposed to be going on a second honeymoon. I hated that it woke me because now I had to deal with my life.

I sighed and swiped at my notifications. Two hours had passed, so the number pending was insane. I went to my Instagram page where the real drama awaited. Pain gripped my throat before my eyes got teary again. The last picture I'd posted was of me waiting for the wedding to begin with the words:

Hair. Check. Makeup. Check. Dress. Gorg. Finally. Forever
   Again.

I dropped my head and rolled my shoulders. A solid ache inched its way up my neck and over the top of my head. I didn't get headaches. I had to be miserable all the way down in my cells for one to work its way up from the dark place headaches came from. I hadn't had one in almost a year. Not since my last miscarriage.

That was the last time I'd lost something that mattered. Then, it was my baby. Today, it was my marriage.

The marriage that began on a whim seemed to end the same. Or had Drew been planning to do this to me? Faithful, reliable Drew plotting nastiness, cruelty, irresponsibility—my hurt. I couldn't imagine a scenario in which that was the plan my husband had in mind. Then I remembered his words: *"I thought if I got dressed, I could go through with it."*

Not a plot or plan, but a decision made after he'd gotten dressed, made somewhat on a whim. He hadn't really thought it through at all. He couldn't have counted the cost to my brand. Drew wouldn't ruin me this way.

I swiped my phone and opened a message to him and typed: Why didn't you tell me how you felt?

My finger hovered over the send icon for a moment. What was I expecting him to say? Could he possibly have an answer that would make me feel better? Didn't I already know? Faithful, reliable Drew hated conflict. That's why he hadn't moved up at his firm. He was lousy at managing bad news.

I pushed the app for Instagram. My comments section was insane—140,000 within hours was high, even for me.

@YourGirlCaseyB What happened?

@YourGirlCaseyB Keep your head up.

@YourGirlCaseyB Forget him. I'm DMing my number. I'll treat you right.

@YourGirlCaseyB This is why you should keep stuff private.

@YourGirlCaseyB I heard you got jilted. Who gets jilted by a husband tho?

I crumbled inside. Who gets jilted by a husband? If you'd asked me last week, I would have said, "No one," but here I was, blazing a trail not made for wedding shoes. Drew wanted a divorce. Not a separation. An entire divorce. I was still trying to process what was happening in my brain.

The ragged nerves in my head and heart pushed pain sensors simultaneously. My dry throat made me aware of the wine bottle I'd brought to the bedroom when I dragged my sad self into bed. I reached for it and turned it up to my mouth.

Empty.

No wonder I'd fallen asleep and no wonder I had a headache. I returned it to the nightstand, careful not to knock over the frame I kept there—a honeymoon picture. It was one of those cheesy instant shots you took in resort photo stations. The kind they hoped you'd overpay for.

The camera caught Drew and me just as I'd turned my head to him. I remember he'd said, *"I'm never going to love anyone the way I love you."* I'd smiled, but the camera caught me just before, right at the beginning of the smile where my lips were about to open. The love in my eyes was real because the love in my heart was the same.

Sure, I'd eloped because my mother wouldn't approve. Flying away and doing it in secret was an act of rebellion. A way to take control. I had to establish myself as an adult, one way or another. A marriage to someone who would clearly have something to say about my life other than her seemed like a great way to communicate that at twenty-nine I was grown—even if it was ten years late.

My mother had diagnosed me with depression. As my mother, she didn't have to study psych to determine such. She had a master's degree in me. How many times had I heard that over the years? I'd lost a contract with Fly Girl Cosmetics. My days on the runway were long over. She couldn't get me booked for anything other than catalog work. I should have been too young to even be considering retiring from modeling, but I wasn't white, which meant there were always fewer opportunities. I hated that. I loved modeling, especially print work, because there were lights, camera, and action. The camera always held my interest. I hoped to be behind one someday.

Maybe I was a little depressed. Whatever was going to be next was scary. Change wasn't a thing I was ever ready for, mostly because the only changing I'd ever really done happened in a dressing room. I'd transitioned through life seamlessly with my mother's instructions, from commercials as a child to editorial modeling as a young teen, and then commercial modeling as an adult. My mother had been my anchor through it all.

When she threw the anchor overboard, declaring I would not do plus-size catalog work, I was done with modeling. I did a few commercials, auditioned for a couple of movie roles, but I wasn't serious about acting, and the casting folks could tell. I wanted to keep modeling, but my mother insisted no self-respecting model went from editorial to commercial to catalog. She'd been turning down work for me for months without my knowledge, declaring, *"We'll figure out something else for you."*

I resented her for making the decision without me. Hence, Drew. Throwing a man in the middle of a relationship that had never had so much as a serious conversation about a man before gutted her. She'd never forgiven me for it. But I didn't care. I was in love.

Drew had caught my eye at a birthday party. Leslie's current man, Robert, also an attorney, treated himself and a bunch of friends and coworkers to dinner at happy hour at The Strong in Soho. Leslie and Robert were new, so she dragged me with her. Leslie paired me with Drew for a game of charades. I hated charades because even though I was graceful, I always felt too big to play. I wasn't like all the other girls. My arms and legs were long. They felt overwhelming most of the time, even to me. But Drew's height—six foot five by my estimation, and right on as I learned later—made me feel comfortable. I could be my tall, long self with this fine-looking stranger.

"I'm Drew Carter." His optic smile lit his coffee-brown eyes, and a tiny flutter filled my belly. "I'm really good at charades."

He was right. I'd later find out he was good because his family—parents and siblings and many cousins—played at Sunday dinners and during the holidays from the time he was in diapers. When we won, and he asked me for my number, I thought it'd be rude to steal his joy by saying no. He called the next day. And the next. And then we met for dinner and lunch and breakfast and coffee and anything we could meet for every day for months. We couldn't get enough of each other. Thoughts of him filled the hours work had filled since I was two years old.

I knew when he asked me to go to Key West that he had marriage on his mind. Not because I was particularly insightful about these things, but because I'd gotten a heads-up. Swearing her to secrecy, Robert told Leslie. Leslie, being loyal, told me.

Just like in the movies, under the stars at the beach, he got down on one knee and asked me to be his wife. It was my idea to elope.

Drew laughed at first, and once he realized I wasn't laughing with him, he asked, "Are you serious?"

He stood and swept me off my feet, once again making me feel the right size in his arms, and I replied, "Of course. Why wouldn't I? You're perfect."

So we made plans not to leave Florida without being man and wife. Casey Carter had a nice ring to it. A ring that was as beautiful as the one Drew slid on my finger.

I had my next act, and I hadn't needed my mother to figure

it out. I was a wife. I'd become a mother. I had no regrets. I was happier than I'd been in years. Drew adored me. But the babies, they didn't come because when the pregnancies did, they didn't last.

I killed a strangled wailing sound in my throat, but I couldn't stop the tears from spilling. I needed more wine. If I was going to have to be awake, I was not going to do it sober. Not with Drew's words squatting in my memory.

"I thought if I got dressed . . ."

Those words lingered like the pain from a stubbed toe. He made it sound so difficult and, in the end, found it impossible to do. There were many times I'd felt sick or just plain tired, and I remembered my mother saying, *"Get dressed and see how you feel."* I always felt better once I had clothes on. Drew had gotten dressed today. He was in the building. He stood inches from me, made me beg, and still, he wouldn't.

Where was that man on the beach? Where was the man I could always count on to make me feel comfortable? The man who made me feel like I fit? I ran my hand over the comforter on his neatly made side of the bed. If actions spoke louder than words, I had my answer.

I left the bedroom, went down the stairs straight to the wine rack, and pulled another bottle. This time I grabbed an architecturally perfect goblet to improve my experience. I really didn't know much about wine. I'd never been a drinker.

Drew's love of wine and all things wine related required me to at least act interested. One of the first things he'd taught me—glass matters. Big glasses for aroma and flavor and small glasses for intensity. Tonight, I fashioned both an aromatic and intense experience by guzzling two large glasses in quick succession. Then I poured a third. I took that one a little slower. I was already feeling like trash. I had no idea why I thought drinking would make it better, but in a mind-and-senses-numbing kind of way, it did.

With Drew's favorite Barski Swarovski goblet in one hand and the half-empty bottle in the other, I traveled back to my bedroom—back to my noisy phone.

"No point running from your fans, girl," I whispered as I opened Instagram.

> @YourGirlCaseyB Please update us. We're concerned about you.

Concerned about me? That comment roused the stink face. "Right. You're nosy @IGbinger."

I raised the glass, missed my mouth, and a trail of burgundy liquid ran down the front of my dress clear to my waist. "Darn it." This dress was supposed to be for my future daughter.

I judged myself for fantasizing about a daughter. I no longer had a husband, and when I did, I couldn't carry a baby. Hysterical laughter threatened to explode from my gut, but I strangled it—held it down. There wasn't a thing that was funny—not even in an ironic what-the-heck kind of way. But I did need to get out of this dress.

On wobbly legs, I made my way to the bathroom. It was a massive combination of tile, marble, and glass that still managed to impress me every day. People lived in studio apartments that were smaller. Real estate like this was hard to come by in the city, even on the outskirts.

I caught my image in the mirror. Mushed hair, smudged makeup, wine stain, and all, I still looked beautiful. *YourGirlCaseyB* was beautiful. That was a fact. And this was supposed to be *her* special day. Drew was supposed to be helping me out of this dress. Being alone right now was surreal. It was a nightmare that I, Casey Carter, had to wake up from.

My phone pinged again, this time with a text message from Drew:

> Would you make a statement on your social media? People are commenting on my work pages.

I frowned. Was he out of his mind? Was I supposed to say something that would save him from the world? He should have anticipated this backlash.

I texted him back: So now you want me on social media?

Fresh tears threatened to spill. I scrolled back through the many other text messages. I had at least two dozen from friends and a few family members. My mother, my staff, even my gynecologist was checking on me.

I dialed Leslie. She answered so fast I thought she might have been calling me at the same time.

"I've been worried about you." I could hear the ache of stress in her voice. "Are you okay? You want me to come over?"

I shifted my weight from one foot to the other, wobbling in the process. I struggled to get my footing, like I was still bouncing on that carpet at the church. "No. I have a headache. I took a nap, but I'm going back to bed."

Leslie grunted—surprise, pity, concern? I wasn't sure. "Do you have food?"

I thought about my packed refrigerator, full of leftovers from our small rehearsal dinner. The wedding planner had ordered too much, more than twice what we ate. "There's plenty."

"I went to the reception for a little while. Your mother asked me to help her."

What a gossipy dinner party that must have been. I didn't want the details, but I needed to move our conversation along. "Was the food good?"

"I didn't eat. I couldn't . . ." She paused, and I could see her shifting in my mind's eye. Leslie always moved when she was uncomfortable with a conversation. "What can I do?"

"Nothing." I spun to face the mirror and removed my earrings.

"What are you going to do?"

I frowned at my reflection and Leslie's less-than-clear question. "About what?"

"Drew. Your social media."

She was sounding like my mother, but she was nothing like my mother, so I didn't mind talking to her about it. I shook my head as if she could see me. "I don't know. I need to make a video."

"You don't owe anyone a video." Leslie's declaration came quickly. "But I think an announcement about the ceremony being canceled would be good. Swella can do it."

Swella was good, but she was not me. Her words would not be mine unless I dictated them to her, and if I had to do that, I could write the post myself.

"Case?"

It was me who grunted this time.

"You should call her. She's dying to come over there. You know how she is. She's freaking out."

This conversation was making my brain tired. First Drew, then my followers, now Swella's need to fix things and confirm she'd fixed them. "She's sent me a bunch of text messages."

"Answer her," Leslie pleaded. "Let her help you."

My throat thickened with sobs. I grabbed a handful of tissues and pressed them against my face. "I'll call her."

Leslie's words came from a swollen heart. "Are you sure you don't want me to come over?" When I didn't answer, her tone became lighter. "I could pick up a white pizza with a ton of extra cheese."

I chuckled over the knot in my throat. "I love you, but I just want to sleep off this day."

A wind of disappointment flittered through the speaker before she offered, "Hugs, girl."

Glad she surrendered easily, I said thanks before ending the call.

I gazed in the mirror.

This is what rejection feels like.

I focused on my reflection. My tears dragged mascara down my cheeks.

And that's what it looks like.

I looked at my text messages again. Drew still hadn't responded. I wanted to fight with him. He apparently didn't want to fight with me.

As if she was demanding attention, my phone pinged in a new message from my mother. She'd be good for a few heated words, but I never won with her. I'd lost enough today.

My mother: I'm leaving the reception. I'll be there soon.

Me: Please don't come over here. I want to be alone.

My mother: Are you alright?

Me: I'm okay. Just tired and embarrassed. I'm going to bed.

The best decision I ever made was not giving my mother a key to my house. Drew had insisted I not, which bugged me, but now I was glad she didn't have one.

My mother: You should make a video. Be transparent. Young women can learn from you.

My thoughts went from annoyed to curious. *Learn what?*

Reading my mind, she added: Hurt happens to beautiful people too. That's a powerful message.

I didn't reply.

My mother: It will work. Pivot. This is a moment.

It was about the angles. Always. The woman never stopped working. Never stopped planning. Never stopped branding. I hated that about her, but hadn't Drew said the same about me?

The extra phone I used for recording makeup videos caught my eye. It was still on the tripod. Maybe my mother was right. I could make a message for my followers that would matter. I turned it on and went to my Instagram page.

Before I changed my mind, I picked up the remote, pushed the Live button, and waited. My Wi-Fi wouldn't connect. The universe was trying to help me, but I wouldn't hear of it.

<hr />

Five minutes later, my image came into view. I looked weary and worn, but I wasn't going to be vain about it. Being transparent was the point right now. A red circle blinked and then fixed solid. The word *live* popped up in the upper left-hand corner of the screen.

"Hey, family. It's me. Casey B.

"I know you're like surprised, right? Casey B's vow renewal a fail. The world is going to hear the deets from me first. My husband left me." I said the words matter-of-factly, but my heart was heavy. "Like how did this happen? I do not know." I chuckled sadly, nervously. "I'm as shocked as you are. I had no idea that the man I was married to would do something like this to me. But you know what?" I paused and stepped back so I was centered on camera. Getting in frame was my special gift. "We're not focusing on him. This is the Casey B channel. We're focusing on me. And I'm here to tell you, I'm going to be all right. Husband or no husband. I'm good. Because this Black don't crack under pressure." I chuckled again, this time less painfully and leaned closer to the phone to read. "Let me see what you're saying."

I swiped the screen. The comments moved so fast I could barely keep up. I greeted a few of the people I knew—mostly other influencers and celebrities I was connected to.

@YourGirlCaseyB I'm sorry.

@YourGirlCaseyB You look beautiful.

@YourGirlCaseyB Can I have the dress? I'm getting married next year.

I chuckled at that and replied, "@Regina_StayinAlive, did you just ask me for my dress? Girl, this thang ain't got a speck of good luck on it."

I stepped back. Humor waned quickly as sadness returned. Before I knew it, my eyes filled with more tears. "You know what? I'm going to be honest. I came on here to try to give a word of encouragement to someone else, but I'm angry right now. I'm hurt. I don't deserve this. He didn't have to do me like this."

@YourGirlCaseyB Get out of that dress. You'll feel better.

"You're right, @Brownsugagirl5810, I will feel better."

I looked down at the stained dress, then up at the camera. "I got dressed with you guys. Seems only fair to get undressed with you too."

I reached up, unpinned my tiara, and placed it on the counter. "This thing survived a whole nap without moving. It wins the award for the best accessory. Shout out to the designer."

I reached behind myself for the buttons on the back of the dress. Tall girls had long arms. I was able to undo them myself and tug the zipper down. The dress buckled and slipped from my shoulders. I read more comments.

@YourGirlCaseyB Have you talked to your husband?

"I have not. I'm not ready right now."

@YourGirlCaseyB I'd kill my boyfriend if he did that to me.

"I hope your man never does this to you." The dress hit the floor. I was standing in front of the camera in my bra, waist trainer, and a crinoline slip.

On some level I knew I was going too far, but I made an excuse for it. "You've seen me wear less at the beach." With a heavy *thud*, the trainer hit the floor. "I'm hurt. I'm disappointed. You hear me out there?"

Silence came back. They could only type comments. I was alone with my hurt and disappointment. These people weren't my tribe. Leslie and Swella were. I should have let them come over, but it was too late. The camera was rolling, and I was a finisher. All videos were a story that had a beginning, middle, and end.

I peered in the mirror. My face was a smeared mess. I walked closer to the phone and angled it the way I did when I was applying makeup.

"You guys know my honeymoon tickets are to Hawaii. You were supposed to go to Kauai with me."

@YourGirlCaseyB Still go. Make it a girls' trip.

"A girls' trip? Sounds cool. I'll think about it." I turned on the faucet and wet a cloth with warm water and held it against my face for a few moments. Nothing but makeup remover was taking this airbrushed mess off. Tears blurred my vision as I searched the counter for it.

Where was it?

My phone rang in a call. I recognized the ring tone as my mother's. I pressed Ignore and waited for the text message.

Are you insane? You have on your bra and a slip. Turn off
that camera.

I rolled my eyes. *You are not the boss of me.* I got into this mess
of a day by myself. I'd get out of it by myself. I moved on to my
hair. I pulled one of my extensions until it came loose. Once I had
a few free, I held them in front of the camera.

"I hate these things. Who did I get them from?" I looked at
the phone for replies. These people kept up with everything I
sponsored.

@YourGirlCaseyB You got them from a struggling hair artist
who sacrificed to send them to you.

I snorted as I dropped them on the counter. "Well, they
suck."

@YourGirlCaseyB Now you're hating them. You liked them
when you were giving us your affiliate link.

I frowned. I was the one who'd been jilted today. "Okay,
you don't have to get nasty about it. I mean they're just fake
hair."

@YourGirlCaseyB It's somebody's business. Someone who
doesn't have all the followers you do.

"You think having followers makes me special? Look at me. My
husband left me today."

That statement caused a burst of hearts. My tears blurred the
comments, but I kept reading . . .

@YourGirlCaseyB You think you're better than everyone else.
    You deserve it.
@YourGirlCaseyB Sorry for you, girl.
@YourGirlCaseyB I guess beauty ain't everything.

I raised a hand to my head. It was pounding, and these people were coming for me like I did something to them. This was not how the video was supposed to go.

@YourGirlCaseyB You spend too much time on social media.
    It's not good for a marriage.

I rolled my neck. "Hey, this being on social media is my work. It's how I pay the bills."

@YourGirlCaseyB Maybe you need a new career.
@YourGirlCaseyB Maybe you can sign up for the Housewives.
    Half of them don't have a husband either. ☺

This shady chick had the nerve to put a smiley face on the end of her comment. I tried to laugh it off with a reply: "I don't think reality TV is for me."

@YourGirlCaseyB @Pressandcurlgirl is right. Social media
    and marriage don't mix.

My followers could barely blend eyeshadow. Now they were all relationship experts. The energy I'd been pushing down in my belly for weeks rose in an explosive burst of anger. I raised a finger and pointed. "Don't come on here with all that. You don't know anything about my marriage. You don't even know anything about me. None of you do. You think you know me because I make videos every day and talk to you. This isn't real. None of it."

@YourGirlCaseyB Your husband leaving you hanging was real.

@YourGirlCaseyB We love you. Ignore the haters.

@YourGirlCaseyB Don't let 'em see you sweat.

@YourGirlCaseyB You gettin' a little out there, girl. You might want to get off camera.

@YourGirlCaseyB Stupid attention seeker.

More hearts filled the screen. What were they hearting me for? Why were they enjoying my pain? Who called me an attention seeker? I tried to focus on the name, but the comment was gone. They were coming in with lightning-fast speed.

@YourGirlCaseyB You need to get off the camera.

@YourGirlCaseyB You made this hard bed you're lying in.

@YourGirlCaseyB Your husband never looked cool with being on camera with you. I'm not surprised.

I snatched my head back. "You're not surprised? You get the gold star for knowing him better than me."

More tears threatened to fall. These people who loved me were turning on me.

Just like Drew.

Hearts filled the screen in an explosion of bright pinks, yellow, and blues. Ordinarily, the admiration was wanted—beautiful— evidence of success, but not tonight. I was grieving, and they were giving me hearts. This was fake love. They didn't care about me. I knew that, but the alcohol made the heat of it rise to my chest like fire.

> @YourGirlCaseyB Girl get off the camera until you fix your
> face.

"'Fix my face.' This was the worst day of my life, and you want me to fix my face?" I snarled. "That's rich."

> @YourGirlCaseyB I'll be back when you have something to
> show us except drama.

Oh really. She had some nerve. A little explosion in my heart fueled more temper. I stepped closer to the camera. I'd had far too much wine. No one could tell me I wasn't bigger and taller than the three hundred thousand people viewing, so I emotionally challenged them to the fight I wanted to have with one man—Drew.

His name echoed inside my pounding head. I couldn't make Drew answer for his behavior. I reached for my phone, scrolled through the messages, past my mother, Leslie, Swella, and other friends. Drew hadn't answered my last text. He wouldn't accept my rage. I looked at the video and directed it at them. These makeup- and fashion-hungry women were the reason my husband was gone.

"You know what? This is trash. You're all trash." My nostrils flared. I was a bull, and every comment and heart on my page looked red. "I'm tired of trying to be everything to you people. You don't have a life, so you sit around and watch mine. So now what? My life has fallen apart. What you gonna do now? Figure out your own stuff." There were more hearts. I didn't care what the comments said. "I'm done. I'm over needing to be everything to you. I'm not here for your entertainment. Not anymore."

And to make sure they really got my point, I rolled my neck and stuck out my tongue—hard and long—before ending the video.

Satisfied that I had gotten them straight, I dragged myself out of the bathroom and crawled into bed. Shoving the pillows off Drew's side, I rolled midcenter into the mattress and fell asleep to the sound of my phone pinging and my heart breaking.

4

—

I FORCED MY EYES TO OPEN AND THEN SQUINTED AGAINST the sunlight streaming into the room through a rebellious mini blind. I rolled over, and I screamed when I discovered I wasn't alone. After which, I fell out of the bed backward.

My head. I held the sides with both hands. Thank God I hadn't hit it. It was aching enough.

My mother stood. "Are you all right?"

All right? I'd fallen out of bed. No. I was not all right, and now I didn't even have privacy to be un—all right. I pulled myself up off the floor. "What are you doing here?"

And then my brain ticked through a list of last night's events:

Drew.

No wedding.

Drinking.

An ugly video.

Nausea made me unsteady on my feet.

I covered my mouth and dashed into the bathroom. I barely made it before emptying my stomach into the toilet. My mother followed. My eyes traveled up from her Christian Louboutin heels, along the length of her silk crepe pantsuit to her fully made-up face. She flipped a damp fingertip towel toward me. I wiped my mouth.

"You've made a mess, Casey." I knew she wasn't talking about the vomit, but I depressed the flusher anyway.

I crawled backward to the wall and raised my knees to my chest. Hot tears wet my nose. The salt mixed with the cruddy taste in my mouth. "I didn't ask you to come over here."

"You got half-naked on social media and told off your followers. Over a sorry . . ." She let the curse word die before continuing, "Over Drew, and you'll soon realize he was *not* worth it."

"You never liked him." My voice trembled on every word.

My mother was genuinely confused. "What does that have to do with what you did to yourself last night?"

"Your voice has been in the back of my mind for this entire marriage: *He's not good enough for you. He's doesn't make enough money. Casey, you could have done better.*"

Why was I blaming my mother?

"You don't think you could have done better than someone who would treat you the way that man treated you yesterday?"

I banged my fist on the floor and cried, "Oh God, Mom, you've done what you came here to do. You gave me your 'I told you so,' which you're always good for, so now will you just leave and let me be sick in peace?"

Our eyes locked, and I held her stare. She sighed and relented. My mother picked up the towel and tossed it into the hamper. She squatted in front of me. "You have an eyelash that needs to come off. It's driving me crazy." She raised a clean towel to my face.

I took it from her. "I'll do that."

"And is that what you think of me? That I would come here to say I told you so?" She rolled her eyes and stood. "I'm here because I'm concerned about you."

I pushed myself to my feet. "I'm not going to go back on social media."

"Well, I'm not leaving you alone. You need to shower and eat something."

"Please tell me it's not your intention to stay all day."

"No. I have a meeting with Isis in a few hours. We're prepping for her meeting with Gucci."

My mother's newest protégé, Isis Ashe, was a stunning, six foot two, Kenyan, Lupita Nyong'o look-alike. She was destined to eclipse every model on the runway this fall, especially with my mother representing her. I knew well what she could do.

"Leslie is on the way. You shouldn't be alone."

I gripped the edge of the counter and fought what I really wanted to do right now, which was cry. "But I want to be." My voice squeaked on the last couple of words.

My mother stepped closer. "No, you don't, and I never should have left you alone last night." She pulled me into her arms.

I pushed away from her. I couldn't ruin her suit.

She reached around me, grabbed a towel, and tossed it over her shoulder like she was receiving a baby.

"What am I supposed to do, Mom?"

My mother's hesitation sent a shiver down my spine. "I don't know, baby, but we'll figure it out. We always have."

~

I was one of the headline stories on *Entertainment This Weekend*. I'd watched others grace their program during their rise or fall, but tonight, this three-minute segment was all about me.

"She's lost a million followers overnight," the news commenter said. "Beauty and fashion influencer Casey B had a meltdown on one of her social media pages last night. The former model stripped, and this is what she had to say to her followers."

The video clip of me raging played. The screen froze on me with my tongue out.

"Ladies and gentlemen, this is what it looks like when social media fame goes wrong."

"I have a hashtag. #KickedtothecurbCasey was trending last night."

Leslie winced. She was in the sixth hour of indenture to me. We'd eaten the omelets my mother made earlier and now moved on to a pizza. I'd never eaten more than two slices of pizza in my life, yet I was working on my fourth. We'd posted a written apology to my followers on all my social media pages. She'd done her duty. "You should go home."

I picked up the remote and pressed Play and then Pause. My distorted image froze again. Smeared mascara and lipstick, tongue out. A wine-stained dress in the background.

"The tongue was a nice finish," Leslie said.

I shrugged. "You know me, it's all about the story. I was going for the childish effect." I looked at the television screen. I'd been successful. I'd been awful.

"Don't scream," Leslie hesitated warily, "but your mother made me join her for a conference call with a brand management agency last night." She bit her lip like she always did when she didn't want to say something. "They handle crisis management."

I let that sink in. "What did they say?"

"All publicity is good publicity. That pointing attention to your mental health would be a good way to go with this," Leslie began. "Did you know just this year the World Health Organization added burnout to the ICD-11?"

Leslie sounded like she was reading off a PowerPoint presentation. "What's the ICD-11?"

"The International Disease Class . . . something. A book that lists what's a real disease or disorder."

I stood and paced around my space enough to work up an attitude. *Mental health? Were they serious?*

Leslie attempted to calm me with a cautiously raised finger. "No one is saying you're crazy."

I pointed at the TV screen. "That's not the least bit crazy looking."

"Being vulnerable is fashionable these days. People respect it."

"But it's a lie. I'm not sick."

"No, but you are a woman who's overworked, stressed, and distraught over the end of a seven-year marriage. It's many women. It's many of the women who follow you, and it's certainly the teenagers who could use a *real* role model instead of a perfect one."

"So you think it's a good idea?"

She feigned innocence and nonchalance with a shrug. "I don't think anything. I'm just telling you what was discussed."

"I was angry last night." I dropped the remote. "Angry at Drew. Angry with myself. Angry at those stupid hearts." I pushed deeper into the sofa.

Leslie took the remote and turned off the TV, effectively removing the frozen news story about me. "Let's not even talk about it."

And we didn't. Not for a few days. Everyone checked in by FaceTime or text. Then Leslie was at my door again. This time with Swella.

Over Jamaican food, we settled in the big, comfortable, overpriced beanbag chairs in the den.

This was also the room where I kept my house plants, which included a number of bonsai, ZZ, jade, peace lily, aloe, red coral, and the most interesting, a corkscrew Albuca. I moved from pot to pot, watering my babies and whispering sweet words to them like I always did. I swear these plants loved me back. It was a good thing, because my husband didn't.

It's just us, little plants.

I didn't dare say it out loud or Leslie would be bringing up the ICD book again. I put my water can down and plopped onto my beanbag. The sign over the plant wall caught my eyes. It was an anonymous quote carved into a piece of wood: "Happiness blooms where seeds of love and joy are planted."

I could keep these plants alive, but I hadn't managed to plant seeds of love and joy with my husband. Was I wrong to be owning this failure like it had been mine alone? What had Drew planted and watered?

"Have you talked to Drew?"

I swear Leslie was psychic, or maybe she followed my eyes to the wall and figured I was bemoaning my situation. "Not a call or text." I picked up my plate and fork. "And I told him I would never forgive him if he walked out of the church. I guess he took me literally."

"Did you mean it literally?" Swella asked.

"Of course I did." But he still should call. He should care enough to check on me. I'd gone viral. Ruined my brand—the thing he claimed had destroyed our marriage—and still, he hadn't called me. How was that possible? And I was waiting to hear from him. I kept checking my phone for his regret, apology, or something. He was a ghost.

I remembered Drew's eyes. *"I thought if I got dressed . . ."*

"Brooke Harris called," Swella interjected.

I was glad for the change in subject, but Brooke wouldn't have made the top one hundred list of situations I wanted to talk about. Brooke was the one making a documentary about my life as a social media influencer. She'd chronicled my story from the very first commercial I filmed, interviewing people from my past—agents, bookers, makeup artists. She had pictures and video footage from my modeling days—behind-the-scenes stuff my mother captured with her video camera—and of course she had the last seven years—my very first social media live video to the last one. I was no Chrissy Teigen in terms of numbers—few influencers were—but millions of followers was rare in this business. I'd achieved it—one video, one photo, one carefully crafted sentence, hashtag, and emoji at a time.

"I've told her you're away," Swella added proudly.

"You probably should take a spa holiday or something," Leslie said.

"I need a real break, not a holiday." I sat forward. "You know I've already worked for thirty-four years." We were all quiet for a moment before I added, "I saw a commercial last night. It was about those ancestry kits. They can tell you all kinds of stuff about where you come from—genetically. I was thinking I should do one of those."

"I took one," Swella said.

Both Leslie's and my eyes fell on her.

"I thought you all knew where you came from," Leslie said.

"White people do ancestry. They're the ones on the commercials." I pursed my lips before adding, "And Swella is adopted."

Leslie's hand went to her chest. She looked like she wanted to suck her words back in. "Why don't I already know that?"

"It's not something to put on a T-shirt." Swella hunched her shoulders. "Anyway, the ancestry thing was cool information."

"Well, you don't need one," Leslie started. "I can tell you what you need to know. You're Black mixed with Black."

I smirked at Leslie. "I want to find out what part of Africa I'm from and go there. Maybe I can travel for a while. I could do like the pray, eat, love woman. You know, like the movie with what's-her-face."

"Julia Roberts," Leslie replied.

"I've never heard of it," Swella added.

"Google it." I pointed at her phone. "I could travel the continent."

"Of Africa?" Leslie chuckled, dismissing me for silliness. "You've never talked about going to Africa."

"Don't all Black people want to visit the continent at some point?"

"No. All Black people don't have Africa on their bucket list." Leslie rolled her eyes at and away from me before giving me the courtesy of eye contact again. "And no offense, girl, but you are the last person I'd ever expect to hear wanted to go to the continent."

Leslie never meant harm, but it bothered me to no end that she was trying to dismiss my Black experiences as if I hadn't lived my entire life in this brown skin. The modeling industry was ripe with racism. I'd dealt with microaggressions from designers and models. Especially models. Some of them literally hated that they had to share a picture or a stage with a Black girl, and then there were those who were so ignorantly obtuse they gawked at me like I couldn't be real, saying dumb stuff like "You should lighten your skin," which would promptly get a response from me that since I was the closer for the show, they should consider darkening theirs.

These issues weren't exclusive to modeling. Some of the brands I'd worked with as an influencer emphasized that they wanted bone-straight hair for the video, with requests to Swella like "Please tell her no plumping lipstick," because a white girl could have big lips, but a Black woman had to minimize hers. And then finally, there was the ultimate insult, "This isn't an urban ad. We need good diction," as if a graduate of Lancaster Preparatory Academy spoke anything else.

My diction wasn't the problem. What they wanted was to not have to deal with the diversity campaign at all, because they couldn't get a vision for their product in the hands of Black women.

Swella raised her phone. "I recognize her from the Lancôme commercials."

God forbid Julia Roberts' prestigious career as an actor ever be reduced to perfume ads, but that's what happened to women. We age and become famous for the last pretty thing we did or the last ugly thing. Currently loading for my legacy was a makeup-smeared video of me raging. I sighed.

Leslie rolled her eyes at Swella. "Julia Roberts is a goddess. When you get home tonight, watch *Pretty Woman* and then watch *Erin Brockovich* and stop being so criminally early twenties about everything."

I chuckled inside. "Swella is here to be young, and I so appreciate it." I looked at Swella's face and smiled. "Ignore Leslie, but do watch *Pretty Woman*. It's a classic."

Swella nodded sheepishly. "Okay."

We were quiet for a while. The sun had gone down on the city a long time ago. Darkness hung outside the wood blinds, and a sliver of moonlight peeked through the top half of the slats.

"I think . . ." Leslie broke the silence. Pacing her words, she said, "You don't have to go all the way to Africa if you want to get to know who you are. You've got relatives right in South Carolina that you don't know anything about."

She was talking about my father's family—or possible family if there was any left. "I wouldn't know where to begin with that."

Leslie released a strained plume of air and flopped back in her chair. The topic of my father's family had come up before. "Ask your mother."

All I knew about my father was he grew up in Georgetown County. After college, he'd joined the army and met my mother at a party at Fort Monmouth in New Jersey. They got married a few months later. They'd been married for only three months when they traveled to his hometown. During the visit, he'd been killed in a car accident. He hadn't even known she was pregnant. I had my birth certificate and a picture of the two of them.

"She's not going to tell me anything."

"You have a right to know about your father's people."

I considered it. It wasn't the first time I'd considered it. It came up in conversation with Drew several times. He was close to his family, and while he didn't judge me, he'd hoped I'd take the time to explore it all. I never did. I'd been too busy. "I could hire someone to do a search. I thought about that once, but then . . . I don't know, I let it go."

"You don't need to hire someone." Angling her head sideways at me, Leslie said, "Go to the county registrar and the archives or something. Find the Blacks. Make finding them a part of the journey."

I looked in Swella's direction. She shrugged. "It sounds like more fun than spitting in a tube and waiting for an email."

"And there are real people on the other end. Not just a report with percentages," Leslie added.

Visit Georgetown, South Carolina. I let it sink in. After a few minutes, I sat up—as straight as you could sit in a beanbag chair.

"You're right. I'm going."

5

I LOOKED AT THE SUITCASES I'D PULLED FROM THE CLOSET. I was chickening out. I was also obsessing over the fact that Drew hadn't called me.

Bile rose in my throat at the thought of him. Seven years of my life wasted. Isn't that what most divorced people thought? You put pictures away, you split friends and family, you had to compartmentalize a good portion of the time you spent with someone because there were emotions and hurt feelings. Would I feel that way?

I just didn't know. I didn't know anything right now except he'd asked for a divorce. I needed a conversation about this. We couldn't just divorce each other without talking.

I'd been lying around in less-than-attractive clothing for days. Because it made me feel confident, I put on my favorite Ivy Park running suit, a hat, and the biggest shades I owned and went to Drew's office building. I stood near a large plant in the lobby. I didn't want to talk to anyone Drew worked with, but I had to keep a keen eye out. There were almost a thousand people in the building. The six elevators dumped them out ten to twelve at a time. Wading through faces got old fast, so I decided to go to his floor, but just as I rounded my hiding spot, he stepped out of the elevator with a few colleagues. I followed them out of the building. Drew parted from them and headed in the direction of the garage he'd been parking at for years. I called his name.

He turned. He seemed stunned, like he never thought he'd see me again, but he looked just like he did every day. Tall, handsome, clean-shaven, well-dressed Drew Carter. He showed no visible signs of trauma or wanting. There was no evidence that his life had been turned upside down.

"Casey." His chest rose and fell, releasing a long, exasperated breath. "I'm sorry. I know I should have . . ." His words trailed off.

"Called? You should have called every day. Drew . . . what is this?"

"Are you still coming?"

The voice came from over my shoulder. A female one. I turned to see one of his coworkers, an attorney I'd seen at a party or two but never met, standing there like she was more important than me. I observed her for a second. She was tall and slender. Her hair was cut in one of those bobbed styles 50 percent of all the female lawyers wore.

I cut my eyes back to Drew. "I'm leaving town for a while." I had no idea for how long I was going, but a while seemed to pique his interest. His eyebrows shot up.

"Really? Where?" His voice carried a hint of excitement. Could we not reside in a city as big as New York? He looked over my shoulder. I craned my neck to see the woman shockingly had not left us. "I'll meet you." He returned his attention to me. I heard the clicking of her heels as she receded.

"Georgetown."

He mulled over my words like his brain was a computer doing a search. I could see the results of his mental query in his eyes. "Isn't that where—"

"My father's family is. Yes."

"Wow. That's good." He stepped forward and placed a hand on my shoulder. "Really good, Case."

He was behaving like I'd told him I was going to rehab. Was this his secret dream for me? That I'd get in touch with my roots like he'd been suggesting I do all these years? I shrugged out of his grip. "Don't you miss me? You can't tell me things were so horrible that you would let all these days go by without checking on me."

He swallowed. "I hurt you. I know that. I've been a coward about calling."

A coward about calling. Not a coward about coming home. I'd told him I'd never forgive him, but looking at him now, I wasn't sure that was true. "What are you doing? Where are you staying?"

He closed his eyes and reopened them. I saw empathy in them—or maybe it was pity. It was caring—I knew that. I could still read him.

As predicted by the weatherman on the radio not even an hour ago, a shower of soft, quiet rain began to fall. It soaked into the shoulders and lapel of his tan trench coat, leaving small dots. Drew hated being caught in the rain. Me not so much, unless I was concerned about my hair getting wet. But I had a feeling getting caught in it today would set the scene for one of the saddest moments in my life. The moment my husband rejected me. Again.

"Casey, go to South Carolina."

Drew had already cut into me with the sharp knife of rejection, but he'd just turned it. He was glad I was leaving. I could see it in his eyes. "Why did you really leave me?"

"I told you."

"No." I shook my head. "You didn't."

"I told you, I couldn't say 'I do' again." His grip on his briefcase got tighter. "I have to go. I'm first chair on this case—"

I turned in the direction of my car and forced my feet to

move without letting my wobbly legs give out on me, eventually picking up my pace until it was a jog. We'd had conversations about my social media before, but Drew wasn't a man who just ended things. He didn't have that kind of temperament. He eased into things and eased out. This breakup was too abrupt. There was something I didn't know.

"Casey!"

I ignored him as I crossed the street and headed to the garage where I'd parked and retrieved my car. The image of him standing in the rain was exchanged with the one of him walking out the door in the church. I kept my emotions together as long as I could, then the raindrops on the windshield triggered the tears in my eyes and made the trip home more regretful than I imagined it ever would be.

There was nothing keeping me in New York right now. Georgetown, a city I'd never been to, held more promise.

6

CHOOSING TO MAKE THE TWELVE-HOUR DRIVE TO SOUTH Carolina instead of flying was one of those decisions to be filed under seemed-like-a-good-idea-at-the-time. People did it in movies all the time. Long car rides were supposed to be soul-inspiring experiences littered with quirky, potential-serial-killer-like characters and questionable diner food. I couldn't think of a better way to begin my little journey of self-exploration, but by the time I got down I-95 in Maryland, a voice inside of me screamed that I was in way over my head.

Maryland's traffic was thick and obtuse, even on a Sunday morning. All these people couldn't possibly be going to work or church. This was almost as bad as New York.

I'd received a phone call from my mother, which was customary on Sunday mornings. Sunday mornings were her time to reflect on the week, and reflection usually included shining a light on my life. I declined the call, opened Settings and went to Location Services, and turned it off. She would not be tracking me.

With a few taps on the volume button, I pushed thoughts of my mother out of my mind and replaced them with Beyonce's *Homecoming* album. It would carry me through this mayhem called an interstate. I exhaled and pressed my back into the leather seat. My hands played a game with the steering wheel, my fingers opened and closed around it, sliding from two and ten to six and eight and back again.

I turned the heat on and then off. I cracked the windows and put them back up, over and over. I couldn't get comfortable. It wasn't the car or the temperature but the very skin on my body that I wanted to crawl out of. I was one of those people who hated showing up at people's houses unannounced, so my anxiety was getting the best of me.

My mind wasn't on this road though. My thoughts were a million miles away. The image of my father was dancing before me, and I wondered if on some spiritual plane he could see me now, driving toward his family home. Would he be proud that I was finally going or disappointed that it had taken me so long?

My eyes stung a bit—they always did when I thought about how I had to grow up without him. How he'd never even laid eyes on me once. It was so unfair. I'd never been able to reconcile how little sense it made.

I was halfway through Virginia before I stopped. Neither I nor the car could go another mile on empty. There were no five-star hotels on the exit, but I found something passably rated with a comfortable bed. The next morning, road fatigue still wore me down. I had to force myself to pull back the duvet and get out of the bed. After a quick shower, I was out of the room.

I managed to figure out the buffet's waffle maker and was pleasantly surprised that my disfigured creation was edible. The side of bacon—my favorite thing—made it almost tasty, but I still needed coffee. Even with tons of cream and sugar, the forgettable brew at the hotel was not worth the calories, so after one sip, I shoved the cup across the table, opened the Google app on my phone, and did a quick search for a real coffee shop. There was one less than two miles down the road.

I tossed my overnight bag in the trunk, started the car, and made a lazy right turn out of the hotel parking lot. The phone rang in another call from my mother. I hadn't called her back last night, but now wasn't good either. I needed coffee in my veins to deal with her. I ignored her again and sent a text message letting her know I'd call her later. Smiley face and heart emoji. It was best to stall our next conversation for as long as I could. I was anxious enough without the lecture that was certain to fill the cabin of the vehicle once my mother found out where I was headed. Delay and deflect. That was my plan.

Once inside the coffee shop, I treated myself to my favorite thing—a tall, hot, mocha latte—and got back on the interstate again. I had five hours left on the drive and no regrets that I'd split it into two days.

As I drove on, South Carolina didn't strike me as being different from North Carolina or Virginia or any other state I'd passed through. Everything kind of looked the same on the highway. I supposed if I'd chosen to drive down the coast, it would have been different, but the fall hurricane season had been unkind. Due to Hurricane Florence, there was still some rebuilding construction on the Intracoastal Waterway, so I opted to avoid going that way.

I was in South Carolina. At first, excitement filled my veins. Before I could enjoy the feeling, though, overwhelm invaded every cell in my body and all the space in the car. What was I thinking coming down here? I had no plan. No information. I hadn't done any research. I'd been rash and impulsive. I wasn't usually either of those things.

I told Siri to call Leslie. She was always good for a confidence-boosting get-yourself-together pep talk.

"Hey, girl. I was just thinking about you," she said cheerfully.

"Good because maybe you can tell me what I'm doing."

"Aren't you driving?"

"Yes. I'm an hour and forty minutes from Georgetown."

"I can't believe you drove that far by yourself."

"Yeah, well, I can't either, and trust, I won't be doing it again. You can pack your little bag and prepare to fly down here to help with the drive home when I'm ready to come back."

"It would be my pleasure. I love the lowcountry. The food down there is crazy, and the shopping in Charleston . . . honey, hush."

Her prattling was unnerving me. I was already nervous. "Leslie, please. Help me. I'm questioning my entire life right now. What made you think this was a good idea? I don't know anything about my father. I don't know his family. I should have hired an investigator."

"This is supposed to be a journey of self-exploration for you. Isn't that what you called it? You're finding your Black half."

"Yeah, but I didn't have to be in the dark to do it."

"You sound like a scared teenage girl. Stop talking yourself into hysteria. Come down from ten."

I took a deep breath and swallowed. "They could be a bunch of really weird people."

"Weirder than our people?"

I didn't have to see Leslie's face to know the scrunched-up expression on it. I laughed inside. Leslie's tone referred to the very colorful living-in-crisis relatives on my mother's side, including Leslie's own mother, but we didn't associate with them. My mother never had the patience.

"I'm serious, Les. There could be bad blood or something."

"If there is, it's not with you. It's with Aunt Victoria. You can't start the what-ifs now. I mean, what if you don't find a single living Black? You can what-if yourself for the rest of that ride, get your stomach to bubbling if you want, or you can think about what could be. You could find some more love, and girl, you need it right now."

"I couldn't bear another disappointment."

"You're a Black woman. That means your DNA is made up of survival genes. You just haven't had to tap in and use the magic lately."

I inhaled deep again. The GPS instructed me to make a turn at a fork. I hadn't been paying attention to my route.

"I'm going to go. I'm about to get lost."

"Put on some music. Turn off your brain and just let this be what it's going to be."

She was right. This was why I called her. "Okay."

"I'm proud of you."

I smiled. "Thanks. Love you."

We ended the call. I did as I was told and put on Mary J. Blige. After listening to a few songs, I hit a wall on being distracted, so I turned it off. I tried to imagine my parents' trip from New Jersey so many years ago. Had they traveled this route? Save for thirty-seven years of maturity, did the landscape look the same?

It was easy to focus on the simple questions when the more complex ones were sitting at the top of my mind. What would I find in Georgetown? Did my father still have relatives there? Would they be easy to locate? And if I found them, would they give a care about me?

I came upon the first sign announcing that Georgetown was in my future. Once again, I bristled from excitement. The ringing of my phone pulled me out of my thoughts. It was Swella.

"Hi, Casey, sorry to interrupt . . ." There was crackling and noise in the background.

"Hold on, Swella." I switched the Bluetooth off and picked up the phone like holding it would help. I had no idea if South

Carolina was a hands-free cell phone state, so I slowed down and pulled over to the shoulder. "My connection is bad. What's up?"

"Brooke says she has to talk to you."

I groaned.

"Her exact words were 'I'm respectfully trying not to involve Victoria.'"

My lips tightened. "She's threatening to call my mommy."

"She said your mother negotiated the contract."

"Fine. Tell her I'm traveling and to *respectfully* give me until Thursday, okay?"

"Okay." Swella sounded relieved. Swella was great, but she couldn't handle a moment of uncertainty.

"Anything else?" I asked.

"Gunerson called about your massage next week. He needs to move it."

"Cancel it."

I could see Swella's eyes widen in my mind. Gunerson was one of the best masseurs in the city, and he was impossible to get an appointment with.

"Don't cancel," I said. "You take it."

"Me?" Swella squealed.

"Yes. You've been through a lot since the wedding. Bill it to my account and book me a slot in a few weeks."

I could feel her heart gushing through the phone. "Thank you, Casey."

"You deserve it. Anything else?"

"I was thinking we need to update the page. Pull up some evergreen content and start posting it."

"Great. I was hoping you wanted to do that."

I could hear the excitement on her end. Swella liked staying busy, and she loved my old modeling and the content I posted in my early years as an influencer.

"And my quotes—the body positive ones—repost them as individual pictures in between the photos. Remind people what I've stood for."

"Will do," she replied, and I could see her saluting me like she always did when I gave her a direct order.

We ended the call, and I looked around at my surroundings. I hadn't heard any cars whiz by since I'd parked. It was a main road but not well traveled, at least today anyway. A sign was posted in front of me that read "Black River."

I looked over the edge of the bridge at the water. The reeds, grass, and marsh danced with the slow-moving water. Shady oaks with moss hung low in some places, and I could hear the faint sound of the birds' wings as they landed and took off again. The water was black, and I supposed that's why the river had its name.

I held my phone up and took a picture of the river and the sign, then I decided to get my camera out of the trunk. My cell was great. Entire movies were being filmed with this thing, but holding my camera made the picture-taking process more authentic and real. It created a richer experience, for me anyway.

Once I snapped all I wanted, a peaceful feeling came over me. I wasn't anxious anymore. I guess I'd needed to stop, enjoy the view, and let the beauty in. I glanced at the sign again. A small smile settled in my heart. Black River. Maybe it was a good omen.

7

Odessa Conway

GEORGETOWN, SOUTH CAROLINA, 1867

THE WATER WAS BLACK. THE NATIVE AMERICAN PEOPLE SAY it's because the white man inked the water with indigo. But the indigo planting in Carolina stopped so long ago. In the warm season, her skin turned darker from the sun, but then by cold season, it was back to the pale-yellow color her mama passed to her, so things didn't stay the same color. Wouldn't the water turn back if the dye stopped?

Odessa Conway plunged her hands in the river and washed the blood off. Her dress was covered in it. She needed to wash it, too, before it stained forever, but there was no time for that. She had to find the nosebleed plant. It would stop the blood. She stood and walked back through the vines. Her eyes searched for white and yellow blooms. She wouldn't be in these woods if she'd listened to Mama. She'd told her to never travel without healing salve.

Just as she was about to give up, she saw movement in the wind on a low-hanging branch not that far, but it was in the swampy part. She walked closer, hoping to see her way clear to get to it, because the closer she got, the more she knew it was what she needed. But she didn't like the low part of the water. Alligators and snakes were in the low parts, waiting for feet and legs.

"I thought you was washing your hands."

Elijah's voice came from behind her. Before she turned good, he slipped close to her. His soothing breath warmed her neck. Everything about Elijah was soothing to her, but still, she playfully banged her fist against his solid chest. "Why are you sneaking up on me?"

"I ain't sneaking. *You* should have heard me coming, gal."

"Is she still bleeding?"

Elijah looked over his shoulder in the direction they'd come from. "Not as bad."

Odessa turned her face back to the plants and pointed. "They're over there."

"I'll go," Elijah said, kicking off his shoes.

She looked at him, realizing if he got wet, he didn't have nothing to change into. The letter she'd wrote to the Freedmen's Bureau came to her mind:

Information Wanted by a son concerning his mother. Elijah, a male born in 1848, formerly owned by Joseph Warton on the Warton House Plantation in Georgetown, South Carolina, seeks his mother, Pearl, of Georgetown, South Carolina, who was sold away in the fall of 1858. Any information may be sent to Bishop Conway, Georgetown, South Carolina. Mr. Elijah Black would be most grateful.

They were going to see his mama—hopefully.

"No! I can go. Now that you're here, I'm not scared."

"You already bloody. No need in getting wet too. Plus, you don't know nothing about walkin' in the swamp."

Elijah was right. She was born a slave, but not in the same way he was. Her family was owned by Papa's half uncle, Bishop Conway. Uncle Bishop was the mixed-race son of an enslaver named Hugh Conway. He set Uncle Bishop free at the age of thirteen and gave him money to start his life. Uncle Bishop bought his mother from his father. Before his mother died, she made him promise he would help her enslaved children. Uncle Bishop bought his half siblings, which included Odessa's grandfather.

And because Odessa was born enslaved to family, she was raised almost like a free Negro. She never had to work in the rice fields.

"It might be 'squitas in the water," Elijah continued. "They'll make you sick."

"You're the one who taught me that fast-moving water doesn't have mosquitoes," Odessa replied. "Stop trying to spook me. I have another dress in my bag. I can change. I don't want your mama to see you looking like wet possum." She slipped her shoes off, shoved them at him, and took the few steps to lower marsh.

"Wait," Elijah said. He picked up a long, thin branch and poked in the water a few times. "If something was there, it would git goin'."

It wasn't deep, but Odessa's feet sank in the wet sand under the surface. She was trying to look for snakes, but the water was so dark. She couldn't see clear, and she *was* scared—scared she'd step on something that would move.

She hummed a song as she pushed through the water. It wasn't long before she reached the other side and made her way to the large tree. She stepped over yellow flower petals until she saw white ones in a bush behind the tree. Where yellow grows, white grows. That's what Mama taught her. Mama was always right.

Once she picked, she made her way back to Elijah, and they returned to their wagon. Odessa placed the flowers on the tailboard and used a rock to grind them into pieces, then she put the pieces in a silver cup and walked back to her patient and got on her knees. Mary was the name of the exhausted woman lying on the grass in front of her, her legs open, blood seeping from her. Elijah was right; the blood was less. Odessa added a little water to the cup. "It's a good thing you have all your belongings, or I wouldn't have a cup to make this in."

She looked up into the eyes of the man who was holding his new baby. Their bags were in a pile behind him—clothes, a cup and plate, a little meal and biscuits. He was scared, but he nodded. "She say the baby early."

"Babies come when they want to." Odessa grinned thinly. Realizing she hadn't asked before, she said, "What's your name?"

"Timothy."

"What are you naming your son?"

He looked at the bundle in the slip of a blanket in his arms. "Mary want Amos. I say Joshua."

"Can't go wrong with either." Odessa pinned him with serious eyes. "I think she's going to be okay."

He nodded.

Odessa looked beyond Timothy to where Elijah was waiting. They had come upon these two on the road. Her pains had come, and her waters had broke. They were alone. She didn't know much about birthing babies, but she'd helped a few times. She remembered what to do.

"Where are you headed, Timothy?"

"Up by Santee House."

"For what business?"

"They lookin' for sharecroppers."

Odessa wondered why they was moving from one field to another so close to Mary's time, and being curious-natured, she asked, "You couldn't crop where you were?"

"Mass—" He cleared his throat. "Mr. Ripley turn everybody out. His missus leave for Pennsylvania, and he say he gon' just stay 'til he die. It's nothing for us there." The baby made a tiny sound, and Timothy rocked him in his arms. "Yauhannah. They raisin' crops—greens, corn, and cotton. Mass—" He forgot himself again. "Mr. Ripley don't have nothing but rice."

Odessa nodded, understanding that the rice was dead for most planters. Only a few could afford to grow it. That's what the man from the Freedmen's Bureau told them when he said hard times was going to get harder. Negro people needed to read and write and be political. Papa took it most seriously.

Odessa pressed the wet flowers into Mary's woman parts. Mary had already drank the tea Odessa made for her. That was part of why she was sleeping.

"She can't walk for a day or two. She needs to rest."

"Out here?"

Odessa considered his question. She certainly did not mean out here. "Do you have money? My man might know where you can stay. He travels doing brick."

"I don't have money. Mr. Ripley couldn't settle accounts."

Odessa tilted her head back and looked at the sky. "It's going to rain."

Timothy bit his lip. "I can see."

Odessa stood and walked to the wagon where Elijah sat, a stalk of straw in his mouth, chewing as he looked at his *McGuffey Reader*. She noticed he took it with him wherever he went.

Odessa had an education. Her uncle Bishop's granddaughter, Elizabeth, was a schoolteacher. She taught in the school for free people of color in Charleston three days a week. On the days Cousin Liz was home, even though it was illegal, she taught Odessa and the other children. Once the war got bad, Cousin Liz taught at home all the time because traveling to Charleston wasn't safe. Cousin Liz told Odessa she had the brains to be a teacher, so she had her mind set on going to teacher school.

Keen on anyone moving by him, Elijah looked up, catching her coming before she made a noise. He lifted a brow. She looked down at her dress. She knew she looked powerful bad.

"I need to put on the other dress."

Elijah closed the book and tossed the straw away. "How dey?"

"*They*," she corrected him. "They don't have money for a room, and she needs to rest."

Elijah grunted.

"They're headed to Yauhannah."

"He told me." Elijah looked thoughtful but not concerned. "It's on the other river. They shouldn't have left so close to her time."

"Maybe we can ride them some—get 'em closer."

Elijah grunted again. "They name ain't on the letter."

Elijah had permission to use the horse and wagon from his former owner, Mr. Warton. Elijah paid him for it for the day. Old masters were doing most anything for money these days. The letter for why they had the wagon included Elijah's name and one female companion.

Mr. Warton was a nasty man. He told Elijah he lost the records with the name of the buyer he'd sold Elijah's mother to. He was trying to keep Elijah on because he helped Elijah get brick work and Elijah split the money with him. He'd been telling Elijah that story about lost papers for almost two years, so on his days off, when he could hire the wagon, Elijah went from plantation to plantation, searching for his mother. Finally, when

Elijah threatened to move on last week, Mr. Warton told Elijah the truth about who he sold his mother to. They were headed there now.

"We can explain the baby. Anyone can see he's newborn."

Elijah looked straight ahead. The tight line of his jaw told her he didn't like the idea. "They not our problem."

"They're God's children, Elijah." Odessa reached into the back for her other dress. She was glad she brought it. Her plan was to change into it if they found his mother so she would look nice. "I'm going to put this on and wash this one as best I can. Please help him get her up."

Elijah looked back at her. "That's you with two men, Dessa. Your pa would have my skin."

Odessa's parents were in Charleston for a political meeting. They didn't know she rode out with Elijah—unchaperoned in public. It wasn't proper, but she rode on the back of the wagon.

"I'll be in back with Mary."

Elijah jumped down from the wagon. Crept up on her slow-like. His warm breath was on the back of her neck again. "If you gon' be my wife, you gon' have to learn to listen to me."

Odessa turned and pushed him away from her. Teasing, she said, "If you gon' be my husband, you will have to learn to listen to me."

As she marched over the grass to the riverbed, she heard him yell, "That's not what the Good Book say."

She turned, walking backward. "How would you know? You haven't read that part yet."

"I know what it say. It say, 'You gotta hard head.'"

Odessa had happiness in her heart as she came to Timothy and Mary. "My man will help you put her in the wagon. We can take you on down the way so you're closer to Yauhannah." She reached into her pocket for a few coins. She closed them in

Timothy's hand. "It's not much, but it'll get you something to eat. Maybe somebody let you sleep in a barn."

Timothy raised his eyes, tears in them. "Thank you kindly. God bless you and your children and they children for what you done."

Odessa appreciated his words. She wished she could do more, but she couldn't. "I'll take the good Lord's blessing any way I can get it." She turned and walked to the trees by the river to change her dress.

8

"WELCOME TO OUR HISTORIC WATERFRONT CITY." IT WAS A very welcoming sign, but it was pretty anticlimactic. I expected to feel something, hear music, experience a quickening heartbeat. None of that happened, especially the music part, but I did have a satisfied sense of accomplishment. I'd driven almost seven hundred miles.

It was one o'clock in the afternoon. I decided tomorrow would be a better day to embark on my mission. I was easing into this hunt for my family in the same way I eased into Georgetown. Front Street was the main road. It was a beachy-looking area, and in the distance, I could see large houses—the big, gorgeous type you found only in the South.

Inside the visitors' center, I chatted with a lovely employee who'd migrated from New Jersey. She gave me brochures and tips on where to dine and get an official tour. I stepped outside and opened one of the brochures, quickly scanning its contents.

"Georgetown . . . founded in 1729 . . . third oldest city in South Carolina, Indigo and rice major industries. *Blah, blah, blah* . . . by the late 1800's, lumber became the most significant endeavor."

Interesting how they skipped the entire chapter about how by 1810, 88 percent of the population was enslaved African Americans. I found that in the African American Heritage brochure.

"Okay, Georgetown, I see you."

It was too early to settle into my room for the night. It was also a pretty day. I went to the car for my camera and walked to the harbor. I wanted to get some good shots of the water and the boats. The breeze carried the pungent smell of the seawater—salt and fish—and gasoline from a boat's roaring engine. The sound sent a flock of seagulls flapping their wings overhead.

I raised my camera to capture a picture of the birds, and once I was satisfied with the shot, I turned my camera to the sea. The sun was made bigger by the glistening blue ocean water. A gust of salty wind whisked past me. The sky was cloudless, making the view across the ocean endless. I looked at the fancy yachts, and it struck me that two hundred years ago, Black people were still being brought across this water in chains. An ache pulsed in my chest, and I took a moment to reflect on that before I raised my camera again.

I returned to Front Street because my stomach was growling. Just that fast, the street had more foot traffic. I entered The Southern Grille. It was one of the Jersey woman's recommendations. The restaurant was a cute little laid-back place with tables of various sizes along the walls and through the middle. A huge bar area took up a lot of the space, and oversized televisions showing different sporting events hung from the walls. I was wrong about the crowd. They were busy. Busy enough to remind me of a New York City restaurant at lunchtime, which I thought had to indicate good business in a small town like this.

"Are you in line?"

A solid, masculine voice that was attached to a decidedly

masculine man standing next to me broke my concentration. He was tall, athletic, with broad lean-on-me shoulders, jet-black hair, and enviable brown eyes. I followed those eyes to where they were focused and noted I'd gotten so caught up in the interior of the restaurant that I hadn't closed the space between myself and the couple in front of me.

"If you're in a rush . . ." I raised a hand, offering to let him cut the line.

"I wouldn't dream of taking your place. I just needed to make sure you wanted it."

I nodded and stepped closer to the patrons in front of me. "Better?"

Amusement entered his eyes. He smiled, and his perfection was confirmed by marvelous teeth and a long dimple in one cheek.

I had to catch my breath for a minute. Dang, is this how they were making the men in the South? I hadn't seen a man this good-looking without makeup and filters.

Focus, Casey.

"Where are you from?"

I cleared my throat. "What makes you think I'm not from around here?"

"I've never seen you, you're taking pictures, and you have brochures sticking out of your pocket."

"Nothing about my accent?" I asked.

He chuckled. "An accent is a choice."

I eased back, meeting his eyes with more interest. He was a smart one.

The line moved, placing me in front of the counter. I looked up at the menu but cut my eyes to him. "I'm a Yankee. Although I'm sure you figured that out."

"Yeah, I kind of did, and for the record, we Black southerners don't have a problem with Yankees. That little war helped us out."

His eyes settled on mine. He seemed to be assessing me—for what, I didn't know. I'd already noticed he wasn't wearing a wedding band. Single men tended to stare like they were concocting a plan for seduction. He wasn't giving that vibe. Maybe he'd told himself to *focus* too. He nodded up toward the menu. "Everything is good here."

Our eyes caught and held for a moment. Now I was inspecting him curiously. He was tall—at least six foot three. Skin was something I always noticed, and he was blessed with what most women worked hard to achieve—even, blemish-free skin with a healthy glow. His complexion was a rich brown, deep—like a sun-kissed sable. His eyes were a shade lighter, and I could see warmth in them. His hair was shaved low, nearly to the scalp, and he sported a tight, neat goatee. He was hot.

I'd taken too long to assess that. His eyes had changed from serious to amused. Embarrassed, I cleared my throat. "What do you recommend?"

He leaned in to me and whispered, "Try the BLT."

I nearly jumped, not from his heat but from the sound of his velvety voice near my ear.

"What can I get you?" the woman behind the counter asked.

I cleared my throat again and turned to the cashier. "I'll have the BLT."

"Sweet tea?" she asked.

"Water is fine."

She gave me my total, and I moved off to the side where I was shortly joined by Mr. Good-looking.

"You never did tell me where you're from," he said.

"New York."

His eyes widened. "The Big City."

I nodded. "Compared to this one, I'd say yes." I reached into my pocket and pulled out the brochures. "Since you have time, which one of these would be good for a tour?"

He looked at each of them and said, "None of them. You can't ask these guys to teach you about Georgetown. They'll be entertaining, but they're not going to show you Black Georgetown."

That 88 percent entered my mind.

"Go to the Gullah Museum. They'll give you the contact information for a tour."

He handed me my brochures. His phone rang. "Excuse me." He took his call, but then pulled the phone away from his mouth and said, "The museum is just over on King Street."

I nodded. After a few minutes, my food was done. Just as I was about to walk out, the guy ended his call. I stepped back to him and said, "Do you mind if I ask you a question?" He stood there, waiting for it. "Do you know any Blacks?"

His features grew tight. "You got some first names for these 'Blacks'?"

I shook my head.

"I can't help you." He went over to the counter to pick up his food.

Although I was sure he didn't hear me, I thanked him and stepped outside with him on my heels.

"Can I ask you one more thing?"

He shook his head. At this point, he found me amusing. "I'm going to start charging you."

I smirked. "Where is the tax office? I need property records."

He pointed to the left. "That's Prince Street. If you take it down to Screven, the courthouse building is right there."

I thanked him again, and he walked to a pickup truck. Before he drove away, he looked at me one last time. "Good luck finding your Blacks."

I walked back to my car, put my camera in the trunk, and slipped into the front seat. After eating my sandwich, which I had to admit that with the fried green tomatoes and jam was notably better than a northern BLT, I opened the email from Swella with the details about my room. Check-in wasn't until 4:00 p.m. It was only two thirty. I could go early and see if they were ready for me, but there was no reason I couldn't go to the tax record office. The only thing holding me back was fear. Fear of not finding what I wanted, and fear of actually finding what I wanted. The latter was ridiculous, but it was my truth. I could find out something that I didn't want to know.

What was that saying about ignorance? Sometimes it was bliss. I opened the Google Maps app and tapped out *Georgetown tax office*. The link for the map indicated it was a four-minute walk. I released a long breath and got out of the car before I changed my mind.

~

After I gave her a brief version of my story—basically that I was looking for my father's family—the woman in the tax office was helpful. There were a lot of businesses in Georgetown with the word *Black* in the name because of Black River, but there were only a few people named Black who owned property, and only one who owned their land at the time when my father was alive.

She pushed her eyeglasses farther back on her nose and investigated her computer screen. "Edward and Ida Black are deeded land on Choppee Road. The first land was purchased in 1870 and then more in 1899 and 1903. In 1945, two hundred acres was transferred to them in their name from Elijah and Odessa Black. The last hundred acres was purchased in 1961."

The clerk and I exchanged a look across the counter. I couldn't tell what she was thinking, but I was pretty sure she could see I was shocked. "Three hundred acres? I don't know. That's a lot of land." Surely my mother would have told me my father lived on a property that big, but she hadn't told me a thing, so why would she have told me that?

The clerk squinted like she was remembering something before she said, "That's Black Farm. They've been around forever. There's a vegetable market there."

I turned the volume of my voice down to that of a conspiratorial whisper. "Do you know if they're Black people, as in race, who own it?"

"Oh yes, the Blacks are Black." She smiled again.

I smiled with her, glad that I hadn't offended her with the question. People were touchy these days.

"I'll print the details for you. You can get there with a navigation app. That farm has been there since I was a little girl." She handed me the printout.

"This is a start," I said. "I appreciate your help."

"And . . ." She paused. "If you find out those aren't your people, your daddy's parents' names should be on his birth certificate."

"I don't know if I could get that. What about a death certificate?"

I read sympathy in her eyes. I hadn't told her he was deceased. "Their names would be there too. Vital Records is at the public health building."

Her hand was on the counter. I reached to her forearm and patted it. "Thank you so much."

I walked out, amazed at how easy that was. If it turned out they were my father's family, my family . . .

My phone rang loudly in the quiet of the hall. My mother.

Not yet.

I closed my eyes and sent it to voice mail. As expected, a text came through. It was threatening, of course: If you don't call, I'm coming over there.

I texted back: I'm not home. I'll call tonight.

There was another text, but I ignored that one. She only wanted details.

By the time I reached my car, it was close to time to check in. Swella had booked me a room at Mays Bed and Breakfast. I pulled up directions to Mays and then added Black Farm to the search. Black Farm was halfway between where I was now and Mays Bed and Breakfast, and both were on the same road.

"Convenient." Especially if this turned out to be the right Black family.

~⌇~

It was close to 5:00 p.m., and the sun was still high. My GPS brought me right to a white brick sign with black metal letters that simply read "Black Farm. Est. 1899." I made a left into the driveway, which opened to several things—an empty, outdoor farmer's market storefront on the left and a small, white brick, one-story house on the right. I stepped out of the car, keeping one foot in and my hands on the door just in case I needed to flee. My heart fluttered as I struggled to grasp the implications of my standing here, but I didn't let myself get caught up. This was my first stop. What were the chances I had the right place?

I suppressed my nerves by focusing on the postcard-worthy property. The house held my attention. It was an old-fashioned farmhouse with a wide sunroom, a blue door, and blue shutters. The porch was furnished with four rocking chairs, and a huge fan hung from the ceiling. If it worked, I could tell from the sheer girth of it that the breeze had to be satisfying. There was more outdoor patio furniture on the ground in front of the house where a bricked-in area provided seating. Tall grass decorated the perimeter, some of which was tied with twine for a decorative effect.

A wooden fence drew a line that separated the house and market from property behind it, and there were five parking spaces marked out in the gravel with parallel rows of brick to separate each one. A wooden sign was posted in front of each space with the word *guest*.

Beyond the house, a bright-red barn with white trim reminded anyone visiting that this was real farmland. I raised a hand to block the sun. I could see water, probably the river that I'd been traveling along that I lost sight of when the road curved about a mile back.

My stomach was in my throat. I was overwhelmed by how massive the property was. I'd turned in to the property planning to just catch a glimpse of it, and now that I was here, I was petrified.

The front door of the house opened, and a young woman appeared. "Can I help you?"

Of course I'd been seen, because of course I'd been heard. Gravel was noisy, and it was quiet out here. Quieter than I'd ever heard in my life.

I reached in for my bag, pushed the car door closed, and mustered the strength to put one foot in front of the other until I reached the steps.

"Is there anyone here from the Black family?"

The woman was young, maybe twenty-five. She was about five-three, plump, if not heavy, with smooth chestnut skin and dark wide-set eyes—really dark and not happy to be looking at me. "It's Black Farm." A hefty dose of "duh" was in those three words.

Of course. I bit my lip and continued, bravely if not foolishly. *Finish strong, Casey.*

I reached into my purse for my birth certificate and driver's license. "May I come closer?"

She perched a fist on her hip. "Come on."

I approached the steps and handed them to her. "My name is Casey Black. My father was a man named Matthew Black. I have no idea if this is the right house, but I'm looking for my relatives."

Her frown deepened. She looked at me and then my license and birth certificate. Multiple lines appeared above her deep ebony eyes. Her energy shifted from annoyed to curious.

"He died before I was born," I added.

She looked in my face again, inspecting me cautiously. "I work here, so I don't know. I'll ask somebody." She handed me my paperwork and stepped inside the house. I was expecting the door to slam behind her, but she held it for me. Nodding, she said, "Come in. Sit for a minute."

I did as I was told, the coming in part, but I didn't sit. I was too nervous. I walked to the end of the porch, folded my arms over my chest, and waited. I inspected the decor. In addition to the blue door, the ceiling was painted blue. It was sparsely furnished, but there were antique metal tables in between the rocking chairs. The floor was partially covered with a knotted wool area rug that included more of the blue and a combination of browns and beiges in a tribal pattern.

A truck pulled off the road and into the driveway. I could see a man in the driver's seat. At this moment, I realized I could disappear into this house and never come out. No one knew where I was. All Leslie, Swella, and Drew knew was Georgetown. I sent a text to Leslie with a picture of the tax record address. Just as I put everything back in my bag, the woman I'd been dealing with opened the main door to the house. "You can come in."

Come in? They weren't sending me away. Was I in the right place? I couldn't move.

"My name is Petra." She held the door open and swayed her

palm toward the inside. It was clear to see she was convinced I deserved an audience with the people in this house.

Emotion swelled within me and moved around until it reached my heart. The heat of tears burned the backs of my eyes. I let out the breath I'd been holding and took enough steps to make it through the door. An elderly woman stood in the center of the room. She had to be close to a hundred years old. She was tall—nearly as tall as me. Her face was familiar, and it was then that I understood. She was not some random distant relative.

"This is Mrs. Ida Black," Petra said, stepping aside.

The only picture I had of my father was one he and my mother took on their wedding day. It was one of those cheap photos that slid out of a slot inside a photo booth. They'd taken it at Funhouse on the boardwalk in Asbury Park where they'd had their honeymoon. I'd been told my whole life that I look just like my mother. I was her twin in some respects, certainly in my facial features. So I knew a person could spit out the exact image of themselves. This woman had. She was an older carbon copy of the man in my keepsake photo. She was my father's mother.

I had a grandmother.

9

IDA BLACK STEPPED TOWARD ME. SHE WAS QUICK FOR A woman her age. Of course, I didn't know her age, but she had to be in her late nineties. I'd never known anyone this old.

She moved closer, staring, inspecting, surmising. Her shock didn't seem as great as mine. What I saw on her face looked like something else beyond surprise and joy. Her tears were happy, but I sensed relief.

She opened her mouth, but the words she wanted to say got stuck in her throat. She struggled, just like me. Petra placed a hand on her back and leaned closer. "What you say, ma'am?"

Mrs. Black shook her head, waved Petra away, and stepped even closer to me. She touched my shoulder and then my chin. "God did not take our seed from this earth."

Her tears spilled over. I raised a hand and allowed her to cup it in hers. Warmth radiated from it, and that warmth crept up my arm and rushed into my heart. I was in instant love.

"You are my Matthew's daughter. Welcome home."

My tongue was locked in the roof of my mouth. I was standing in the middle of a room in a house in South Carolina with a grandmother I never imagined I had. "I . . ." I paused. "I don't know what to say. I didn't expect . . ." My words stuck in my throat. I took a deep breath, and a tear might have streamed down my face, but then the door opened.

I turned to see who entered. It was Mr. Good-looking from the restaurant in town. His surprise matched mine.

"What are you doing here?" we asked each other in unison.

Not waiting for my reply, he stepped around me. "Ma, what's going on?"

He and I weren't the only ones confused. "How do you know her?" Mrs. Black asked.

He looked at me suspiciously. "I met her in the city this afternoon."

Mrs. Black let go of my hand and stepped back to a well-worn recliner and sat. Stress melted into the gentle folds of her face. Her skin was wrinkled but smooth and soft-looking at the same time. She raised her eyes to his curious ones. "Nigel, this is my granddaughter."

My thoughts swirled. A hand touched my elbow. I looked to see it was Nigel's. Did he think I was going to faint?

"You should sit down," he said.

I shook my head and pulled my arm from his easy grip. "I need to make sure. I need to know that you're the right family." Suddenly I was questioning what I'd just been sure of. This woman looked like my father with her golden-brown skin and her big brown eyes.

"Victoria," she said, "you have your mother's features. Strong and beautiful. I'd know that face anywhere." A shadow of pain shrouded her face. My mother's name evoked sadness. "She kept you from me. All these years."

She looked up at the ceiling and closed her eyes. She mumbled words I couldn't discern. It wasn't English. It sounded like a chant, and then she said, "'Though He slay me, yet will I trust Him.'" She opened her eyes, and they were filled with heavier tears.

I looked like my mother, and she looked like my father. This was the right house. She was my grandmother. I said nothing, but I felt everything. Relief, happiness, confusion, and there was still shock.

Petra handed her some tissues. She pointed to the chair on the other side of the table next to my grandmother. "You makin' her strain her neck. It would be better if you sat."

Once again, I followed Petra's instructions. I found the house to be a little warm, so I also slipped my jacket off my shoulders.

"Ma," Nigel said, getting my grandmother's attention. "I'll come back."

She frowned. "No, you stay." She pointed at an empty chair.

I looked at him. Inspecting him with different eyes this time. Looking past his handsomeness and seeking out common facial features. "Are we related?"

He shook his head. "I call her Ma Black. Most people do."

Petra smiled. "Miss Casey, it's nice to meet you. I work for your grandmother. I'm a live-in health aide."

I nodded at her and then looked at Nigel when I said, "I'm Casey Black." My lips split into a smile, and a tear slid down one of my cheeks.

Petra handed me some tissues. "Can I get you something? Tea, lemonade, or water?"

"I'm fine." My emotions were rolling around inside of me like they were trying to find a place to settle. I was not fine.

Nigel hadn't taken his eyes off me. He cleared his throat and glanced at Petra. "Lemonade." He sat back and crossed a foot over his knee. He raised a hand to his lips and assessed me curiously, in the same manner he had at the restaurant. I turned my attention to my grandmother.

"How did you come?" my grandmother asked.

"I drove from New York. I arrived today."

Nigel interrupted. "I think she means how have you come to be here?"

I looked at him again. "Oh," escaped my throat. I returned my attention to my grandmother. "I decided I wanted to know more about my father."

"You're thirty-six?"

I nodded. "Yes, ma'am, thirty-six years old."

"Your mother . . . is she still living?"

"Yes. She's in New York."

That hurt her. I could see it. She squeezed her eyes tight. "Eddie," she cried. "I'm sorry for this sin." She wiped her eyes.

"Eddie was her husband—your late grandfather," Nigel offered. "He passed in 1997."

I nodded. "Oh." I squinted at Nigel and whispered, "Should I go?"

He frowned and shook his head.

I looked at my grandmother. I was a teenager in 1997. I had no way to meet my grandfather on my own.

My mother kept me from these people. She made me miss knowing my grandfather. A heated surge of anger rose, tightening my jaw. I had to push these thoughts out of my mind to enjoy the moment I was in.

Petra came back in the room with two glasses of lemonade, one for my grandmother and the other for Nigel. It looked fresh-squeezed, pulp floating on the top. I wished I'd said yes. I needed something to calm the swell of emotions rolling through my body.

"Are you alone?" Nigel asked.

"Yes. This was something I wanted to do on my own. I'd like to know more about my father and"—I looked at my grandmother—"you, of course, and any other relatives."

My grandmother nodded. "We will learn each other."

Nigel took a sip of his lemonade. "Where are you staying?"

"Mays Bed and Breakfast."

Petra grunted. My grandmother frowned. Nigel pitched an eyebrow and put his glass down.

"No," my grandmother said. Disappointment replaced the joy that had been on her face. "You can't stay there." She said the words softly but firmly.

"I can't?"

"It's an old plantation." Petra's short fuse and smart tone were back. "Now I know you from the North, but, ma'am, just no. We don't stay on old plantations." She walked out of the room and disappeared down a hall. I had a feeling she'd had all she could take from the northern girl.

"The land is unhealed. There are too many souls and too much blood in the ground. You can't stay there." My grandmother squeezed the arms of her chair like she was wrestling the fabric. "No Black will ever stay there."

Nigel came to my rescue again. "The Mays enslaved nearly a thousand of our people and were said to have been very harsh owners. Turning the house into a bed-and-breakfast doesn't erase the evil that was done."

I took a deep breath. I hadn't even thought about what the word *plantation* implied. What it must mean to Black people here in the South in particular. "I'm sorry. I had someone make my reservation. I didn't even think . . ." Swella hadn't thought, but there was no way for her to know this was problematic.

"It's okay," Nigel said, looking to my grandmother. "We'll figure out something else."

"There isn't an empty bed here. The rooms are full," my grandmother said. "We have cabins, but our migrant workers are staying in them. They come every year at this time." She was thoughtful for a moment before offering a suggestion that surprised me. "You can stay at Nigel's house." She pushed up on the arms of the chair to her feet.

I stood with her, and so did Nigel. "Excuse me?" I looked at Nigel for help.

"I rent my house on Airbnb."

"Oh," I said, understanding. I wasn't sure this was a good idea. What if I hated the house? I didn't want to offend him after I saw it. "I'll find another hotel in town. I'm sure there must be something." I recalled Swella telling me most were booked and the one she reserved was the nicest thing that was left.

"It's spring break. I don't think there's much left in town. I mean you might find something out on Pawleys Island, but that's out of the way."

I didn't even know where Pawleys Island was.

Nigel said, "And what you find out there might be more of the same, if you know what I mean."

I knew what he meant. More bloody land. More for my grandmother to disapprove of.

"Nigel's house is nice. It's not as old-fashioned as this one. It'll do," my grandmother inserted, settling the matter.

Nigel cleared his throat. "It's a few miles down the road. I'm sure it will be sufficient. It's clean and as renters say, 'well appointed.'" He smiled and my heart thumped.

"You get her settled and come back for dinner. Six." My grandmother stepped closer and pulled me into her arms. Her hug felt like it belonged to me. "My peace," she whispered. "My lost one has come home." She smiled, warm and tender, before she turned down the hall. Utter silence filled the room for a long time, or possibly a short time that seemed long. I was still reeling from all that had happened.

Nigel moved toward the door, opening it for me. "Ma has an appointment with one of her clients. I should get you settled."

I picked up my bag and walked toward the door. "Thank you," I said, and I stepped outside. I heard the door *snap* together behind us. Nigel fell into step with me. It was then that I accepted I was legit in shock. My head started spinning.

"It seems you found your Blacks," Nigel said.

"The ones you didn't know." I couldn't keep the snark out of my voice.

"I'm protective of her," he said soberly, and I appreciated him. My like for him was as instant as my love for her.

I released a long breath. I shook my head. "I didn't expect . . ." My words trailed off; they were stuck in my brain. "I figured I'd meet some distant cousins. How old is she?"

Nigel smiled. "Ninety-nine."

I closed my eyes against the thought. "I don't know what to say or think. How can we all be sure?"

"She's sure, but you'll figure it out at dinner." Nigel pulled the door open to my car. "She has pictures and other records."

"Did you know my grandfather?" I asked, tossing my purse in.

He nodded. "I worked here during a summer camp they held for the 4-H club."

I bit my lip and put one foot in the car. I spent most of 1997 in Paris. Nigel had to have been a teen himself when Grandfather died. He wasn't much older than me.

"You're close to her," I said. There was no denying that.

"She's like a second mother."

I couldn't believe I was staying at his house. I wanted to ask him for the address. I wanted to look at the Airbnb reviews. I wanted to google him. He was a stranger to me, but the usual alarms didn't go off in my head.

I pulled my eyes away from his and looked at the white

house with the blue door that my ninety-nine-year-old grandmother lived in. This house was safe, and so was everything
and everyone connected to it. I could feel it. So I decided to
trust my gut. Trust the grandmother I'd known all of twenty
minutes.

10

I HADN'T OBSERVED MUCH ABOUT THE HOUSE DURING MY earlier visit. That wasn't like me, but I'd been stuck in my emotions. Now that I was back for dinner, I received a tour. If old houses had character, this one had a strong, welcoming personality. It appeared small on the outside, but inside, it was twice as big as I imagined. Off to the left of the front room was a dining room with a smooth, ebony clawfoot table with six chairs around it.

There were three bedrooms—one for my grandmother, one for Petra, and the third was my grandmother's War Room. She said we'd visit that room after dinner. There was one other tiny room. It was so small it could have been a closet that was converted to a room. It had another recliner like the one in the living room and two other straight-back chairs across from it. Along the walls were shelves filled with jars and bottles with wet and dry herbs in them. The bathroom, the only one in the house, had an enormous clawfoot tub. Claws were a thing in this house. There was no shower.

Finally, she took me to the kitchen, if *finally* was the right word. The house was all kitchen. It had to be one-third of the square footage. It was the most modern room in the house, boasting a tremendous granite-top island, two ovens, and a double farmhouse sink where each side was large enough to bathe a small child. It also had one of those fancy pull-down faucets that I imagined washed tons of vegetables from a farm easily. There were open cupboards with glass doors filled with food and dishes. There was love in this room, love in this house. I could feel it.

"I like to cook," my grandmother said, reading my mind. "It's what I do best these days." We went into the dining room.

The dinner party included Petra; a cousin who was a few years younger than me named Lachelle; and Lachelle's grandfather, Roger Lance. Everyone was staring at me like I was an alien who descended upon them from Mars. I suppose I had dropped from the sky.

Iced tea, which I was politely schooled to understand was sweet tea in the South, had been poured into glasses. Petra and Lachelle entered from the kitchen with platters of food.

There was fried fish, baked chicken, a jambalaya-type rice, a shrimp-and-okra dish, macaroni and cheese, greens, and fried hush puppies. The aroma of garlic, onion, oregano, and bacon tickled my senses and made my stomach lurch forward, begging to be filled. Something was spicy. I could feel the heat of the pepper in my nostrils. I liked spice.

"I don't think I've ever seen this much food on a Monday night." I rubbed my forehead with my fingertips.

"If we knew you were coming, there would be more." My grandmother smiled. "Your uncle Roger and aunt Thea own a restaurant. Uncle Roger brought the food."

"Thank you, sir," I said. I was a quick study. Lachelle and Petra said sir and ma'am, and I caught on.

"Thea is in Greenville." I could barely make out Uncle Roger's words for his thick accent. It wasn't just southern. No one else talked like him. "She be back before the week out."

"Are you allergic to anything?" Petra asked.

I shook my head.

"Good," Lachelle said. "You would not survive in these parts if you couldn't eat seafood." She laughed.

"Let's bless the meal," my grandmother said, looking at Uncle Roger.

Everyone bowed their heads and closed their eyes, so I did too. I didn't give thanks before meals. Leslie said grace, therefore I was used to being respectful when it was happening. Uncle Roger was speaking in a completely different language now. Once he was done, we opened our eyes.

Lachelle bumped my knee. She whispered, "In case you were wondering, Grandpa is Gullah."

"What does that mean?" I hadn't asked Nigel what that meant when he suggested the museum earlier.

Lachelle leaned closer. "The Gullah are a group of people who lived on the sea islands during slavery. Because they were separated from the mainland, they kept their culture. Their language is a mix of English and West African dialects."

I had heard about these people before, but *Gullah* wasn't the word. "I thought they were called Geechie."

Lachelle nodded, confirming I was right. "Gullah and Geechie are used interchangeably."

Uncle Roger pulled us from our side conversation with a question to me about my trip. The dinner conversation was lively, and I was grateful it wasn't focused solely on me. Uncle Roger was full of stories. I didn't understand everything he was saying, but I could see he was a master storyteller. Embellishment could be recognized in any language.

"Gullah is a whole vibe, as you can tell from Grandpa," Lachelle added.

"Is Aunt Thea Gullah?"

"No, but Grandpa says unofficially—by marriage—any person married to a Gullah is."

Lachelle continued. "Grandma Thea has lived in Plantersville in the Gullah community for a few years. For most of their marriage, they were in Greenville. They retired down here."

"She's a cook?" I asked.

"Grandpa does a lot of the cooking in the restaurant, but she helps. You'll meet her later this week."

"Casey, is that your given name or a nickname?" my grandmother asked.

"That's what's on her birth certificate, ma'am," Petra interjected.

"Well, it's pretty," she said. "Your name is important." She paused for a moment and stood. "Come with me. All of you."

We followed her into the kitchen and out the back door. Once we were on the deck, my grandmother closed her eyes. When she opened them, a look of deep reflection filled her face. We waited until she was ready to speak.

"Black wasn't our name. Not at first. Enslaved people didn't have last names. They were property. Some kept they masters' names after Freedom came, but others changed their names.

"Mr. Elijah, your great-grandfather—my Eddie's father—was born and freed at Warton Plantation. Warton is abandoned land now, but it was closer to Georgetown city, where the two rivers come together—Black and Waccamaw.

"When Freedom came, Mr. Elijah was seventeen years old. He walked off the plantation. He didn't have no family tying him to the place, and he had money from being hired out as a brickmason, so he decided he was going to make his own way. He stopped by the river, caught a fish, and cooked it."

My grandmother paused to smile through her words. "He was a man who could catch his own fish and sit there all day if he wanted to. He said *that* was freedom. He loved the river so much for the feeling it gave him that he stepped into it to wash away the dirt, pain, shame, anger, and indignity of slavery."

She looked at all of us as she spoke but settled her eyes on mine more than anyone else. "He didn't say it like that, but it was the residue, you understand. That's the word for what he was trying to say. He saw that the color of the water was the same as he was. He decided to make his name the same as the water. The natives called it Wee Nee, which meant black water. So we are named for Black River."

Once again, my heart filled. My grandmother had a melodious voice, soothing and powerful. Everyone slipped under its spell when she spoke; I wasn't the only one.

My grandmother took my hand and pointed with her free one. "You see that water there?"

I nodded. "I followed it from the city."

"That's Black River. Elijah Black died owning land on the river that made him new."

After slices of caramel cake, my grandmother and I went to the War Room.

"This where I take my peace. I study my Bible, read, and keep my herbs for healing." She walked to a metal case near a table at the far end of the room and opened it. She took out a few scrapbooks and photo albums and then a pile of notebooks, which she told me were family journals.

There were newspaper clippings and all kinds of other items from the past. She showed me pictures of my father from his birth until his military years and two with my mother. She was so young and vibrant, pretty, and in love. I spent time with those photos, absorbing the special gift they were. There were also pictures of my father and his brother.

My grandmother's steady hand hovered above the first picture of her sons. "Matthew and Mark were fraternal twins, but they looked a lot alike."

My heart stopped beating. I felt as if air was being sucked from my lungs. *Twins?* "I didn't know my father was a twin. My mother didn't tell me that. Where is he?" I asked, excited to have an uncle.

"He passed. Long time ago." My grandmother didn't dwell on that. I had a feeling there was a lot my mother hadn't told me, but I tucked that disappointment away and focused on what I had in front of me.

"We only have one video of the twins. Those cameras weren't that popular when they were young, but I have one with their graduation. I'll find it," she said. And then she got to the family journals. There were thirteen of them. My great-grandmother Odessa had written ten, Great-grandpa Elijah had written one, and Grandpa Eddie had written one.

My grandmother said, "I'm an old woman. I've been waiting for God to call me home. But I didn't have no one left to give the Black story to. No one here who wants it. Not really. And now you've come."

She put her hands on the stack of journals. Some were made of leather and leather-like hide and other materials. She reached near the bottom. It was little more than a piece of muslin cloth bound with rubber bands. She opened it, and the pages of paper were glued together at the edges. It was a homemade binding. She placed it on the table between us. "Your great-grandmother, Mama Odessa, taught me how to be a woman after I married Eddie. My mama, Laura Wilson, died in childbirth when I was three, and my daddy didn't take another wife." She pointed to the first page. The paper was old and barely legible. "Mama Odessa was a writer and a teacher. She also taught me about herbs for healing."

Thinking about the bottles and plants I'd seen earlier, I asked, "Is that what's in that room next door over?"

"Yes. Tinctures and salves for healing, but we'll get to all of that." My grandmother paused. "Mama Odessa wrote her story in these books so the family could know who she was. Your story begins with her story."

I leaned closer to get a look at the artifact.

"Mr. Elijah has a small book in here too. It's mostly records from his brickmason days, but he did write a letter about his life before Freedom and the farm."

I moved my eyes from the stack, back to my grandmother's face.

"How long can you stay?" A hopeful light filled her eyes. They begged me to say forever. She didn't even know me, but I sensed it.

"I don't have a time limit really. I own my own business. I'm taking a break from it."

She picked up my left hand and touched my ring finger where there was just a tan line as evidence there had been a ring. "You taking a break from this too?"

I dropped my eyes to my finger. "That's a long story."

"Well, if you can stay for a season, we can learn each other's stories and much more." She handed the journal to me. "Touch it. Feeling it matters just as much as the words." She pulled the cover back.

"This farm is a dream fulfilled. Do you know what it is for our people to own three hundred acres of land?" She pressed her lips together, and her eyes were wet again. "You, Casey Black, did not come from nothing and nobody. Do you understand?"

I nodded. "Yes, ma'am."

Petra's presence was felt in the doorway before she spoke. "Mrs. Ida, it's time for bed."

I stood with my grandmother. She pulled me into an embrace. It was the second time today, and both times it felt comfortable and good.

"Come on, ma'am. I know Casey is a shiny new toy, but she'll be here tomorrow." Petra winked at me.

My grandmother pursed her lips and slapped Petra's hand. "You sassin' me."

Petra chuckled. "No, ma'am. I know you need to get proper rest."

"You can read a little before Petra locks up," she offered. "Tomorrow is a special day. Be here by ten?"

I nodded yes. She walked to the door but then did a half turn when she reached it. "And Nigel . . ." Her expression was serious. "You can trust him."

She left. I heard Petra's chatter until they reached the end of the hall where my grandmother slept. I sat in a chair by the window with Mama Odessa's journal and opened the cover.

My heart swelled with anticipation of the journey I had ahead of me, but also from the sadness.

I focused on the first page of my great-grandmother's writing and read the words:

December 20, 1872

Yesterday, I married Elijah Black. I pray our children and theirs and theirs will read it in the same way the stories in the Good Book were passed through the family line.

The days have been dark, and the times are hard, but there has always been love, even before Freedom. Find love and keep it. It's the only thing that no man or woman can take away.

Love,
Odessa Conway Black

I read until Petra came to put me out. The words from my great-grandmother from 150 years ago caused emotions to stir that shook me at my core. And her writing—it was so eloquent and beautiful. I knew the words would change my life in some way, and that was a good thing. I needed a change. I thought about the river behind the house and the pictures I'd taken along the way. Black River was more than a good omen; it was a part of me. I looked forward to finding out just how much.

11

Odessa Conway

GEORGETOWN AND CHARLESTON,
SOUTH CAROLINA, 1869–1872

HER FATHER NEVER WANTED HER WITH ELIJAH BLACK, BUT
Odessa lost her heart to him between lunch and dinner on a hot
summer day.

Papa didn't like the fact that he was uneducated, so Odessa
taught him to read and write. He was pretty good with numbers
already, but she also taught him arithmetic. Now Papa didn't like
the fact that he traveled so much for work. The only thing she
didn't like was Elijah wasn't willing to move up north. Teaching
and moving north, those were the two things Odessa wanted
most.

Odessa focused on the teacakes she was making for the children in her class. She was teaching at the church school every
day and had promised them sweets if they all did well on their
exam tomorrow. Elijah was repairing some of the brick on the

kitchen hearth for Mama. Odessa turned her attention to him. Her next words were going to anger him, but they had to be said. "You have gone to every plantation left in Georgetown. She's not here, Elijah."

"I ain't been to every plantation. You know how many people was farming rice? And I got letters out all over the network."

"You don't have to tell me about all the letters you have out in the network. I wrote them."

He grunted as if that didn't matter in this discussion, but it did. Odessa was invested in finding his mama, too, but she was not going to pretend she wasn't growing weary.

Elijah stood from the floor. He walked to his tools and moved them around, seeking out another before getting back down. "I'm gonna hear something about her."

"Papa will telegram us if you get a letter."

Elijah didn't say anything.

"What if she doesn't"—Odessa hesitated—"come back?"

"Don't do that." He banged a fist on a wood plank next to him. It was the first time she'd seen Elijah slam something on account of her words. He didn't have a temper. Odessa looked through the door that joined the kitchen to the keeping room. Her mother was there, close enough to chaperone but far enough not to hear every word they spoke. She didn't seem stirred by Elijah's tone.

"I'm sorry." Odessa smoothed her hands down her dress like she could wipe her foolish words away. She knew she shouldn't have supposed his mama wasn't coming back. "I was thinking she could be married and have more children."

Elijah pulled his head out of the hearth and stood again. "She would see 'bout me."

Odessa agreed she would, so she asked if he had considered the worst—that she might not be living?

"You don't understand, Dessa. You got people."

"I'm your people. I'm trying to be." She shifted closer to him and took his hand. "I won't marry anyone else, so Papa will have to let me marry you, or he'll turn me into an old maid."

"I'd prefer your father want me to be his son-in-law."

Odessa stepped back. She was just over seventeen years old. Papa's blessing was going to be hard to get. "He'll come around."

But deep down inside, Odessa worried. She'd overheard words between her parents. Mama disagreed, but Papa wanted his daughter to marry a light-skinned man. He saw the difference in treatment, even after slavery. But Papa could desire that all he wanted. She wasn't going to change her mind. Elijah was all the way in her heart. There wasn't any room for anyone else, light or dark.

"Never you mind about Papa. *My* mind is made up."

Elijah's eyes said he wasn't sure.

"We don't need to talk about marrying until you finish school." Elijah was thoughtful before speaking again. "I've been thinking on it for a while. I can help pay."

Odessa shook her head. "Papa is saving."

"He's a country preacher. How long you think it'll be before he have enough to send you to Fisk or Philadelphia?"

"But you're saving to buy land."

"I'm saving for our future." His eyes darted toward the keeping room door to make sure Mama hadn't moved from her chair before he took her hand. "Your father will have to see I care about the family enough to educate his daughter." He kissed the top of her head. "You apply to whatever school is best for teaching. I'll talk to your father." He placed a hand under her chin and tipped it up. "It's settled now."

Her eyes sank into his. If he wouldn't go north with her, they'd be separated while she went to school. She didn't want that.

She thought her heart would spin out of her chest and spiral into the earth if she couldn't see Elijah, but he was right. Odessa knew her father, and so did her man. He was high-minded about what he wanted for her. He would give them his blessing if Elijah did this. Her father had respect as a pastor, but little money. Nothing would make him prouder than to have an educated daughter.

A few days later, when her father went to Charleston for business, Odessa went with him. Uncle Bishop owned a second house in Charleston. These days, her cousin Liz was there because she was able to teach full-time.

Things were changing in the state. Papa talked politics at dinner every night. The year before, a new constitution was written, and 73 of the 124 delegates were men of the race or mixed race. All of them were Republicans. They passed voting laws, laws for education, and even some laws for women's rights. On the local level, the Freedmen built more churches, schools, and mutual aid societies. People started newspapers and opened more stores. There was so much going on in the city.

But though there was progress, some things remained the same. Charleston was divided. Before Freedom, they were divided by free and enslaved, with free people of color keeping themselves separate from the problems of the enslaved by creating their own communities and networks. After Freedom, they were divided by class and color. Uncle Bishop, being white enough to pass, purchased his home where other nearly white mixed-race people did.

Odessa had been to Uncle Bishop's house on Coming Street only once. She hadn't seen Cousin Liz in months. Having considered herself cooped up for years during the war, Liz no longer came to her father's house in Georgetown. A maid let Odessa into the foyer of the two-story brick house.

After a short wait, Cousin Liz joined Odessa at the dining

room table where Odessa had been seated, kissing her cheek before she sat. "I was happy to receive your post last week." Cousin Liz rarely wasted time with unimportant talk when a matter was pressing. Tea and lunch were brought in by a maid. "I have good news. I went to a meeting just yesterday. Training for female teachers will begin"—she paused for what looked like dramatic effect—"here in Charleston."

Excitement rose in Odessa's chest. Training here. She was overcome. She had been praying for teacher training in Charleston.

"I only taught you to about seventh or eighth grade, so you'll have to complete secondary classes before and pass an exam, but once you're done with those, you may apply for enrollment. I'll provide the necessary letter of recommendation, of course." Cousin Liz paused again. Odessa knew she liked to break up her speech, and she didn't like to be interrupted, so Odessa waited. "And there's money from the American Missionary Association for fees. You would have to pay for your room and board. To that end, you may room here. We're family. I'm sure you won't eat me into the poorhouse."

Another wave of emotion rushed through Odessa. Like a strong wind, it nearly toppled her out of the straight-back chair she was sitting in. "Cousin Liz, thank you." Odessa wanted to reach for the woman's hand and squeeze it, but Cousin Liz didn't like to be touched that way—even the kiss she'd placed on Odessa's cheek had been to the air. "I don't know what to say about all of this."

"Say you'll be a credit to the race."

Odessa smiled and picked up her cup. "I can promise that."

<hr />

Moving to Charleston held some excitement, but it was also hard. Odessa hated leaving her mother. Now that she was packing, she wondered how she would fare when she eventually went north. Mama and she had never been apart her whole life.

"I has some Jimson Weed, Fever Root, Mullen, Yarrow, and mint." A paper tag wrapped with colored ribbon closed the fabric around each set of leaves. "And witch hazel."

Odessa looked at the stack of healing herbs and salves. "Mama, I can't tote all this. I need room for my clothes and books."

"You gon' need it. You get an ache in your head or a stomach pain, and you gon' wish you had your tonics." She stacked the plants she was sending, adding a piece of muslin between each plant so they didn't mix, and then rolled the bundle and tied it.

"They have doctors for the pupils. Colored ones." Odessa said it to her mother like her mother didn't understand the details about where she was going. She'd explained it to her a hundred times since the acceptance letter had come.

Stipends from the AMA were only for the teacher training classes. Odessa had to pay to take high school classes for a year. The public school did not have many students ready for high school because most were still at the primary school level learning to read and write. The only schools with high school classes were the private ones. They'd been operating in Charleston for free people of color for years, way before Freedom. They had fees that were greater than most colleges. Elijah paid every penny without hesitation.

Odessa finished packing the lunch bag she would be carrying with her. Fried chicken and buttered biscuits with muscadine jam were what she would eat until she got settled in Charleston. She put her food into her shoulder bag with her novel and handkerchief. Her mother handed her the plants she'd bundled. "Everything don't require a doctor. You goin' to school to get more knowledge, not to forget what you already know."

Mama stepped back. Her face was stormy with worry. Odessa understood now. This was all her mother had to give her. A healer was who she'd always been, so prayer and healing is what she had.

"Yes, ma'am. I'm sorry I made it seem as if this wasn't important." Odessa pushed the cloth into her overstuffed bag.

Mama's eyes filled with tears. "I don't know what I'm 'posing to do without you. I just don't understand. What's wrong with you teaching the colored here what you already know?"

"We've talked about this. Getting more education will help me to be a better teacher."

"But you know most everything you need to know. You know 'bout much as Liz."

"I do not." She said the words in a tight whisper. "I need to learn more history and science and writing."

"For what?" Mama asked. "You gonna marry Elijah. That man has a good trade."

"I know all that Elijah is. I know better than anyone, but I want to teach. We'll never move forward as a people without education."

Mama was slow to speak, like she was nervous. Odessa felt a warning coming on. "You have to be single to finish at the school. That be three years more after this one . . ." Her mother's voice broke off for a second. "If'n you follow those folks' rules, you gonna lose your man."

Odessa's back had been to her mother. She turned now and looked at her. So this was it. She thought she would lose him. "Elijah and I love each other. He believes in me and what I want to do. If he didn't, he wouldn't be paying."

Odessa moved to get her bag and the crate she was taking with her books. Once she reached the door, she put both down and rushed to her mother for a final hug. "I love you, Mama. I'll see you soon."

Heavy tears fell from her mother's eyes. She was behaving like she wasn't going to see her again. Papa traveled to Charleston a few times a month for business and meetings. She could travel with him and see her. But Odessa understood—they'd always been together.

The door opened, and her father stepped in for her things. He took them to Uncle Bishop's carriage. Once loaded, she and her father climbed into the carriage.

"You be safe," Mama said, tears streaming down her face, pain echoing in her voice. "You mind your ways."

Odessa wanted to believe her mother was being nonsensical, but Mama had told her why she worried so.

They were enslaved before Freedom. But Odessa never worked like most enslaved people. She had daily chores, lots of them in her estimation, but combined, they didn't take more than half a day's time. She'd heard stories about how the enslaved on cotton fields worked before sunrise to after the sun went down. That the women delivered babies and went back to work the same day. The lash of the whip on backs that were already broken from cruel labor.

Mama hated that Odessa was so spoiled.

"You just like milk someone left out for a week."

She blamed Papa for not preparing her to be a woman of the race. Slavery had not made Odessa tough in the way she needed to be.

Her mother had been right, because now that she was off the plantation, city life among angry, poor white folks was dangerous and scary. Negro women were still being beaten for just existing and certainly for speaking up when they were wronged. This was the reason her mother didn't want her to go to Charleston.

Odessa settled into life at Cousin Liz's house. When she wasn't in class learning, she was studying. She also taught reading and writing two nights a week plus Saturday mornings and Sunday afternoons. She had fifty-one adults in her class and only eighteen *McGuffey Readers* to be shared among all of them. They were also short on slates and chalk. No matter how much they asked for more and more were provided, there were never enough supplies.

⁓

Her high school courses took two years to finish. Once completed, she applied for the program at Avery, but was denied. They already had a few female students and would not enroll more. Odessa was crushed.

Although Odessa found it rewarding to see the adults in her class learn their letters and writing, she had a dream to teach literature. It would never happen this way. Elijah could see her heart was broken. He tried to encourage her to continue her education.

"Odessa, you can apply to Avery next quarter."

"There's no point. They only want a certain kind of Negro from the right kind of Charleston family. Cousin Liz tried to help me, but anyone who was born a slave isn't their kind of people."

Elijah was as disappointed as she was. "What about the school in Columbia?"

"They're closing for teacher training."

He'd been standing across the living room, pacing near the large window that faced the street. "Fisk?"

"No." She stood and walked to him, raising her hand to touch his face. "Let's get married, love," she said. "We've been waiting five years already."

Elijah kissed her hands. "You sure? I don't want to get my heart excited for it."

"There are people who need teaching in Georgetown. I can do what I'm doing now and be married. With my stipend and your pay, if you move in to Uncle Bishop's place, we can save for our own house."

Elijah smiled. "Ain't I supposed to ask you for your hand?"

"Then get to asking." She returned his smile.

Elijah got down on one knee and proposed marriage to her. On December 20, 1872, she became Mrs. Elijah Black. As she said yes to that dream, she let the dream of graduating as a full teacher go.

12

OAK TREES WITH KNOTTED ROOTS WEIGHED DOWN WITH Spanish moss lined the entrance to Nigel's property. Branches and leaves rustled in the persistent breeze. There were a thousand stars in the sky—all looked as if they begged to be touched. The beauty of the sky was closer here. Of that, I was certain.

I parked. I hadn't had time to do a full inspection earlier, but I thought it was nice. He'd been right. It was sufficient to meet my needs.

The flooring was a walnut hardwood that contrasted with the gray white-washed wood on the walls. The stark difference between the two was a handsome touch. A contemporary brass chandelier hung over the coffee table in the great room. It rivaled the one in my own house that I'd had custom made and shipped from Canada. The area rug was like the one on my grandmother's porch. It included hints of the blue but also various shades of gray, brown, and orange. The walls displayed paintings of rivers, beaches, and the marsh. Sweetgrass baskets held glass fruit on the kitchen table and decorative balls on the end tables. The overstuffed living-room furniture and cushions added a fashionable touch.

Who decorated this for him?

After setting down my bag, I stepped outside on the front porch. The breeze carried a chill, but it was welcoming. I hadn't seen it before, but now I noticed a bottle tree made from a wire frame was pitched near the shrubbery on the edge of the property. I'd seen several of them today.

I sat in the swing, opened my phone, and scrolled through my messages. My mother's calls waited returning. I wasn't ready for the conversation I needed to have with her. She didn't know it, but she wasn't ready for me either. I called Leslie. She was the more deserving of the two.

"You're kidding!" Leslie said after I told her about my day. "You must be in shock. It came together so fast. It was meant to be!"

Leslie said everything I was thinking. "She's so sweet. Everyone is so nice. If Lachelle and Uncle Roger are anything like the rest of them, I'm going to love them all."

Leslie scoffed. "No one loves all of their relatives, but that's a nice fantasy."

I laughed. "I know, but I mean they aren't mean or messy."

"Not on the surface," Leslie teased. "Your mother is nagging me. She knows I know where you are."

"I'll talk to her tomorrow."

"She's worried. It's not like you to ignore her."

"Maybe I *should* be doing this to her. The consideration I give to her isn't returned."

"Don't get down there and get new."

"Leslie, my grandfather died when I was fourteen. There was no way for me to see him without *her*. She made sure it didn't happen. I'm angry about that."

Leslie's sigh was filled with agreement. "Auntie does have some explainin' to do, but don't . . ." Leslie paused. "Forget it. It's not my place to tell you how to feel."

"I appreciate you saying that. I'd never disrespect my mother, but I can't act like this is okay."

"I'm so sorry," Leslie said. "But hey, you didn't get a spell cast on you."

"They are obsessed with spirits down here. Bottle trees and haint blue paint everywhere."

Leslie sucked her teeth. "I told you. Watch ya back."

We talked about a few things and then she got a call from her new man. Ending ours was necessary and quick.

I reentered the house. Due to the openness of the floor plan, I could see clear through the kitchen and out the rear door, where there was a bright light in the yard. I crossed the room. With a tug, I pulled back the sheer drapes. Nigel lived in an Airstream trailer in the backyard. I could see the end of his truck behind it.

I stepped outside and followed the light. As I got closer, I began to think my behavior was right out of a horror movie. What was I doing out in the dark, walking across this yard? Woods were less than twenty-five feet from the Airstream. I walked around the side where the light was coming from and found Nigel sitting in a hot tub.

"Hey, neighbor," he said, greeting me cheerfully.

I stepped closer. "Aren't you fancy?"

"Farm work leaves me achy."

The man wasn't wearing a shirt of course, because men don't wear shirts in hot tubs. I turned my head for a minute, looking around at everything in the vicinity except him.

"Are you comfortable over there?"

I stuck my hands in my pockets and cleared my throat. "Everything is great. It's a beautiful place. Looks like it has a designer's touch."

"It does. In fact, one of your cousins decorated for me. She moved to Texas last year." He smiled. "You're going to learn the Blacks are quite industrious. If you need something, somebody in your family does it. Your aunt Thea will explain." He reached for a beer bottle and took a sip. He assessed me with that curious gaze he'd planted on me twice today. He was looking through me, trying to inspect what lay beneath the surface.

"I'm curious about something that's been bugging me. Why were you at my grandmother's house?"

"I *am* the farm manager. I have been for five years."

Managing a three-hundred-acre farm had to be a big job, so that would make Nigel a big shot. I made a low whistling sound, acknowledging his status before saying, "Okay. That's kind of wow, but why were you so full of no help earlier when I asked you if you knew Blacks?"

"People have been sniffing around that land for years. When you mentioned the Blacks and tax records, you became suspect."

It really is a small world. The thought was less fleeting than it ordinarily was, but I reckoned Georgetown was small. "Can I ask you something?"

He shot me a good-natured grin. "Here we go again. You've been asking me questions since I met you."

"Sorry. I'm new in town." I had to laugh at myself. I was being repetitive. "What is a season?"

His squinted at me. "Do you mean a planting season?"

I shrugged. "My grandmother asked me to stay a season."

"Well, yeah, she'd be talking planting." Nigel stood and stepped out of the hot tub. He wiped his face with a towel. "A season," he said, moving closer to me, "is from seed to harvest."

My breath had left my body. I scratched my head and tried to stay focused on our conversation. Nigel's body glistened in the light coming from the moon. Water dripped from his chest and shorts.

He is fine.

"I *umm* . . . get my vegetables from the supermarket. How long is seed to harvest?"

He wrapped the towel around the back of his neck.

"The spring season officially starts tomorrow. Your timing is perfect. The seed blessing ceremony is in the morning." He continued, "To answer your question, harvesting begins in May, June. It depends on the vegetable."

"I can't stay until May."

Nigel reached for the hot tub cover and flipped it over. "You must have said something to make her think you could."

"I told her I was on a break from my business."

He picked up his near-empty beer bottle. "Ah, that's all you had to say. She expects you"—he tipped his bottle toward me— "to stay." He paused, looking through me again. "Besides, you seem like someone who's looking for somewhere to be. Maybe Ma Black sees that."

I sighed. There was witchcraft down here. This man was reading me like a medium, but I wasn't going to let him get away with basically calling me lost. "You know if you weren't like family, I'd be offended by that statement."

"Don't be offended. I'm simply an intuitive man."

I stuck my hands in my back pockets. I couldn't argue with that. "Maybe you're right."

Nigel said, "You seem to be intuitive yourself. I am like family, but what clued you in?"

"My grandmother asked you to stay for some pretty sensitive family business today."

He nodded. "That she did." Nigel's eyes searched me for a few seconds. I couldn't discern what he was looking for, but I didn't turn away. A slow, lazy smile slipped through his lips. "You did a lot of driving. You should get some rest."

"I am pretty worn out." I took a step away from him. His wet body seemed to be inching toward me.

"Let me know if you need anything," he said and then added, "in the house." As if he needed to clarify what he meant. Was he flirting?

"I will." I turned and started for the steps.

"Oh, and Casey . . ."

I stopped moving. I looked at him, waiting for him to say whatever it was he was going to say while trying not to be distracted by the fact that he still wasn't wearing a shirt. "I never *ever* claim a beautiful woman as a relative unless there's blood or marriage tying us together." He *was* flirting. He smiled again, and I couldn't help feeling some kind of way about those good-sense-stealing eyes of his.

"Good night, Nigel." I turned and headed toward the house.

"Enjoy my well-appointed accommodations!"

Smiling to myself, I gave him a backward wave. He was going to be interesting.

13

ONE LID AT A TIME, I OPENED MY EYES. UNFAMILIAR FUR-
niture came into view. The pervasive quiet was like noise in my
head. In New York, I awoke to street sounds, honking horns,
and garbage trucks starting, stopping, and banging. There were
sirens, people, vehicles, things. But here it was still. Silence was
a different kind of noise. It was intrusive. It made it possible for
everything I thought to reverberate like a cymbal against my
consciousness.

I rubbed my eyes and out of habit, reached for my phone.
Before I swiped, I put it down. Not yet. The world locked inside it
could wait until I had coffee. The South was changing me already.

I stood and walked to the window. It was still dark, but there
was a light on in Nigel's trailer. He was an early riser, too, of
course. He was a farmer.

I pulled the door open. Before I stepped out, I heard a noise.
It sounded like the hum of the dryer. I stepped back in and
reached for my robe. My pj's were short. The last thing I wanted
was for the dirty-clothes burglar who'd broken in to see me half-
naked. He might get ideas for me while his clothes were on the
cool-down cycle.

I looked around the room for a weapon and saw a set of golf

clubs in the corner. I grabbed one, raised it over my shoulder, and opened the door. I stepped out just as the bathroom door opened. I flipped the light switch.

Nigel stepped out in a towel. I screamed and dropped the club. "You scared me to death."

"I was taking a shower."

I let my eyes wander up and down his nearly naked body. "I can see that."

Using the hand that wasn't holding the towel, he raised an index finger. "I forgot to tell you. This is a shared rental."

"What's that?"

"It means we share the common areas—that's this bathroom, the laundry room, and the oven on the rare occasions that I bake something. I do everything else in the Airstream."

I huffed. "I'm not used to sharing space."

Nigel quirked an eyebrow. "The tan on your finger is not for a missing wedding band?"

"You're nosy."

"I'm observant."

"Marriage is different." I thought about it for a few seconds. I didn't want to move. I liked his house. "It would be nice to know when you're here."

"Some mornings at about six and in the evening one or two nights a week. I shower at my parents' house. I'm there most days after work. I get my farm dirt off there."

I bit my lip. I wasn't used to this kind of deal.

Nigel's voice interrupted my thoughts. "If you're not comfortable, I know of another rental that you can look into."

"No. It's fine. I'm already unpacked. My grandmother all but ordered me to stay here."

Seemingly satisfied we'd resolved that, he walked to the laundry room door. "You're up early."

"I'm usually up before seven."

He pointed into the room. "My clothes are in here, so I'll just close this door and get dressed."

He disappeared, and I forced myself to mentally mind my business. I padded my way to the kitchen. "Do you want a cup of coffee?"

"Black would be great!"

His Keurig looked new. "Is this thing already clean?"

"Yep!"

I set up a cup for him. By the time he finished getting dressed, the coffee was ready. He took a sip and thanked me.

"Everything dry?"

"It was already dry. I put it back in to get the wrinkles out."

"Is that replacement for an iron?"

"On some days. Usually, I don't care much about wrinkles, but today is the ceremony. I don't want to look bad."

"I meant to ask you what that was last night."

"It's an annual ceremony some of the farmers observe. They pray for the planting season. Because this is one of the biggest farms in the region, the mayor comes, folks from the USDA office, and other important people. It starts at ten thirty."

Now I understood why as I was leaving dinner, I was charged with being at the farm no later than 10:00 a.m. "Well, I'll see you there later."

Nigel did that thing he'd done last night—it was a look; I was readable. He took a few more sips of the coffee, rinsed the mug, and put it in the sink.

I followed him to the door, watched him walk to the Airstream, and minutes later, he exited and got in his truck. I locked the door and took my coffee back to the bedroom with me. As I walked past the bathroom, I stopped and peeked in. Save for the steam, it didn't even seem like it'd been touched.

I could smell cleanser, so I know he cleaned the shower after. This wasn't a problem. It was just a shower and laundry. I had a private en suite bathroom.

Back in the bedroom, I picked up my phone and scrolled through my social media. The comments there were depressing. I still had close to a million followers. I wondered if they were hanging around to see if I'd act out again. I checked emails. More depressing. I was losing revenue daily. I had multiple requests for interviews and a heated email from Brooke confirming per Swella I would reach out to her by the end of the week.

It was early, but my mother was an early riser, too, so I called her.

Before she could say a word, I spoke. "I'm in Georgetown. I arrived yesterday. I've met the Blacks."

There was a long beat of silence before my mother asked, "Who have you met?"

"My grandmother, Mrs. Ida."

A soft gasp came through the speaker. "I can't believe Ida is alive. She must be nearly a hundred."

"She's ninety-nine."

I heard the bed creak on my mother's end. "Mr. Eddie?"

"He'd be almost 120, Mom. He died in ninety-seven."

"I'm so shocked. I can't believe you're there."

"Did you think I would never try to learn more about my father?"

"You didn't care about it, and now you do, and that's *only* because you're avoiding what really matters."

"Are you serious? You don't think I cared about my father? About my family?"

"You're the one meeting them at thirty-six." My mother was right about that. She added, "The Blacks were never *my* family."

"I'm a Black, Mother. I came from two people. I don't just belong to you."

My mother sighed. "You do just belong to me because Matthew is dead."

I rolled my eyes. She had zero remorse, and that was unacceptable. "I'm going. I'm angry with you right now. I'll call when I'm not."

"Casey . . ."

"Say goodbye, Mother." I ended the call.

14

I PULLED INTO THE DRIVEWAY OF THE FARM. THERE WAS A news van near the house, and the rest of the lot was overflowing with cars and pickup trucks. I eased into an empty parking space. I was surprised it had been empty, but then I realized why. There was a sign made of wood, painted white, with my name etched into it. Someone had been busy early this morning.

I got in my feelings for a moment. The emotions swirling in and around me had been overwhelming because this trip was turning into the very most. And I still hadn't decided what I was going to call my grandmother. Granna was the name on the tip of my tongue. The grandmother from my favorite childhood book was called Granna. As a child I'd thought if I had a grandmother, I'd want to call her that. I had no idea if my grandmother would like it.

I sent a text to Leslie: I don't know what to call her. "Grandmother" feels formal.

I can't say Grandmom or Grandma.

Leslie replied: Why not?

I replied: I don't know. I think it's different when you meet them when you're older.

Leslie replied: Girl, you are hilarious. You'll figure it out, but you're right, Grandmother is too formal for the country.

A tap on my driver's side door startled me. I locked eyes with Nigel. I pushed the button for the ignition, and he pulled my door open.

I stepped out. Before I could greet him, he cocked his head toward the sign.

"Casey Black." He shoved my door closed. "You're important around here."

I pushed my keys into my jean pocket. "She shouldn't have."

"It made Ma Black happy to see it."

"How did it get done so fast?"

Nigel pushed on the post to make sure it was steady. "One of the employees works with wood as a hobby. She asked him to do it, and he got right on it."

I fell into step with Nigel as we walked around the back of the store, past my grandmother's house to the entrance of the farm.

There were about forty people gathered around the stage where my grandmother was sitting. I recognized reporters from the extended-range cameras they held. Most of those gathered were farmhands. The gentleman on the stage looked familiar, but I couldn't place him.

I leaned into Nigel. Once I had his attention, I asked, "Who's that?"

"The mayor of Georgetown."

That was it. I'd seen his smiling face on the city website.

"I'll see you in a few," Nigel said. He raised his hat to me before walking to the stage to join my grandmother and her other distinguished guests.

It was seventy-eight degrees and balmy. The sun broke through a thicket of white clouds in the distance and provided the perfect cerulean backdrop for the events.

I removed my phone from my pocket and took a few pictures of the stage and then the setup in front of it. There was soil, seeds, a water can, and some other soily-looking stuff labeled "Compost." I filmed a video.

Two of the farmhands lit candles on tall wooden stands at either end of the stage.

There was noise from the podium. Nigel had stepped up and taken the microphone.

"Good morning. My name is Nigel Evanston. It's my pleasure to thank you all for being here for the seventy-sixth seed ceremony for Black Farms."

There was a round of applause from everyone.

Nigel continued, "I welcome the members of the press who support local farmers with media coverage for our events throughout the year. Sometimes I think we'd disappear and be forgotten without you, so we appreciate you being here again. We look forward to a long, productive, and collaborative season."

My grandmother tugged at Nigel's arm. He leaned toward her. She whispered something to him, and his eyes fell on me. He cleared his throat and said, "Casey, would you come up here?"

I thought I'd be a spectator, but I was on my way up to the dais. The crowd near the steps parted, and one of the men assisted me up the steps and handed me off to Nigel. His fingers closed around mine. Electricity surged between us, throwing me off for a few seconds. He covered the mic and whispered, "Your grandmother wants you introduced," then he returned his attention to the crowd.

"Mrs. Black would like you all to meet her granddaughter, Casey Black." A gentle applause came from the attendees. Nigel covered the microphone again and whispered, "She just sprung this on me. Do you want to say something?"

I blushed, pulled my hand from Nigel's and raised it to wave at the small crowd. Being "on" was something I knew how to do. I leaned toward the mic. "Thank you for allowing me to be a part of this planting season. I'll try hard to stay out of everyone's way."

A few of the men laughed.

Nigel leaned in to the mic again. "This is Casey's first season planting, but we don't want it to be her last, so let's help her out today."

I stepped backward, closer to my grandmother's chair. She enclosed my hand with hers and held it on her shoulder. It was wrinkled by time but warmed by her affection for me. The love had been instant on both our parts. I guess we needed each other. I was hoping she would like Granna. It was all I saw when I looked at her. That and pride.

I knew she had Nigel and all the other employees, but Grandpa Eddie had been gone for twenty-two years. She kept this farm going. She was a baddie.

This was a legacy. I wondered if my father would have farmed after he finished his military career. Would my mother be here in Georgetown instead of up north? My father's death had changed the direction of my mother's life, I was sure of it, but I'd never had a conversation with her about the plans she and my dad had. His army career would play a part, but the details—why he had joined, was he planning a long career in the service, or was he planning to serve some time and get out—were a mystery to me.

Nigel introduced the mayor and a representative from the USDA extension office—whatever that was—and they spoke briefly. Then it was time for my grandmother to have words.

The warmth of her hand left mine. I looked at her as she pushed off the arms of the chair and stood. She had strong, determined movements. Her height added to her prestigious presence. She walked to the podium and began speaking.

"Ezekiel 36:34 says, 'The desolate land shall be tilled instead of lying desolate in the sight of all who pass by.' Every year, the words I say at this ceremony become less because God becomes more. This is a time to honor the earth that He has given us to eat from, but I'm glad the mayor is here and other important people from the county leadership. I hope you will continue to serve the land here in Georgetown County because in serving the land, you feed the people and preserve our way of life.

"During the early 1800's, Georgetown was the largest exporter of rice in the world. This was due to free labor of thousands of enslaved people in the rice fields. Since emancipation, more than forty thousand acres of land from those former plantations have been abandoned—given back to the alligators and the marsh. My hope is for our government officials to work with the people in the county who want to grow food and farm to be able to access this land instead of selling to developers. I pray we see more Black farmers have access to what their ancestors worked. Developers bring in some tax money, tourists, but what they take away as they build hurts the earth that God has entrusted to us. Thank you. I believe they call that a TED Talk."

People laughed.

My grandmother stepped to a large whiskey barrel filled with soil. She placed her hands in the soil, moved it around, and raised her hands with a fist full.

"Oh majestic God, Your Word says, 'The earth brought forth grass, the herb that yields seed according to its kind, and the tree that yields fruit, whose seed is in itself according to its kind. And God saw that it was good.'"

She returned the dirt, mixed compost with it, and scooped out a few holes. She reached into a small bucket and removed a few seeds.

"You provide seed, water, and nutrients."

She placed the seeds in the soil, poured water in a circle around the seeds, and added more compost.

When she was done, she prayed, "Divine Father, bless the

work of our hands, the earth below our feet, and the heart of the seed we return to her. Give us grace, good weather, and protection from everything that would harm our bounty. In Jesus' name, I pray. Amen."

Nigel returned to the podium and said, "Let's plant."

Music erupted from the speakers.

Everyone cheered, and the employees dispersed, tossing punch cups in the trash as they went their separate ways to different locations on the farm.

I stepped off the stage. My grandmother and Nigel were busy with the politicians, and I wanted no part of those conversations. After a few minutes, Nigel walked the big shots out the gate. My grandmother took my hand. "You come with me."

I followed her into one of several massive greenhouses on the property. I watched while she planted five things. Two from seed, two from little plants I learned were called seedlings, and pieces of what looked like a potato. She planted those in a burlap bag.

"Okra, tomatoes, kale, onions, and potatoes. You can do all your survivin' with just these things." My grandmother put sticks with the name of each plant inside the pots. "The tomato is the only one that has to stay in the greenhouse. We have to wait for the last frost to put it out."

My face must have read *overwhelm* because my grandmother chuckled. "One day, one plant at a time." She pointed at a table. "You put these over there. Everything on that table goes outside. Nigel'll have somebody take it out."

I moved the okra, kale, onion, and potato pots to the table. There was a lull of a few seconds in my grandmother's work, so I took advantage of it. "I need to ask you something."

My grandmother looked at me with a sweet kind of expectation. Her face was so open, it welcomed any and all questions, and that made me less anxious.

"There are a lot of things people call their grandmothers. There's one name in particular that I like, but I want to make sure you like it too."

My grandmother's lips split in a small smile. "I'd be pleased to hear it."

"It's Granna. I know it's not that common . . ."

She grabbed my hand and gave it an emotional squeeze. "I like it. I like the way you say it. I can hear the affection." Wetness filled her eyes, and I could feel her affection for it too.

I released a heavy breath. I was glad that was decided.

Her warm eyes swallowed me. "I'm so glad to have you here."

We shared a moment with each other holding hands until the door opened. Nigel entered, pulling a wheelbarrow behind him.

"You have good timing. I need to go walk the farm." She turned to me again. "I like to see the seeds go into the ground. Nigel will teach you." She left us.

"I just watched her do those." I pointed to the table. "And this tomato plant."

"Okay, let's do some more," he said. Nigel showed me how to repot seedling plants. There was a lot of repotting to be done. It only took watching twice to get it, but he still didn't leave.

"Are you afraid I'm going to kill everything?"

"My people have their assignments. Per my boss, I'm to work with you."

We worked together side by side in silence with only the hum of machinery from outside in the background. The door creaked open and closed with the entrance of employees bringing something in or taking something out. It was peaceful work and surprisingly satisfying.

Nigel was fast, doing two or three pots to my one even while taking calls on his cell and walkie-talkie with questions from his employees.

"How did you learn all this?" I asked.

He stopped, giving me his full attention to answer. "I studied agriculture at Clemson, but I learned most of what I know from my father."

"You grew up on a farm?"

"Ten miles from here. It's not anything like this. There aren't many farms this big in the whole state. My father has twenty-two acres."

Nigel cocked his head a bit, and though his lips didn't open, a smile hinted at his mouth enough for that dimple to appear. A rush of warmth flooded my body. I was too young for a hot flash. We'd exchanged too much direct eye contact, so I busied myself by reaching for the hand shovel I'd been using and made a hole in the pot I needed to plant next. "That's still a lot of land," I said, giving him my attention again.

"He grows some vegetables, but he also raises goats and sells them and their milk."

"If you have a farm in your family, why aren't you there?"

"My brother runs my father's and my uncle's farm. There isn't enough work for both of us."

I scooped compost into a hole I made and then put the plant in. "I'm an only child. I've never had to deal with those dynamics. Do you get along with him?"

"We get along great most of the time. He thinks I think I know more than he does."

Finished, I wiped my hands on my apron. "Do you?"

"I know what I know." I saw confidence, not arrogance in his eyes. "I need you to help me plant some more tomatoes."

I followed him into a separate room in the greenhouse. "This is my private space." He moved a small barrel of soil out of the way to make room for me to pass.

"*Ooh*, what are you cooking up in here, master gardener?"

"Exotic varieties and a few experiments too. Sometimes they do well. Sometimes they don't."

"Unpredictability in your lab."

He shrugged. "We can't control nature."

"It must be hard to invest months and not get anything."

"You have to be growing something that's worth the risk." Nigel stared in my eyes. "All tomatoes aren't the same. Some are more valuable. They're worth the work."

I broke our stare and turned to the table. "So what are the steps here?"

Over the next thirty minutes, Nigel had me repot large tomato seedling plants in whiskey barrel containers. Soil, Epsom salt, lime, compost, and to completely gross me out, he added actual heads of fish.

"Fish heads are one of the best fertilizers you can use for tomatoes, and since we have access to many heads here in low-country, I use them in here."

I watered everything the way he showed me—deep. He inserted markers with the letters *BB* on them and pushed the containers to another section of the greenhouse.

I had an odd sense of satisfaction. The only work I'd ever done with my hands was in applying makeup and doing my hair. I removed my gloves and checked my nails to make sure I hadn't broken one. I'd have to cut them down to work out here. "What does *BB* mean?"

"It's a secret. You'll find out when we harvest them."

"How long will that be?"

Nigel turned up his lip like he was deciphering scientific data. "I planted the seedlings in early February. They take about eighty days. May to June-ish."

"Seeding is a lot of work. They'll be planting for a week."

"We succession plant." Nigel walked me outside where he

pointed left. "They'll only get this part of the farm done this week." He pointed right. "That part next week." He continued to explain the process. "We don't want everything to come up at once. We'd have to sell it all at the same time."

We walked to a patch of land. I was grateful it was dry because my sneakers would be a mess by now. Nigel told me only a third of the land was used for vegetables they sold locally. The rest was used to grow commercial products—soybeans or corn. "This year, it's soybeans," he said, handing me a hoe. He grabbed one for himself. "This row is yours."

I watched what Nigel did and plunged into the soil the same way. We worked side by side digging, turning the soil over, looking for rocks, and repeat. I noticed workers in the rows down from us using a machine to do what we were doing. "What's that?"

"A tiller. It turns the soil."

"So why aren't we using one?"

"You have to learn by hand before you automate a process."

I wiped sweat off my forehead. "Seriously, are you sure you're not trying to see what I'm made of?"

"I know what you're made of. You're a Black."

~⌒~

My bathtub didn't fill up fast enough for me. But even after a good soak, I wanted water with bubbles. I put on a swimsuit and cover-up and left the house with one intention in mind—to get in Nigel's hot tub.

I found him relaxing, the smooth voice of Sade creating a vibe.

"I'm here to crash the party."

Nigel removed the cigar he had planted in his mouth. He put it out in a nearby ashtray. "Welcome."

I placed my towel on a table, removed my robe, kicked off my flip-flops, and stepped down into the water. "This feels good."

Nigel couldn't hide his admiration. He clipped the end of his cigar and reached for his beer like he needed it. "Can I get you a drink?"

I shook my head. "So you're a cigar man."

"Not really."

I waited for his explanation. There had to be one since he was, in fact, smoking a cigar.

"The mayor gives me one every year, and every year, I smoke it." He added, "It's celebratory."

I nodded, swishing my feet around and adding to the agitation.

We were quiet for a stretch before Nigel said, "Ma Black was happy today."

"Seventy years. That's legacy."

"She was happy about you." He took another sip and placed the bottle down. "I don't mean to be nosy."

"Which means you're about to put your nose in my situation."

He tilted his head at me. "Yeah, I am. Ma hasn't been happy in a long time. Why are you two just meeting each other?"

Granna not being happy added to my nagging guilt. I blamed my mother for never meeting my grandfather, but this late sojourn to Georgetown was on me.

"It's complicated, obviously. But there was no easy way to get the truth out of my mother, and in a weird way, I was being subconsciously loyal to her by telling myself I was too busy to figure it out myself."

"But now you want the truth."

"I need the truth about a lot of things." I stood and stepped out of the tub.

"I'm not running you off with questions, am I?"

I slipped into my cover-up. "Not at all. I'm tired, and I don't soak more than ten minutes. It's bad for the skin. I take care of mine."

"I can see that." The admiration in his eyes tinged his tone. "And on that note, you need some farm attire. I get the sense from what you were wearing today that your luggage is full of clothing that shouldn't get dirty."

I smiled at him. "I feel seen."

"We have an account at Wilson's General Store. Tell them I sent you and you need to be outfitted for the farm. Charge it if you want. It adds up."

Nigel knew I pulled up in a new Mercedes, but still hadn't chosen to assume I had money for my farm gear. Something about that struck me as generous and thoughtful. "I'll go in the morning. Thank you," I said. "And thanks for today too."

"Today? Did I do something special?"

"You worked the snot out of me." I chuckled. "I needed a distraction."

"Farm work is good for that."

"I can see. Maybe I'll stay for a while. I could use the distraction."

My words seemed to settle in a good place for him. "We'd be glad to have you, Ms. Black."

I left him to his celebration and went into the house.

15

I HAD DINNER WITH MY GRANDMOTHER THE FOLLOWING DAY and the day after that. Soon we fell into the habit of dining together every evening. She shared stories—stories about herself, her father, Grandpa Eddie, and my great-grandmother Odessa, whom she adored.

In addition to letting me read the journals, Granna told me stories. We also cooked. I mostly fetched ingredients, chopped stuff up, and stirred pots, but I had my hands wrist deep in dough a few times and could officially figure out what a dash of this or that looked like. I picked fresh basil, oregano, and other herbs from the garden. The homemade sweet potato pie we ate, I helped with that.

My time with Granna was enjoyable, but she did not talk about my father—not once, and I didn't want to push her to go there.

I'd been in Georgetown for one week when we had another visitor for dinner. A short, stocky woman with steel-gray hair worn in tiny shoulder-length braids walked in. Her nose was straight, but it flared wide at the end; round cheekbones and pouty lips made her face open and friendly. She rushed into the room, bringing wind like a human tornado. "Is this her?"

Granna nodded. "Who else? Casey, this is your aunt Thea."

Aunt Thea pressed her lips together. "Well, stand up, honey. Give me a hug."

Aunt Thea was technically my cousin. She was my grandfather's great-niece, therefore my second cousin, but she was sixty-eight. Granna said she was Aunt Thea, so that's what I called her.

I stood, and Aunt Thea enveloped me in warmth and the smell of coconut and lavender. She, like Granna, drew feelings of connection from me instantly.

"I can't believe it," Aunt Thea said, holding my hands and shaking her head. "She looks like him." Her eyes teared. "I know you look like your mother, honey, but you also look like your father." Aunt Thea released my hands to swipe her tears away.

I agreed. I could see it in the pictures I'd looked at. It was hard to even narrow down which features, but the resemblance was there. The thought of something of him in me made me emotional.

Granna interrupted our moment. "Fix your food. Our plates are getting cold."

Aunt Thea went into the kitchen. I could hear her saying, "Look at what God has done. I can't believe this."

After she joined us, we said a quick grace. Aunt Thea shoved her fork in her rice and ate a mouthful before returning her attention to me. "How long are you staying?"

"I don't have set plans."

"And you're from New York City?"

"Yes, ma'am."

"That's so far." She looked at Granna. "Who all has met her?"

"Just Lachelle and Roger," Granna replied.

"Well, what you keepin' her for?"

"Because I got the least time here," Granna said.

"Oh, go on with that talk." Aunt Thea waved her hand. "We need to have a little welcome-to-the-family reception."

"You don't have to make a fuss. I'm sure I'll meet people eventually."

"No, I'll figure it out."

"Are there a lot of relatives?" I asked.

"Enough. Uncle Eddie was one of eight—well, seven really . . . not counting Earl." Aunt Thea sighed around some sadness. "Then there are a few people on the Wilson and Ladson side."

Done eating, Granna put down her fork. "I've heard all of Thea's stories. I'm going for a walk." She picked up her plate and took it to the kitchen. I could hear the *pop* of the screen door behind her as she went outside.

"Should she be walking alone like that?"

"She's old, not dead. If walkin'll keep her, she gonna live forever." Aunt Thea threw me another smile. "I can't believe it. Matthew's daughter. Lord Jesus. You right on time."

I wasn't sure what she meant. "Right on time for what?"

"To get to know her. I mean, she's in good health, but she needs some joy in her life. Finding out about you is the medicine God has for her old heart." She continued to stare at me. "I can't believe you are real. Uncle Eddie always said he felt like a piece of himself was still on the earth."

"You mentioned an Uncle Earl and then sort of dismissed him."

Sadness entered Aunt Thea's eyes. "Earl was Eddie's brother. He disappeared when he was eighteen."

Instinctively, my hand went to my heart. "That's terrible."

"He and Eddie had a fight, so the last thing Eddie said to him wasn't good. He carried a lot of guilt about Earl." Aunt Thea pursed her lips and heaved a heavy breath. "And that's why your grandmother doesn't have a bottle tree. The boys fought under the tree. The next day, Earl didn't come home. Eddie always felt responsible for his brother's disappearance. He believed he cursed him." Aunt Thea propped her fist under her chin.

Great-grandma Odessa and Great-grandpa Elijah must have been devastated by the loss. I pressed Aunt Thea for one more fact. "What did everyone else believe about Uncle Earl?"

Aunt Thea drew back in her seat. "What they always believed when a Black man disappeared without a trace back then: trouble with white folks."

I sat there for a moment, processing that he might have been murdered or lynched. I think every Black person wished they didn't have a story like this in their family. I hoped those journals at the end of the hall didn't reveal much more in this vein, but whatever it was, I would endure it. If they lived through it, I could read about it.

"I didn't mean to upset you, but it's a heartache for the family." Aunt Thea stood. "That's enough sad talk."

Aunt Thea told me all about her children and grandchildren. I told her a little about my life. Before I got too far into my story, Granna returned just in time to save me from probing questions.

Aunt Thea noted the time. "I have stayed too long. I'm exhausted after my drive from Greenville, but I had to lay eyes on you."

We all stood together. "It's time for me to get you to bed, Granna," I said. Petra had two nights off a week. This was one of them, so she slept at home.

"Look at you, helping your grandmother." Aunt Thea put her hand on her chest. She squeezed her eyes tight for a few seconds. Tears escaped anyway. "You don't know what you've done coming here." She patted my shoulder. "You just don't know."

Aunt Thea hugged us both and left.

I took care of the dishes while Granna washed up for bed. Once she was in her bedroom, I asked the question that I'd been pondering the entire time I was washing the dishes. "Shouldn't there be someone else here on Petra's nights off?"

"I don't want anybody in my house. It took a year to get used to Petra."

This didn't feel right. A ninety-nine-year-old in a house by herself. "I don't like you being alone."

"I'm not alone, baby."

She was talking about God, but I didn't know God like that. I wanted a human being in this house. I considered curling up on the sofa, but it was too short. I wouldn't get any sleep, and there was the matter of Granna not appreciating me being there when she woke.

She was elderly, but she wasn't helpless. I had to respect her choices. I gave her a kiss on the cheek, locked up, and left her to the God she trusted.

16

GRANNA HAD A SCHEDULE. SHE WAS UP AT FIVE THIRTY IN the morning. She spent an hour praying and doing devotional reading. She ate breakfast, and by seven, she was out of the house. She bathed at eleven thirty, ate lunch at noon, read from whatever novel she was enjoying at twelve thirty, and then from one to two thirty, she took a nap. From three to four thirty, she received healing clients. There was someone nearly every day. At five o'clock, she prepared dinner, served at six sharp, and then she watched an hour of TV or news from seven thirty to eight thirty. She was in bed for the night by nine. She ran her life like I used to run mine, on a timer the whole way through, and I loved that she and I had that in common.

The only thing I didn't know about her schedule was that when she went out at 7:00 a.m., she wasn't in her herb garden, not for at least an hour. Nigel disclosed that she walked every morning. He slid his hands into his pockets. The sun and sky bled blue and white behind him. Against the backdrop of the sky, I was reminded of how handsome he was. "Unless the weather is bad, she walks to the river."

Alarm made it easier not to focus on his chiseled face and bulging biceps. That was a long walk. "By herself?"

133

"The workers keep an eye on her. Her fitness tracker has GPS."

I cocked my head at him. "It's got to be over a mile."

"It's two," Nigel offered unapologetically.

"Is it okay for someone her age to walk that far?"

Lifting his shoulders defensively, Nigel said, "I'm not her doctor."

"What about her heart?"

"I hear it's as fit as a sixty-year-old's."

I raised a hand to my hip. "It seems like a lot."

"It may be, but it's not like you or I could stop her." Nigel cupped a hand over my shoulder. "We watch her, Casey."

"I didn't know people her age could be that physical." I released my anxiety on a long plume of air. "Where is she right now? I want to meet her."

Nigel reached into his pocket for his phone. "I can tell you where she is without looking, but just to be certain . . ." He tapped a few times. "The river." He raised his hand and pointed to the strip of land that split the farm in two. "She comes up that way."

"Thank you." I started to walk, but I noticed a bicycle against the side of the house and figured that would be faster. It took a few minutes for me to get used to riding on uneven grass. I probably could have walked faster.

A few minutes into my ride, I saw Granna. She was flying up the path, nearly as fast as I was pedaling. When I reached her, she smiled and asked without slowing down, "What are you doing all the way down here?"

"Looking for you." I got off the bike and pushed it. "You told me to come before the sun gets high."

She patted my hand like my obedience pleased her.

"So you walk around the farm every day?"

"Half of it. There's no fountain of youth. The secret of staying young is walking, water, and vegetables."

Granna's legs pumped nearly as hard as I could move my own with the bike beside me.

"I'm getting ready for the Waccamaw Senior Games. It's at the end of April. It's like our countywide version of the Olympics. I compete every year."

"Doing what?"

"Walking laps. I ran five years go. I don't much feel like running anymore. I don't have anything to prove."

I didn't think there was a limit to the things this amazing woman did. I'd heard of the Senior Olympics, but I had no idea people competed at her age.

"How far do you walk?"

"We do laps 'round a track. Last year, I did thirty-one. I didn't win though. A seventy-two-year-old did thirty-four and made me second runner-up."

"Granna, that's amazing."

"You can do all things through Christ, baby. You set your mind, commit in prayer, and get to work. It's that simple."

One of the workers stepped into our path. He greeted Granna. She spent a few minutes talking to him while I took pictures of the sun over the river. I'd been to twenty-eight countries, but I didn't think I'd ever seen sunshine this radiant.

I heard Granna call my name, and I fell into step with her again. She picked up our conversation where she'd left off. "This is my last competition. I'll be a hundred. I can't compete after that." Granna squeezed my hand. "I hope you'll come."

"I wouldn't miss it."

I was aware I was committing more time here than I ever planned to, but it felt right. The house and farm were molding around me, providing a cocoon of warmth and safety that I hadn't known I needed.

~⁓~

"Some of the best desserts are the simple ones," Granna said. Today was the day I was going to learn a simple recipe for a fruit cobbler.

Granna stood on one side of the island, and I was on the other—the cooking side.

"First, you take your butter, put it in the glass dish, and stick it in the oven. You just want it melted, so you'll need to keep checking it."

I did as I was told and followed her directions for the fruit mixture, which included blackberries, blueberries, raspberries, sugar, and fresh lemon. Other ingredients included flour, sugar, extracts, and eggs for the crust.

I mixed the ingredients for the crust in a mixer, and after I pulled the ball of sticky dough off the mixer, Granna taught me to put it in a bowl with plastic wrap so the dough could rise. After that, I stretched and flattened it with a rolling pin. I had flour everywhere—my apron, cheeks, arms—but Granna's face held a constant look of contentment. "You're easy to teach. You're a bit of a natural."

"I find that so hard to believe with the mess I'm making."

"It's true. I don't lie about cooking and baking."

I looked at Granna, trying to imagine a scenario in which she would lie about anything.

She seemed to sense my curiosity. She chortled, saying, "I may tell someone they have a nice hat on at church when it's not really so nice, but that's not real lying."

I laughed with her. "I think that's a kindness." I picked up the mason jar labeled cayenne pepper. My curiosity about what we were using this for had gotten the best of me.

"A pinch brings out the flavor in the fruit. It's a little trick. It only applies to berry pies."

I nodded. The scents of fruit, vanilla and almond extracts, brown sugar, and lemon mingled, making promises they were sure to keep.

Once we had that in the oven, we moved on to the main course item, a one-pot shrimp-and-rice dish. We had the kitchen smelling like spices and cilantro, but it was mixed with the smell of my cobbler, which was doing its best to dominate.

"All that cream. I'm going to have to join you for your daily walks to keep from gaining weight."

Granna patted my hip. "Chile, you got a nice shape. A little cream ain't gonna hurt you."

"I'm just not used to having it."

Granna's eyes said I'd cursed. I could see she was serious about cream. "Why? Are you lactose intolerant? I know a lot of Black people get that way. I never did."

"Not yet." I chuckled. "I used to be a fashion model. I had to watch my figure, or I wouldn't get booked for jobs."

Granna's lips split in a wide smile. "I knew there was something special about you. You have a presence. You take up the whole room when you're in it."

I smiled slightly. "Thank you, Granna. That's kind of you to say." I picked up the measuring cups we were using and walked them to the sink to wash them out.

"So, tell me, what kind of modeling?"

I answered over my shoulder. "I started doing commercials when I was two, and then I did print work for designer children's clothing. By the time I was a teenager, I was a runway model."

"Casey, that's wonderful."

"I stopped modeling when I was twenty-seven. I tried a few things, but eventually became a social media influencer."

"What's that, like posting pictures on Spacebook, and what's that other one?"

She tickled me. "Facebook and Instagram. I use quite a few others too."

"How do you make money doing that?"

"Sponsors. If you have enough people following you, you get paid to share products."

"That's interesting," Granna said. "Is that all you do?"

I appreciated her interest, but I wondered if she thought it was a simple job. "It's all I have time for. It's busy."

"It sounds like you might be famous if you have a lot of followers."

The fact that I'd gone from three million to less than a million didn't need to be discussed right now. The fact was, at nine-hundred-thousand plus, I still had a tremendous following. "I'm not famous. The only people who would recognize me would be people who were really into fashion when I was modeling, and now anyone who follows me is into makeup and clothes."

"*Mm-hmm*," Granna said. "That sounds like a famous person to me."

My phone rang, and I recognized the number. I sighed. I needed to have this conversation and stop running from it. I groaned inwardly and looked at Granna. "I have to take this." I tapped the icon as I walked out the back door to the deck.

"Brooke!" I ducked like she was physically with me, attempting to throw something at me.

"Casey! Seriously?"

"I'm sorry."

"Yes, you are, and that's shocking. Victoria told me you were in South Carolina. We must meet."

"I won't be in the city for a while." I thought about my conversation with Leslie about burnout and felt validated in saying, "I'm burned out, Brooke. I'm resting, and this is a good place for it. It's beautiful down here." The sky was clear, and I could see straight down to the river. I wasn't exaggerating.

"I have relatives in the Carolinas; I know what's there. When are you coming back?"

I sighed. "I'm not sure. I—"

"No *I*. This is not about you. It's about me. I have a deadline. Burnout or no burnout, I need to wrap up filming."

"That's the thing though. How are you going to wrap it up?"

Fear stole my breath while I waited for Brooke's response. She hesitated for a few seconds like she had more than one scenario in mind, and then she stole my hope. "With the truth. You imploded, and whatever else you want to say about the fiasco. And your final thoughts about social media, being an influencer, etcetera."

"So basically, you want to turn me into a cautionary tale."

"We can soften it at the end, but you legit *are* a cautionary tale."

Did Brooke realize I was an actual person on the other end of the phone?

"Look, I didn't even want to do this fluff piece. I'm a serious storyteller. I need to finish so I can move on to something in my wheelhouse. Unless you have another way for us to take this story, I have to go with the one that's in front of me."

I sighed.

"And, Casey, if I can't get footage from you, I'll tie it up anyway with someone else's thoughts about your situation and a statement about you not being willing to come back on camera. You've got to know that's worse."

"Wow, Brooke, say you're going to humiliate me without saying it, why don't you?"

"I'm just doing my job."

The phone call ended. I sat there for a long time trying to think of ideas about what we could do to put a spin on this story. I googled myself and scrolled through the many links to the video and every blogger's take on my life. There were pages of links. So many people had written about me. This was tragic, and it made Brooke's job of finding others to talk to easy.

I was two seconds off texting my mother to ask if the crisis management people came up with anything other than me claiming mental health, when I heard Granna call me.

"Casey, come get your cobbler out of the oven!"

No wonder people burned food. Just like that, I'd forgotten I was baking.

Once it was out of the oven, I marveled at how pretty it was. Not perfectly symmetrical or anything like that, but very comfort-food-looking.

"It's perfect," Granna said. "That's exactly the way it's supposed to be."

I was proud of myself. I was going to wait for it to cool and stick my entire face in it. That was what it was going to take to deal with Brooke's threat. The words *comfort food* had more meaning now that I was eating them. The cobbler was right on time.

17

AUNT THEA WAS QUICK ABOUT PULLING TOGETHER MY reception. She and Uncle Roger decided to make it an informal pop-up event at their restaurant that following Sunday.

Rice N' Tings was a small building on the corner of US-701 and County Road. It was in a strip next to a gas station, laundromat, and convenience store. The outside did not lead one to believe the inside would be so nice, but the counter and tables were made from a gorgeous butcher block wood that was finished in stripes of dark and lighter browns, white, haint blue, and a cherry red. Red café chairs were around the tables. There were only ten tables, but between the wood-grain and sawgrass centerpieces, they looked attractive. A menu hung behind the counter, and on the walls were various pictures from lowcountry settings that included fishing boats. There were a few pictures of Uncle Roger holding a fresh catch, and he and Aunt Thea posing with groups of children for sports teams they'd sponsored.

The patio in the rear was large enough to accommodate seating for about twenty. An awning kept the area cool. Uncle Roger was having a spirited conversation in his Gullah tongue with a young man attending an open pit grill. A buffet was set up with a cake that read *We Welcome Oona! Oona* meant "you" in Gullah.

Lachelle and Aunt Thea carried pitchers of sweet tea to the table. When they were satisfied that everything was ready, we took pictures. We exhausted our smiles and poses just as people joined us.

Meeting family was emotional but fun. There were so many names and faces. I'd never remember even a tenth of them, but Granna's nieces and nephews and their children and children's children were a joy to my soul. Not many of Granna's family were present because there weren't many Wilsons and Ladsons left, but the people who showed looked just like Granna. Strong genes were evident on that side. I had no idea how often or even if I'd see many of them again, but at least I had pictures. I had proof I was connected to people other than the five relatives we talked to on my mother's side, Leslie's older brother included, and three of those five were rare.

After the party, I took Granna home, handed her off to Petra, and spent some time reading Great-grandma Odessa's journal. Although I was worn out from hugging, laughing, dabbing new tears, and picture taking, this sacred room pulled me in, and so did the words that were left behind. My mother and I didn't have artifacts of any kind. She had one small photo album with a few pictures of her parents and some pictures from her childhood. She didn't look happy in any, except for a birthday party photo where she received a bike. She owned a scarf and brooch of her mother's, but it was like her parents were storks. She had nothing of her father's in her personal belongings. She said things were burned in a fire, and Leslie confirmed that was true, but it was all so lonely. It left empty spaces in my past.

I opened a box of photo albums and looked through them. If being a hoarder of pictures was a thing, Granna was it. She had multiple pictures of the same things. Photo albums were in duplicate and then she had a picture box, which I found had the same photos in the albums. I was slow to get it. She'd been keeping two albums—one for each son and then her own set. I couldn't in any measure imagine the kind of pain she experienced when she looked at this collection.

I'd been so focused on the photo albums from way back when my father was a child that I hadn't looked at anything recent. There were photos from the farm, Granna's church, running events, birthday parties, and holidays. A few of the winter pictures included shots at the vegetable stand. The items stacked inside were jars of fruit, jam, pickles, and Granna's chow chow relish.

As I turned the pages, I noticed there weren't many that didn't include pictures of Nigel. He was there for every occasion. In many cases, he was standing closer to Granna than any of the Blacks. I thought about the sign I had posted in my houseplant garden at home:

"Happiness blooms where seeds of love and joy are planted."

Nigel's role was more important than managing the farm. He was a surrogate grandson. My heart warmed around this thought because Granna needed him. He brought her happiness and joy, and for that, I was grateful.

───○───

I walked into the house, placed the plate Aunt Thea sent for Nigel on the counter, and looked out the window facing the Airstream. I got my phone from my bag and texted him.

Aunt Thea sent you dinner.

Before I could put the phone down, it vibrated with a new message.

I'm starving. I'm in the back. Will you bring it over? Please. ☺

Great. More of him wet and half-naked. I wondered if there was a limit on the number of hours a person should spend in a hot tub, and if Nigel had, in fact, hit that number.

The food was still warm. I grabbed a fork out of the drawer and walked out of the kitchen door.

Just as I rounded the corner, he was stepping out of the tub. I stalled, watching as he raised a towel to his chest and wiped the water off. Either he was a bit of an exhibitionist, or I was a voyeur, because this was a show. He had a solid chest, strong arms, and . . .

"It's time to get out of there anyway."

Nigel's words broke through my thoughts about him. I hadn't realized he'd seen me.

He accepted the plate like it was a treasure, removed the foil covering, and moaned. "Seriously, her sticky chicken, oyster mac and cheese, greens, and corn bread when I wasn't expecting it." He couldn't hide his excitement. "I feel like I've died and gone to heaven."

I raised the fork. "And you won't be hungry when you get there."

"I'm going to warm it up. I like it hot." It seemed inconceivable that Nigel could sense I wanted to talk, but his excitement piped down, and he was looking at me like he did. "You want a drink or something?"

"I . . ." I paused. "I don't want to bother you, but if you're going to be eating, yes."

He hesitated, reading my face, which had to be in large print. He cocked his head in the direction of the door. "Come on."

I followed him into the Airstream. I expected an unkempt bachelor pad, but it was clean and neat, just like his house, but much sparser, holding only a few pieces of key furniture and an oversized television as the centerpiece.

"I'm going to get out of these trunks. Have a seat."

I reached for the plate. Heat rushed into my chest when our eyes connected. The interior of the Airstream felt intimate. "Let me stick that in the microwave for you."

Nigel's eyes seemed stuck to mine for longer than they should have been, then he nodded and walked through a door that led to the bedroom. I pulled the microwave open and put his food in for ninety seconds. It seemed to take only that much time for Nigel to return. He was wearing sweats and a T-shirt.

He handed me a glass of water.

"Thanks," I said.

Nigel stretched his hand to the chair at the small table for four next to me. After getting butter from the fridge, he removed the plate from the microwave and sat across from me. He smoothed butter on the corn bread, and the combination gave the room, which had been devoid of a distinct odor, a homey smell. "How was your party?"

I painted a picture with the highlights.

My mind went to the story the photos told about Nigel's history of being at Black events. "I'm surprised you didn't join us."

He dug into his food like he hadn't eaten all day and took a few bites. "I had something to do," he replied without elaborating.

After swallowing half the plate in three mouthfuls, he returned his attention to me. "So what's up?"

Nigel had a nice face. That was not a new assessment, but I'd never sat across from it at a forty-inch table face-to-face this way.

I took a deep breath and forced myself to stop thinking about how completely good-looking this man was. He was my friend. I'd never had a male friend before. It was nice.

"I'm reading my family journals."

Nigel wiped his mouth. "Having those is a trip."

"I can hear their voices in my head."

He nodded. "Mr. Elijah's journal was a lot."

"You read it?"

"Ma had me reading them when she hired me for the farm. She wanted me to understand the vision." He put an elbow on the table and spun his fork in the empty plate as he talked. "I've read slave narratives and other memoirs from Reconstruction before. I love history. I like learning about people, but it has to be like on ten for you. This is your family. Your history. My family doesn't have anything like that."

"I know. His words jump off the paper . . ." I paused. "I felt like I was being ripped in two when I read about his mother being sold."

"I wish he had written more."

"We're lucky to have that. According to Great-grandma Odessa's journals, she had to make him write that one." I chuckled, imagining her using her wifely influence to get him to cooperate in this thing she found so important.

Quiet fell between us as I continued to reflect on some of her words about the poverty after the war.

Nigel's hand was on mine. "Are you okay?"

"I'm overwhelmed and sort of unsettled, but I also feel like I'm a part of something."

"You are."

"Am I?"

"You're a part of a lineage of great people, but you didn't know that. Now that you do, it's okay to feel a way about it."

"I'm still in awe that I have a whole ninety-nine-year-old grandmother with journals dating back to the 1800's."

"You're lucky. Most of us don't know anything about our family. I did that ancestry thing, and I got nowhere. Asking my parents and other relatives . . . no one in the family knows much. Nobody carried the history. You at least get to go back."

I reflected on how fortunate I was as we sat there not saying anything. Then I recalled another subject we had to discuss. "We need to talk about rent."

"Casey, I'm not taking money from you."

"You aren't being sexist, are you? I can pay."

He frowned. "No. If you were Ma Black's grandson, I wouldn't take your money either."

I sighed. Why couldn't he just let me do the right thing and let me pay him? "I'm not leaving anytime soon."

"Really?"

Granna had less time on this side of life than she ever had. I didn't need to think I could pop back down here and see her like she was going to live forever. "I'm enjoying getting to know her."

Nigel's face showed no emotion, but his eyes revealed his happiness. His eyes told all his thoughts. "Is your work situation flexible?"

"I run a small business. I have a few staff who are taking care of what needs to be done. Anything that involves me can be done from my phone or laptop." I cleared my throat. "It's all kind of in a slow season right now." I was clandestine enough for him to look curious but not ask questions. "I should go. I get up early because I want to. You get up early because you have to."

"It's no rush," he said. "I like talking to you."

Our eyes caught and held for a few seconds before I popped out of my chair. "About that business, I need to send some emails."

Nigel stood too.

"Thanks for listening to me."

He shoved his hands down into his pockets. "Anytime."

We walked to the door just as the bedroom door opened. A little girl stepped out. She was wearing pink pj's with the

Disney character Ariel on them. She was a thin little slip—all face and perfectly almond-shaped eyes that would be one of her best features one day.

Her head was tied in a scarf. I knew that all too well as a child. My mother was relentless about protecting my hair.

"Daddy, I'm thirsty," she cried.

Daddy? Okay.

"What's the rule about getting out of bed?"

"I can't dream with a dry mouth."

Nigel walked to the water cooler on the counter, took a pink cup from the cupboard, and put a little water in it.

"You can have this after I see some manners." He leaned against the counter.

I don't think she'd really noticed me standing there. She raised her eyes to mine and said, "Hello, ma'am."

I pushed my shock aside with a toothy smile. "Hi."

"Star, this is Miss Casey. She's Ma Black's granddaughter." He handed her the cup.

Her eyes widened like he'd just told her I was the Little Mermaid. "Really?"

I nodded. "Yes."

Star's eyes traveled from her father's face to mine. "But she's all big."

I chuckled inside. "I've been big a long time."

"How come I never saw you before?" Her little face was full of confusion. She had questions.

"I live in New York."

"Little Miss, that's enough. Drink and go back to bed," Nigel said.

She took a few sips and handed him the cup.

She twisted her mouth like she was unsatisfied about not having her questions answered. "It was nice to meet you."

"It was nice to meet you too," I replied.

She didn't even try her daddy. She went back to her room.

"Wow! She's sweet. How old?"

"Seven. She stays in Plantersville through the week. She goes to the private school where my aunt works. I have her Friday nights through Monday mornings."

My feelings about the fact that he had a child were lodged in my chest. I didn't know if I felt a kinship with people my age without children or that I was jealous of those who had what I wanted. Maybe it was both. As if he owed me an explanation, I said, "I didn't see her last weekend."

"Her mother took her to Charleston."

I nodded again. Of course, there was a mother attached to this situation. Nigel had a history that had nothing to do with Black Farms.

"And this past week, she was away for spring break with my brother's family." He cleared his throat. "I've missed her."

"I'm sure." I swallowed. "Where do you sleep when she's here?"

He pointed. "The pullout."

"Nigel, is her room the locked bedroom in the house?"

"Yes."

I'd stolen a piece of a child's happy place. "You should let her have her bedroom."

"It's just weekends. She knows when I have a tenant, we stay here."

I tossed my hands up. "I'm not a tenant, because you won't take rent."

"Casey, she's a kid." His eyes swept the room. "She loves this thing. Trust. It's all good."

I looked around. I could see it being an adventure for a child. "She'd probably be glad to be with you in a tent."

We stood there for another moment of awkwardness. "You have to get her to school in the morning. I'm going."

He nodded, but the gesture and his eyes did not agree. He hung in the opening as I walked across the grass. Once I reached the door, I turned and waved before going inside. He had a daughter. A beautiful baby doll. And she had a mother who no doubt was just as pretty.

We are just friends.

Of course we were. I was only four weeks out of my seven-year marriage to Drew. I looked at my empty ring finger, felt the ache of emptiness in my heart, and wondered whether I would ever experience love again.

18

I'D GONE TWO WEEKS AND ONE DAY WITHOUT HEARING FROM my mother, but now she was on the other end of the phone. I guess she assumed enough time had passed and she could pick up like she'd never broken my heart.

"I've been calling you all day. Why aren't you answering your phone?"

"I've been busy."

"Doing what?"

"I help out on the farm."

She cackled. "You cannot be serious."

The energy needed to explain drained right out of me. It was replaced with irritation. "Mom, you said you've been calling. You have me."

"I'm in Charleston. I got in this afternoon, but it's a turn-around trip. I've got to fly back tomorrow. Come have an early lunch with me."

I seriously doubted my mother had to fly to Charleston. She wanted to put eyes on me.

"You couldn't have come to Georgetown?"

"I don't have time. I told you I have to fly back out tomorrow."

"Why would you fly down here without making sure it was okay? I have something to do tomorrow."

"I know. You have to see me. And it's not just about me. It's about Drew, so let me know when you arrive. I'm at the Winchester."

She ended the call. Now I had to emotionally deal with her and some Drew drama at the same time. I could hardly wait.

⁓

The Winchester Hotel was Charleston's answer to the Ritz-Carlton and my mother's answer to all things luxurious in lodging. It was elegant and exclusive. A horse drawing a carriage trotted up to the entrance as I handed the valet my keys. The lobby's cream marble floors shined so bright under the skylight I still needed my sunglasses. Flocked wallpaper and expensive artwork in heavy gold frames decorated the walls. Whatever they were pumping into the vents was a combination of orange and mint—refreshing and crisp. I swept through to the elevator bank and rode to my mother's floor. The door to her room was propped open. A server was setting food on a table near the balcony. I dropped my bag on the sofa and headed to the bedroom.

My mother was on the phone, ranting while she paced. I located the bathroom. I went in, washed my hands, and patted my hair. A debate over whether to straighten it or let the curls live wrangled my thoughts this morning. Curls won. I stepped out of the bathroom just as the temper dissipated from my mother's tone. When she spotted me, she ended the call and walked toward me. After a hug, she raised a hand to the unruly strands.

"Natural hair." She held a frown and forced a smile. At least she was trying to play nice. "You look fresh."

"I'll take that as a compliment."

"It was intended to be." My mother's greetings were always initial assessments. She'd been checking me for damage my entire life.

I was wearing a marigold silk knit tunic, an ivory denim vest, and my favorite ripped jeans. Mother wasn't a huge fan of ripped anything, but she understood fashion trends. She touched the hem of my top. "I like this."

Of course she did. She liked fine things. We both had plenty in that regard, but it hadn't always been that way. Not in the beginning when she was a struggling single mother weaving through the busy streets of Manhattan with me for auditions. Then, she'd had two good suits, one black, the other taupe, and five blouses to coordinate with them. She called that her struggle wardrobe. It was a long way from the Donna Karan, Veronica Beard, and St. John's collection she owned now.

"Why are you here?"

"Meeting with Miss Teenage South Carolina. She wants to model."

With a few folded bills in hand, my mother walked into the living room. "We'll serve ourselves," she said, handing the server the money. She left us.

I reentered the living room and sat on the arm of the sofa. "So you did have business."

"Of course I did. Why else would I be here?"

"I don't know, to see if I'd gained weight."

My mother smiled and dismissed me with a wave before giving her pinging phone attention.

"So," I said, interrupting the text message symphony, "how did it go with Miss South Carolina?"

"Well . . ." She stuck her phone in her pocket. She clasped her hands in front of her waist. She was about to lecture me. That

Mary Poppins stance was a precursor. "Casey, it's been five weeks. You *are* a social media influencer. You need to be on social media. What are you doing?"

"Taking a break."

"You've had a break." She tamped down a spurt of annoyance and softened her tone. "You can't let this one mistake destroy your life."

"You don't understand."

"You're right. I don't. You've lived your life in thirty- and sixty-second reels for years. Why can't you get over this?"

"Because it's not just about Drew or the video. It's me. Now that I'm here, I realize how exhausted I was. That's why I blew up on camera. I'm tired."

"Baby, I understand being tired, but there's a time element here. Social media doesn't stop."

"I know. That's why I've been thinking it might be time for me to do something new."

If my mother's eyes could have fallen out of her head, they would have. "Something new? Like what?"

I shrugged. "Maybe photography. You do remember I have that little degree from FIT."

My mother did not acknowledge my photography degree— ever. It was like I got a master's in stripping or something. She was disappointed I'd chosen to go to a fashion college when I'd been accepted into the business program at Columbia University.

I'd applied to Fashion Institute of Technology's Fashion Merchandising program, claiming an interest in becoming a buyer for Macy's or Saks. But weeks into my first semester, I began to notice a difference between myself and the other students enrolled in my program. Mainly that they worshiped clothes and the designers who created them. I simply liked clothes.

I also liked fashion magazines, but I merely flipped through them and turned down the pages on stuff I thought was cool and my favorite pictures. I had an epiphany. Just because I liked clothes didn't mean I would be good at merchandising them, so I began to think about what did interest me. There was one thing, a scary thing: photography. The next semester, I changed my major.

My mother steepled her hands in front of her. We'd had this conversation before, after I stopped modeling. She didn't believe in me then, and she obviously didn't believe in me now. "You can't become a photographer. It's an insanely crowded space."

"So was modeling and becoming an influencer."

My mother closed her eyes for a few seconds. Her chest rose and fell hard. "Sweetheart, do you know how hard it is out there for photographers? Female photographers? Black female photographers?"

"What business is easy for women?"

My mother reared back in her seat. "Okay. We can talk about that later. Let's get back to Casey B. You don't want to end your influencer career as a failure. Your parting video to the world can't be that video. You have to at least put your brand back together, then you can go do something new."

She was right. I didn't want to be remembered for that video. It would follow me all over the internet forever. It would follow my mother, too, and she despised failure. That's why she had always been able to help me attain success. "I'll think about it."

"Good." I heard the relief in her voice. "I'm starving. Let's eat."

We sat at the table. It would take only five mouthfuls to knock the air out of my mother's stomach. When she had those five, she put her fork down, and I moved us on to the topic I wanted to discuss.

"Mom, why didn't you ever bring me down here?"

She raised her water glass and took a long drink. When she was done, she said, "Because I don't get along with the Blacks."

"Why not?"

"Because they blamed me for your father's death."

Anxiety crept into my stomach. What didn't I know? "Why would they blame you for a car accident?"

My mother leaned forward, giving me an eye roll that said, *duh*. "Who else was she going to blame? They couldn't blame your father or God." My mother shook her head. "What has Mrs. Ida told you?"

"I haven't asked her."

"What about Thea?"

"She says it's not her story to tell."

"Aunt Thea minding her business." My mother rolled her eyes. "My, but the South has risen."

"She's been very good to me."

"I'm glad to hear that." Her face did not match her words.

"The accident was in Georgetown?" I knew that. I wasn't sure why I was asking her what she'd already told me.

"Yes, not far from the house. The car ran into a ditch. He died at the scene." Her words were slow. She closed her eyes, visibly emotional. "Mrs. Ida . . . tolerated me through the funeral. She never liked me. They'd picked out a local girl for him to marry. Lane or Lacy something. He'd known her since kindergarten and dated her midway through college. They broke up, but his family figured he'd get back together with her. But then he came home with me." She played with the rim of her orange juice glass. "That was my first sin."

"What?"

"Why, stealing his heart, of course. He was hers . . . the Lane girl, or maybe he was simply Ida's." My mother picked up the glass and took a sip, then she reached for her fork. "Can I just eat?"

I picked up my fork too. I twirled it around in my salad a few times, inspecting it for cabbage worms. Now that I knew what they were, I looked for them daily. We partially finished our meals, as was our way. My mother drilled into me that women who didn't want to gain weight didn't clean their plates. Models couldn't gain weight.

"I'm getting to know my grandmother and some of my other family."

"Other family. They were all old as Methuselah a long time ago."

"They've added some since you knew them."

My mother crossed her leg over her knee and pushed back in her chair. "I guess they would. There's nothing else to do in that place."

I tuned in to her, remembered her words. "What was the second sin?"

My mother frowned.

"About my father. You said the first sin was stealing his heart."

My mother grunted.

"The funeral. It wasn't Christian enough. They were weirdly religious and superstitious." She took a deep breath and blew it out like she was an engine letting off steam. "Are you really going to make me relive all this?"

"I want the truth."

"The truth is, they said some horrible things to me, especially your grandmother. Once I got back to New Jersey, I swore I would never go back down there and that bitter woman would never get a chance to hurt me again. They would certainly never hurt you."

"But that was so long ago."

My mother huffed like her strength was gone. "Casey, I'm done talking about those judgmental people."

"My grandmother is a good Christian woman. She's not judgy of anyone."

"You wouldn't know a good Christian if they fell off that balcony." My mother flicked her finger in the direction of the windows.

I bit my lip. She was right, but something about Granna was so gentle and good, it had to come from a connection with God.

"You're escaping down here. Running and hiding is for criminals and victims of domestic violence. You are neither."

She stood and walked to the desk, coming back with a manila envelope. She placed it next to my plate.

"What is this?"

"I told you we needed to talk about Drew."

I opened the envelope. There were several pictures of Drew—at restaurants, walking into a building, holding hands. The woman in the pictures was familiar. My mind went back to the conversation I had with Drew in the parking lot.

"Are you still coming?"

His coworker. The one waiting like a . . . like a girlfriend, not a coworker at all. How had I not seen that?

"I have talked to Drew about your divorce. The papers are ready to file. You can do it electronically. I have a friendly judge who'll push it right through."

"You talked to Drew about our divorce."

"Yes. He initially pushed back a little on the postnup terms, so I hired a private investigator." My mother pointed to the envelope. "I wasn't going to show them to you, but I didn't want you questioning the decision. As you can see, Drew has moved on. It's possible he had moved on before he left you. The sooner you file, the better."

Bluntness was my mother's special gift. It wasn't welcome right now. "Don't I get to grieve, Mom? Can I just have a minute to think about all that's happened?"

"You have money, Casey. File while he's agreeable." She eased into her next statement. "Sometimes we have to grieve the dead thing in the quiet of the night. When we lie on our beds, we can shed our tears, because life doesn't allow us to stop moving."

"I've had to grieve in the wee hours of the night before." I stood and walked to the sink. "You know that. You've watched me get up and go to work the next day after—" I stopped. I couldn't speak about my miscarriages. I was hurting enough.

"That was insensitive," she said. "I'm sorry."

I stood, walked to the sink, wet a paper towel, and wiped it over my face. I thought about Drew's insistence that he could not do it again. The "could not" was the most painful part. He wouldn't even help me save face.

"I told Drew if he left that church, I would never forgive him." I looked at the manila envelope again and released a long plume of air. "You're right. There's no reason to drag it out. Let me know what I need to do."

Telling my mother that put her in commando mode. She had the lawyer on speed dial who was more than happy to do a video chat with me. I could e-file, and in thirty to sixty days, I'd be divorced. It was that simple.

When we were done, my mother went into the bedroom for a few minutes. I hadn't noticed it before, but her carry-on suitcase was already at the door. "I have to go."

I stood, picked up my bag and the offending envelope. "You should have planned a longer trip. We could have had a spa day or something."

"Come home. You can always visit again after you get your business on track."

"I'm not ready yet."

My mother sighed deeply. Irritation pressed into the creases around her lips. She pulled me into her arms and squeezed tight. I don't know when she'd ever hugged me quite this way. It reminded me of Aunt Thea's clutch, only faster and more desperate. She raised a hand to my hair and looped a finger around a stray curl. "You're beautiful, baby."

Before I could respond, she turned and did what she always did before she walked out the door: she looked at her reflection in the mirror. A shadow of sadness fell over her face. I caught it just before she smoothed her hair, and I wondered what vulnerability had scratched her emotions. But there was no way for me to find out. She was done talking to me. If she'd wanted more conversation, she would have stayed longer.

Once she was safely in the hotel airport shuttle, I had the valet bring my car. I looked at the envelope on the seat next to me. I thought about the way this woman stood behind me as I talked to my husband.

"Are you still coming?"

Her voice emitted a certain level of power. It wasn't a question. It was a reminder of his obligation to her. His time didn't belong to me, it belonged to her, and that didn't happen in the short period of time after the wedding. Drew had been cheating. He couldn't say I do again because of her, not me.

"Liar!" I gripped the steering wheel and tried to push all of the hurt and negative energy out of my body.

When had he stopped loving me? Every time I asked that question in my mind, I wouldn't let it cycle. I wouldn't let my brain process the answer. But now I couldn't fight it. I knew. He stopped loving me last year . . . maybe even before that. He'd said it during an argument about my back-to-back business travel.

"I can't do this much longer. I can't stay in this marriage. I don't even know if I love you anymore."

A few weeks later, we were celebrating a positive pregnancy test and then grieving a second miscarriage. He'd taken those words back, but he meant them then, and I'd been too deaf to hear him. I looked at the envelope again. Drew had left me a long time ago.

19

THE NEXT DAY, I SPENT TIME IN THE HERB GARDEN WITH Granna. "Our ancestors didn't have medicine. They had to use what God put on the earth. Clove for dental problems. Dandelion for kidney issues. Garlic and ginger have a lot of uses." She reached for a plant with a white and yellow flower bud. "This is feverfew. It's good for headaches and fever. Herbs and roots kept our people alive since time began."

I didn't get sick much, but I figured if she was ninety-nine and nearly as spry as I was, she knew, so I listened. The growling sound my stomach made ended the lesson.

Petra already had warm bowls of Aunt Thea's crab-and-bacon chowder and yeast rolls on the table. We also had a salad with fresh lettuce and kale, tomato, cucumbers, mushrooms, and red onions, which I'd picked from the garden. This back-yard farm-to-table lifestyle was undeniably the third best thing about being here—family and the slower pace were the first two.

Petra hadn't set a place for herself. She joined us most days.

"Aren't you going to eat?" I asked.

"I need to run to the bank." She placed a hand on Granna's shoulder. "I'll be back before you get up from your nap."

Granna picked up her spoon. "Don't rush on my account."

Petra winked at me but said to Granna, "You know you need me, and I need you."

"What you need is a social life so you can get married," Granna said. "You're not going to get a husband while you're working for me."

I waited for Petra's balk. This was an ongoing conversation between the two of them.

"*Um-hmm,*" Petra murmured. She picked up her bag. "I'll be back."

She left the house.

"How old is Petra?"

"Twenty-seven," Granna said. She picked up her roll and broke off a piece. She dipped it in the soup and popped it in her mouth. "She had a boyfriend last year, but he wasn't the marrying kind. He couldn't even take care of himself."

Even though it wasn't funny, I laughed at the way Granna spoke about Petra's ex. "Is she the first aide you've had?"

Granna wiped her mouth with a napkin. "Yes, and I *do* want her to quit so she can have a life."

I gave Granna a disbelieving, wry look. "You know you and Petra are attached at the hip. Who would help you around here if she left?"

"I don't know. Maybe my granddaughter. I could put a shower in that bathroom." Granna hiked her thumb in the direction of the hall. "In fact, we could add on an entire bathroom."

"Is there a Black for that too?"

"There's a Black for everything, sugah," Granna said.

I placed a hand on hers and squeezed. I was eventually going back to New York, but I didn't like the idea of her needing me and me not being here. "I believe in crossing bridges when I come to them." I dipped my soup spoon into the bowl. "And I don't require a new bathroom."

I smiled before slipping my spoon into my mouth. Thoughts of showers and bathrooms faded away when the bits of bacon and corn blended with the creamy broth and fresh seasonings on my tongue. "Aunt Thea is going to have to teach me how to make this."

Granna reached for the chain that secured her eyeglasses around her neck. She pushed them up her nose. "Good luck getting her to. I think she's trying to take some of those recipes to the grave."

Granna's medicinal recipe book was on the island next to her. She pulled the book closer. "Speaking of recipes and Thea, I need to make something for her. She's been having trouble with her stomach."

"Does she know why?"

"I think she's worried about her granddaughters. Thea likes to micromanage them."

I dipped bread in my soup. "Do they need it?"

Granna shrugged. "I don't know." She looked down her glasses at me. "Do any of us want people running our lives?"

I couldn't believe I'd asked that when I was tired of my mother trying to run mine. "I don't think so."

Granna grunted. She flipped pages until she found what she was looking for. "I've tried some simple things. Maybe swamp willow would work for her." She put a marker in the page. "You should copy some of this. Healing is in your blood on your daddy's side."

I'd already discovered that from reading the journals. "Your grandpa Eddie was a community medicine man. Some people called him a witch doctor, but it wasn't no magic. It was pure knowledge of what God gave us. He learned it from his mother."

I nodded and then recalled something I'd meant to ask her about. "Great-grandma Odessa used to make a cream for her hair. I was wondering about that."

"What's in it?"

I reached for bread as I recalled the list. "Oils, aloe, lemon and lavender, something called mars root."

She pivoted her head from side to side as she inspected my hair. "Your texture is similar to hers. It would probably work for you."

"I don't know what mars root is."

"Maybe marshmallow root or alma. Both are good for hair. Alma is a mars plant. It don't grow here in the low. It's not hot enough. She would use something she could get here unless she brought it from the Caribbean. The ships came in, and people could get things that way too. The marshmallow is in the garden. You could experiment with it. Pick some, and we'll figure it out."

I got a warm feeling inside. The thought of making a hair product that my great-grandmother Odessa used pushed tears to the backs of my eyes. I didn't allow myself to cry. I cried way too much yesterday. I was an emotional mess right now.

Granna pushed her chair back. Right on schedule, she announced she was tired and went to take her nap. I washed the dishes and went back outside to the herb garden and looked for the marshmallow root stuff. She had everything marked. I squatted down and examined the plant. Sniffed it and checked the condition of the leaves. It had full flower blooms on it. I took my garden shears and cut off a few branches.

"Ma Black is going to make an herbalist out of you yet." Nigel's voice came from the door.

I hadn't seen him all day. There were days when he spent all of his time in his office dealing with paperwork.

"She's trying. I have a bunch of houseplants, so I've got a green thumb, but this is different. I'm a bit overwhelmed by it all." I stood from my knees and put the shears back with the tools. "What else is new, right?"

"I don't know. You seem to be doing pretty good to me. But

are you learning because you're interested or because Ma Black wants to teach it?"

I considered his question. "Probably a little of both."

He searched me for a moment. I thought he was going to say something else about it, but then he said, "Aunt Thea asked for some lettuce for dinner. You want to help me pick some?"

"Sure," I replied. I followed him out of the herb garden. I was a pro at this lettuce clipping thing. The lettuce and other greens grew on a piece of land flanked on both sides by tall, shady trees. I'd learned that lettuce needed partial shade and didn't like heat. I was thankful for the coolness the shade provided. The sun had been oppressive today. "Did she specify a kind?"

"Nope. Pick what you like."

I chose a crisp Bibb lettuce and cut enough for a large salad. Removing my phone, I took pictures of the harvest and the immediate area.

"You've been taking a lot of pictures lately," Nigel said.

"I know. I want to record the beauty of everything here. I think I've been taking it for granted."

Nigel didn't respond. He cleared this throat. Then he looked away and back at me. I was convinced he had something on his mind, something to say, but then my phone rang.

It was Petra. I finished up with her and said, "They need me to work in the market today."

Once again, I noted a kind of lost-moment look on Nigel's face before he said, "I'll see you later."

I took the lettuce into the house and went to meet up with Petra.

⁓

The Black Farm Market was a wooden canopy with shelves built into the three walls that held bins and oversized whiskey barrels on waist-high stands in rows on the floor. All were packed with vegetables.

The market was open half days from Thursday through Saturday. Two of my teenage cousins worked at the stand. They were seventeen-year-old college-bound twins. They rarely missed work, but on this Friday they had a debate club event. With Petra's help at the register, I managed to handle the vegetable stand. As always, by 4:00 p.m., it was busy. The line of cars was out of the lot and down the road. People traveled from work to home, stocking up on their vegetables for the week. We had an abundance of greens, lettuce, squash, cucumbers, broccoli, cabbage, and eggplant from the greenhouses.

Granna walked the line holding a tray with sample-sized honey biscuits and shot glasses filled with sweet tea. I figured she knew most of the people as I overheard conversations about spouses and children and quick summaries of people's current story. When she didn't know someone, she introduced herself. It was obvious to me that Granna never met a stranger. I understood why I'd instantly fallen in love with her. She was lovable at first sight.

When it came time for her to make dinner, she left the tray on one of the tables at the entrance and went into the house. Petra followed, and before I could question if I could keep up, she was replaced by Nigel.

We worked through the line. A pro, he was faster than Petra and me, with his only delay occurring when he was slowed down by a flirtatious woman. There were quite a few of them. Young women, old women, and women our age. It was amusing to watch him keep the subject on the vegetables.

The rush was over by 6:00 p.m. When we were done, we made a few trips with the utility cart piled with the produce we hadn't sold to the temperature-controlled storage building that kept the vegetables safe from heat and bugs. There was also a section that was refrigerated. This is where the market food was stored. Nigel and I emptied the contents of the cart into the shelved walls and onto tables until everything was done.

Nigel's eyes connected with mine, and he tilted his head, inspecting me more deeply than he should have been. He was hesitating again, the same way he had back in the herb garden.

"Do you want to go to a movie tonight? After dinner. I feel like all we do is work you." He paused seconds more before adding, "Star is with my parents this weekend."

A movie? Wasn't that a date? I was so surprised I could hardly respond. My throat tightened, stopping the effortless flow of words. "I . . . uh . . . I don't know. I . . ."

He raised his hand to stop my stuttering. Maybe he sensed rejection was coming. "No pressure. If tonight's not good, maybe some other time." Nigel's lips and eyes told two different stories. His eyes said he'd been gut-punched.

I wanted to say of course another time. I wasn't even sure why I couldn't just say yes right now, but my words died on my tongue when Nigel walked out of the storage house, waited for me to follow, and locked the door before leaving me there wondering if I'd made a mistake.

———∽———

"You are a real buster."

I looked at the screen. Leslie's face was covered in a clay mask. "I can't believe he asked me," I said, still seeing the disappointment on Nigel's face in my mind. "It was so out of the blue."

"You're never without words," Leslie said.

"I know."

"So why didn't you say yes?"

"I'm not dating." I slipped an earring into my ear. I repeated the process and then fluffed out my hair.

"You look like you want a date," Leslie said. "Where are you going anyway?"

"For a ride into town. I saw a flyer for a Gullah pop-up market when I was coming from Charleston yesterday. I want to see what that is." I hunched my shoulders. "I might drive over to Pawleys Island. Maybe I'll watch the sunset at the beach and take some pictures."

"I'm sure Nigel would have been glad to show you the island at sunset," Leslie teased.

"I can't start something with him, Les. He works for Granna, and I don't live here." The thought of any more heartache and accompanying drama made me sad . . . instantly. "He shouldn't have asked."

Leslie scrunched up her face. "It sounds like he was just trying to go see a movie. Maybe he's one of those people who doesn't like to go alone. You are friends, right?"

I sighed. Leslie had probably nailed it. Of course he was looking for company. I closed my eyes to shut out my image. When I opened them, I was still looking at myself and feeling foolish. "Now I feel rude."

"You can always ask him to go next week to make up for it. Men live to be asked out." Leslie's lips slipped into a smile. "I love that you're rocking your natural hair, chica. It looks good. You look younger."

I raised my eyes to the mirror and squinted. "Do I need to look younger?"

Leslie smirked. "You'll be gorgeous forever with Auntie V's genes."

"My mother's are not the only genes in me."

"Speaking of which . . ."

Leslie had a way of making you think about something without posing a whole question. I knew where she was going, so I bypassed her question. "We haven't talked about my father. I'm waiting patiently. I can tell Granna's not ready. I'm not going to push her."

"What did your mother say?"

"She said she and the Blacks had nasty words. My father was supposed to marry someone else." I reached for a lip liner. "I don't know."

"Girl, this is going to be a drama saga before it's over."

I lined my lips and picked up a lip gloss. "I think so, but it already makes me sad. This story did not have a happy ending."

Leslie grunted. "I know. I'm sorry I made light of it."

"No." It was my turn to wave her words away. There was no need for an apology. She was right. There was more to this drama. "It's fine. I know what you mean."

"So Aunt V didn't say anything new, even though she knows you're there and you'll eventually get more of the story? I'd think she'd want her side on the record first. You know how she 'likes to get in front of things,'" Leslie said, making air quotes with her fingers.

My mother did like to spin a story first. "Nothing. But something is bothering her. She could have overnighted the pictures or even emailed them to me."

"True, but she's probably jealous, Casey. You've been her entire life, and now you're off trying to get your groove back with people she doesn't know anymore. She seems nervous to me, but it might be fear of having to share you. She's never had to."

I considered that for a moment too. "I guess. We'll see."

"Anyway, with respect to work, let a sister know if I should be updating my résumé."

"When I come back and we hit the ground on the next thing,

you'll be glad you had a chance to breathe." I opened the lip gloss and swept it across my lips. "Besides, your résumé stays current. You're ready to leave me once a quarter." I smiled, knowing that was true. Leslie was always trying to figure out if she wanted to do something else besides manage my books with my mother. The dissatisfaction had more to do with salvaging their aunt-niece relationship than it did with me. When the books got to my mother, she nitpicked operations to death.

I stood and stepped back so Leslie could get a full look at me. "Cute or nah?" I pulled on my favorite periwinkle denim jacket.

"Always cute. The question is why so cute?"

I shook my head at her antics. "Because I'm still Casey B, which means I encourage women to be beautiful for them-selves, not for others," I said, repeating the quote I used in all my videos.

"If you were here, I would give you a high five."

I laughed. "Casey B incognito." I picked up a dark pair of sunglasses. "I need to go before the sun goes down. I don't want to get lost. It was nice getting dressed with you. Wish me a good time or whatever it is I should be having."

"Fun. A good life," Leslie said. She ended our video call.

A good life. That we could agree on.

~

I drove to downtown Georgetown. I had a picture of the sign for the pop-up market on my phone, but there were signs posted on the side of the road directing me to the location on King Street. To my surprise, it was in front of the Gullah Museum Nigel told me about.

The street was blocked off for the event. While looking for a parking space, I spotted an SUV pulling away from a corner spot. I slipped in and grabbed it. When I turned off the car, it jerked a little. I noticed it had done that when I started it in Charleston yesterday. I made a mental note to find the local Mercedes dealership and have it checked out.

I left my vehicle with my camera around my neck and cash, phone, and credit card in my jacket pocket. Festive drum music floated through the cool night sky to my ears before I reached the sawhorses at the entrance. There was a sign posted in front that read:

"We Outchea! Gullah Geechee Corridor."

I joined the throng of folks entering. Once inside, I saw the vendors. Tables were set up on both sides of the street selling various things like jewelry, scented oils, lotions and creams, and hair products made from shea, mango, and cocoa butter. There was an elderly woman who reminded me of Granna, surrounded by not only seagrass baskets and hats but children from about ages five to twelve. Each held a piece of seagrass in their hands, and they carefully followed directions she gave them to interlace the grass.

On the opposite side of the street were booths with quilts, clothing, paintings, and books. At the end, I saw fruit and other food. It reminded me of street festivals in Brooklyn. On any given Saturday in the summer, there was a street fair or market somewhere.

I raised my camera, made adjustments for the lighting, and took pictures as I walked the length of the market. I continued walking until I came to the entrance of the museum.

The Gullah Museum was a pale-yellow building that was jammed between a barbershop and a chiropractic office. From the outside, it didn't look like much, but inside was a nice little cultural surprise. The place was chock-full of information about the

Gullah people. I took my time inspecting the art, jewelry, clothing, artifacts, story quilts, baskets, and books. I joined a group that was huddled around one particular quilt. It was displayed on the wall in the back corner of the museum. The owner shared the story of how his wife was commissioned to make the quilt about Michelle Obama for the White House quilt display during President Obama's inauguration. Mrs. Obama's paternal grandfather was from Georgetown.

When he was done, I went to the gift shop area. My first stop was the books. The one that stood out at me read *De Nyew Testament.* I opened one and noted it was a New Testament Bible translated entirely into the Gullah language. I purchased it and a few other things before I left. I understood why Nigel told me to visit.

As I walked past the vendor tables in the market, I bought something from nearly everyone. I hauled everything to the car, put the bags in the trunk, and slipped inside the driver's seat. I pushed the button for the ignition, and the car didn't start. I tried again; it was dead.

"Great." I reached into my pocket for my phone and used the app for roadside assistance, then I got out and popped the hood. Why I did that, I had no idea. I guess I was expecting a huge wire to be sticking out with a note that read *Stick me back in,* because I knew nothing about cars. I closed it and got back inside.

I called Aunt Thea.

"Where'd you say you are?" she asked, worry rising high in her voice.

I told her. She grunted and asked, "Who are you with?"

"I'm alone."

"What? We're going to have a conversation about this later." She grunted again, this time angrier. "Your cousin Jason is a mechanic. He'll be there as fast as he can."

"I already called my roadside service. I just wanted someone to know where I was."

"You can't be sitting out there waiting for roadside assistance. Call and cancel. When I told you there's a Black for that, I meant everything. Jason will take care of you. Give him a few minutes."

I'd barely gotten off the phone with my roadside service when there was a double tap on the passenger side window. Startled half to death, I cracked the window.

"Hey. I'm Jason."

I was so relieved. I pushed the button for the hood and popped out of the car.

"Ma Black's granddaughter. Ain't that something," he said, rubbing his chin.

I smiled. "Yeah, it is for her and me."

"It's sweet anyway. I know she's glad." He walked around to the front of the car and pulled the hood up. "Everyone calls me Jay." He leaned in.

I leaned in with him, again like I knew a thing about what I was looking for. "I've never had a single problem with it. It did do this little jerking thing yesterday, but I didn't think much about it, then it did it again tonight when I parked."

"It's probably a sensor. Sensors don't give much warning. You should have gotten an engine light code."

"I didn't."

"*Hmm,*" Jay said. "I won't know what it is until I put it on my machine. I got my truck over there." He pointed in the direction of a shiny, orange flatbed.

"I don't want to take you away from your work. I have roadside assistance."

"I'm a mechanic. My side hustle is towing cars. I'll take it to my shop. If I can't fix it, I'll take it to the Mercedes service center in Myrtle Beach."

I thought about Aunt Thea. She'd sent him. I needed to trust that he could at least diagnose the problem. I nodded. "That sounds good."

He walked to his truck, got in, turned it around to face the back of the Mercedes, and got out again. "I'll drop you off at Nigel's on the way."

"Are you sure that's not out of your way?"

"It's not out of the way, and that don't matter. I'm taking you home." Jay chuckled. "This isn't New York, but G-town has its share of crime."

I grabbed my camera and took my shopping bags out of the trunk as Jay lowered the flatbed. He noted me struggling with the bags and rushed to help me. "Dang, girl. You bought out the market."

"I tried," I said, climbing inside his truck's cab. Jay tucked the bags in the seat behind us and then finished with my car. When he was done, he got in the truck with me.

I reached into my purse for my phone. "I better call Aunt Thea and let her know you made it."

"I already did," Jay said.

We didn't talk much more because Jay's phone rang, and he had a long, troublesome back-and-forth with his woman about how he needed to deal with their child's soccer coach's overly rigorous practice schedule.

Once we pulled in front of Nigel's house, Jay put her on hold, jumped out of the truck, and opened my door.

I reached in the back for my shopping bags. "Your wife?" I asked, letting him cradle my elbow as I stepped down.

"Ex-wife. I would remarry her, but she's a worse nag than she was the first time."

I shook my head. Poor girl. We got out, and Jay helped me take my bags to the porch. "I can get them in," I said. "Thanks so much. I appreciate this."

"I got you, cuz. Look for a call after nine. I'm in the shop by eight thirty-ish."

Relief washed over me. I sensed my car was in good hands. Being called "cuz" was kind of cool in a solid, "I got peeps" kind of way. I turned and walked into the house with my bags.

I dropped my keys on the foyer table and locked the door. Just as I switched on the living room light, I saw a figure. My heart leapt into my throat for the second time tonight. I raised a hand to my neck. It was Nigel. "You startled me."

"Sorry. I figured you were out, so I'd get my laundry done." He looked at the bags around my feet and said, "You're in early."

"My car is on the back of my cousin's tow truck."

Nigel frowned and stuck a hand in his pocket. "That Benz is a recent model, right?"

I shrugged. "It still wouldn't start."

Nigel's mouth became a little circle. "Where were you headed?"

I hesitated. "Nowhere really. I was just out for a drive. I went to a pop-up Gullah market, and I saw the museum you told me about." I reached down and pulled my shoes off and put them against the wall. "I was thinking about driving over to Pawleys Island. I haven't seen it."

Nigel couldn't hide his hurt. I hadn't intended to let him know I turned him down to do nothing specific with no one because it wasn't really like that.

"If you're going to see Pawleys Island, you should go in the daytime."

I shrugged out of my jacket. "You sound like Jay and Aunt Thea. I'm full-grown. I've been going out at night for a long time—in New York City."

"I can see you're *full*-grown." Nigel's eyes swept my body, and heat rose to my face. "What I was saying before you assumed I was going to lecture you is that there's a lot to see on Pawleys. You should go with a local who can share that."

"Oh. My bad."

"And your people are right. Driving around at night alone isn't safe. It's a good thing you broke down where you had a phone signal."

"Well, it's a Mercedes, so I don't really need a phone signal to get help."

Nigel raised his index finger. "You're right. That Benz roadside would locate you at the center of the earth."

"But in any event, I've been sufficiently chastised for being lax about my safety."

On the heel of my words, my stomach growled like I hadn't eaten in two days.

Nigel's eyebrow hitched. "Hungry?"

"I'd planned to get food while I was out." I walked into the kitchen, pulled the cabinet open, and removed a can of soup.

He walked to the fridge and pulled it open. He removed a plate covered in aluminum foil. I recognized the precise double-wrap method Aunt Thea used to secure a take-home meal. "I finished up late, and on my way out, I ran into your aunt. She was dropping your grandmother off. She asked me to bring it just in case her darling Casey was hungry."

I took the plate from his hands. "I thought she wasn't cooking tonight."

Nigel folded his arms across his chest. "Maybe she didn't, but they always have food at church revival. That's why I go sometimes."

I laughed at his silly admission. "Bless all of you." I removed the foil and inspected the food—fried chicken, perlou rice bursting with hunks of what looked like smoked turkey, a fluffy corn fritter, and well-seasoned collard greens. I put the plate in the microwave. "Did you eat? There's enough to share."

"If you want my company, I have dessert waiting for me next door."

He was always welcome, but I wondered if he asked because I'd chosen to forgo his company tonight. I sensed he wanted me to say it. "Why eat alone when we can share this lovely table?"

He looked surprised I'd said yes. Was his ego really that fragile? I couldn't imagine a man who was so good-looking and smart and easy to be around would think anyone wouldn't want his company. But his truth flickered in his eyes. Once again, I hated that I'd turned his movie invitation down.

It was only minutes before he returned. He went to the laundry room first, and again in minutes was back at the table with me. He'd already folded the few pieces he'd had in the dryer and piled them into a small laundry basket. The smell of his citrus dryer sheet overpowered the aroma coming from my plate.

Nigel dug into his red-velvet cake before saying, "So we talked about me last week, but you never told me what you do for a living."

I hesitated for a moment, still feeling insecure about telling him who I was because if someone told me they were an influencer, the first thing I'd do was google them to check out their pages. The last thing I wanted him or anyone to do was google me. The top links included a TMZ blog post titled "Influencer Goes Nuts After Being Left at the Altar" and that picture—makeup smeared, teary eyes, tongue stretched out of my mouth like an iguana. It wasn't the real me, and I didn't want it to speak for me.

"I'm in marketing. I help companies get their brands recognition with potential customers." That was easy and true and not Google-worthy.

"Sounds cool," he said, showing interest in his eyes. "Is it advertising?"

"Some of it is ads." I was brief, hoping lean responses would not require expansion. I stood and went to the cupboard for hot sauce. Nigel had several different kinds. Hoping that was the end of that part of our conversation, I delayed returning to the table by studying the bottles, removing them one by one and looking at the labels. "You are a connoisseur of hot sauce."

Nigel stood too. He opened the fridge, removed a beer, and used the bottle opener on the wall to pop the cap off. "Your job must have really stressed you out. Your entire face shifted."

"It did," I said, choosing a bottle and returning to the table.

Nigel leaned back against the counter. "We don't have to talk about it. It's just work. It's not your identity." He tipped his bottle in my direction. "You want a beer?"

I shook my head. "I haven't tried many, but I've never met a beer I liked."

Nigel chuckled before taking a drink. "I don't know if Aunt Thea mentioned it to you, but the family is having a birthday party for Ma Black. They have one every year. I thought you should know in case you needed to get back . . ." He hesitated, clearly not wanting to say the words *to New York.*

"You being here will make it special."

"One hundred is a special birthday anyway. I'll have to see if I can help. I'm kind of good at planning things."

"I would think someone in marketing would be." He curled his lip and added, "And you look like someone who would be good at marketing." His eyes settled on mine. Unexpectedly, a tug of friendship or something else pulled between us, and the tension from earlier melted away. It was only fair that he learned about my work, or thought he did, because I knew everything about his. "Let me know if you need a ride to Jay's shop or whatever. I'll be around most of the day."

"I will," I said, looking at the wall clock. It was only ten. Early still. Nigel's eyes had followed mine. I wanted to say, "Hey, it's still early enough for us to catch the movie you wanted to see" or even invite him to hang out and watch one here, but I'd rejected him, so now I was stuck with the evening being a loss, and I didn't want it to be.

Nigel went to the sink and poured his half-empty bottle out before tossing it in the trash. "I'll see you tomorrow." He picked up his laundry basket, walked to the back door, and pushed it open. The screen door snapped behind him. I missed his presence immediately.

I washed our forks, and after making a cup of green tea, I turned off the lights and padded to my bedroom. I needed a good distraction from all the thoughts that were circling the perimeter of my brain . . . my career, the documentary with Brooke, Drew's unfaithfulness, the ever-pressing desire to know the details of my father's death, and surprisingly . . . Nigel. There was so much uncertainty in my life right now, but what I did know was this trip delivered tenfold. It was much more than a distraction from my life in New York. My new family was everything I never knew I had, and the pages of Great-grandmother Odessa's journals were everything I didn't know I needed.

20

Odessa Black

GEORGETOWN, SOUTH CAROLINA, 1876

SOMETHING WAS TRYING TO MAKE A MEAL OUT OF HER. THE rain from the night before last drew gnats and flies from all over. They had to smell the wetness on her skin.

"You see, I do this with all the jobs." Elijah took a stick and carved the letters *EB* in the mortar.

Odessa squatted to inspect his work. "It makes you proud to have your initials in the buildings?" she teased.

"Brickwork is art. I want my name to last forever."

"I don't know how Papa will feel knowing you're marking the foundation of the house of the Lord."

Elijah's eyes twinkled with mischief. "Your pa is glad to be getting his own building. He ain't gonna care one way or another what I write in this brick."

The sound of a horse whinny interrupted their conversation. There was nothing out here but them, God, and the promise of a new temple, so it was as loud as a trumpet in the quiet stretch of land.

Out of the corner of their eyes, they saw them coming up the road, and she prayed they would keep going, but they didn't. White men could not let them do anything in peace.

There were two of them. One small and hungry looking, the other tall and overfed. Blood stained their clothes. They'd been hunting. Odessa could smell them off the horse.

The small one asked, "What y'all doing here?"

"Laying the foundation with brick, sir," Elijah responded.

The two of them looked at each other. The big one had a piece of long grass in his mouth. He took it out for his question. "Boy, where did you get this brick?"

Elijah knew not to look them in the eyes too square. Odessa stood behind her husband and let him do the talking. "I bought this from Mr. Hershey. I did some work on his house, and he sold it to me—the extra." Elijah reached into his pocket. "I have the bill of sale here." He handed it to the tall, thin one.

The big one was looking at Elijah like he was trying to think on where he knew him. "You worked for Mr. Warton?"

Elijah cleared his throat before replying, "Yes, sir."

The small one looked at the paper Elijah gave him and then attempted to hand it to his partner, who didn't accept it.

Odessa wondered if either of them could read. Poor whites were no better educated than freedmen. They returned Elijah's receipt.

"I seen him before. He did the steps on my uncle's church," the big one said.

"What you buildin' a foundation for?" the small one asked.

"A church, sir."

"Another colored church. Y'all putting a church every mile." He turned to his friend. "Why can't these darkies worship together?" They cackled like suffocated roosters.

Odessa wanted to say, *"Because we don't have horses like you. We have to walk too far,"* but she knew better than that. She kept her eyes down. She was supposed to be invisible.

"Well, y'all get back to it." They tapped their horse reins and rode away.

Elijah and Odessa stood there like brick statues until they disappeared. "Next time you stay home," Elijah said, releasing the energy from his fear. He walked to the wagon and unhitched the horse. "Go tell your pa to get some men out here to help me, and whoever he send, they have to come ready to sleep here."

"Why?" she asked. Before Elijah could get cross words out, she added, "In case Papa ask."

"Your pa ain't gonna ask, but since you need to know, they might come back and mess up the brick before it dries."

"What makes you think they would come back?"

"Dessa, I know those boys. They'll do it for sport."

"Everybody respects the house of the Lord."

"So why they burnin' Black churches? They burned that church in York." He shook his head. "I should have known better than to bring you." He pressed his lips to her cheeks, hurried and hard, then took her hand and helped her up on the horse.

"If this is what you know, we need to leave. I told you I want to go north, Elijah. It's safer for Negroes up there."

"And harder to make a living."

"But my cousin say—"

"Woman, is you going to get me my help?" Elijah's frustration was rising. It was going to meet the sun if she didn't go on.

She closed her mouth at first. This wasn't the time, but it never seemed to be the time. "Not talking about things won't change them. We can have a better life."

"Without family?" Odessa knew beneath it were the words

without knowing about my mother. They lined every decision Elijah made. "When the babies come, who will help you if you teaching?"

The babies? Odessa swallowed the lump that rose in her throat. The babies that hadn't come yet, no matter how much lovin' they made? She pushed the emptiness out of her heart. "We would figure it out." She knew her words on the subject were as unwelcome as the fly Elijah had just swatted from around his head. "I won't have anything if I don't ask for what I want." She gathered the horse's reins. "I want to leave the South, Elijah." She bumped the sides of the horse and rode home.

21

THE BLACKS WENT TO CHURCH ON SUNDAY. GRANNA HADN'T insisted before, but she let me know I was going today. Fortunately, I had something to wear. I never went anywhere without a few all-purpose dresses and a few good pairs of stilettos.

I stood in front of the mirror and pulled the dress over my head and thanked the God of southern food that I could still fit into it. I inspected my profile in the mirror. I sucked my stomach in and twisted to inspect my backside. I had put on a few pounds thanks to Granna and Aunt Thea's cooking. I didn't look bad, and I'd always told my followers: *No matter your size, no matter the fit, believe no one could wear it better, and the world will believe with you.*

I heard noises outside my window and walked over to peek out. Nigel had locked the door to the Airstream, and Star was walking a doll across the hood of his truck. Granna had to be at church obscenely early for prayer, so I'd opted to meet her at the start of service. However, I wanted to follow Nigel so I could enter with him, just in case I couldn't sit with Granna. I grabbed my bag and rushed outside.

As promised, Cousin Jay fixed my car and checked all my

sensors and belts so there wouldn't be any more surprises. He even drove it to me so I didn't have to pick it up.

"Good morning, Miss Casey," Star said cheerfully.

I returned her greeting and said, "Don't you look pretty."

Blushing, Star shrank inside into the wide collar of her dress.

The *click* of Nigel's truck locks interrupted us. I raised my eyes to his. Nigel looked good in the turquoise-colored dress shirt he'd chosen. I was sure the wrinkles had been removed not with the dryer but by a hot iron. It was crisp and pressed along the seams. The top buttons were open, exposing the strong lines of his masculine throat.

Nigel stared for a moment like he was seeing me through fresh eyes. I suppose he was; I was wearing church-appropriate attire. "If you're going to church, you should ride with us."

I hadn't considered riding with them, but it sounded nice. "Are you sure?"

"Of course." He pulled the doors open. Once he hefted Star in, he turned to me. "You look nice. And tall. Very tall."

In my three-inch heels, I was eye-level with him. "Thank you."

We piled into Nigel's truck.

The trip to Choppee Church by the River was short. The paved parking lot was full, so we had to park on the grass.

"Daddy, it's April," Star cried from the back seat. I heard the *snap* of her seat belt right before her door opened.

"Leave the doll," Nigel said, getting out.

Star's lips morphed from a smile to a pout within seconds. "But she'll be hot."

Nigel opened my door. When my hand slipped into his, warmth spread up my arm and throughout my body. Our eyes held for seconds longer than they should have. Once I was steady on my feet, he tore his attention from me and spoke to Star. "There is no playing with dolls in church."

"I have an idea," I said. He hadn't moved back, so my breath was a wispy slip of air against the side of his face. I was looking at Star, but I could feel his eyes on me. "How about I put her in my bag? She'll be cool in there." I returned Nigel's stare. "And I promise I won't play with her either."

Nigel's chuckle brought back the return of Star's wide smile, which was sunshine against the cloudless sky. She handed the doll to me, slammed the door, and rushed to enter with her friend.

"You spoil her," he said.

"Little girls need spoiling."

Nigel peered at me curiously. "And why is that?"

"Because they need to know that they can get what they want. It fosters ambition."

"And a bad temper."

I smirked. "I prefer to call that *fire*."

"Did you always get what you wanted?"

"No, but my mother had enough ambition for the both of us."

He nodded and closed my door. "I have to give you a heads-up. These folks are gossipy. We're going to be the talk of Choppee."

"Why is that?"

"Only couples ride to church together."

"Is that so?" I took my arm and looped it through his. "I've been talked about before. If people are going to talk, I prefer to give them something juicy."

Nigel reared his head back and inspected me. "Yeah, you got your way." We walked in sync. "You'll have to tell me about why you were the talk."

"Maybe later. Let's get inside."

Nigel and I sat just as the service began. I looked for Granna.

Dressed all in white, she was seated on one of the front pews that faced sideways. Her eyes were closed. She was praying. Prayer was one of her ministries. I recognized a few Blacks but resisted the urge to give finger waves. Everyone was facing forward and looking serious.

I inspected the grainy black-and-white photos on the back of the program. They dated back to the 1800's when Great-grandma Odessa's father was pastor. It was nice that the church history was honored, especially for me, because in their own way, both my great-grandfathers built this church.

The program was detailed and followed to the letter. The service began with singing. All singing required standing, as did Scripture reading. There was a lot of singing and Scriptures, so I didn't understand why we just didn't stand period. There were several recitations: the call to worship, doxology, and the decalogue. I found those to be compelling. I was introduced to the A.M.E. Hymnal. It was a humungous book that I flipped through curiously until I heard Uncle Roger's name called.

I looked up.

"Your uncle says the Lord's Prayer," Nigel said, handing me a Bible. He'd been educating me during the entire service.

It was open to the book of Matthew, chapter 6. Nigel pointed to verse 9 and said, "Follow him down to verse 13."

Uncle Roger closed his eyes, raised his hands, and began to pray in Gullah. "*We Fada wa dey een heaben, leh ebrybody hona ya name.*"

I flipped to the beginning of the book of Matthew. I let my palm settle on the first page. My father was named for this man. I suddenly wanted to know more about him.

That evening, I settled in with the book of Matthew. I used the Common English Bible version because it was plain English, but I was going to go back and use the King James Version because that was what my grandparents used in their time. I wanted to compare them.

As I read, my insides filled like I was carrying something. The stories pricked at my mind, made me conscious and aware. My nerve endings were exposed, exposed to something—maybe the truth. My own thoughts pressed in, saying, *Maybe a lie. These are great stories that made people feel hopeful enough to guide their lives.* I didn't know. But what I did know was my ancestors weren't fools, so if this was their faith, if it had got them through their rough times, how could it lead me wrong?

~⁓~

I woke early the next morning. Earlier than I usually did. Dirty from a game of basketball after dinner, Nigel showered last night, so I wasn't expecting him. I got in my car before the sun rose and drove back to the church.

I wanted to photograph the building at dawn. My photographer's mind told me it would be a beautiful sight in the rising sun. I was right.

The early-morning sun cast a shimmer of light that burst through the glass on the bottle tree, creating a hologram prism. The bottles sparkled like parts of them were coated with tiny diamonds. I walked to the tree and touched the strong oak trunk. The bottles weren't just blue. Some were red, yellow, green, and clear. I wondered what the various colors meant. I took a few pictures and then turned my attention to the building, especially the brick foundation beneath the wood frame.

"What you built is still standing," I whispered. I placed a hand against the building and closed my eyes. Could he have imagined that 150 years later, his great-granddaughter would sit in his church?

I squatted low enough to touch the brick. I pressed my fingers into the roughness of the texture. Then I took a few pictures. As I was looking at my work in the LCD screen, I caught sight of something. I looked at the brick again. There was an inscription in the mortar. I wiped away a web and some dirt. It was small, but it was there. The letters *EB*. Elijah Black.

I placed my hand against it. "I bet you left your mark all over the state of South Carolina."

I pointed the camera and took more pictures. I heard a car pull into the parking lot. My heartbeat sped up. Who else would be out here this early? I rounded the corner to investigate and was relieved to see it was Nigel's truck. He stepped out and approached me.

"What are you doing here alone at this time of morning, Casey? This isn't safe."

Ignoring his chastisement, I said, "I had a strong desire to take pictures."

"At six thirty in the morning?"

"Obviously," I replied smartly. I squatted again. "You've got good knees. Join me so you can see this."

I knew he had great knees. I'd seen him squat on the farm. I pulled his hand to the engraving. "See, right there."

Nigel inspected it.

"Do you think it was him?" I asked.

We stood.

"The foundation is the original. It was common for artisans to carve their initials in their work."

"Their contribution to the beauty in the world," I stated.

Nigel added, "Their way of telling the world they were here, and they did things—built things that mattered."

I reflected on that for a moment when Nigel said, "I guess he called you out of your bed this morning so you could come discover this. It's early spring. In a few weeks, the wildflowers will cover it."

I glanced at the bottles and raised my camera for another shot now that the full sun was behind them. "Why does this tree have different colors?"

Nigel cocked his head. "Blue, you know, is for haints. Evil spirits. And the other colors represent health, prosperity, fertility, freedom. They represent all the issues people bring before the Lord."

I took another picture.

Nigel tugged at my camera strap. "Come have breakfast with me."

I raised the camera and took a few pictures of him in rapid succession. "Only if you're treating."

"Enough." He raised his hand to the lens. "I wouldn't have it any other way."

We entered The Low Flavor Diner. The takeout line was long, but the tables were empty, so we sat. Before I studied the menu good, a waitress was upon us. She placed mugs on the table and poured Nigel a cup of coffee. "Morning, Nigel." His name came off her lips slow and sweet as chilled syrup.

"Morning, Tanya." Nigel rubbed his chin, and I fought to hide amusement at her flirtatious stance. She was standing so close to him that her hip touched his arm. "This is Casey. Casey is Ma Black's granddaughter."

She forced her eyes away from Nigel's and said, "I heard about you." I didn't get the smile Nigel got. "Coffee?"

"Please," I replied, and she poured.

"How long you stayin' here?"

Obviously too long, I thought. "A few weeks." I picked up the cream and lightened the ink-black coffee.

"Ma Black is everybody's grandmother around here. She's sweet."

"She is," I replied. "Thank you."

She turned her attention back to Nigel. "The regular?"

"You know it," he replied, taking a sip of his coffee.

She turned back to me, and I said, "I'll have whatever he's having."

"I bet," she said and then she sashayed away.

"Subtle much?" I laughed.

"Not her." He shook his head, opening a pack of sugar and pouring it into his cup. "It may be hard to imagine, but I'm considered a great catch in these parts."

"I think you'd probably be considered a great catch just about everywhere." I didn't wait to see his reaction to my frank statement. Handsome, educated, employed, with an athletic body—he was a commodity on all seven continents.

I scanned the restaurant's interior. It didn't look like much, but I knew some of the best food was cooked in places like this. I'd seen it in my overseas travel.

Nigel had been reading my mind. "This place has the best shrimp and grits in the county."

"I said I trust you."

He eased forward, meeting my eyes. "That wasn't hard to earn."

"Granna trusts you, so you're trusted by association."

"We know them by the company they keep. Somebody was paying attention in church."

I took another sip of coffee. "I have a confession."

Nigel waited for it.

"I've never been to church before."

He frowned. "Really?"

"I've only been in churches for weddings and one funeral."

"You're a unicorn, Casey Black." His tone was light, but his frown deepened. "Are you atheist or agnostic?"

"Neither. We just didn't go to service. My mother talked about God. She would quote Scriptures, mostly when she was frustrated or something, but I had no idea where they came from."

Nigel's expression softened. "Are you going back?"

"I've been told the Blacks go to church."

A smirk curled the corner of his mouth. "Not all of them."

"I guess the ones my grandmother can make."

"Yeah, that's some of it, especially those young ones." He pushed his back into the chair and gave me one of those Nigel stares. The one that made me think he already knew the answers. "Did you like the service?"

Star's chatter about the upcoming Vacation Bible School had not stopped the entire ride home after church. I was unfamiliar with VBS, so I'd indulged her, asking questions, so Nigel hadn't had a chance to ask me this before. I considered it for a moment. I'd opened my Bible last night to research my father's name, and I was back there today, curious about the building. It had left an impression.

"It was nice, but long. I felt like I was supposed to be there, if that makes sense." I played with the handle of my mug, still processing my thoughts. "Uncle Roger's prayer stirred something in me, but I thought the Gullah kept themselves separate."

He picked up his mug again. "They did before Freedom. There weren't opportunities to meet other people. The enslaved stayed on their plantations."

"Except the lucky ones like Great-grandpa Elijah. Because he had a skill."

Nigel pitched an eyebrow. "Casey, they all had skills. Some were more valuable off the plantation."

Of course, he was right. I was embarrassed I'd said that. "I didn't mean it that way."

Nigel reached for my hand. Even though I'd gotten a questioning brow, there was no judgment in his eyes. "It's fine, Casey. I'm just saying, growing and harvesting rice was a skill; otherwise, why would the enslavers have specifically sought out the Angolans and the Sierra Leoneans?"

I released the guilt I'd felt, perhaps when he'd taken my hand. I looked at it now, covering mine, and then raised my eyes back to his. There was that tug again. The one that made me want to be with him all the time, every day. I pulled my hand back and tried to keep my chest from rising and falling so hard.

"Anyway," Nigel continued, "as for the Gullah, some still stay separate, but we're a community down here. The Black people in this region would never survive without each other. Not with all the developers and shady land takeovers and other things that go on in the name of increasing tax revenue."

I picked up my cup. "I want to understand. Our people were so much more than what I learned in history in school."

"I know you do, and for good reason. Those three hundred acres of land and the blood and sweat it took to get it is a part of you. You're a part of it."

Tanya arrived and placed our plates in front of us. When I saw what was on it, my mouth dropped open. "What is all this?"

Nigel chuckled. With his fork, he pointed, "Shrimp and andouille sausage, potatoes, grits, eggs, and a biscuit with homemade muscadine jam."

"Are you seriously eating all this for breakfast?"

His forehead wrinkled. "Farm work is hard. I need the carbs."

"You could have warned me you were ordering a truck driver's meal."

"You were quick to say ditto." His eyes were full of mischief before he closed them to bless the food.

I raised my camera and photographed my plate, then I took another picture of Nigel. I wanted to remember everything about this time, and that included him.

When we arrived at the farm, we found Granna on the porch sitting in her rocking chair. Nigel gave her a brief greeting while handing her a plate from the restaurant.

"You are good to me," she said, like this wasn't their every Monday routine.

He turned to me and said, "I'm going to work on the fence on the outer left. Rabbits have been getting in, so I won't be up this way much today."

"Okay," I said, missing him before he left.

He backed out of the door and went down the steps. I kept my eyes on him. Right before he turned the corner, he looked back at me. My heart skipped a beat.

"How are you this morning, Granna?"

"I'm blessed. Still in the land of the living." That was what she always said. "You're early."

"I decided to go by the church and take some pictures." I sat and told her about discovering the initials.

"Eddie showed them to me once."

"Nigel told me it was something the people did back then . . . sign their name."

"*Uh-huh.*" Granna smiled. It was a knowing smile like she had uncovered a secret. She opened the cover and raised the plate to her nose for a deep sniff.

"Can I get you a tray for your plate?"

"No. I like to eat it like this. This the best shrimp fritter I ever had. Don't tell Thea." She took a bite.

I sat there while she ate, listening to her moans of delight, and then continued to sit there when she was done. And while she was reading her Bible. Before long, she handed it to me.

"My eyes are tired." She pointed. "You read from here down for me, please."

I'd been bamboozled, but it was okay. If she wanted me to read the Bible, I'd read it. When I was done, she said, "Nigel is a good man. He'd be good for you."

I gave her a probing stare. "Where did that come from, Granna?"

She raised her fork and shook it once. "Y'all are a pot on simmer, baby. I'm old, not blind."

"We're just friends."

Granna snorted. "That's a waste of a perfectly good man, making him a friend."

I couldn't stop the laugh that escaped. "I don't even live here, Granna."

She leaned away from me, inspecting me the way she did when she was about to plant something deep into my spirit. "You don't really live up there either."

How did she know so much? I had work and Drew, and now both were gone, Drew for certain. "I can turn things around when I'm ready."

"You certainly can, because you are a Black." Granna's smile was honest. "As for Nigel, distance can be overcome, and those divorce papers will be final before you know it."

Granna had no idea how inexperienced I was. I married the first man I dated. I sighed. "I can't jump from one relationship into another. I have to get over my husband."

Granna's probing stare became more serious. "I can see you're grieving something, but it's not that marriage. You're not a woman overcoming a romantic heartbreak."

My mouth dropped open, and I closed it. I didn't even know what to say to that.

Granna touched my hand. "I don't believe in making love wait. Time don't always belong to you."

"But we can't live our lives trying to do things because we might run out of time."

"Why not? I've always understood the urgency of time." Her tone was nearly chastising. "I also trusted the Spirit to guide me. You don't have to wait for anything. Do what you want."

I sat there with her words filling empty spaces in my heart. And then she spoke again, and this time the words tore at my heart. "Do you want children?"

I couldn't stop my eyes from filling.

"Oh no, now. Come on." Granna put her plate down. "Tell me about these tears."

I folded my hands and unfolded them. "I've had two miscarriages."

"I'm sorry to hear that."

"It's been less than a year since the second one, and . . . I don't know. I guess now that I'm starting over . . ."

"You wonder if you'll ever have them."

I nodded. I raised a hand to swipe at a tear. "My husband and I . . . we needed that baby."

"A marriage that needs a baby isn't much of a marriage."

I stood, walked to the window, and looked out. Since I was baring my soul, I decided to tell her all my hurtful truths. I turned to look at her. This woman who had carried so much weight in her own life would now have to carry the burden of my heartbreak. I knew she would feel it all, but I needed her wisdom.

"Right before I came here, Drew and I were going to have a seven-year vow renewal service. A few minutes before I was supposed to walk down the aisle, he told me he couldn't marry me again. It was embarrassing because as a social media personality, it was a public wedding. There were lots of cameras and eyes on me."

"Why are you just telling me this?"

"I didn't want to talk about it. I wanted to focus on you and getting to know the family."

"I knew you were in some pain. I've been praying for you, but I sure wish you would have told me you were carrying this."

"He did me a favor." I pressed my palms into each other, pushing my emotions from one side of my body to the other. As if that would work. Energy didn't disappear, especially this kind. I looked in Granna's eyes. She'd been waiting for me to speak. "It's better to know your spouse wouldn't say I do again, but I would have walked down that aisle."

"It's always good to know the truth. A lie shouldn't make your heart its home. But were you walking back down that aisle for the right reason?" Granna looked me over with keen eyes that told me she knew the answer to her question. "The first thing you said about him not doing the vow renewal was that it was public. I wonder if embarrassment outweighed your heartbreak." Granna's mouth was taut with emotion. "Do you still love him?"

I thought about it for a full thirty seconds before shaking my head. "And for some reason, I feel guilty about that. He was my husband for seven years, but I don't miss him, Granna. I think about him. I get angry with him, but I don't really miss him, so what have I been doing? Going through the motions every day? Has my life been one big show on and off social media?"

Granna squeezed her lips together like she always did when she was thinking hard. I knew words of wisdom were coming. "Sometimes when a woman ends a marriage, she don't have no grief left because she grieved the end of that marriage while she was still in it, moving day-to-day, waiting for the change to come that would separate her from her husband. By the time she is legally free, the emotional healing was already done."

Granna paused, giving me a few minutes with her words. I needed them. They were powerful. "In gardening, there's a process called turning the soil. You do it every year after harvest and before you plant again to prepare the soil for the new seeds.

"Baby, you need to turn the soil of your heart over. Unprepared soil never grows a good harvest. Talk to your husband. Close everything up between you. You have to make your heart good ground for the next season of your life."

I nodded. My emotions were so full, I couldn't muster a thing but a nod.

Granna stood. "Now come here and let me hug you."

I walked to Granna and folded myself into her arms. She felt like love, hope, and a good macaroni and cheese rolled together. I took it all in, every bit of what she had to offer. I needed it. It was going to take all three to turn the soil in my heart.

22

WARM WEATHER WAS MY PREFERENCE, BUT TODAY WAS HOT. The air was juicy and thick with humidity. My task for today was checking leaves for bugs and disease. Afterward, I escaped into the air-conditioned house.

I found Petra in the kitchen pouring fresh coffee. One of the counters was covered in the herbs we'd picked. Basil, rosemary, and thyme created a savory aroma. The oregano in my basket added to the scents in the air.

I rarely drank coffee in the middle of the day, but to be sociable, I accepted the cup Petra offered.

Loaves of baked bread served as the island centerpiece. Stacks of the same in plastic wrap were on the counter. There was always something sweet in this house.

Noting my observation, Petra said, "It's zucchini bread. Ma made it last night."

"When?" I remembered she was in bed when I left.

"Sometimes she gets up to bake. Older people don't always sleep through the night."

I'd heard that before. It made me sad for Granna. Not getting a full night's sleep was hard on me. I would think it would be worse for her.

"That's why she never skips her nap." Petra's reply indicated she was reading my mind.

Inspecting the loaf, I said, "I've never had it."

Petra frowned. It was that same "chile, your life is all wrong" frown she always gave me when I told her I'd never had something. "What do y'all eat in New York?"

There were dessert plates next to the bread. Petra reached for two and placed a slice on each and slid one to me.

"It's not a New York thing. *I* didn't have sweets growing up. My mother didn't think sugar was healthy." I raised a slice and took a bite. It was moist and sweet and packed full of nuts with a muffin-like texture. I closed my eyes and savored the flavor. "This is delicious. I can taste the zucchini in it."

Petra cocked her head in the direction of the pile of zucchini on the counter. "Yep. Everything she cooks this week will have zucchini." Petra put a piece of bread in her mouth. "Whatever is harvested is what she eats."

"How long you been working here?"

She took another bite of the bread. "Three years. I've lived in the house for two."

"How's her health overall?"

Petra chuckled. "Better than ours. Her blood pressure and sugar are good. Her heart is strong. The only thing she deals with is arthritis. You can't escape that."

I enjoyed every crumb of the bread. "Granna will have to teach me how to make this." Having this snack and coffee in the middle of the day was such a sweet treat. It couldn't be wrong to enjoy a simple pleasure like this.

Finished with her bread, Petra went to the pantry and returned with plastic wrap. She tore off pieces and wrapped a few slices of the bread and put it at the end of the island. "Your grandmother will give a slice to her clients. People leave here with more than they came for."

I stepped to the entrance of the kitchen, leaned against the doorjamb, and glanced in the direction of Granna's room where she held her healing meetings. I had yet to observe one because they were private consultations. "What does she do in the meetings?"

Petra yawned like I'd woken her in the middle of a nap. No doubt, Granna's middle-of-the-night baking exploits robbed her of sleep. "She does different things with different people. Some clients have medical problems like eczema or rashes, aching knees, headaches. She recommends an herbal solution. Sometimes she gives them something she has, and sometimes they have to come back for something she makes. Other people want counseling."

"Like therapy?"

"*Um-hmm*. For problems with depression or their marriage or kids. They ask her questions about the Bible. Sometimes they just want to talk to an older, wiser woman or they want prayer. She helps with whatever. She's what you call a *doctress*. Some people say medicine woman. They take care of the physical, mental, and emotional needs."

"She sees a lot of people." I raised my coffee mug to my lips and hid behind it when I asked the probing, if not nosy, question on my mind. "Does she charge?"

"She takes donations, but she gives it all to a food bank."

The door to the room opened, and I skirted to the island and sat like I'd been trying to avoid getting caught eavesdropping. It wasn't like I was standing close enough to hear anything—the room was down the hall—but I didn't want to just stand there staring at her client. Petra moved a few of the zucchini from the counter and placed them next to the wrapped slices of bread.

I could hear Granna and her client walking up the hall, having what sounded like parting words. Granna entered the kitchen. She picked up a slice of bread and a zucchini and handed them to the woman before she let her out the door, then she joined us in the kitchen.

"Two of my favorite people in the world." She smiled, but her eyes were weary. She walked out the door to the back deck.

"Sometimes the sessions wear her out," Petra said, once again reading my thoughts. "That was Mrs. Coakley. Her son died last year. She comes about her grief."

Granna rocked in one of her chairs. The rhythm was slow and unintentional.

"She always bakes the night before she comes. I think talking to Mrs. Coakley reminds her of her sons." Petra took our dishes to the sink.

I walked outside and joined Granna.

"How was your session?" I asked.

She turned her attention away from the view and looked at me. "It was good. Helpful to her. Did you try the bread?"

I perked up like the sugar wanted to answer her. "Yes, ma'am. It was so good. I was telling Petra I've never had it before."

"It's easy to make. I'll show you how." She stood and walked back into the house. "It's too hot even for me." I agreed and followed her inside.

She stopped at the sink, looking at the pile of herbs in the draining sink. "I see you picked a bunch more." She plopped a hand on her hip and assessed it all like it was a mess. "I overplant. I can't seem to stop myself." She sighed. "Let's hang the ones that are already dry."

I couldn't help but notice Granna looked tired. "Why don't you rest, Granna? We can do that tomorrow."

"I don't put things off for tomorrow when I can do them today. I keep busy. It helps my mind," she said. "Right, Petra?"

Petra smiled. "Yes, ma'am."

Granna opened a drawer and removed twine, scissors, tags, and a permanent marker. "The batch you washed has to dry first. We'll hang those tomorrow." She moved to a pile on the counter that wasn't wet. She smoothed the pieces out and tied the ends with the twine on the bottom of the branches. Then she wrote a tag out for rosemary and slipped it through the twine and tied it to the bundle. I followed her into the pantry where a bunch of bundles hung around the room. "We store them in here. They need to hang until they're completely dried and cracklin' like the way you buy them in the store. That's when you take the leaves off. Just like that, you have dried herbs."

She reached for a hook, attached it to the end of the twine, and pushed it up on another hook. "They hang upside down. You want the oils and juices to flow down from the stems into the buds here," Granna said, rubbing one of the oregano leaves. "It makes the flavor more intense."

I nodded. "Granna, do you think I'll ever learn all this?"

"I like to teach you, Casey, but some lessons come by living and trying things. It can work both ways. Just don't be afraid."

"I can be a bit of an overthinker."

"I see that, but you can't break nothing around here, baby, and if you do, we'll grow more or replace it." Granna pulled me into a hug. She whispered, "I love you."

I drew in the hug, inhaled her clean scent from her handmade sage soap, and took all the emotion in. This time with her was all like a dream. A wonderful one. The best kind ever. I squeezed one last time before she let me go. "I love you, too, Granna. So much."

23

Odessa Black

GEORGETOWN, SOUTH CAROLINA, 1882

MAMA WAS SICK, AND INSTEAD OF GOING TO SEE A DOCTOR, she put all her faith in headache tonic, stomach bitters, and liver pills from a charlatan. This was a drastic change from the woman who grew up using plants from the earth and taught Odessa how to do the same.

"I can't get her to see reason, Papa." What she didn't say was she didn't feel like she knew her mother anymore.

She'd just come from her parents' bedroom. Mama was sleeping. She'd been in bed most of the day, complaining of tiredness and stomach pain.

"And there's something else. Her thinking is off. I had the hardest time convincing her that today is Tuesday and the date. She wouldn't believe me. She seemed confused."

So focused on the latest issue of the *Missionary Record*, Papa had let his dinner plate grow cold. Politics and news seemed to be the only things that held her father's attention these days. As a somewhat prominent pastor, he was called to meetings in downtown Georgetown and Charleston every week, sometimes several times a week. "Your mother will be all right, Odessa. Don't you fret too much about her. She's strong."

"I don't believe so, sir," she said with the most tempered voice she could muster with the feelings she had. He was ignoring her, preferring his work to his wife, and that was not what God would want him to do—or maybe he knew something was wrong and he didn't want to see it. He had just lost Uncle Bishop last year. He'd left for Jamaica shortly after the war. Other than for extended visits to handle business, Uncle Bishop stayed on the island, but he was special to Papa. He'd saved their family from the hard labor of slavery.

Papa dropped his paper on the kitchen table, removed his spectacles, and put them in his pocket. Concern etched his forehead. Odessa wasn't sure if it was regarding the issue or her tone.

"What makes you say such a thing when you know the power of your tongue on these matters?"

"God gives us wisdom to *do*, not just words to believe." She placed a hand on her belly and walked to the shelf where Mama kept her potions and pills. "Look at all of this. Mama is trusting northern carpetbaggers to heal her. She's put her hope in these colored waters that don't do anything but give her more time on the pot. I'm scared for her." Odessa walked to her father and placed a hand on the lapel of his suit jacket. A handsome, store-bought, black suit she and Elijah gave him for Christmas last year that Papa wore proudly to all important meetings. "Something is wrong. She needs to go to a real doctor."

"She has been to the doctor."

"He hasn't helped. There's a doctor in Charleston—"

"Charleston?" Alarm filled his voice. Papa was friends with

the local doctors. "There are two perfectly good Negro doctors here in Georgetown."

"Perfectly good is not the best." She could read the concern on his brow. Papa was a man you had to wrangle, but when you got his attention, he listened. "Why can't you take Mama on one of your trips to Charleston?"

"Who is this doctor you talkin' about?"

Odessa took the newspaper from under her purse and unfolded it. "This is the write-up about him. He moved from Atlanta a few months ago. He cures stomach problems. The ones that can be . . ." She paused. Her words stuck in her throat like a dry biscuit. Fear locked her tongue. She desperately wanted her mother healed, but she knew it was bad. She'd seen the evidence.

"She has blood in her pail." Odessa turned her back to her father. She fussed in her purse for a moment, more to hide her wet eyes than any shame over talking about her mother's pail. She removed a handkerchief and wiped her eyes.

"I've got to get home. Elijah will be waiting for his dinner." Papa was as still as one of the dummies in the store window downtown. She kissed his cheek. He'd heard her. Finally. Blood was always a bad sign. "You let me know when you're taking her. If you need me to go with you . . ."

He placed a hand over Odessa's. "Your mother is my responsibility. I'll see about getting her to Charleston early next week."

~⁓~

Next week was too late for Mama. Three weeks or even a month before would have been too late. The doctor in Charleston said she had a mass in her stomach. She needed a surgeon to remove it, and she needed the surgery a long time ago. Mama lived only a few more weeks.

Losing her was Odessa's first real loss in life. She could hardly make herself get out of bed to care for her children, who seemed to come all at once after a slow start. The truth was, breathing was hard. It was good that it was summer. She taught reading and writing at the Colored Academy three days a week during the school year. Going to work right now would have been impossible, but school was starting again in a month. She'd have to find someone to help with the children—Pearl, Liz, and the one in her belly that only she and Elijah knew about.

She finally understood why her husband would never leave here. Why the man who claimed to love her so much would not suffer to step foot out of Georgetown County no matter how she begged. He'd lost his mother as a boy. Odessa had hers all these years. Her heart was broken in pieces that would never come back together.

She rolled on her side and wrapped her arms around Elijah from the back. He cupped her hand, raised it to his lips, and kissed her fingers.

The only sound was the shrilling of crickets and an owl in the distance.

"You gonna survive this, Dessa."

"I know," she whispered. "I'm sorry."

Elijah turned onto his back. She propped herself up on an elbow and looked into his eyes. They held the question before he asked it. "For what?"

"Your mama. I'm sorry for every time I asked you to leave."

He pulled her into his strong, able arms, and another dam burst inside her heart. She sobbed into his chest until she couldn't cry anymore.

24

THE PHONE CALL TO BROOKE WAS GOING TO BEGIN WITH screaming on the other end. She communicated with her emotions. I'd witnessed the full range over the months I'd worked with her. She'd given me grace, so now whatever she said, I had it coming.

"You are lucky." Brooke's voice was even, low like she was whispering.

"Am I? I don't feel very lucky." I actually did because she wasn't screaming.

Though I heard her on the phone, it took Brooke a full minute to reply. "I've been in Vancouver for the last two weeks. And now I'm taking family leave for two, maybe three weeks. That buys you time to get your story together so we can finish."

Three weeks. That put me at early May. Maybe by then I'd have some clarity about what I wanted to do with my life so we could focus on that instead of my meltdown.

I closed my eyes and released my anxiety. A reprieve. That's what I needed.

"Okay. Family leave, though. Is everything okay?"

"My father had a stroke. I need to take care of him and get some things in place."

"I'm sorry to hear that."

"Me too. I'm thirty-one. I never expected caregiving responsibilities to begin this early." Brooke's sigh was heavy in my ear. I could only imagine how heavy it was on her heart. "I will text you when I'm back, but Casey, be prepared."

The line went dead.

I dropped the phone and fell back against my pillows. I could not go down in history as the social media influencer who lost it. I'd become a case study in some college curriculums. I needed to offer her something else, something more interesting, and I had to come up with it fast.

I'd taken hundreds of pictures since my arrival in Georgetown. I sent some of my favorites to Leslie, including the ones of Granna and me in the kitchen and a few selfies we took on the farm.

Minutes after I sent the pictures to Leslie, my phone was ringing with a call from her. "This girl in the pictures has never, ever looked this free."

"This trip was long overdue. Thank you so much for telling me to venture down here. I never would have thought of it on my own."

"I'm glad I could help a sistah out."

"I talked to Brooke. Email me the contract. I need to read the fine print."

"Was she on your case?"

"No. Fortunately, she's on family medical leave." I scrunched up my face. "That didn't come out right. But because she's out, it'll be a few weeks before she's ready to work again. She's threatening to drag me. I know my mother wouldn't have had me sign a contract that didn't offer me some protection from a negative story."

We talked about a few other things and got off the phone.

I lay on the bed, swiping through the pictures again. I opened

Instagram. A reboot would excite my followers. They were out there, waiting and wanting me to answer the question: What are you doing now, Casey B?

I tapped a few times and created a new page. I decided it would be a cool place to catalog my pics. I was a visual person. An online journal would be a forever keepsake. Well, "forever" as long as the 'Gram lasted. I tried several names; most were taken, and then the hashtag Black Mixed with Black came to mind, so I used @IAmBlackMixedWithBlack as the account name. It was perfect. I was a Black, and this experience was the true essence of our culture—family, history, food, fun. I scrolled until I found the pictures I'd taken at the church.

"And faith," I whispered. "The faith of my ancestors."

What would I believe if I had been introduced to it as a child? What did I believe now?

I picked up my phone and went to my business page and clicked on the recent comments. The positive comments far outweighed the negative ones, but I couldn't look past the negative ones.

> @YourGirlCaseyB Have you killed yourself? Girl, the man isn't
> worth.
> @YourGirlCaseyB For real, you just giving up on life.
> @YourGirlCaseyB I'm so #disappointed in you.

"Seriously, disappointed in me? I'm not your mother or your child." I tapped the screen and went to my @IAmBlack MixedWithBlack page and uploaded more pictures.

I had some on my camera too. I captioned each of them. It was a private page, but I sent it to Leslie so she could see more.

Leslie texted me: Catchy page name. Make it public.

I texted back: No. I'm showing off to you.

Almost two hours later, I stopped because my phone battery was at 2 percent. I could be so hyperfocused, it was criminal.

I hopped off the bed and went into the kitchen for water. Through the blinds, I saw Nigel stretched out on a lounge chair on his stoop. He looked like he was sleeping. I pushed the door open and walked over. All he was wearing was a pair of jeans and a baseball cap that covered his face. It was embroidered with the words, *We do it better in the lowcountry.* I quirked an eyebrow at that. Nigel's long, athletic body was tanned a darker brown on his folded arms than it was on his torso. He wasn't wearing shoes, but it was his lack of a shirt that I found distracting. The rise and fall of his tightly formed abs—doubly distracting.

The good Lord took his time with this one.

A rowdy snore escaped from under the hat. The voyeur in me was rattled, but I didn't stop watching his chest go up and down. I'd been avoiding the inevitable truth I hadn't let process in my conscious mind—I was more than a little attracted to him. I'd worked with a lot of male models, so it took a lot for me to admire a man just on his looks, but I was here. Standing over him like a perv. In what world could a man do what I was doing right now? I had no right ogling him like this.

Another snore, this one louder, caused the hat to blow up a bit. I removed the hat. He stirred, but he still didn't wake.

"Nigel," I called softly as to not startle him.

One of his eyes opened, then the other. He unfolded his arms and sat up. After a few seconds of being disoriented, he grabbed his T-shirt from the table next to him like he was aware he was half-naked and it mattered.

"Don't clothe on my account."

He cleared this throat. "Was I sleeping?"

"Hard and snoring. You could have been robbed."

"By who? You?" He retrieved his hat from my hand and slapped it back on his head.

"If I wanted to rob you, I wouldn't have woken you up. I wanted to save you from being eaten alive by bugs."

He stood. His full height putting me eye level with the chest I'd been admiring. "Bugs don't bite me."

I thought, *Why not? You look yummy.* I said, "Ever?"

His dark eyes settled into mine. "Not often."

"Well, they tried to eat me whole."

"That's because you're sweet."

We stood there for a moment with the sound of the crickets filling up the night, his masculine presence filling up my senses. That compliment filling my head. I took one step back, away from him. "I've done my good deed for the night. I'm going to go."

Nigel took one step forward, toward me. "I appreciate you being a good neighbor."

I cleared my throat and tried to ignore the fact that my heart lurched. "And not robbing you."

He smiled, and all those beautiful teeth he owned lit up the night sky.

"I'm going." I turned and practically ran back to my house. Once inside, I fell against the door. I was already looking forward to seeing him tomorrow. I needed to watch my feelings for him. This season in South Carolina would end, so falling for him was a bad idea. Long-distance relationships rarely worked. I couldn't even keep one with a man I lived with. I kept telling myself we were friends, but I also wasn't lying to myself. Nigel was the kind of man a woman wanted more from.

25

MY PHONE BUZZED, AND I LOOKED AT A TEXT MESSAGE FROM my mother.

Your divorce is final. I'll email a copy.

Just like that. Divorced. I tried to fight them, but it wasn't long before feelings of sadness and disappointment invaded my thoughts. My emotions were a pesky fly that I couldn't swat away. I understood why people called it a failure. It felt like one.

But then I watched as Nigel moved across the grass—powerful arms, tight abs, nice strong thighs. He was headed in my direction. I thought, *Drew who?*

Lord have mercy.

He was in a cheerful mood, but he could tell I was not because his first words to me were, "What's that face?"

"I just found out that my divorce is final."

He displayed the right amount of sympathy. "You need a soak. You have a space reserved tonight in my hot tub."

"That sounds good."

"If you don't want me around, I'll disappear, but if you want the company of someone who's been through what you're going through, I can be a shoulder to cry on."

I'd just been looking at those powerful shoulders. Who was I to reject them? "I accept your invitation to the hot tub, and you may stay, but there is one requirement."

"What's that?"

"You have to supply me with a beverage that is not a beer or soda or sweet tea." I raised a hand to the side of my mouth and whispered, "Don't tell anyone about the tea."

Nigel laughed. "Wine?"

I turned up my nose. "No wine. That was my ex's thing."

"Okay," Nigel said, pushing a fist into his palm. "Tell me what the single no-wine-drinking ladies are consuming these days."

"Good old-fashioned lemonade."

He chuckled. "I can manage that." He walked away, and I stared at him going in the same way I stared when he was coming. I didn't know which view was better. My brain asked the question again.

Drew who? But deep down inside, I was still hurting.

<hr />

The day didn't end fast enough. I was glad to put on my swimsuit and climb into Nigel's hot tub. He had my lemonade. Fresh squeezed right out of Granna's kitchen on special request. And he had surprised me, quite pleasantly, by mixing it with peach Schnapps. By the time I was done, I was a little buzzed and in a much better mood.

"I wasn't a horrible wife."

"I know."

I dropped my head to the side and smirked at him. "You don't know."

"Well, you'd have to be a horrible person to be a horrible wife."

I snorted. "No, you don't."

Nigel laughed with me. "I'm supposed to be making you feel better."

I kicked my legs in the water, let gravity lift me up a little. "I was a good wife most of the time. I worked a lot. Maybe too much, but so did he. He's a lawyer. You know they work all the time too."

"You're a hard worker. I've seen the way you go after weeds."

I dropped my head back and laughed again. "You're teasing me."

"I just think you need to stop trying to find a reason to blame yourself. It's not your fault."

I let that statement roll around in my head for a minute before saying, "I know he was cheating. I found that out a month ago."

Nigel's eyes widened. "Really?"

"I have proof. Pictures."

His eyes widened again. This time he reared back his head. "So why are you blaming yourself?"

"Because for one, statistically, men who cheat don't leave their wives unless they get caught and their wives make them." Nigel raised a finger to insert a "but." I grabbed his hand. "And two, I guess I'm one of those women who thinks if her man is cheating, she did something wrong."

We sat there in the middle of the tub with me holding his hand and our eyes sinking farther into each other. It was quiet. All I could hear was crickets and an occasional bird in the trees. I looked down. "The water isn't moving."

"I turned off the heat. I know how you are about your skin."

I released his hand and giggled. "So this is now a kiddie pool."

"A big, expensive one."

I raised my hand to cover my face. Sorrow still had a hold on me. Nigel's hand was on my shoulder. I opened my eyes and dared to look at him again.

"I don't know the statistics, but people are unfaithful because they choose to be."

I was too fuzzy in my brain and emotions to be this close to Nigel. I pushed away from him to the other side of the tub. "It's complicated between me and Drew. Some of the disappointments were pretty bad."

"It's complicated between all couples. Don't own his crap, Casey. If he's a dog, let him be a dog. You no longer have to cover him or protect him."

I nodded. "Wow. That was kind of what I needed." I thought for a minute before saying, "Granna helped me to see that I'm over him, but I'm still stuck with wondering why it ended the way it did."

Nigel's eyebrows knit together. "How did it end?"

At first I thought I'd said too much, but then I realized, Nigel was my friend. Who was he going to tell? And why was I keeping what the world knew from someone who actually cared about me?

"We were supposed to renew our vows. There were over two hundred people in the church. Some of my business partners were there. It was an event." It all felt so long ago, but the sting of Drew's betrayal was still fresh. "My husband didn't go through with the ceremony."

Nigel blinked a few times. He was stunned. I could see that. "You mean like on the day?"

"The hour. Nearly the minute. He came to the church and told me he was leaving."

Nigel shook his head. "I . . . wow . . . what a jerk. I'm sorry you went through that."

"Yes, he was a jerk," I said, "and it affected my business."

"Hence the break."

"Look at that. Can't get anything past you." I scratched my head. "What about me was so unlovable that he had to embarrass me that way?"

"I don't have his answers. All I can tell you is some things aren't meant to be. Maybe from the start. Maybe they break down in the middle or simply unravel at the end, but either way, they were never going to last."

"Marriage is supposed to last. We're not supposed to give up on each other."

Nigel cocked his head. "And yet, we do."

We sat there not saying anything for a long time before I said, "Thank you for tonight. I didn't want to be alone."

"I'm here for you." He got a serious expression on his face.

I let my arms float to the surface. I played in the water, fanned it until it made waves, and then looked at Nigel. Granna was right. Friendship was wasted on him. "What if I want more?"

"Here comes the rebound divorce move." He shook his head. "No more Schnapps for you."

"I asked you for lemonade. You gave me a lemonade mixed drink." I couldn't keep the silly grin off my face.

"You're not drunk, Casey. You know what you're saying. That divorce rejection can hit hard. I've been there."

"You're saying I'm only making a *little* fool of myself." I raised my hand and pinched my index finger and thumb together.

"No. I'm saying you're not allowed to ask me that question today. You can ask tomorrow, because I would only consider dating a woman who was divorced for at least a day."

I flicked water at him, rested my head back against the cushion, and closed my heavy eyelids. My heart felt lighter.

26

Odessa Black

GEORGETOWN, SOUTH CAROLINA, AND
PETERSBURG, VIRGINIA, 1886

GOD WAS ANGRY.

Odessa knew that for sure because He shook the earth. Yesterday, when her daughter Beth lied to her about eating the last of the molasses, she grabbed her shoulders and shook her once. She shook her because she was angry.

Elijah was on the way home. He'd been working in Columbia for two weeks. Odessa made his favorite dinner—pork chops, Hoppin' John rice, oyster fritters, greens, and biscuits. He liked his biscuits with molasses. But Beth stuck her fingers in the bottom of the barrel and finished it. Odessa was upset about it. Upset enough to shake a child she never shook.

"Mama, I can't find my ribbon." Pearl, her oldest child at age eight, came into the kitchen holding a ponytail she'd brushed out perfect.

"What ribbon?" Odessa asked, knowing she had only three

colored ribbons. Pearl was wearing a red dress, so she wanted the red one.

Odessa opened the oven and put the chops in. It wasn't as hot as it should be, so it was going to take longer to cook.

"Red, Mama." Pearl's expression was tired, like *she'd* been cleaning and cooking all week for her husband to come back.

"If you can't find it, use another color."

"Beth took it on Sunday."

"If she did, it'll turn up. Finish dressing. I need you to go to Miss Francine's house to get me some molasses."

"I have to finish the picture for Daddy."

"You had all morning to finish, and you dawdled, so now you have to do what I say."

"But Mama . . ."

"No *but* to me." Stress climbed up Odessa's back. This was a bad week. There was an earthquake—in the South. She learned in school that wasn't something that happened here, but it had, and it was a bad one. God shook them.

God shook her when the letter came. She looked at the envelope sitting atop the icebox, out of the way, safe so the girls—Pearl, Beth, and Ann—wouldn't reach it. The letter her father gave her at Bible study that Tuesday night in reply to an ad Elijah placed in *The Colored Tennessean*.

Odessa remembered the words. They had changed over the years as they learned new information, but they'd been the same for a long time.

INFORMATION WANTED BY A SON CONCERNING HIS MOTHER.

Elijah, a male born in 1848, formerly owned by Joseph Warton on the Warton House Plantation in Georgetown

County, South Carolina, seeks his mother, Pearl, of
Georgetown, South Carolina. In 1858, she was sold by
Mr. Warton to Abercrombie Riley of the Riley Plantation,
but then was sold again about a year later to the highest
bidder at auction in Summerton, South Carolina. Any information may be sent to David Conway, pastor of Choppee
Church by the River, Georgetown, South Carolina. Elijah
is now known as Elijah Black. Mr. Black will be eternally
grateful as his mother is his only relative.

How many times had she written that letter? Now information was here, waiting for him to return to it. Odessa dared not
open it. No matter how bad she wanted to know, to prepare him
for good or bad news. She didn't even know when to give it to
him: as soon as he arrived, later in bed, or the next day when he
was rested. Odessa didn't know what was best. He'd looked so
long. They'd had so many conversations.

Elijah told her she didn't understand the pain in his heart
about his mama. He was right. Odessa didn't understand. She'd
only gotten a glimpse of the ache when her mama died. She
missed Mama like she'd died yesterday. So she had pain, but not
the kind that was persistent. She didn't ache.

"I hope it brings closure for him," Papa had said as he pressed
the letter into her hand. Odessa gasped when she looked down
at it. She was shook to her core. The heat mixed with her nerves,
making the walk home unbearable. She was sweated out by the
time she put the girls to bed. She'd climbed in the tub for a
bath, and just as she was getting out, the house shook—hard. The
earth moved all around her.

"Mama!"

Odessa turned to her daughter, lowered her face and yelled,
"Stop calling me, Pearl!"

She didn't even know what the girl wanted. She didn't care. She wanted her husband. Now.

Pearl stepped back. Spoiled and not used to hard discipline, she burst into tears.

Odessa released her frustration on a wind of breath and softened her tone. She gave Pearl the mother she was used to. "I'm sorry. I didn't mean to speak so rough. I need some molasses for your daddy's biscuits. Would you go for it, please?"

Pearl nodded. She wasn't hardheaded like Beth, but she fought for her share of attention. Between the baby and Beth, sometimes Pearl disappeared from Odessa's consciousness.

"I'll let you wear my red ribbon. Be a good girl and put on the black one for now."

Pearl nodded again and then walked back to the bedrooms. Before long, she was out the door headed down the road.

Hours later, clutching a warm glass of lemonade in one hand and the newspaper in the other, Odessa stood on the porch, watching for Elijah without moving. Not even a little. She'd read about the earthquake damage. The paper reported it was felt all over the Southeast, but Charleston had been hit the hardest. She also read about the lynchings of Negro men. They were happening every day now. Jim Crow had blanketed the South with evil. White people were able to exercise their absolute power and take out their hatred on the Negro people.

Columbia was only about six hours by horse and cart. Elijah always left at sunup, so he was long overdue to be home. Odessa worried about him all the time. He wasn't alone. His work partner, Monroe, traveled with him, but still . . . Negro men on the road with tools and money. It wasn't safe. Not with those night riders. They did evil in the light of day too.

Finally, she heard the clomp of horses' hooves on the gravel before they stopped in front of their house. Elijah's shadowy figure climbed down. Darkness had swallowed the light hours ago, but she knew him. The horses started up again, and Monroe crept back down the road.

Elijah carried bags and tools, bringing them into the house as Odessa followed.

They had a routine. Normally, he'd enter, put his things down, hug the girls, and then kiss Odessa hard on the back porch. But it was late. The girls had fallen asleep on the living room floor, so she had him first. They walked to the kitchen.

He pulled her into his arms and kissed her, long and sweet and necessary. Odessa whispered against his lips. "I was so scared. I have never been so scared in my life. The paper says it's more dangerous than it's ever been with the night riders, and now with the earthquake, people might be more desperate." Elijah had to feel her heart beating. It was nearly coming out of her chest.

"I know what people are doing, Dessa." Elijah pulled away from her. He wiped his hands over his head. "I don't want it to be the first thing I talk about when I come through the door."

The words *I'm sorry* were about to slide off her tongue, but Elijah said them first. Not literally; instead, he told her what he knew she wanted to know. That was apology enough. "The roads are damaged in some parts. I've been coming all day."

"Papa says Charleston was hit bad. People are dead. A lot of the buildings were destroyed. Churches, schools, businesses."

He raised a hand to stroke Odessa's face. His eyes sunk into her. He rubbed the pad of his thumb across her lips and half smiled. "Everything looks good here."

She knew what he meant. He was talking about her, but still, she shared their minor losses. "A few glasses and plates broke. A lamp. Nothing much."

"There'll be work for me." A flicker of guilt crossed his face, and he sighed. "I don't mean to be thinking about that."

Odessa understood. Elijah never wanted to see anyone hurt, but he was a businessman. Masons would be in demand to repair damaged buildings. He'd have plenty of work in Georgetown and Charleston Counties, so he wouldn't have to travel so much.

She placed her hands on his arms and ran them up to his shoulders. "I'm glad you'll be working closer to home."

She heard a noise in the living room and seconds later, squeals of delight, before the girls converged on him in the kitchen. Elijah took the time to pick up each one, starting with Ann, the baby. He kissed them and hugged them, and when the excitement was over, Odessa sent them to bed, asking Pearl to take care to get everyone changed.

"Your hair is pretty, Pearl," Elijah said as she walked out.

She reached up and twirled the red ribbon before giving her daddy a toothless smile.

"I'ma be in for prayers in a minute," Elijah called to their backs, and they sped up. They knew that meant hurry on.

Odessa fixed his dinner and watched him eat, stealing glances at the top of the icebox the whole time. Once he finished his meal, he washed his dishes, his gift to her for being gone so long and leaving everything on her.

"I'm tired. I need to wash the road off me. I want to go to bed." Again, he stroked her face. They'd gone two weeks without each other. He wasn't trying to sleep. Not right away. Odessa wished this night would be like every other night he came home, but it wasn't going to be. Not at all, and she couldn't hold off a minute longer.

"Something came for you." Her voice trembled on her words. She crossed the tiny kitchen to the icebox, reached for the letter, and stretched it in his direction. "It's word, Elijah. It's about your mother."

It was Christmastime before Elijah and Odessa could travel to his mama's grave. She had work and the children had school, so they waited until their break and took the train. His mother had long been gone—thirteen years now. She'd passed from a cough and fever.

Elijah's mother was buried in Petersburg, Virginia. God's maneuvering put her husband, Tom Williams, in Tennessee with his employer where he saw the ad seeking his dead wife. Pearl was sold in Summerton to Raleigh and then on up to Virginia where she was when she was freed. Her years as a free woman gave Elijah much comfort. The fact that she had a husband gave Odessa comfort. A woman shouldn't be alone in this world. No one should.

"You can tell Tom still misses her," Odessa whispered as they looked down at the rock that marked her grave. She leaned down and put the flowers they picked on top. "She had love."

Tom approached Odessa and Elijah at the grave after giving them some time alone. "She was trying to go back to see you before she got sick. She dreamed about it 'most every day," Tom said. "We couldn't save the money. We didn't have nothing after the war. We 'bout starved. All I knew was fieldin', and Massa—Mr. Sollaway—wasn't paying us nothing but ole meal and salt pork and the quarters. It took me a year to save for shoes and a better dress for her.

"And we didn't know nothing about the newspaper ads. Nobody at Sollaway Plantation knew 'bout the paper. Everybody there was with they kin. Pearlie and me was the onliest new slaves they bring in, and Sollaway got us fa debt Massa in Raleigh had to pay."

"You pick cotton?" Elijah asked. Knowing what kind of crop grew on a plantation told a lot about the kind of life the enslaved had. Some things were harder than others.

"Tobacco mostly."

Everybody knew cotton was bad. It was almost as hard as rice, but cotton days were longer, and the overseers were cruel.

"I kept some of her things. We got dinner for you. It ain't much."

Odessa touched Tom's forearm. "We thank you kindly."

It took a long time for Elijah to pull himself away from that grave. Over a meal of chicken and sweet potato that was cooked by Margaret, Tom's gal—not a wife yet—they talked some more.

They left Sollaway Plantation, carrying with them his mama's handkerchief and some needlework and leaving Tom with thirty dollars to buy whatever he needed so his life could be better.

They took the train home with Elijah deep in thought. He finally spoke what he'd been thinking all these years. "I'm glad I can stop looking and wondering, but I wish I could have seen her one more time."

Odessa squeezed his hand. "She's in heaven. She can see you. She saw what you did for Tom, and that made her glad." She smiled at him. "And you know what else? She's so proud of you. You have a trade and a family. You're a good provider and a good man."

Wetness made his eyes shiny. She wasn't used to seeing that. "It's okay for you to be however you have to be with me. I love you."

"I love you." He kissed the side of her head.

Odessa held his hand for hours while he wept inside his soul. She tried to absorb as much of his pain as she could, but she knew from losing her mama that it was mostly a burden you had to carry on your own.

Once they were home, they settled back into their routines. Fortunately, Elijah had a local job. For that, Odessa was grateful. He needed her and the children right now.

It wasn't a week since they'd come back from seeing his mama's grave when after being sweet to each other, he took her in his arms and said, "I want a farm."

"I know. We've talked about it."

"I want to start buying the land."

Odessa sat up. He was talking serious now, and when he did that, she looked him in the eye.

"There are twenty acres available on Choppee Road by Black River. I want to buy it."

She nodded.

"I'ma still brick, but land is costing more. We need to buy now even if we don't live on it."

She nodded again, but she wasn't sure this was all settled. Once they found his mother, they were supposed to be free to go north. Odessa was frustrated here and scared most of the time. The South was a pot on a hot fire with too much water in it— threatening to boil over. Everything they had gained politically after Freedom, including the seats of the seventy-three Negro and mixed-raced Republicans, was lost when the Negro politicians were defeated—crushed by the Democrats in 1877. She'd thought fragility ended it, that either party would hold a majority in some elections and be voted out at the successive election, but now, nineteen years later, as the situation for Negro people became worse, she realized it hadn't been frail.

The 1867 election that seated the Negro representatives had

been a fluke. It was the steam off the boiling pot—a gas that disappeared, never to be collected again. Because the day of the Negro Republican politician was over, South Carolina was more miserable and violent than it ever had been.

Even with all this swirling around in her head, Odessa told her grieving husband what he needed to hear. "We'll do whatever you think is best for us."

He pulled her to him. Kissed her gentle and sweet. She curled her body next to his, her back to his strong belly. He put his powerful arms around her. She always felt safe in his arms.

"And Dessa, one more thing."

"What's that, honey?"

"Ann is almost four. I love my daughters, you know that, but I want you to stop doing whatever you doing to not get in the family way. I need a son to carry the Black name."

27

THE WACCAMAW SENIOR GAMES WERE HELD THE LAST WEEK in April every year on High Market Street in Georgetown. Granna was the only person in her late nineties competing.

The Blacks had our own cheering section, with Black Farm being a sponsor. We took up an entire third of the stands on one side of the field. Nigel and some of the employees were here too. I looked over my shoulder at him. He was engaged in a conversation with a few of my male cousins, but he tipped his head up at me.

My heart did a little dance, and I sucked my belly in to quell the fluttering. This crush was ridiculous.

Lachelle's entrance was the distraction I needed. She rounded the bleachers, her mass of curls lifting with the light breeze as she put enthusiastic, spirited pep in her bounce down the steps. She slid in on the row next to me.

"Hey," she said, angling a popcorn barrel in my direction.

I shook my head. "It's been a few weeks since I saw you."

"I know. I was in Miami. I took a travel nursing job—a short-term one."

"Really?"

"Yeah, that's what I do when I don't have enough per diem

work around these parts." She swept her long hair up in a ponytail and put a holder around it. "I'm so glad you're here."

"Me too. I can't believe she competes."

"This is her last year."

"I'm just in time."

"You're just in time for a lot of things. I heard you're helping with the party."

I nodded.

"How long are you staying?"

"Until the party, and then I'll be going back to New York."

"The first time I met you, I thought you were familiar, but I couldn't place you." She looked off at the field, stuck her hand in the popcorn, and put a few pieces in her mouth before returning her attention to me. "Casey B."

I cast her a quick, awkward smile. I'd been discovered. I knew it would happen eventually. "Instagram is doing its job."

"I'm not on social media much, but, yeah, I follow you." Lachelle's lips pinched together, and her nose crinkled. It was a mix of admiration and teasing in a closed-mouth smile. "You are like a celebrity."

I released a gentle puff of a laugh. "I'm not."

"Millions of people want to look at you and know what you think and what you're wearing. How is that not famous?"

Sweat caused my sunglasses to slide down my nose. I pushed them up. "I don't feel famous. Not anymore."

Lachelle's mouth fell open. "You've modeled all over the world. It's all so impressive."

"You haven't told anyone in the family, have you?"

"No, but I was going to."

I shook my head. "Don't, please. I like the idea of just being Cousin Casey right now without anyone knowing what I've done or where I've been."

Lachelle looked disappointed. "Our little cousins would look up to you."

My stomach knotted. "Breaking down online, I don't think so."

Lachelle shook her head. "On one out of thousands of videos." She removed her sunglasses and wiped them with the hem of her T-shirt before sliding them back on. "You're still fabulous." Lachelle was big on using descriptors to speak for her.

"That's not how it works. Disgrace is rarely overcome." I hated that what I was saying was true.

She threw up a hand. "Okay. I won't breathe a word, but you should give everyone a chance to be proud of you. I'm going to sit with my brood." Lachelle stood. "I'll talk to you." She walked back up the bleachers.

Shortly after, Nigel joined me on the left. I felt his presence before I looked to see who had slid in next to me.

"She has her camera-camera," Nigel said.

"I told you I'm not just another pretty face."

"I would never think that." He made a serious expression. "The face is beautiful. I think anyone with eyes can see that, but it doesn't take knowing you long to know there are layers." His voice thickened. "Smart ones, deep ones, caring ones, all the necessary ones."

"That's some first-class flattery."

His eyes searched my face. "I see all the layers."

The beating of my heart was loud enough to lower the volume on all the sound in the noisy stands. He saw me. I saw him too. Nigel had a quiet strength and a masculine beauty that rose like the green stems of plants from the dark earth under our feet. It promised something—a depth of character and understanding that naturally emanated from him. He was unpretentious, and I liked that because underneath it all, so was I. He had his own layers.

"Daddy, I want popcorn." Star's voice popped the bubble that had formed around us. She came down around the side of Nigel and pushed her body between us.

"Excuse me," Nigel chastened. He cocked his head toward me. "Hello, Miss Casey."

She raised a hand to her forehead like she would faint from embarrassment. "Excuse me. Hello, Miss Casey."

She was just sweet enough. "Hi, Star." She looked especially adorable today, except for her hair. It was coming undone. "I like your shirt." She thanked me and told me all about where she got it, but the whole time, I was staring at her hair. I couldn't let her go off like that. "Star, one of your braids is coming loose. Can I fix it for you?"

She nodded. "My mommy didn't have time. She was rushing."

I pulled her between my legs and reached into my bag. I didn't have much, just a pick and some conditioner. I undid the rubber bands on the two plaits in the back, added some conditioner and did flat braids to her scalp. When I was done with the back, I did the front, creating a little style by swooping the very front braid horizontally across the width of her head.

Appreciation filled Nigel's eyes. "That looks nice."

I opened the camera on my phone and showed it to Star.

"It's pretty, Miss Casey. Thank you." She wrapped her arms around me and squeezed. To her father, she whined, "Daddy, can I have my popcorn now?"

Nigel threw his hands up. "I have to pay Miss Casey. I don't have any money."

Star giggled. "You do not, Daddy. She's not going to make you give her money."

Nigel looked at me. "Was that free?"

I laughed at his silliness. "Give the girl her walking-around money."

Nigel reached into his pocket for a five-dollar bill and handed it to her. "No candy."

Star took the money and skipped away. She joined a few older kids—her cousins, I assumed, based on the obvious closeness I observed between them. One of them touched her hair, and I saw Star point at me, and the girl looked. It would have been nice to grow up with a bunch of cousins. All I had was Leslie, and we saw each other only a few times a year in the summer. My mother had me working or auditioning nearly every weekend of my life. There was no time for family gatherings, even on holidays.

"I didn't even notice it was bad until you fixed it," Nigel said.

"It wasn't bad, but it could be better," I replied. "I'm all about helping women feel their best." I stood. "I'm going to go take a few pictures of the contestants. Save my seat for me."

"Certainly. I owe you," he replied, and the warmth of his voice brought the bubble back.

I walked down the neatly trimmed path to the area where the seniors were standing, sitting, and/or stretching. Granna noticed me, and she reached for my hand.

"Everyone, I want you to meet my granddaughter." She pulled me into the center of a small group, and they all marveled at me and offered compliments about how beautiful I was, and how I got my height from Granna, and any other compliment they could share. Granna added, "She lives in New York, but she's been visiting me for the past couple months."

They all thought it was nice and said so.

"I know you've had enough photographers taking pictures, but if you don't mind, I'd like to take a few for an album I'm making."

They didn't hesitate to gather together for a group photo. There were ten of them in Granna's huddle, and another twenty in other parts of the waiting area.

I took pictures and made a short video with each of them sharing their reasons why they competed every year, finishing just as the organizer came in and asked them all to get prepared to begin.

When I returned to my seat next to Nigel, I was a bundle of nerves. Granna had been doing this for years. She walked every day, but a race, even a walking one, had me concerned about her overdoing it.

Nigel took my hand and squeezed. "She'll be fine, Casey."

"Am I that obvious?"

"Yes."

"I feel like a worried mother."

A whistle blew, and the walkers lined up at their yellow cones. There were ten of them on each row. The first ten were Granna's group.

Once the race got underway, the first ten walkers took off. When they were about a third of the way around the track, the next ten started, and then the final ten.

The crowd was on its feet the entire time. The Blacks, a good forty of them, were yelling, cheering, stomping, clapping, whistling, and anything else they could do to cheer her on. I was just trying to breathe. I was trying to survive it. But when the last heat came around and Granna was in the lead, I cupped a hand next to my mouth and screamed, "Go Granna!!!"

I was recording, but this was the most difficult video I'd ever made because I wanted to put down the camera and cheer. My heart was in my chest during every lap my grandmother made around that track. In the end, she did thirty-two. She'd won. Recording her victory was almost as sweet as watching it.

Afterward, the local media converged on all the runners. They interviewed them and took pictures while the seniors wiped off sweat and rehydrated. Awards were presented right after the race, and Granna smiled for my camera as I captured the moment the medal was put around her neck.

Granna was still catching her breath and drinking water when I reached her. Once she stopped panting, a medical person checked her vitals. "I don't see anybody taking blood pressure and heart rates at the real Olympics," she said, groaning. "See how they do us?"

I laughed at how feisty she and her teammates were. They did not appreciate anyone inferring that they didn't know their own bodies.

Nigel slipped next to me just as the medical person was finishing up. "Way to go, Ma!" he said, giving Granna a congratulatory high five.

"Granna, we want to take you out to a celebration lunch."

She frowned. "Casey Black, you have known me long enough to know I have a ritual. I eat out with my team after we watch the other folks compete."

Sufficiently chastised, I said, "Yes, ma'am. What's the next event?"

"You are leaving." Granna's lips pinched.

I thought I heard her wrong. "Why?"

"Nigel has something to show you on Pawleys. It's a good day for it."

Granna turned to her teammates and joined their conversation. I had been dismissed.

Nigel planted his hands on his hips and said, "What can I say? She's busy."

Amused, I shook my head. "*Busy* isn't the word for her. What are we doing on Pawleys?"

He raised a finger. "Give me a minute to get Star settled."

Nigel walked away and joined the group of kids who were hanging out eating ice cream and everything else from the concession stand. He pulled a teen girl, someone I recognized as a cousin of mine, to the side. I couldn't remember her name. It was funny. I had very few relatives on my mother's side, and I knew them all. Having a relative I didn't know by name—several of them—was foreign to me and a little cool. I had people. I'd never really had people. I grew up hearing my mother say, *"It's just us. We're all we have."*

"And we're a team," I whispered, repeating my mother's words.

Nigel's voice cut into my thoughts. "All set."

We left downtown and got on US-17. As we crossed over the bridge, Nigel said, "This is where the three rivers come together— Black, Pee Dee, and Waccamaw. It's called Winyah Bay."

I remembered Granna sharing the story about how my great-grandfather stepped in Black River where the rivers came together. As we traveled on the massive concrete bridge, I tried to imagine this area without the modern construction, but I couldn't. The fancy boats around the perimeter didn't help either, but I could still see the water was dark. "Why is the water so dark?"

"The simplest way to explain it is that black water is water that moves slow and picks up decayed leaves and branches that release tannins into the water."

"Interesting."

We drove farther down US-17 to a large, abandoned house. Flanked by massive oak trees with overgrown, mature branches, it was a good distance from the other houses in the area. The beach was about an eighth of a mile from the entrance. Seeing as though everything in this area was a resort of some kind, I was surprised it was like this.

Nigel seemed reflective before he said, "This is the home of former enslaver William Tate. It's in foreclosure right now. I'm thinking about buying it. I have some investors."

I looked at the tabby ruins of the antebellum plantation house.

Shock locked my mouth in a perfect little O before I managed to move my lips again. "For what?"

Nigel pulled his eyes away from the building and looked at me. "I want to turn it into a resort. There are quite a few resorts on this island that were converted from plantations. Some of the land used to belong to Black people. A lot of it was stolen in tax schemes and shady land deals and heirs' property claims. Because of that, a lot of our people won't vacation here. But Pawleys doesn't just belong to white people. The lowcountry—all of it—belongs to us too."

The hot sun sat high, right above us. Even with my sunglasses, the light cut my visibility. I raised my hand over my eyes and looked at the beach. "Will Black people want to come to a resort just because it's yours?"

"I think so. Reclaiming what was lost to us is different from visiting what was stolen." He was quiet for a moment before he continued, "Ma Black wrote a prayer of restoration for Black people. She shared it once in church, and I memorized the words. 'Lord, repair and return to the descendants of enslaved Africans what is theirs. Give Your children what we worked for. Give an inheritance to those in their bloodline—emotionally, physically, financially—all that was stripped away from us through the generations . . . return it. Let what we built come back to us—righteously.'"

The emotion in his voice stirred feelings inside of me. He continued, "Enslaved men and women built this place for Tate. After they built the house and the cabins, they grew the rice that made him very wealthy. He owned over seven hundred people during his lifetime. He liked to buy children. They were cheap, and he could start them young. The mortality rate for children was high on rice plantations. A lot of them died before they reached their eleventh birthday."

A pain radiated from my chest outward to my back. Dead children for financial gain? What kind of people were these enslavers? I'd heard all the arguments—it was a different time, it was the system in place—but the dead bodies of children were dead bodies of children. Who could look on and call them *property* and continue to watch them die because they could buy more? I don't care what the law or the system permitted, these people lacked humanity and needed to be remembered as the monsters they were.

"Are you okay?" Nigel asked, and I met his eyes. "I didn't mean to upset you."

I was scarcely okay, but I swallowed the knot in my throat and said, "I'm fine. I'm glad for the history lesson." I forced a smile, but I didn't feel it. This was not to be smiled about.

Nigel continued, "Tate was overextended before the war. He lost everything when he lost his free labor. A record from the Freedmen's Bureau recorded that the enslaved left this plantation in droves and didn't go back. Anyway, he died a penniless drunkard or something like that."

I sensed contrition in the lift in Nigel's voice. It was for me, certainly not the man who deserved a worse death.

Nigel squatted. He picked up a fist full of the sandy dirt, squeezed it, and then let it slip back through his fingers before he stood. "This land has changed hands sixteen times over the years. No one can keep it or make anything out of it."

I raised my camera again and captured a shot of a black bird on the roof of the worn building. It looked like a vulture, which was appropriate for the rot and decay everywhere.

"My great-great-great-grandparents were owned by Tate. What was stripped away belongs to me. This land owes me an inheritance." He turned and looked at me. "I want what's owed to me."

❧

We were back in the truck. Nigel was quiet, and I respected the solitude he needed. I was also still recovering.

"This is what Granna wanted you to show me."

He nodded.

"Why?"

"I don't know. She just told me to show it to you. I didn't question why." He looked out the window away from me, but then turned back and started the engine. The air in the truck was full of longing. Again, we were quiet until he said, "Let's get lunch."

I nodded.

"The place we're going is not fancy. In fact, it's the opposite." The quality of his voice wasn't as heavy. He was back to himself.

I looked down at my attire. "I'm wearing jeans, a Team Black T-shirt, and flip-flops."

"True." He smiled at me, and I blushed like a girl in high school. He turned his attention back to the road. "Anyway, the owner and I went to school together from kindergarten through high school. I never come to Pawleys Island without stopping in his spot."

I grinned. "Sounds like a plan."

"The food is really good."

"You don't have to keep selling me on it. I trust you."

Nigel tightened his hands on the steering wheel. "Okay. You just strike me as someone who's eaten at a lot of fancy restaurants."

"I have, but I'm a New Yorker. I know how to eat street food. There's nothing like a hot dog stand in the city."

"All right. It's settled. Let's go."

Mike's Grill was a small place. It was a rustic hut with a full-service tiki bar. There was outdoor and screened-in patio seating. Crushed oyster shells filled spaces in the parking lot where grass or decorative rocks would be. I thought it was cool. The place was very beachy. It looked like a hard wind could take it down. People were sitting outside soaking in the beauty of the day. And the aroma floating from the kitchen made me want to order everything on the menu without even seeing it. Nigel ordered a beer, and then I told him since they had such a collection of beers to order one for me.

"Let's see if I can meet a beer that I could finally like."

He chose Jamaican Red Stripe. It was a premium item.

"For a premium woman," he said, and we clicked out bottles together.

I tasted it and, surprisingly, I kind of liked it. Well, I didn't dislike it. I told myself that's what it was, but maybe it was the company I liked. Maybe I liked what Nigel liked. He couldn't do any wrong. He literally seemed perfect. I wanted to know more about him.

I had a burning question that came to my mind, so I asked him. "Tell me about your divorce. It was easy for me. I don't have children. What was it like for you?"

"It was rude, but it could have been uglier." He sighed and took another long sip of his beer. "Ava was unreasonable."

"About what?"

"Money." He raised his bottle and took a sip like it didn't bother him anymore. I was glad I hadn't brought up a sore subject.

"Do you get along now?

"Yep. No reason not to. She got everything she wanted, and

I forgave her for being greedy enough to take everything she wanted." He twisted his watch around his wrist. "That and for the most part, Star is here in South Carolina and not in Atlanta. She doesn't belong with her mother. Visits are sufficient, and because Ava gives me that . . . we're cool."

I lifted my bottle again and took another drink. "Any plans to remarry?"

A thoughtful glint entered his eyes. "Definitely. I'd like to find someone special."

I trolled him with a sweeping eye action. "But are you looking?"

Nigel examined me carefully, after which his face got even more serious. "My eyes are open." He said the words slowly, cautiously. I sensed a double meaning, but I didn't have time for a follow-up question. A server interrupted us, requesting Nigel come to the kitchen to see Mike, so he left.

After he was gone, a woman approached the table and asked, "Are you Casey B?"

She hadn't spoken loudly at all, but I looked around at the nearby tables like she'd screamed it. I struggled to reply. I didn't feel like Casey B here.

"You are! Oh em gee. You're so gorgeous."

"Thank you."

"I miss your makeup tips and stuff. Wow! Here at Mike's. So cool."

I tried to give her a genuine smile, but I was hoping this interaction wouldn't last long.

"Can I take a pic with you?"

"I'm kind of trying to be incognito."

"I know, but I've been following you for years."

I could see through the kitchen's pass-through window that Nigel was still with Mike, so I stood and moved into her space enough for us to take a selfie. She raised her phone, and we smiled.

"A pic with Casey B." She stalled. "When are you going to start posting again?"

"Soon. I'm on a little break."

"I'm sorry about your husband. He was such a jerk."

She looked down at the cell phone. I could see she appreciated the memory captured there. "Thanks for the pic." She walked backward into Nigel. She looked up at him and then winked at me. After apologies, she waved and walked away.

"You know her?" Nigel asked.

"Let's just say, she has an appreciation for my sense of style."

He nodded and looked back at her and then back at me. "Okay. Woman stuff."

"How's Mike?"

"He's good. Glad to see me. He'll make his way over to introduce himself when he can. Did you get a chance to look at the menu?"

"I did." I glanced at it again. "I'm trying the gumbo. What else is good?"

He picked up the menu, leaned back in his chair, and pushed his chest out. "You, Casey Black, are about to do some mad overeating."

"Bring it on," I said, drumming my fingertips on the table.

Nigel had not exaggerated. I had gumbo filled with every kind of seafood you could put in the pot. We had fried oysters, gator bites, pit-cooked barbecue, jalapeño corn bread, and left Mike's so stuffed, we laughed about it all the way to the truck.

"We made pigs of ourselves," I said. "We need to go for a walk."

Nigel groaned. "You're right. Let's do that."

He backed out and drove about a mile down the causeway

to a road that gave us beach access. He opened my door, and I stepped out. Nigel tilted his head in the direction of the water. "The sand will give us a good workout."

He grabbed a blanket from his back seat. We traveled almost a half mile down the coast, sat and talked for a while, and walked back. Like I'd been doing all day, I took pictures. Nigel and I took one together, and after I gave him a quick tutorial on my camera, he took a few of me.

We wiped sand off our clothes and rinsed our feet at a hose before getting in his truck.

"You owe me a date to the movies," he said. Nigel must have felt the same way I did—like he wasn't ready for our time together to end. He cleared his throat. "Star is sleeping over. It's a good day for it." His Adam's apple bobbed. He was nervous. "Not that I can't get a babysitter pretty easily for another time."

"I'd love to go to the movies." Those words were comfortable, but what I really wanted was for him to kiss me. I had never wanted a man to kiss me as much, but I couldn't say that.

The muscles in Nigel's face and neck relaxed. He nodded. "There's usually an early show. Let's go."

We ended up going to the theater in Myrtle Beach. It was only fourteen miles north of where we were, and it was showing a movie we both wanted to see. Afterward, we played mini golf until Nigel worked up an appetite again. After we ate, we had ice cream and started toward home, but the sun was so beautiful over Murrells Inlet that we parked and watched it set. Completely drawn to each other, we went for another walk and talked some more about music, movies, books, even politics.

"Do you know what time it is?"

"Almost eleven," he said. "Which means it's either time to go home or time to go dancing."

"You aren't tired of hanging out with me?"

He took a lock of my hair and swept it off my forehead. His eyes were serious, and his voice was husky when he said, "Not in the least."

This magical chemistry reminded me of the early days with Drew. But Nigel had more of a silent, sensual energy, and I wasn't a wide-eyed innocent. This was different.

My chest swelled with anticipation. I hadn't danced in a long time. "Where are we going?"

"Back north."

"You're kidding. There isn't any place in Georgetown?"

"Not anywhere I want to go. Besides, I don't want people in my business." He turned the truck back onto US-17. He drove toward Myrtle Beach but turned off the highway before we got to the city and parked at a small bar.

"Are you sure they're good with flip-flops and sandy jeans?"

"They'll be lucky to have you inside." He opened the door, and within minutes, we walked into the dark club. If it could be called that. It looked smaller inside than it did outside. The DJ was playing Afrobeat music for the ten couples who occupied the dance floor. Most were older than us.

"This place is for the grown-and-sexy crowd."

"I can see that," I replied, looking around. "We should be able to keep up."

We took a table, and a waitress came right away to take our drink orders, which included soda for both of us. Shortly after they arrived, "Love Nwantiti" came through the speakers. Nigel stood and took my hand. "Let's see what you've got."

We moved onto the dance floor. I really liked the song. Nigel had the kind of rhythm to his movements that made me want to flow with him, so I did. It was fun and freeing.

The next song brought the pace down. Nigel took my hands. He placed one on his shoulder and held the other. His free hand went to the small of my back, and he stepped closer, removing most of the space between us.

"Follow my lead?" It was more of a question than a command. I nodded. The club didn't have sufficient air-conditioning, and the movements to the sexy song made it hotter.

The music stopped. Our faces were inches apart. I could smell the sweetness of his soda on his breath and feel the warmth of his breath on my neck.

We stood there staring at each other for a long time, possibly thirty whole seconds. My brain was screaming for him to kiss me. Just as I started to take control of the situation and kiss him first, he said, "Let's finish our drinks."

We sat, drank, and then played pool and darts. It was a whirl-wind of a date. By the time we left, it was 2:00 a.m., and almost three before we made it home.

At the door I said, "I learned about Tate Plantation, I found a beer I like, I will forever visit Mike's Grill when I go to Pawleys Island, and I danced for almost two hours straight, so Mike's food was canceled out."

Nigel took both my hands in his. He stared at me for what felt like a long time. Again, just like at the club. I didn't know about him, but I was forcing myself to show restraint. "Thank you for a good time."

Our eyes held each other. I saw want fill his. "You're welcome."

I knew he would kiss me before he did, because I'd wanted it so badly for hours, maybe weeks. He had to know it. He had to hear my heart beating. Nigel cradled my face between his palms. His warm breath teased my mouth before he pressed his lips to mine.

I leaned into him, inhaling the faint fragrance of his body wash that had been awakened by the heat of the perspiration on his skin. I raised a palm to his chest, felt the solid mass against my fingers. There was no resistance between us, only the melting of our lips and tongues together in a dance that went on and on until we needed to catch our breath.

There was no doubt I'd wanted this . . . needed it. And it was worth the wait, worth the risk, worth remembering. Having only been kissed by three men in my life, I was practically a kiss virgin. I'd been a quick study under Drew, but Nigel's kiss was deeper, more searching and probing. Everything I'd been fighting awakened from deep inside me, including a healthy dose of fear.

When we finally pulled away from each other, I asked, "What are we doing?"

"I don't know what you're doing, but I just did something that was inevitable," he replied. "I've been moving toward this moment since the first time I saw you in Ma Black's house." He swept the back of his hand across my cheek and chin. I thought he was going to kiss me again, but he only looked at my lips and smiled. "I'll see you tomorrow."

"It is tomorrow."

He walked out the door and across the grass, looking back when he reached his own door, where he hesitated before waving. My whole body warmed but then froze when I saw the figure in the door next to him. A woman. She stepped out onto the porch.

"What are you doing here?" Nigel asked.

"Where's Star?" she yelled.

I heard Nigel's exaggerated groan. "She's with her cousins."

"Why, so you can . . ." I didn't hear anymore. She followed Nigel into the house. She was asking for Star. She had to be his ex. Just like that, the magic spell was broken.

28

I COULDN'T SLEEP. I WAS IN MY FEELINGS. I WAS EXHAUSTED, but also way too nosy to rest with Ava next door. I kept walking by the window and peeking out, hoping to see something. Wanting to know what kind of hold this woman had on him. I know what he told me yesterday, but I wasn't walking into this situation by faith without using my sight. I had learned a Scripture well enough to make it work for me. Granna would be proud.

While I was struggling, Nigel's only problem with sleep seemed to be that his ex-wife wanted to talk. He was laid out in his favorite lounge chair with a South Carolina State blanket over his chest and a Clemson Tigers hat over his face. I didn't need to hold a glass to the door or window to hear Ava. The houses were close enough that with the temper her voice carried, I could make out some of what she was saying: Ava had come to surprise Star. She didn't bite, so why didn't he come inside? She wanted to know what he was doing coming out of his tenant's house so late, and finally, she missed him and wanted him to come back to Atlanta.

Nigel's low, no-doubt confident responses were not discernable. His annoyance for the intrusion was. I did hear his final words for the night, and they were, "Ava, are you going to get in that bed and go to sleep or am I?" She stormed into the Airstream, slamming the door behind her, and that was the end of their discussion. I finally went to bed.

The sound of gravel crackling under a set of tires woke me. I peeked at the clock on my nightstand. It was noon. I flew out of bed and rushed to the window. Nigel's truck traveled up the driveway and a little red sedan driven by Ava followed. Star was in Ava's back seat. Nigel exited the truck with bags of takeout and went into the Airstream, followed by a dawdling Ava and Star.

I'd never seen a picture of Ava. I observed her now through the small slit in the blind that was available to me without widening it and getting caught stalking them.

As most women were, Ava was petite compared to me. Probably five foot four, thin, but curvy in all the right places. She had honey-colored skin and full, glossy lips, and a long high-quality weave hung down her back, hitting just above a very voluptuous behind. Butt job? Probably. A good one? Definitely. God did not give out butts that perfect. Her face. Gorgeous. Now I knew for certain why Star was such a pretty girl. Her mother was lovely.

Nigel hadn't mentioned the fact that she was so stunningly beautiful. I guess there was really no opportunity for him to do that. Learning she was an actress was a clue, as most actors were good-looking people. And I can't say I would have much cared before last night—before he kissed me, leaving me with sweet dreams about what could be between us. But now that she was here, I couldn't help feeling like I wasn't the only pretty girl in his world anymore.

She and Nigel had made a handsome couple. Like, for *real* real, the very picture of enviable love.

Kind of like Drew and I had. That's what everyone said. But we turned out to be beautiful on the outside but broken on the inside. Why didn't those two beautiful people go the distance? Why couldn't Drew and I? Was it a lack of love or a lack of commitment? People who'd been married for a long time swore above all else it was a commitment to the marriage. They had an unwillingness to ever get a divorce, but where did that never-say-die kind of steadfastness come from? It had to be rooted in both people. Commitment doesn't work without a self-sacrificing kind of love. I refused to believe anything different. I'd been committed to my marriage, yet here I was peeking out the window at Nigel and his beauty queen, hoping that kiss I had last night was the first of many because it made me feel desirable again.

After I showered, I went into the kitchen to make coffee. There was a bag on the table with a note in Nigel's familiar handwriting.

I thought you might be hungry when you wake up. We both know you can eat. He'd drawn a smiley face, which made me chuckle. I looked out the window again. All was quiet over there. I put a K-cup in the maker and opened the bag. It was a plate of Hoppin' John rice and chicken.

The audacity of him to buy me food when he was with Ava. I mean I knew they were long divorced, but still, he couldn't have wanted to hear the "who is that for and why you gotta get her food" questions come out of her mouth. She had a big mouth. I'd heard it last night. And I knew she was asking.

I sat down with my coffee and sent him a text: Thank you. This is thoughtful.

Nigel: Thoughtful because I can't stop thinking about you.

This time the smile pressed its way through my lips. My heart fluttered. I knew his ex-wife was next door, but I couldn't stop these feelings if I tried. Another text came in.

Nigel: I just saw you smile . . . in my head. ♥

A heart emoji?

"Okay, Nigel. I see you coming hard."

I giggled and typed out another text but then hesitated, deciding not to send it. He was with his family—or rather, he was with his daughter. He and I could talk later.

I uploaded pictures from our exploits yesterday to Instagram and FaceTimed Leslie. She was sitting in her car, but she wasn't driving. I could see the parking lot behind her.

"Hey, girl," she said. Cheer as bright as the yellow dress she was wearing tickled her greeting.

I observed her face. "Your makeup is gorg. Did you go to church today?"

"I did. I can see you did not. You look like you crawled out of bed a few minutes ago."

"Twenty to be exact."

"What's going on down there on the farm that's got you sleeping this late?"

I took another sip of my coffee before answering. "I'll get to that, but first off, Granna won the grand prize yesterday."

Leslie squealed and clapped. "Your grandmother is a century-old baddie."

"I know. I was so happy for her."

"You said it's her last time competing?"

"Yep. She went out like a boss."

"Did you all celebrate?"

"No. She had her own victory party situation with her team. I didn't have a place at the table. But"—I raised an index finger—"I did do something interesting yesterday."

Leslie pursed her lips before asking, "Did Nigel just get out of your bed?"

"Oooh, Leslie, now you know he did not."

"I can't think of anything more interesting."

"Then that means you need more church."

Leslie clucked her teeth. "I know. That was not the work of the Lord."

I waved a hand to shush her. "Anyway, I did spend the day with him. It was like a marathon fifteen-hour date."

"Stop!" Leslie exclaimed.

I filled her in on the details, including the kiss that I could still feel on my lips.

"Wow!" Her mouth hung open long after the word came out, then she repeated it. "Wow, girl."

"I know."

"Is that how they're doing it down there, because if they are, move over and make room in that house for me."

"I don't know if it's southern. I doubt it. I think it's just"—I let my affection for him settle in my chest—"him."

Leslie's head bobbed like it was on a spiral wire. "Him is very likeable, honey."

My heart melted just thinking about him. "So likeable."

"That's great."

I struggled to keep doubt out. "I don't know. I don't live here, Leslie. I mean if we get something started, how's that going to work?"

"It's going to work how you work it. Take one day at a time and see how you feel about the man. Kiss him again. Twice." She laughed.

"I know how I feel about the man, and that's what's got me feeling confused."

"Confused is normal when you like someone."

"I've been out of this game for over seven years, and even before Drew, I wasn't really dating."

"Yeah, and because it sucks so much, I want to encourage you that if you got lucky enough to meet a man without having to sign up for ten woefully raggedy dating apps and swipe left and right for two years on narcissistic, undatable idiots, then you should thank God and try very hard to see if you can make it work."

I sighed. "I'm not ready for a relationship. I shouldn't be, right? Two months ago, I was renewing my vows. Am I moving too fast?"

"Only you know if you're ready to move on. Don't let fear or somebody else's idea about how long it takes to recover from a divorce get in the way of your happiness. You've always deserved to be happy, Casey."

"I know. I do. I just need to make some decisions about Casey B first," I said, switching gears. "I went over the contract for the documentary. I have some creative control. She can't just run over me and tell the story the way she wants to."

"Of course she can't. Your mother negotiated that deal."

"That she did." I thought about my mother's savvy. One thing she was always going to do was make sure contract terms were in my favor. "I have an idea for it."

"What is it?"

"It has to do with my experience here. I need to fully flesh it out in my head first."

"Okay, but you do know you're leaving me hanging." Leslie rolled her eyes. "I have to go. I'm headed to a baby shower."

I dropped my chin on my fist. "I miss you. Have fun!"

"I miss you, too, but it sounds like you are having more fun than me. You have your hands and eyes full with the plants and the man." She cackled.

I laughed and stuck my tongue out. "Bye, Leslie."

"See. It's that tongue. You need to keep it in your mouth."

The screen went blank, and I fell against the chair. I did miss Leslie, but I didn't miss New York. I didn't miss feeling rushed all the time, or the traffic, or the crowded spaces everywhere, or the smell of the city in places—the steam from manholes filled the air with a moldy smell and the doorways of empty buildings were rank from urine. I didn't miss looking for parking or even that five-second worry that entered my mind every time I handed over my keys for valet parking. Would my car come back in one piece?

There were great things about the city—food, shopping, shows, the diversity, and energy, but I never felt like it was where I wanted to live for the rest of my life. I was born there. I worked there. I lived a life with a husband there, but traveling to locations that were less densely populated made me long for elbow room and more nature. I had plenty of it here. Thinking about nature made me think about my plants. I sent a text to Swella:

Hey, you. How are you? How are my plant babies?

Swella: I'm good. The plants are great. I'll send you a picture when I water them again.

Swella: I miss you. 😞 😔

I put my phone down. My food had gotten cold. As I waited for it to warm in the microwave, I peeked out the window. Nigel was outside. My heart thumped like a lovesick teenager. This reaction was too much.

He was leaning under the hood of his truck. I craned my neck to see if the red car Ava had been driving was there. It wasn't, so I opened the door and walked out.

Nigel's smile was wider than the expanse of land behind him. He wiped his hands on a rag and walked to me.

"You are so considerate."

He crossed his arms. "Like I said, you're on my mind."

"Where's your houseguest?"

"They messed up her order, so she went back to get them straight." He pitched his eyebrows. "Real straight, I'm sure."

I put a hand on my hip and shifted my weight from one foot to the other. "She's beautiful."

"I guess I've gotten lucky again because I'm looking at a beautiful woman right now."

I smiled and twisted my lips shyly. "What's wrong with the truck?"

"Nothing. I check my fluids on Saturdays. I was busy yesterday, so it didn't get done."

I smiled again. "You were really busy."

He dropped his arms and stuck his hands in his pockets. "I had an amazing time with you, Casey. I . . ."

He was interrupted by an approaching car. I turned. Ava was back.

Star popped out of the car and ran toward me. "Miss Casey." She wrapped her arms around my hips.

"Hey, Little Star." I squatted to her level.

"Did you see Ma Black's trophy?" she asked.

"I did, and I'm going to see it again today."

"Did you take a picture?"

"You know I take a picture of everything."

The feeling that Ava was approaching was stronger than the light grind of rocks under her shoes.

I stood.

"Baby, take this in for Mommy," Ava said, and Star took her bag and went to the Airstream.

"Change your mind about switching it out?" Nigel asked.

"I did. I figured I can always eat some of your food since you ordered what I like." She moved her eyes from Nigel's to mine. "You must be the tenant."

Nigel released a little sound, a mix between a grunt and chuckle before saying, "Ava, this is Casey, and Casey, this is Star's mother . . . obviously, Ava."

"'Obviously'? Has someone talked about me?" Ava asked, extending her hand for a shake, which I cooperated in. "You're Ma Black's long-lost granddaughter."

I nodded.

"That is so beautiful. There's been so much tragedy for her. I know she's thrilled to have you here . . . from New York, right?"

"Yes. And meeting her has been amazing for me as well."

"I know it has to be." Her fake smile dropped when she looked back at Nigel. "You done with the truck? I was going to set your little table."

"You and Star go ahead. This is your time."

Ava visibly fought hiding her disappointment, but it flickered in her eyes. "Fine." She turned toward the Airstream and then did a half turn toward me. "Did you enjoy your food?"

I hiked a thumb over my shoulder. "It's waiting for me, but I always like the food from there."

"I'm sure Nigel knows what you like." She cut her eyes at him. "Anyway, it was nice meeting you."

"Likewise," I said.

Ava looked down at my feet and let her eyes rise to my face before turning and taking steps to the trailer. I'd been thoroughly inspected.

Once the door snapped closed, Nigel said, "She's leaving tomorrow night."

Ava leaving had a nice ring to it, especially since Nigel and I had finally moved an inch over the friendship line to more, but Star needed to see her mother. "I hate that you're all crowded in there. Maybe you should tell her she can stay in the empty bedroom in the house. It's one night. I don't mind."

"Ava's mother lives twelve miles down the road. She caught me off guard this morning, but she will be sleeping under her parents' roof tonight."

"She wants to be with Star."

"That's debatable." He groaned. "I shouldn't have said that. I don't want to pull you into our drama. Twelve miles is nothing. She can take Star with her to her parents'. She's choosing to inconvenience me. That's the story of us."

"She's inconveniencing you because she wants you to come back to Atlanta. I heard her say it."

He inhaled deeply and then exhaled slight frustration. "That's never going to happen. Our marriage was over before we ended it."

I looked at the Airstream. "I'm going to go in. I don't want her thinking anything about us."

"Too late for that. And Ava's had like five boyfriends in the last three years. We're grown single people. I don't care what she thinks."

"Nigel, simple in life is easier. We'll talk when she's gone. Thanks again for the food. That was mad sweet."

"Like you." His eyes smiled. "I'll see you at work tomorrow."

I turned and went back into the house. It felt good to be around him. So very good.

~

I didn't go to the farm. I spent the day doing research on Black southern family documentaries. I even went to the public library. I needed to talk to Brooke tomorrow, and I wanted to have my selling points together.

Granna had her book club meeting. Even though she'd insisted I come over for dinner, I decided to let her have her time with her friends. Plus, I was in a funky mood. Ava's car was at Nigel's for most of the day. Now he was home, and it hadn't moved.

"Jealousy is an ugly thing," I whispered to myself.

I spent time scrolling through social media looking at all the pictures Swella posted of me. She'd started with my first diaper print ad and worked through everything I had up until my final photo shoot. I'd shared many of those over the years. The followers I had left were loving them.

My stomach was going to eat my back if I didn't feed it. I popped out of bed and went into the kitchen. I'd frozen several containers of food from the many times Aunt Thea had given me too much. Just as I was about to put a container in the microwave, I heard a knock at the door. It was almost nine, so it was dark.

"Hey," I greeted Nigel. I could see Ava's car over his shoulder.

He stepped in. "I missed you at work today." He pushed the door closed.

"I had some nonfarming work to do."

Nigel hiked an eyebrow. "Okay." He seemed to want to say something but felt uncomfortable.

"What's up?" I asked.

"Ava is drunk. Really drunk."

"She drinks?"

"When she's sad about her work, and from the looks of it, her career is in trouble. She's sleeping it off."

"Where's Star?"

"With my parents. She has school tomorrow."

I put the container in the microwave and turned it on. "Sit down. You want something to eat? I have some food."

He sat. "I'm good. I had something. What are you doing tonight?"

"Nothing, really. Reading. Streaming a movie. Trying to get up the nerve to talk to a colleague."

"The nerve?"

"I have to make a pitch tomorrow."

"You're impressive. You'll be great." He smiled. "Would you like some viewing company?"

I pointed toward the backyard. "Is she going to be okay over there?"

"I'm not a babysitter. Ava is grown in Atlanta. She's grown here. I did, however, take her keys, so she won't be driving."

"Good."

Nigel and I got set up in the living room with a movie, but we talked more than we watched. He left to get ready for bed. I watched him bring his blanket and pillow out to the lounge chair. No way was he sleeping outside. I crossed the yard.

"Come stay in the house," I insisted.

"I don't want to get in your space."

"I don't need an entire house, Nigel. Come on."

I could hear the shower running in the extra bath as I washed my dishes and the bowl from the popcorn we'd shared. I took a shower and changed into my pajama shorts and tee. Nigel's side of the house was dark and quiet. He'd already gone to bed. I went to my room and read for a while. I couldn't focus with him down the hall. I tried to watch a little more TV, but that wasn't what I wanted. If Nigel was close, I wanted to be near him, so I padded my way down the hall.

Nigel hadn't closed the bedroom door. The slits through the blinds provided enough light from the moon for me to make out his silhouette on the bed. He rolled over, and I stepped back, forcing a creak to rise from the wood floor.

"Come in. I'm awake." Seconds later, light from a lamp cast a warm glow in the room.

"I didn't mean to . . ."

Nigel pushed himself up on the bed. He was sleeping in men's pajama pants with no shirt. "What did you need?"

I couldn't stop the smile that threatened to break through.

He was sitting there half-naked, looking like a literal African god of some kind, and he was asking me what I needed? I needed to be held and loved. I needed to know I wasn't alone in how I was feeling about him. I needed a lot of things.

But instead of saying all that, I replied, "I couldn't sleep. I was checking to see if you were asleep."

He stood, reached for a T-shirt, and pulled it over his head. He dropped back on the bed. "Come, sit with me."

I hesitated at first, but then walked around to the other side of the bed. I put my phone on the nightstand. Nigel got in, crossed his legs at the ankles and locked his hands behind his head. "We could watch more TV. Listen to music. Read together."

"You could tell me a ghost story," I said, sitting. "Like the one about the Gray Man on Pawleys Island or maybe a Gullah story."

"Ah, the spiritualism in the low. Who told *una* about how we stay down here?"

He sounded like Uncle Roger using Gullah language.

"Actually, I spent the day looking for documentaries about history in the lowcountry."

He quirked an eyebrow. "Did you find something interesting?"

"A few, and they mentioned some of that stuff."

Nigel propped himself up on pillows and reached for my hand. He cocked his head. "Come closer."

I bit my lip and swung my legs over on the bed and inched back against the headboard with him.

"You don't need to hear a ghost story right before bed."

"I'm not easily spooked," I said, poking him in the chest.

"Yeah, well, I am." He chuckled and took my hand in his. "I don't want to think about the Gray Man. I grew up with the stories my entire life about the ghost who wandered Pawleys looking for his lost love."

"And people have seen him," I teased.

"They say so. I don't want to."

I laughed. "Do you think they're true?"

"Why not? Between the war and slavery, there probably should be ghosts. The land keeps no secrets."

"I've never heard of most of the stuff I've learned."

"I grew up here and didn't learn our history until I went to college."

I settled back into his arms more. Remembering he told me he and Ava were high school sweethearts, I said, "You two were together a long time."

He nodded. "Yeah, we were, but the marriage only lasted four years. She was in California for half of that."

I didn't know what to say. I didn't want to say "that's too bad" because this conversation with him, his warmth next to me, the date we'd had on Saturday, made me happy.

"You asked me about my divorce the other day, and I talked about Ava's shortcomings. I'll be honest and share mine." He swept a hand across my temple, moving a curl back before kissing me on the side of my head. Then he continued, "During the marriage, I could have believed in her more. I could have supported her career, but I didn't." He paused. "I couldn't wrap my head around the whole acting thing. It wasn't something we ever talked about and"—he paused briefly—"it's not like she had acting talent."

I couldn't hold back a chuckle. "None?"

Smiling, he shook his head. "Ava has other gifts. Acting isn't one of them."

I grinned, keeping another laugh inside. "It's hard to believe in something when you don't see the potential in it."

Nigel sighed agreement. "Once we moved to Atlanta, the reality TV bug bit her. Untalented people make it big all the time, but that's luck. I didn't think luck was going to happen for her," Nigel said. "So that's my failure."

"It doesn't sound like a failure to me," I said, thinking about the differences between Drew and me. "A marriage rarely works when people want different things."

"Maybe not, but you compromise in relationships, right?" His eyes said he really wanted to hear a yes from me.

I gave him what he wanted. "Of course, but my ex might accuse me of the same thing."

"Not believing in him?"

"Not seeing that I needed to compromise. I was a workaholic. I could have done better."

We were silent for a minute, and then Nigel spoke again. "So we've had the ex talk. Now that that's out of the way, we can go deeper on getting to know each other."

I hadn't even realized we were having "the ex talk." I didn't know there was a such a thing, but it was a good idea. No surprises.

"I want to know more about you, Casey. You've been giving me half answers to questions. I need whole ones at this point because . . . I'm into you, so before this thing gets deeper . . ." He stopped speaking, but his eyes finished his sentence.

This *thing* he was talking about had escalated—fast. He was into me, and I was into him.

He raised a hand and traced the outline of my chin. "Tell me something I don't know about you. Something important."

I hesitated again. One of the biggest parts of who I'd been was easy to share. "I used to be a fashion model." I released the words fast. I needed to get them out fast before I wouldn't say them at all.

He sat up straight. "Really?"

"I started doing commercials right before I turned two, and I stopped modeling when I turned twenty-eight. There was a lot of work in those twenty-six years." I reached for my phone and went to the Instagram page. I swiped down so he didn't see the number of followers I had. I showed him the collection of pictures I'd looked at earlier.

His brows were locked together as he scrolled through each one. Every once in a while, he let out the word "wow" as he continued. He smiled appreciatively when he came to a bikini pic. "This is incredible." There was no mistaking, he was impressed. "I'm shooketh."

I laughed. "People are always shook."

"Why'd you stop?"

"Models age out young. Not everyone, but most. My business manager, otherwise known as my mother, didn't want me to go from high fashion to catalog work, so I retired."

Nigel handed me my phone.

"Why aren't you on any social media?" I asked.

"I don't have a use for it."

"It could help with your consulting business."

He raised a finger and stroked my cheek. He followed that by moving his finger to my throat and collarbone. "I have more business than I can manage." His voice was low, husky, sexy.

Heat flooded my body. I had zero business in bed with this man. I pulled away from him. Although it was only a queen-sized bed, I put some space between us. "You'll have to be on socials for your resort."

Nigel smiled knowingly about why I moved away from him. He cleared his throat. "I'll pay a teenager."

I wagged a finger at him. "You never pay someone to do something for you until you at least know a little about what you're paying them to do."

"Is that like using a hoe before a tiller?"

"Exactly," I said, laughing. "Let me have your phone."

He groaned, opened it, and handed it to me. I downloaded the Instagram app.

"I am not going to use that."

"You can follow my new page. It's all about my experience here in Georgetown."

It took minutes for me to set up his page. I took one of the pictures of the two of us and put it on his page.

"Your page is private. No one can see it but you and me." I had him follow @IAmBlackMixedWithBlack.

"I wouldn't mind following the page with your bikini photos."

"This is more of who I am right now than all those pics of me modeling. Besides, the real me gets in your hot tub a few times a week."

"Aren't I lucky?"

I scrolled through a few hashtags for farmers and showed him their pages. "See? This is how you use Instagram to market a farm."

Nigel squinted. I could tell he was out of his depth. He put the phone on the nightstand. "Enough of that. I've been wanting this since I walked in the house." He raised a hand to my cheek again, stroked it for a few seconds before touching my bottom lip with a finger. He leaned forward and kissed me. I didn't pull back. We explored each other's mouths until my heart burst wide open.

"I'm glad I told you about the modeling."

He nodded. "Me too."

I threw my legs back over the side of the bed and pushed myself up. "I should go."

Nigel extended a hand to me, and I took it. Wordlessly, I asked him what he wanted. He tugged once, and I was leaning over him. He put his free hand behind my head and pulled me down for another kiss. I climbed over him and back into the bed.

I hadn't felt this good in a long time. Nigel held me until either he or I fell asleep. I wasn't sure who was first. He exited the bed without making a sound. I woke up late and was pleased to find a note on the pillow he'd vacated.

That was the best platonic sleepover I've had since elementary school.

Nigel

I laughed and got ready for the day. Granna would be wondering where I was . . . or not. She seemed not to worry about anything in life. Just as I was about to step out the door, I saw Ava's face in the window. She startled me. I opened it.

"Good morning." She raised a mug. "Can I bother you for a cup of coffee? All Nigel has over there is instant coffee, and I cannot."

I stepped back. "Help yourself."

I went to the bedroom and busied myself with nothing for a few minutes before I came back into the kitchen. Ava was standing there taking a sip from her mug. She had no intention of leaving without talking to me.

"You're Casey B. I recognized you yesterday." She grimaced and put her mug down. "Recovering from shame in the lowcountry."

"Ava, if there's something you want to say, say it."

"Other than my ex-husband hates social media?" She folded her arms over her chest.

"Nigel and I are just friends."

Ava snatched her head back and dropped her arms. "Girl, please." She picked up her mug, walked to the sink, and poured out the coffee. "I put too much water in that." I sensed it was more like she wasn't here for coffee by the way she was looking me up and down. "I'll get right to it. I know you had a rough breakup this year. So woman to woman . . ." She paused. "I need to tell you that Nigel is not a good fit for you. I'm not saying this because I want him back." She paused again. "He has no interest in me. My only motivation is that I care about him."

I shifted my weight from left to right and then pulled out a chair. "Sit down."

Ava did. "My career was a problem in our marriage. Not the success or failure of it but the public aspect. I had a few reality TV jobs. Nigel hated it. He hated that I had to be on social media and sharing my life with people. He's intensely private."

"I gather the private part."

"Your worlds won't fit. He wants a simple country girl. You are not that. You'd stand out like a sore thumb around here even in overalls. Nigel hates social media. He thinks it's destroying our society."

I chuckled. "He does not talk like that."

"Not yet." She smiled tightly. "Anyway, I know he couldn't possibly know, so you need to tell him what you do and let him choose before he gets more than his nether parts invested in you."

"Wow. Did you just say 'nether parts'?"

She cocked her head. "I'm trying to be southern-lady about it."

"You're trying to make sure I'm not interested."

"Not really. This isn't a catfight. It would be if I thought I had a chance to get him out of here, but he's more loyal to the Georgetown dirt than anything or anyone else, and I can't stay here." She stood, and I stood with her. "I went to LA to try to find some work during pilot season. I was there for a few months. I kept waiting for him to join me or come drag me home, but he never did. After all the years we'd invested, he just let it all fall apart. Kind of like your husband did when he didn't remarry you. I don't know your story—"

I interrupted. "That's for certain."

"But I know what it's like when someone gives up on you—the one person who you thought would at least try." Her eyes clouded over with tears, and she reached up and dabbed at the corners. Nigel was right. This was some terrible acting.

She locked her fingers together at her waist and continued. "He's not leaving the lowcountry and the Casey B I've followed is not coming here. Don't break his heart. He doesn't deserve it."

She'd gone a bit far with this last warning, but I wasn't going to get into any more of a discussion about Nigel with his ex-wife.

Ava took a deep breath and pushed back her shoulders. "Thanks for the coffee. Tell Ma Black I said hello." She opened the door, stepped out, and went to the Airstream.

"I'm not letting you get in my head, Ava," I whispered, but she already had.

I gathered my things and got in my car. My stomach churned, and I fought to keep from rolling my eyes at the trailer. She was probably watching me through the blinds the same way I'd been watching her.

I refused to think about her on the drive to the farm. Just as I was about to get out, my phone rang with a FaceTime request. It was Leslie.

"I was scrolling through your new page. These pictures of you are getting more and more righteous. What are you going to do with all this content?"

"It's for me. I want to be able to look back and see the revolution that was my life."

"You have found your joy, and you look happy with Nigel."

I swiped through a few of the pictures she was talking about. "Yeah, but my home is in New York."

"Your home has been in New York. That doesn't mean you have to stay here. The thing about home is, it's not a place. It's a feeling. What I'm seeing is that feeling has found you right where you are."

"Are you seriously trying to talk me into not coming back? Won't you miss me?"

"Of course, and I'm not saying don't come back, but I am saying that season your grandmother asked for seemed like the balm you needed, but it could also be the change you need."

"What would I do down here?"

"Accept the challenge of figuring it out."

"Starting over is hard."

"Is ease a requirement?"

I didn't respond. Maybe it was and I was ashamed of that.

"You're a photographer. A good one. And I don't know what you're supposed to do next, but I will tell you this, the only thing keeping you from the life you want is *you*. Do you understand what that is? It's a privilege. Don't squander it. Too many women wish they had some." Leslie smiled at me. There was love and empathy in it. She really understood me like no one else, and she didn't judge me—ever. "My new client has called twice. I need to go."

Her words settled in my heart. I was a photographer. I'd been thinking about it more lately. Thinking about how to use that to solve the problem with the documentary.

I sent Brooke a text.

My phone rang, and it was her.

"You are psychic. I was just about to call you," she said.

"Good. We're in sync. I have an idea. I want to meet about it."

"The only thing I want to meet with you about is the end of this production."

"I know, but hear me out, okay? Let's get on FaceTime."

We ended the call and got on a video chat. I was more convincing on video. I filled her in on the idea I had for the end of the project. When she heard the words *hundred-year-old grandmother, three-hundred-acre farm, lowcountry, Gullah, journals that went back to Emancipation*, all starting me getting my groove back after disaster, she was practically salivating.

"Are you serious? Can you get everyone on board with this?"

"I'm pretty sure I can. My family doesn't want our stories to die."

Brooke squealed. "When will you know for sure?"

"Give me a week. I need to talk to a few people and—"

"Casey, if you can pull off this part of your story, I will, like, kiss you."

"I think I can do it. I'll be in touch."

We ended the call, and I went inside to talk to Granna about my idea.

29

Odessa Black

GEORGETOWN AND CHARLESTON,
SOUTH CAROLINA, 1899

"I WANT YOU TO STOP TRAVELING."

"What you mean?"

"Times are different. You need to be home where it's safer. The children are getting older."

"How you expect me to earn a living?"

"Working in Georgetown."

"That ain't enough to be steady, and the pay not as high."

Elijah and Odessa had had this talk before, but this time, she was not letting him win. "It's dangerous, and you know it. How do you think I'd live without you? We have all these children and one on the way." At forty-nine years old, Odessa was pregnant again with their eighth.

"You are letting fear rule you."

"Yes, I am, sir. Fear that my husband will not come back home."

"I'm surprised you not saying we should go north."

She resented him for that. It was almost like he was teasing her about it. That had been her dream since she was a teenager, and she'd sacrificed it for him—for love. Many Negroes were moving north now. They were going to Ohio and Chicago, but Odessa hadn't thought about it in years. "Papa is too old and alone for that."

"Your daddy might be marrying again."

"Really?"

Elijah nodded. "Don't say nothing or he'll never trust me again. Took thirty years to gain what I have."

"I'm not thinking about the North anymore. We're settled, but I do think we need a change."

He looked at her with intense interest. "To what?"

"The farm. It's time to buy more land."

"We got twenty acres."

"You said you wanted each of our children to have five acres. We need to buy more before the laws make it harder."

Now she really had his attention. Elijah was wise to what was happening politically and economically. There were some places where Negroes couldn't own land. They were being burned out, robbed, and even hanged just because they had the money to better themselves.

"Sir Wright is the only farmer with vegetables for the market, and he's old. With no children, that farm will end. We can build our business."

Elijah was all thought on this. Odessa saw his mind turning over her words.

"There's one hundred acres for sale on the river."

"A hundred." Elijah laughed like she'd said something funny. "We don't need that much."

"He won't split it."

"'He' who?"

"Mr. Sanford. He is offering the land to people who are close. The Mitchells are thinking about it, so we need to decide."

Elijah walked to the back door and looked out at the yard. Their garden didn't take half an acre, and they paid someone to help with it because Elijah was gone so much. The thought of a hundred more was overwhelming, but God was finished with the earth. He wasn't making no more land. They needed to get their share of it. Their children deserved an inheritance that would last.

"I'm three years away from that plan."

"The land is available today." Odessa paused. "Tomorrow is a hope, not a promise. I want you home."

~

Buying that much land wasn't going to be an easy thing to do. Georgetown had changed politically, and the land white people abandoned after the war, they wanted back, even though many had been gone for over thirty years, hadn't paid taxes or maintained it, and even if it had *never* been their family land. The law was working for them.

For that reason, they had to be smart about the purchase, and because they were smart, Odessa traveled to Charleston with Papa the next week.

"Elijah in agreement with this plan?" Papa asked.

"Yes, sir."

She was glad the days when Papa disliked her husband were behind them. But now Odessa was at the very end of her patience and tired after thirty years of enduring Elijah's traveling.

Papa stopped the coach in front of Cousin Liz's house and helped Odessa down.

"Tell Liz I had business to rush on to. I'll see her when I come to fetch you." Papa hugged her and said he'd be praying for them to come to an agreement.

Minutes later, Odessa was sitting in the parlor waiting for Cousin Liz to receive her. Her maid served tea and left her alone with her own prayers for success.

Cousin Liz walked in with a flourish and promptly hugged Odessa before sitting. She hadn't seen her for a few years. Her husband had died in the war, and she never remarried. She'd been traveling—Chicago; Boston; Philadelphia; Washington, DC; even England for a while. She taught some, but mostly just got away from the life she lived with the husband she mourned here, but now that she was older, over sixty, she'd come home. There were rumors about her in the family—that she was set on a married man with a sick wife. Odessa didn't care. She wanted her help.

"My dearest cousin Odessa. It's a joy to see you."

They exchanged words about how each of them looked well and how the good Lord had kept them in these perilous times.

Cousin Liz poured herself a cup of tea and sat back. "I've been meaning to get over to Georgetown to visit with you and the children."

"And I had thoughts of bringing them here, but they keep me busy."

"I can only imagine, but we'll talk about them later. Your note was so curious. Please tell me what I can do for you."

Odessa explained their situation. Cousin Liz was political before she left the South. Even with her life up north, Odessa couldn't imagine that Liz hadn't kept up with everything that was happening down here. She knew how Georgetown County had changed.

"We were fortunate for a long time," Odessa said, putting her teacup down. "Reconstruction ended in 1877, but in Georgetown, it seems like it's lasted more like twenty years."

"What the people of color did politically was marveled at all over the North. Twelve Negroes in the South Carolina House, near the same port where so many of the race entered on ships. Simply amazing." She sipped her tea.

Odessa bristled a little. She'd supported none of the efforts here, certainly not while traveling all these years.

"That's over now. With the 1895 elections, there are only two Negroes in the entire state. Some days it feels like we've been set back thirty years."

"It's challenging for sure, but I believe things will turn again. They always do." Cousin Liz reflected for a long minute, and Odessa wondered what she was thinking about. "What can I do to help with this land purchase?"

"Your father's name still matters here. Your name," she added, knowing they shared the same maiden name, but Liz's *Conway* was different than Odessa's. Odessa's grandfather was Hugh Conway's property, not his blood. "I was hoping you could deed the land with us and then transfer it over."

She nodded. "Do you have the money?"

She couldn't possibly think Odessa was asking her for a loan. "Yes, ma'am. We expect to pay $4.50 to $5.00 an acre."

"My, your Elijah has done well for himself."

Odessa kept her lips parted in the smile Cousin Liz liked. She had no idea. They could buy three times that much land and still have money put away. They had saved every bit of extra that they didn't use to help others with. Elijah always made good money. His work was in demand, and she taught before all the children came. She still tutored a little.

Odessa continued, "We can also take care of all the fees for your lawyer's paperwork. We need the land to be willed to us until we can handle the full transfer of the deed."

"I can do that. I'm sure our attorney knows how to make sure the paperwork is what it needs to be, so it'll never be questioned. Daddy did it quite often for our common Negro family."

Common.

Odessa was certain that it was Cousin Liz who taught her what *common* meant. Of no special distinction or quality. Average. Ordinary. But that's not what Cousin Liz meant. She was talking about class.

If Odessa was really common, it wouldn't bother her so much to hear Cousin Liz say it. But she was a teacher, just like Cousin Liz, and nearly as educated. Heat from her temper boiled just below the surface. Slavery was done over thirty years and mixed-race Negroes like her still thought they were better. But Odessa was here, asking her for her advantage, so what right did she have to be upset that Cousin Liz was acknowledging it?

Cousin Liz stood. "Let's go in for an early lunch. I'm starving, and I want to hear all about your children."

Odessa's stomach had been in knots the entire time she was sitting there. Cousin Liz could have said no, she didn't want the trouble, but she hadn't. Odessa was grateful for the Conway blood that ran through Liz's veins.

Not only was she agreeable, but she was also fast. Three days later, she and her lawyer were in Georgetown purchasing the land, and a week later, Elijah's and Odessa's names were added to the deed and Cousin Liz's will. With their existing land, they owned one hundred and twenty acres on Black River. The water that Elijah had dipped his body in and declared himself baptized as a free man and changed his name to. It was theirs.

Six months later, Cousin Liz transferred the entire deed into their names. On the way out of the county records office,

Odessa's water broke—early, she knew she was early. They made it to a local Negro midwife just in time to deliver their son, Edward Black. The midwife cleaned him up and wrapped him in a blanket.

"Edward is such a grown name. I think we'll call him Eddie until he grows into it." Elijah took the baby from the midwife and placed him in Odessa's arms.

"Now you have three sons, and I'm an old woman. Can I be done?"

Elijah kissed her on the forehead. "You could have been done after Lawrence and Earl, but I'm glad for him."

She was tired of carrying and raising children, but she looked down into the face of her sweet boy. In this complicated and imperfect world, she marveled at how perfect he was.

"He's a gift from God," Odessa whispered.

A gift to her and Elijah, because as sure as her name was Odessa Black, she knew *this* son was the future of their farm.

30

I REACHED FOR THE TOMATO PLANT AND PULLED OFF THE fruit. I had grown this tomato with my own hands. There were peppers. I had grown those too. They were almost ripe; so were the eggplant and the zucchini. I had grown food, and I was proud.

I heard the squeak of a wheelbarrow. I turned to find Nigel a row over. It was good to see him. I didn't see him as much anymore during the day. He spent most of his time in his office. Apparently, managing a farm was a lot of paperwork. After he walked through certain parts of the farm and drove through others, he was a man behind a desk.

Nigel parked the wheelbarrow and said, "Walk with me." I liked when he said that. I always felt like there was a promise of a little adventure.

He took me to the tomato plants. His special ones. He stopped, crouched, and pinched a few weeds off a group of plants before asking, "What's on your mind, Casey?"

I hunched my shoulders. "What makes you think I have something on my mind?" The pitch of my voice was so high that I would have been suspicious of myself.

"You have been hanging around here long enough for me to recognize when something's bothering you. When you're struggling, you wilt like a tomato plant that's had too much sun."

"Is this some kind of farm psychology?"

He stood and placed a hand on his hip. "You haven't answered the question."

"I had a conversation with my mother earlier. She thinks I'm running away from my life down here. She thinks it's time for me to come home."

"Is she right?"

I walked past him and asked about some spots I saw on a leaf. "What is this? Is it healthy?"

"It might be a virus. That's why I've separated it. I'm treating it." He pinched a few leaves off and repeated the question I'd avoided. "Is your mother right?"

"No."

"Good. Don't let her ruin your day."

He was on the move again, and I followed. We went into the back room of the greenhouse. "You have a full-grown plant in here." He pointed.

It was at least six feet tall. I looked and noted the little *BB* marker we'd placed in the pots on the day we planted the seedlings. "Wow, that's big."

"I was going to wait until the fruit were larger to show you, but . . ."

I leaned closer to the plant. "I thought it was a tomato. It looks like an eggplant."

Amused, Nigel smiled. "This is a Black Beauty. It's one of the most delicious tomatoes you'll ever taste."

I stared and then touched the rich blue-black flesh. "I have never seen a black tomato this big before. I've only seen the cherry size."

"It's not even half the size it could get. Beefsteak heirloom varieties can get as large as cantaloupe."

"Really? Why are they called heirlooms?"

"Because they're special. They've been grown by master gardeners for generations without crossbreeding. Ma has been growing this one for fifty years. She guards the seeds. Keeps them under lock and key."

"It's like a tomato . . . heirloom." Gaining understanding, I nodded.

"Exactly, and because this one is special . . ." He paused. "Because it reminded me of you."

"A tomato reminded you of me?"

"Yes. First there's the name, Black Beauty." He stepped closer. "It's exotic and special. People love it for its dark, smooth, shiny skin. You know you have that farm tan on you."

I smacked his arm.

"A little color never looked so good on someone." His voice was husky with emotion. He cupped my chin. "And the taste . . ."

Our lips were inches from each other. "What about the taste?"

"It's unique, strong, and . . ." He paused. "Honestly, I don't think it compares to anything else."

Kissing him was becoming addictive. I melted inside. I actually melted.

He pulled back before I did. Nigel was always the disciplined one. "You can't leave until you eat one."

I removed my phone and took a few pictures. Leaving him was the last thing on my mind.

~ ✧ ~

I had a ton of new pictures to upload to Instagram. After a long soak in the tub, I flopped on the bed and opened my app. I blinked several times. I couldn't believe what I was seeing. Black Mixed with Black was public. I had nearly a quarter million followers. I went to @YourGirlCaseyB and what I expected was there. A post that read, *Follow Me and See What I've Been Doing.*

I went back to the page. I scrolled down and looked at what people had seen, what they were liking. Pictures of my gardening, food and cooking shots, pictures of Granna and Aunt Thea. My trip to Pawleys Island, everything I'd chronicled over the past months was there. The largest number of likes were on my own pictures. Selfies of my makeup-free skin and big, wild, natural hair. They loved those, but undeniably the largest number of likes and comments were on the pictures and the short video Nigel and I took at the beach.

> @IAmBlackMixedWithBlack Who is the bae?
> @IAmBlackMixedWithBlack Casey, you have to share your
>   hair products.
> @IAmBlackMixedWithBlack Is Casey B done?
> @IAmBlackMixedWithBlack You look amazing and so healthy.
> @IAmBlackMixedWithBlack So you were the one cheating
>   'cause this is fast.

I groaned and video called Leslie. "How did my page become public?"

Leslie frowned. The television in the background went mute. "What page?"

"I Am Black Mixed with Black."

"I don't know. Are you sure you didn't publish it?"

"There's a post on Casey B directing people to it."

Leslie winced. She was quiet for a moment and then she gasped, obviously seeing the post. "I'm sorry! I was going to tell you. I was looking at pictures, and your mother saw."

"You let my mother see my page?"

"She only looked for a few seconds. I didn't think it was a big deal. She said something like, 'Oh, she's back to that photography thing.'" She shrugged it off.

I sighed. "She doesn't have access to my password bible. It's in my safe and . . ." I closed my eyes. "Swella." I groaned again. "Let me call her."

"Okay. Call me back. I'm going to look."

I FaceTimed Swella, and she answered right away. The tick at the corner of her mouth gave her away immediately.

"Did you give my mother my password?"

"She said you were ruining the business, and she had to save it. She threatened to fire me."

"You work for me, Swella."

"She threatened me. She said she would get me blackballed. You know how your mother can be."

I grunted. "You could have at least warned me she had it."

"How did she find out about the new page?"

I clicked my Instagram app and started scrolling through the pictures. "She saw it on Leslie's phone."

"Are you starting over?"

I was not starting over, and now I regretted that I didn't make a blog or a secret board on Pinterest or something. "No. It was a personal kind of photo journal."

"The pics are gorgeous."

"Thanks."

"You look happy." She was right, I was happy. "Who's the guy?"

I rolled my neck back. She was prying. "He's the manager for the family farm."

"Is he like a kissing cousin?"

I laughed. "He's not related to me."

"You two look friendly." Swella giggled. Then her face became serious. "Are you coming back?"

"My grandmother's hundredth birthday party is next week. I could come home after that." I said the words. They made sense in theory, but I wasn't sure I wanted to.

"Really? Do you want me to reach out to some of the brands to see if we can generate some work?"

"The people who've canceled me? No. We'll brainstorm what's next."

"Okay." Swella nodded. "Casey, I'm sorry."

"It's okay. I can unpublish it and take down the post."

"You could . . ." Swella hesitated like she wasn't sure if she should say what was on her mind. "But I don't think you should. If you're coming back in a week, leave it. See if the comments generate some conversation we can use when we all meet."

Sometimes Swella surprised me with a good idea. I don't know why. I hired her because I thought she was smart. "I like that."

She smiled like she'd gotten an A-plus on a physics exam.

My next call was to my mother. She rejected my FaceTime and then a few minutes later called on the phone. I could hear traffic in the background, so she was either driving or being driven.

She greeted me with the words, "Well, if it isn't the little photographer."

"Mom, how could you do that?"

"Be glad I did. Because of it, you have an offer from Now Cosmetics. They want to talk to you about a new natural, anti-aging skincare line they're launching. They're looking for a brand ambassador."

I took a deep breath. Now Cosmetics. This was pretty huge. "Really?"

"Really." I could hear the self-satisfied sound in her voice. "Do I have permission to talk to them on your behalf?"

"If they're serious."

"They are serious. And you do realize, they'll need you in the city."

I nodded. "My grandmother's birthday party is in a week. I'll be home shortly after."

"Good. Finally. You haven't gained weight, have you?"

I rolled my eyes. "You looked at my Instagram. Have I?"

"No. You look good. Must be all that fresh air in the fields. By the way, you need a stronger sunblock. You look like someone put you in a toaster oven."

Lord, my mother was too much. "I can hear you driving, so I'll let you go."

"Wear a hat too," she said. The call ended.

I dropped back on the bed. I picked up my phone and googled Now Cosmetics. Although I knew who they were, I went to the About page on the website anyway and read. "Industry leader, authenticity, diversity." They definitely had a diverse line of cosmetics. I went to the home page, and at the top it listed, "Coming Soon . . . New! Natural Anti-Aging Skincare Line."

I put the phone down. Images of myself as the brand ambassador skittered through my mind. This was a big deal. I guessed it was true—all publicity was good publicity—because this . . . after that makeup-smeared video?

Interesting.

I had two minutes of rest before I heard Nigel's truck. He wanted me to stay longer. I knew that's what the conversation about the Black Beauty was about. I was falling for him. Hard. Soon, I wouldn't be able to leave. Maybe it was already too late, and if it was too late, how would Now Cosmetics fit into my world?

31

SIXTY-TWO OF THE NINETY-SEVEN BLACKS LIVED IN SOUTH Carolina. All sixty-two attended the party. Depending on who it was, Granna was an aunt, great-aunt, or great-great-aunt on down, and out of respect, no one missed the matriarch's annual birthday party. Although they were much smaller families, there were Wilsons and Ladsons from Granna's side of the family in attendance too. With spouses, significant others, special friends, employees, and folks from the church, we hosted 235 people.

Large cast-iron pots were set up over coals on cinder blocks for outside cooking. Whole pigs lay across metal grates. A mix of peppers, onions, and other seasonings lined the insides of their bellies like silk fabric in a casket. They'd begun roasting last night. The rest of the menu included steamed clams, oyster perlou, okra and shrimp, shrimp fritters, collards, barbecued chicken, corn bread, ginger beer, and homemade muscadine wine. The wine was Uncle Roger's specialty. Lachelle and I spent the morning making peach and berry cobblers—ten of them. People could eat until they ran out.

One of Aunt Thea's granddaughters was a baker. She brought the five-tier cake from Greenville and had it set up for decorating with lilies and magnolias—Granna's favorite flowers.

Aunt Thea's assertion that "there's a Black for that" was true. I had cousins who had a balloon and flower decorating business in Charleston. They created floral centerpieces set in sweetgrass baskets for the tables, none the same, and made festive balloon arches. Purple, silver, and black jumbo-size balloons with long tassels floated to the top of the tent. Silver and black were the centenarian colors, but purple was Granna's favorite.

The weather cooperated. It was only eighty degrees, and there was a light breeze off the river that carried the heat west. Nothing else could have been done to make it more beautiful. My people were down to earth, but not simple. This was fancy.

Cell phones caught video footage, but I took pictures. I was the Black for that. People were staring at me, but the comfort of my camera blocked my self-consciousness. I could focus on them in a way that made them conscious that they were focusing on me. I took pictures for the first hour or so of the party and then went inside the house to check on Granna because she'd yet to appear.

She was dressed in a silk deep-amethyst caftan with metallic silver and black embroidery across the chest, and braids of silver and black piping down the sides and across the bottom. Lachelle's sister, Michelle, fussed over the placement of an enormous crown on Granna's head. It was woven from sweetgrass and fashioned with shells and pieces of the same kind of glass that was in the bottle trees. She'd also done Granna's makeup.

"Granna, you are gorgeous."

She gave her shoulders one good shimmy and said, "I go all the way sometimes."

I took a few pictures before we went outside for the festivities. Granna took a seat on a throne at the head table. One by one, the heads of the families took a mic and made a speech.

I wanted to take more pictures, but I was instructed to sit with her so I could meet family I hadn't met yet. After speeches and eating and dancing, it was time for the cutting of the cake.

I was back on picture-taking duty. Just as I raised my camera, a hand slipped into the small of my back—a familiar one—and I inhaled a scent I'd grown to love. I craned my neck in Nigel's direction. "Where have you been?"

"Two of the horses went into labor at my father's farm. I had to go help him. I sent you a text."

"Did you?" I asked. I pulled my phone from my pocket. Not only had he sent me a text but he'd also taken a selfie with his dad and mom. "The reception out here is spotty."

"They want to meet you," he said. "My mother said she could tell I was happier. I said it was too early."

I looked into his face, took in every curve and line, his beautiful brown eyes and kissable lips. It was early, but I was happy.

I was happy when I eloped, but I was like a kid defying my parent. It was more of a high than it was pure bliss. But this feeling with Nigel took root in my belly and pushed up to my heart. The emotions were consistent. They never changed except en masse as they grew. I wanted to see him more and more. I wanted to be with him more and more. He made me happy more and more. This had to be what love was. Love was more.

I avoided his question about it being too early with a kiss on his cheek. "I missed you."

He kissed my forehead. "I missed you too."

Lachelle walked up and said, "Congratulations."

Nigel's eyes held an uneasy interest. "What's happening?"

"The Now Cosmetics thing," Lachelle said, hugging me. "It's so cool, and I'm happy for you, but I'm going to miss you too." Lachelle walked away, leaving Nigel and me both confused.

"I don't know what she's talking about." I opened my phone and went to my Casey B page. There was a cross-posted video about the Now Cosmetics line. I don't know why they would do this before we signed a contract, but the woman in the press release basically said I was at the top of their list to be the new face of Now. My mother had gone too far.

Nigel looked over my shoulder.

"You have a lot of followers. What kind of marketing do you do?"

"Can we talk about it later?"

Nigel nodded agreeably, but he knew I'd kept something from him, which made me even angrier with my mother. I took a deep breath and tried not to think about it. This was a big day for Granna. Not only were we at this party, but she and I had agreed to do her interview for the documentary afterward. She said she was only going to get dressed up with makeup once, so this was it.

It was time for Granna's presentation. Her speech was humble and sweet. She thanked us all for making a big fuss over her and thanked God for allowing her to reach a hundred years, and then we toasted with Uncle Roger's muscadine wine and had cake that tasted like a piece of heaven floated down on a cloud and turned into whipped frosting.

Afterward, I took Granna back inside the house. Michelle followed. She needed to touch up Granna's face before leaving.

"The real dancing'll start as soon as the rest of the old folks go home," Granna said. "They gonna go on all night like 'nary one of 'em is saved or sanctified."

I laughed.

"Babies always come in this family in January because them babies get made after they finish grinding up at my party."

Michelle smirked. "She's telling the truth. I have two January babies myself." Michelle pointed the makeup brush at me. "Watch yourself. Nigel Evanston ain't nobody to dance and drink with if you trying to stay unpregnant."

My laughter died, and the ache babies caused pushed into my chest. However, the idea of babies with Nigel was swoonworthy.

Michelle asked, "Are you going back to New York?"

Granna threw up a hand. "Today is my day, and I don't want to hear a word about Casey leaving here." She looked at me. "Let's do this interview."

I reached for the tripod I'd put in the corner of the room earlier and set my camera on it. Granna's soft, sweet-looking, chestnut skin was a friend to the camera. So was the purple and silver. Other royalty couldn't compare.

The documentary about my life had become bigger than me. It was bigger than Casey B, the social media influencer who lost it on camera. Brooke and I turned it into the story of a woman who went on a journey to find herself and in doing so found family, culture, faith, and love for a farm. It was the story of a woman who pivots. Brooke wanted to do a more serious project, and I'd given her one that had the potential to make her career.

I asked Granna questions I knew people would want the answers to. When and where she was born. What her childhood was like, education back then, dating, marriage, her work. I knew they'd want comparisons between then and now. The best moments of her life, and of course questions about her diet. Although I'd already gotten plenty of footage about it, I asked about her commitment to walking. Some things I knew the answers to, but one I didn't was the one I needed her to answer. What was the most painful experience in her life?

"That ain't for the world to know," she replied.

I stood and turned off my equipment.

Granna removed the crown. "It's time for me to tell you about my sons."

Shock pushed adrenaline up from my gut. I hadn't expected this. "Okay" was all I could say. I slid into the chair next to her.

Granna reached into the holder on the table on the other side
of her and pulled out a few facial tissues. She was prepped for
being emotional. "I'm sorry it's taken so long."

"It's fine. I understand."

"Eddie and I had been married for seventeen years before
I got pregnant. Eddie thought he was carrying a curse around.
He buried two young wives and now here I was . . . barren. He
assumed it was him. Something he must have done. He always
felt like he was paying for Earl's disappearance. So when I come
up carryin', he was the happiest man in the world."

"How old was he, Granna?"

"Fifty-eight." She smiled at the memory. "I was forty. One
of my aunts dreamed about fish and woke up to a double-yolk
egg, so she knew somebody was pregnant with two babies. I was
hopin' it was true because we waited so long.

"They were good babies. Good boys all the way through.
You couldn't separate 'em until high school. They got a little
competitive about their grades and sports. Both were smart, but
Mark was lazy. He relied more on his looks than I wished he
would."

She paused for a long moment. "When they finished high
school, Matthew went to Allen University in Columbia. He
graduated, but then he signed up for the army. We thought he'd
come home from college and marry his old girlfriend, but she
married someone else as soon as she found out your father joined
the army."

"Why did he join the army?"

"He said they was gonna pay his loans off. He didn't want
us to have bills. Me and his daddy didn't care nothing about
the bills. The farm was doing good enough. We could afford the
school, especially since Mark didn't go.

"Anyway, Matthew signed for three years. After basic training, he was assigned to Fort Monmouth in New Jersey. He was a communication specialist, and they trained them there."

"That's where he met my mother."

"Yes. Matthew married Victoria without our blessing, which wasn't done in our family, but he brought her down here to meet us."

Granna got quiet. Her eyes had finally gotten wet.

"He applied for Officer Candidate School. He had a degree, and it was more money. Victoria quit her job before coming. There was nothing for her to go back to really, and he couldn't take her to OCS with him, so he had her stay here. I wanted her here. I wanted to get to know her." Granna frowned. "I don't think she really wanted to stay. It was country—much more country than it is now, and you know she was a northern girl. But he was only gonna be gone twelve weeks, so she settled in.

"Mark had been in Chicago for over a year. Nothing he tried to do would work out for him, so he came home. Eddie was afraid for him in Chicago. He thought he'd get himself involved in something bad and end up dead. He was always afraid of one of them disappearing, Casey."

I could only imagine how much Earl's disappearance weighed on my grandfather. That kind of trauma couldn't be healed.

Granna was reflective for a moment and then continued. "Mark did good being home. He was helping with the farm and taking on responsibility he never took on before. He and your mother became friendly. They were both young, so he took her around with him a little."

Granna lifted her hand to her cross necklace, rubbed it a few times like she was pulling strength. "Midway through his training, Matthew had a holiday weekend, so he came home. He was planning to take your mother back with him. She could stay at a hotel near the base. He hadn't been back for a day before . . ."

"Before what?"

"He and his brother started quarreling about old stuff, new stuff. It was obvious that Mark was jealous of your daddy. Matthew had a college degree, a career in the army, and a pretty wife."

Sadness settled in my chest. This story was not going to end well. I knew that. They were both dead, but now it seemed it was going to be worse than I ever imagined. "How did my father feel about Uncle Mark?"

"Matthew wished he had a little more of Mark's charm, but he wasn't the difficult one. It was Mark." She stared at me intently. She wanted me to know. "I hated that they weren't close anymore."

Granna's breathing was heavy. "Mark was the one who started the fight. He picked with him, made comments about Matthew being a slave in the army. Then on Saturday night, out of nowhere, we heard their voices, angrier than they'd ever been. Your mother was in the middle pleading for them to stop and insisting Matthew was wrong. I knew something terrible had happened. Before we could figure out what was going on, Mark left and then Matthew followed him. A few hours later, we got a phone call from the sheriff. They were in a car accident."

Granna looked at me. Grief shrank her, drew her into herself and stole the sparkle from her eyes. "Matthew was killed immediately. Mark hung on for a year in a nursing place, but he was gone that night of the accident. His heart and brain hadn't stopped enough to take him off the machine, but then he had a stroke and died." She wiped her eyes. "They were only twenty-four when they crashed that car."

"Granna, I'm so sorry." My mother had told me my father was coming from a bar and that he'd been killed instantly in a car accident, but she hadn't ever told me about Uncle Mark.

"We were both devastated, but Eddie . . . he changed. He blamed himself. Just like he did about Earl."

It wasn't just hard to watch Granna cry. It was impossible. I couldn't burden her with this. Not tonight. "Let's stop now. You're too upset to keep talking about it."

"I'm not going to open this wound again. I'm too old to bleed this heavy."

The back door opened and closed with that familiar *snap*. I heard Aunt Thea's voice and then saw her and Uncle Roger. Aunt Thea curiously took in Granna's appearance. I heard whispering, and Uncle Roger went back outside.

I gave Granna my attention again.

"What about my mother?"

"She left the house after Matthew's funeral. She took his ashes. We never heard from her again. We kept hoping she would call or come back to see us, but she never did."

Aunt Thea entered the living room. "Aunt Ida, are you all right?"

"We were talking about Matthew and Mark," I replied. "And my mother."

"This is too much. You're already tired," Aunt Thea said. She looked tired herself. "Petra is still at the party. Let me get you into bed."

"I'll do it tonight," I said.

Aunt Thea stepped back, concern deep in the folds of her face.

Granna stood. She was unsteady, so I handed her her cane.

"Can I get you some water or something?" I asked.

"I'll bring some," Aunt Thea said.

I helped Granna undress, removed the jewelry and pins from her hair, and wiped the makeup off her face. She washed up and settled in her bed. She was tired before we started talking.

"My sons were a blessing. We didn't have a curse." She pressed the right side of her face into the pillow and whispered, "Eddie forgave me. I forgave Victoria. Long time ago. Maybe I need to ask her forgiveness too." Her eyes closed, but she mumbled a prayer before giving in to sleep.

Now that Granna was in bed, I allowed myself to process my emotions, to think about what she'd said. My father and Uncle Mark were together in the car. They'd been arguing. About what? And my mother forgiven. I needed more. What had Granna forgiven her for? What did Granna need forgiveness for?

I met Aunt Thea in the kitchen where she was wiping down Granna's spotless appliances. Waiting for me. That's what she was really doing.

"Where's Uncle Roger?"

"Probably playing spades."

I nodded.

"So she told you."

"My dad and Uncle Mark were arguing and got into an accident. Uncle Mark was jealous of my father." I leaned against the back door and looked outside to make sure no one was coming up from the river before I implored Aunt Thea to finish this story. When I saw it was clear, I said, "Something is missing. Granna doesn't want to talk about it, but I need to know. What's missing?"

"Your mother is missing and has been for a long time."

No prodding was required. I waited for Aunt Thea to unpinch her lips. "Your grandmother can't speak it." She shook her head. "I didn't think she would be able to, so now I'm going to tell you everything."

She took a deep breath and plowed in. "The argument between Mark and Matthew was about your mother. Victoria was with Mark while Matthew was gone—or at least something made Matthew believe that. Victoria was pleading with Matthew to 'leave it alone.' She insisted that nothing was going on. That's what your grandparents overheard. 'He's lying. Nothing happened.'"

Aunt Thea bristled with anger. "Eddie had been refereeing fights and arguments between his sons since they were in the crib, but he was eighty-two years old. He couldn't break up that one. He wasn't strong enough—not his words or his muscle." Aunt Thea hesitated again. "Mark had already been drinking before he left to go to a bar. There was only one around . . . over there on Brown Ferry Road." Aunt Thea pointed to her left, and I looked, like I expected a hologram of the past to appear.

"Matthew went after him. Once Matthew found him, they argued some more." Aunt Thea raised a hand to her heart. Her lips pinched again, and her eyes got wet. "People told us the story later, you know, after the funeral. There was talk. They said Matthew hit Mark like he wanted to kill him. Mark was drunk, so the bartender wouldn't let him drive. He didn't have no choice but to get in the car with Matthew and your mother."

"Mom was with them?"

Aunt Thea looked shocked that I didn't know. "Yes. Victoria followed Matthew out of the house."

Now it was my face that was contorted with bitterness. The heat of tears burned my eyes.

"Victoria walked away from that accident without a scratch." Aunt Thea huffed. "But the accident wasn't the worst of it." Aunt Thea looked like she was trying to gather herself. "Because Victoria was Matthew's wife, she had all the power to make the funeral decisions. We wanted a church funeral, but she arranged for a service at Beaufort National Cemetery. It was far, so many of the people who knew Matthew couldn't attend. She did it without talking to anyone in the family."

Aunt Thea stopped and shook her head. "She was married to him for three months and wouldn't even discuss it. We went to Beaufort expecting a service and an internment, but they took the casket away for cremation. Your grandparents didn't believe in cremation. We had no warning. No one was expecting that. She and your grandmother fought bitterly about it.

"Other things came into the fight—the relationship with Mark. It was ugly. Your grandmother regretted the things she said to your mother. Victoria was young. She wasn't a Christian. Aunt Ida drove her away, and it caused a rift between her and Uncle Eddie. That rift lasted a long time. They weren't able to grieve together. Aunt Ida never quite forgave herself for how she talked to Victoria after the funeral."

Aunt Thea put a hand on her hip. "But I understood Ida. Your children . . . losing them has to be a different kind of pain. I loved those boys like they were my own. Before God, I can't lie. I had to pray for years about my feelings about your mother. Both those men were gone. The woman in the middle didn't even need a Band-Aid, and she dishonored their parents like that. It was difficult."

Tears flew from Aunt Thea's eyes like they'd been shot out of the cannon of her heart. I walked over to her and put my arms around her. She pulled back and looked in my eyes, managed a version of a smile. "But now I realize she walked out of that accident with you. You were a part of God's plan."

Aunt Thea's voice croaked with heaviness. "How do the young people say that thing? 'If understanding it better by and by was a person, it would be you.' You were our miracle. Eddie's heart was broken on the side of the road that night and then crushed at the funeral, but his bloodline was not wiped out."

I raised my head and looked out the window, over the farm and beyond the tent. Because of the lights at the party, I could still see the river rushing past my relatives, carrying the spirit of the people before me, people who believed God always had a plan—even if it was difficult to understand.

My heart ached for a man I'd never met. Grandpa Eddie didn't deserve this. Neither did Granna. On the tail end of that thought, realization that my mother hadn't been honest with me slammed into my chest with a sharp bang. She'd never told me she was in the car too.

"No wonder she didn't want me to come down here. All these years, she was hiding her secret."

"*Hmm*," Aunt Thea mused. She moved away from me, picked up the dishrag she'd been using, and started wiping the island again. She clearly wasn't going to defend my mother's choices in that regard. Aunt Thea had given her grace. Said she was young, but my mother wasn't always that *young* woman who fled Georgetown.

My thoughts churned and spat out puzzle pieces that I tried to put together. My mother was responsible for my father's death. It was an accident, but what if cheating started a chain of events that led to that accident? And on that thought, my brain got stuck on the words *cheating* and *father*.

Matthew Black.

That's all I ever knew. All I had was a picture and edited short stories my mother shared. No one knew she was pregnant when she left Georgetown, which meant she hadn't been pregnant very long. My father had been gone for training for six weeks. There was a six-week window in which both Black sons could have . . . I let my thought end. I pressed it out of my head.

Festive music rose from the river—louder. The DJ had increased the volume. January baby-making dancing to the sound of sexy beats had begun. But if there was a mouse in this kitchen, you could hear him pee on a napkin. Aunt Thea didn't make a sound. She let me process and process. As a result, one question turned repeatedly in my mind.

"Whose"—I hesitated before finishing—"daughter am I?"

Bitterness creased Aunt Thea's face. "Honey, the answer to that question is between God and your mother because the dead can't say nothing."

32

I DIDN'T SLEEP WELL. MY MIND WOULDN'T TURN OFF. I KEPT replaying the story Granna and Aunt Thea told me. It was like a movie. I could see it all scrolling across the screen in my brain. Two brothers fighting, two women trying to break it up, and an old man wishing he was young enough to stop them.

It was a tragedy.

But even still, I couldn't imagine a scenario in which three months into my marriage to Drew, I would have cremated him without having a conversation with his family about it. He'd been my husband, but he didn't belong to me. And that was the problem: my mother always thought she owned the people she loved.

I'd spent an hour staring at the ceiling. I couldn't come up with a reason not to be furious with her. She lied and denied me the love I was due all because she had secrets. This was unfair. Why didn't she believe I deserved better than this? Why didn't she trust me with the truth? Who were we to each other?

I was headed back to New York, but this conversation couldn't wait. I opened my Mac and called her using the FaceTime app. It was Sunday morning. Sunday was the only day she permitted herself to sleep in, so I wasn't surprised to find her in bed. Her ivory leather tufted headboard was behind her. She was wearing a cotton-candy pink silk pajama top. She still had her headwrap on, and a mug of coffee was in her free hand.

"You're early."

"Yesterday was Granna's party."

My mother frowned. "Granna. Is that what you call her? That's different."

"I'm sure, especially since you meant for me never to call her anything."

My mother took a sip of coffee before putting the cup on her nightstand. "Are we back to that?"

She was far too unapologetic for my liking.

"Last night, I learned *everything* about your time down here."

My mother's face stiffened. She couldn't hide her concern, but she could delay responding. She made a fuss of adjusting her body on the bed to push up higher on the pillows. When she was finished, she took another sip from her mug. "Now you think you know everything."

"I want to know why my father died."

"Well, that's easy. He died because he lost control of a car."

"Why didn't you tell me that you and his brother were in that vehicle?"

"Because I didn't want you to know." She said it as if that answer was good enough.

"Maybe it was because you didn't want me wondering which of the Black men is my father."

I could see the statement threw my mother off guard. "Matthew is your father! Is that the lie they planted in your head?"

"No one said that."

"Then why are you saying it?"

"Because of the situation."

"I wouldn't lie to you about that."

I laughed. It was the kind of laugh that got a kid smacked in the mouth. But I wasn't a kid. I was a grown woman, and she was going to tell me what I wanted to know. Today. One of my mother's triggers was anything that even remotely called her integrity into question, so I pushed her. "This is the thing. You've kept so many secrets that now you look like a liar."

"Watch your mouth. I'm still your mother." Her eyes sliced into me. "And my past is *my* past."

"No." I pointed a finger at my chest. "Your history with my dad is a part of the beginning of my life. I lost him, too, and I needed him more because God help me, all I had was you."

She reached up and untied the knot that secured her headwrap. "I'm a terrible mother now that you've gotten someone else's version?"

"It's the only version I have. Why didn't you tell me yourself? Do you feel guilty?"

Neither of us said anything, but we were quiet for different reasons. I was waiting on her to answer my question, and she was visibly trying to answer it for herself.

I pushed again. "Please, tell me."

"I wasn't guilty. I was grieving."

"I'm thirty-six. Have you been grieving that long?"

"Grief doesn't have an expiration date."

"That's a tired cliché." I wanted more from her. Maybe I should have waited until I was back in New York, but she'd deflected when she was in Charleston. Being face-to-face wasn't going to change her answer. "Why did you cremate him like that?"

"Because it was my decision. Matthew was my husband." She banged on her chest. "He was the only person in my life who loved me. You think you had a hard time growing up, traveling, having money, being famous? I grew up in the projects with a mother who had no choices and the ones she had made her crazy, and then she died." She raised her hands to cover her face.

After a few seconds, she dropped them. Tears wet her eyes. "Matthew made me promises, and he kept every one of them. If he said he was going to call, he called. If he asked me on a date, he showed up. If he upset me, he brought flowers. I loved him, and I was not ready to let him go. Maybe I was wrong, but I needed those ashes. I needed a piece of him with me."

My mother reminded me of Granna last night—small and wounded. I understood wanting a piece of something you lost. Clinging was natural when one was still processing grief, but he wasn't just her husband. He was a son. He was my father, and I'd lost my family for years because she had to have those ashes.

"They were his family, and they should have been my family. They could have been your family."

"No." She shook her head. "They didn't think I was good enough for him. We could never be family." Half of her upper body disappeared when she reached into her nightstand. When she came back on camera, she had a lit cigarette in her hand. She'd aged ten years during this conversation, but I couldn't stop. Now that I had this door open, all the skeletons needed to come out.

"What happened with Uncle Mark?"

My mother inhaled and blew out a long plume of smoke. "Nothing." She paused briefly before continuing. "Mark was nice to me. He got me out of that house, and we had fun. He was an instant brother—at least that's how I saw him." Although her eyes stayed forward, she wasn't exactly looking at me. She was gone to a place she'd left thirty-seven years ago. "He wasn't like your father. Mark had more of a gritty, streetwise edge to him. Where he got that from, I don't know, but I recognized that from the projects. Matthew was not like that. But Mark was still a part of him. When I was with Mark, I kind of had a little piece of Matthew."

"Why were they fighting that night?"

"Because Mark had fallen for me—or at least he thought he had." My mother shook her head. "I knew it. That's why I told Matthew I needed to come to Georgia. I blamed it on Mrs. Ida. I told him I didn't feel welcome because I couldn't tell him the truth about his brother." She took another drag off her cigarette. "I couldn't tell him that his brother walked in the bathroom on me and peeked through the door when I was dressing. I couldn't tell him those things.

"He believed me about Mrs. Ida. He understood mothers and daughters-in-law don't always get along, but when he got there . . ." She shook her head. "Mark lied. He told Matthew we'd kissed, and he hinted it went further." Her bottom lip trembled. "Casey, *that* wasn't true. Mark wanted to destroy us. Matthew loved him, but Mark . . . he didn't love Matthew, not enough to not want to hurt him."

My heart broke for the good brother who loved his twin and trusted him, who died because of him and left a widow and a baby behind that he probably would have loved forever, if he'd had the chance.

"After the accident, I told Mrs. Ida about Mark. But by that time, Matthew was dead, and Mark should have been. She only saw one thing in common with all the pain she and her husband were experiencing, and that was me."

My mother dropped her head back and let out a long breath. "She told me she never wanted to see me again. She said it with such a visceral hate that I swore to myself she *never* would." My mother stubbed out her cigarette. "So, dear daughter, I wasn't guilty. I was keeping a vow."

My mother looked like she'd been through a war. I felt like I'd watched one. Tension in my back crawled up my neck and strangled me from the rear. I wanted the answers to my questions. Now I had them, along with every bit of sorrow they'd carried through the years.

"Do you believe me?"

The question came out of my mother's mouth carrying a near-childlike lilt. I looked at her. I saw her differently now. I saw the grieving widow that she still was.

"Yes. I believe you."

"Are you sure? Because I don't want to rehash this, Casey. It's too hard."

Granna didn't want to rehash it either. I had to give my mother the same grace to not have to dwell in her pain. "You've never lied to me. You've kept things from me, but never spoken a lie to my face, so yes, I believe you."

A tear fell from my mother's eyes. I'd only ever seen my mother cry once. It was at her mother's funeral when I was five years old. Since then, if she got misty, it was over something like a heartwarming TV commercial or movie. She didn't cry about real-life issues.

But then again, of course she did.

"*We have to grieve the dead thing in the quiet of the night. When we lie on our beds, we can shed our tears.*" She cried, but she'd hidden her tears from me.

My mother pressed her lips together. She pulled the collar of her pajamas together too. She wasn't often vulnerable with me. Maybe she didn't know how to be. Maybe I'd failed to make her believe she could be. My mother was fifty-six years old. She didn't really have friends. She wasn't close to any family. She hadn't dated over the years, not seriously, so if she couldn't be vulnerable with me, who could she be vulnerable with?

"I love you, Mom. I wish I could give you a hug right now. You've always hugged me, and it made it better."

More tears escaped her eyes. "Grief really doesn't have an expiration date, Casey." She released a heavy breath. I didn't know if she'd even heard me about the hug. She'd been transplanted back to a time and place where she'd suffered the most pain. "That's not a cliché."

I thought about the greatest loss I'd ever had—my babies—and realized that grief was still fresh. I nodded. "I know."

33

SOMETHING WAS WRONG. I SENSED IT THE MOMENT I WALKED through the door. And then it was confirmed when Aunt Thea turned, one arm folded over her belly, the other raised with her hand pressed against the side of her face. A hollow sadness in her sunken eyes.

"What is it?" I asked, walking closer, just to the edge of the hall that led to Granna's bedroom. "Is Granna okay?"

Aunt Thea moaned. The sound was weary, hurt, pained. A heavy tear fell from her eyes. "Baby, your grandmother has gone home to be with the Lord."

A pain spread through my chest like fire. It was a hit—hard, sudden, injurious. Home with the Lord. Her home was here with me.

"No." I wasn't sure if I was speaking or just thinking. "No."

I backed up. Backed toward the door. Maybe if I left and came back in . . .

"She passed in her sleep."

"Alone?"

"Peacefully."

She'd been alone. That thought stuck with me. "No." I shook my head. "No, no, no, not yet!"

There were noises outside. I turned and looked through the door. An ambulance and a hearse rolled in front of the house. I put a hand over my mouth. "Is she still here?"

Aunt Thea nodded, and I closed my eyes.

"If you want to see her, you can go in now."

"See her? Dead?"

No, no, no!

"I can't. I don't want to. Am I supposed to want to?"

"You don't have to do anything you don't want to do." She stepped around me and pulled the door open for the men and women who were coming to take Granna away from this place. Away from me. Forever.

I moved to the farthest corner of the living room and then ultimately decided to go into the kitchen and out on the back porch. Through the glass panes, I could still see them—entering, pulling and pushing a gurney through the door, in the living room, and then into the hall where it disappeared from sight.

The wind that left my body had still not come back to me. My chest had that heavy feeling like a weight was pressing against it. The pressure had a sharp edge to it. It wasn't the first time I'd felt this. I'd struggled with this heaviness when I had my second miscarriage. I'd wanted my babies. I wanted Granna. Why did I lose what I loved?

I turned away from the house, out to the farm. The sky was clear as far as my eyes could see, which today was down to the river and its slow, lazy current. Was it carrying the soul of Granna out to the sea, back to land our ancestors came from, to give her a final resting place?

"Casey."

Startled, I turned to see Nigel behind me.

I shook my head.

"Aunt Thea called me." He stepped closer. I would have

stepped back, but there was no place for me to go except down the steps, and I knew my legs were too wobbly for that. Besides, I didn't need to run from him.

"I'm in shock. She was fine last night, Nigel."

"I know." He stepped closer still. "I'm so sorry."

"You loved her too."

"Of course."

I heard a loud noise inside the house. "I should help Aunt Thea."

"You stay here," he said. "I'll go back in."

"No!" I walked past him. I placed my hand on the knob and looked at him. I wasn't an observer or a visitor, not anymore. I wasn't their spoiled, estranged, lost little relation from New York who everyone had to coddle and teach things. "I need to be strong for Aunt Thea."

I turned the knob and swept through the door. I found Aunt Thea in the bedroom. Granna's body was already on the gurney.

Granna, no.

I cried inside for few seconds, but then pushed my way to Aunt Thea's side.

"What can I do, Auntie? Can I make some calls for you?"

Aunt Thea looked at me; light shined in her eyes. She raised a hand to push back curls off my forehead. "Baby, you don't have to do anything. You being here is enough."

"No, it's not. I want to help. Give me something to do."

"I sent a text out on the Blackline so family will all know soon. I also called the pastor and her doctor already. You can call the newspaper about the obituary."

"Is that it?"

"That's it for now. The funeral home will make some time for us later. She already had her funeral planned out, so we just have to put the pieces in place."

My throat was as dry as two-day-old toast, but I managed to croak out the word "okay."

Aunt Thea asked, "Where's Nigel?"

"I left him on the deck."

She squeezed my hand. "He'll take care of letting the employees know."

"Did you want me to tell him that?"

"Nigel does what needs to be done without anyone having to tell him."

A member of the EMT team caught Aunt Thea's attention. "We've confirmed her death, so they can remove Mrs. Black from the home now."

A little sound escaped Aunt Thea's throat. Her free hand went to her chest. I clutched the other one more tightly.

The men from the funeral home rolled the gurney out of the room. The creaky floorboards cried out from the weight above them, or maybe they cried for the loss of the woman who'd walked on them for over eighty years. Some people believed houses had energy contained in them from the owners. If that were true, the house was mourning too.

Once the body was gone, we were left with a space full of nothingness. It seemed like we should be doing something. Petra arrived. Nigel was out with the staff, so it was just the three of us sitting in the living room absorbing each other's grief.

"It's not fair. I only just met her."

Aunt Thea's arms were around me. The warmth of her hug was necessary and effective. I needed this love. "Your grandmother lived a long, full life. She lost her sons and then Eddie. It's been hard for her."

"But I'm here. I'm one of the people she loves." I inhaled and tried to push my selfish thoughts from my mind. I wanted more time. "I needed more time."

I walked to her chair, touched the worn, smooth fabric and then the chenille throw that had been her cocoon. I pulled it to my nose and took a long, intentional sniff. Granna was there, inside this blanket. The fiber held her scent, but it was a promise that wouldn't last long. I could already feel it slipping away, or maybe it was me, slipping, falling, sliding into my despair. Granna was gone. Gone from this world. Gone from me. A piece of me, the happy piece, the stable piece, had gone with her. I dropped into the chair and pulled the throw around my shoulders.

I raised my eyes to Aunt Thea's. Heavy teardrops sat on the rims of my eyelids. My lips trembled. "What am I supposed to do now?"

"Today, you weep. Tomorrow, you remember."

I removed my phone from my pocket and sent a group text to my mother and Leslie.

Granna died.

From Leslie: I'm so sorry. I know you loved her.

My mother didn't reply for a long time. More than an hour. When she did, it read: My condolences to everyone.

Nothing specific for me. This was a Black loss, and in my mother's opinion, I was not a Black. Just when I was about to get angry about that, she replied again: Let me know if you want me to come be with you.

I lifted an eyebrow. *Come here to bury Granna?*

Another text came through: I know it wouldn't be appropriate for the funeral, but I could stay at a hotel. I don't want you to be alone.

My mother was reading my mind. I had to give her credit for caring. I replied: I'm not alone. There's a lot of family.

My mother didn't respond to that, so I followed up with: Granna forgave you.

My mother: Still doesn't mean she'd want me at her funeral.

I returned my phone to my pocket. "What kind of service are we having?"

"A grand one," Aunt Thea replied. "That's what we do."

Before she could go on, the door opened, and Nigel came in with Pastor Ridgill behind him. We all stood. Petra walked to me and said, "I'm going to clean up the bedroom."

"Should I?" I asked.

"It's no problem, ma'am. I've done it before. First I'll strip the bed, and then I have some special cleanser I keep in my trunk."

I nodded, and Petra disappeared down the hall.

I half listened, half tuned out Pastor Ridgill as he offered Aunt Thea and me words of comfort. I was not ready to be comforted yet. I was still in shock.

Nigel entered the house and took the seat Petra had vacated.

"Pastor, can I get you a cup of coffee or water?" I asked as soon as he took a pause.

"No, thank you, Sister Casey."

I looked at Auntie. "What about you, Aunt Thea?"

"Water would be good."

I excused myself to the kitchen and came back with a tray that included three glasses and a pitcher of ice water. I poured for Aunt Thea and Nigel. Nigel's eyes caught mine as I handed him a glass.

I slid the pitcher in front of the pastor, just in case he changed his mind, then escaped back into the kitchen. I leaned back against the island and looked at the cabinets brimming with all her secrets—spices and herbs. I stared at the mixer and recalled the mess I'd made when I put it on high and sprayed the wall with cake batter. I smiled a little inside. I wanted to believe Granna's spirit was still here, but it didn't feel warm or cheery now. The sense that she was completely gone from this place was overwhelmingly sad. I wanted to comfort myself, even if it was with a lie.

"*A lie shouldn't make your heart its home.*"

I nodded and whispered into the emptiness. "You taught me so much, Granna."

Nigel walked into the room and came over to where I stood. I released a pained puff of air. "I feel like I should be cooking something."

"There will be lots of food coming here today."

"That's what Aunt Thea told me."

"Food for weeks," Nigel said.

"You'll have to take some." I was already thinking ahead. What would we do with lots of food and no appetite?

"You and Aunt Thea will sort it out," he said. "But I need you to know that your aunt isn't the only person who is here for you. Ma Black would want me to take care of you."

I reached for his hand and squeezed it. He meant every word he said. His actions said so, and that made him a good friend. And he was right. Granna was pushing us together from day one. What had she seen in him and me that made her know that he and I . . . My thoughts trailed off. I let go of his hand and walked over to get an apron. I pulled it over my head and walked to the cupboard and opened it.

"Granna would want every person who walked through this door to have something sweet." I went to the deep freezer and removed some bags of fruit. "We have berries. We can make a cobbler or two."

Nigel smiled and shoved off the island. "Let's bake."

<hr />

The service for Granna was held on Friday. The Blacks who had traveled for the party were still here, so Aunt Thea didn't want to delay it. I hadn't asked my mother to come. I didn't want to see anyone who didn't love Granna. The family took care of that requirement. Love—there were many Blacks for that.

We had to have the ceremony at one of the larger A.M.E. churches in the area, and even still, the five-hundred-seat sanctuary was packed.

Pastor Ridgill preached about Granna's giving heart. He told one of her favorite stories, the one about the shepherd losing one of his hundred sheep and searching for that one.

"Sister Black's ministry was in encouraging and teaching. She knew how to love just enough to win the heart of anyone she was talking to. She was the shepherd who was always trying to bring one more sheep closer to God. She looked tirelessly for the lost one, and for that, God rewarded her on this side of heaven by reuniting her with a granddaughter she never knew she had."

I wiped a tear. Nigel pulled me closer. They opened the service for words. Each of us could say something about Granna. I wasn't going to speak, but then right before the pastor closed it, I stood and accepted the microphone.

"Love was my grandmother's special gift. Making people feel better. Offering them somewhere to share their hearts—the good and the bad. Many of you know she had a healing ministry. She held sessions with people here in the community. She took the time to pray with people, offer them medicinal solutions and a listening ear. Her ministry was healing. She wanted everyone to have it.

"When I met my grandmother, the first thing she said to me was 'My lost one has come home.' Before I came to Georgetown, my life had been turned upside down. I was a little lost. I was searching for somewhere, something, someone, some purpose.

My grandmother taught me that everything I needed, I already had inside of me. I wasn't lost. I just needed a comfortable place to grieve. My grandmother made me feel safe and comfortable. Then I could rest, and once I rested, I grieved, and when that was over, I found my joy. My grandmother gave me that. In the same way she gave it to many of her clients.

"We'd only just begun, and she's gone." I stepped away from the podium and walked to the casket. "But if going to be with the Lord is *home* for you, Granna, I want you to be there. Get some rest, and find your joy in heaven. Give my daddy a hug for me." I kissed my fingers and placed them on the casket.

Nigel stood. He joined me at the casket. An usher took the microphone. Under the sound of applause and amens, we returned to our seats, where he wrapped an arm around my back and pulled me close. I sobbed until I couldn't cry anymore.

34

I ENTERED GRANNA'S HOUSE AND WALKED THROUGH IT, touching all the things she loved before going to her private room, the place where she prayed and had her quiet time with God.

The room smelled of lemongrass and lavender. Those scents would always remind me of her.

Great-grandma Odessa's journals, Granna's prayer journals, and books were neatly organized in the box. I would be the keeper of the family treasure now, and the weight of the responsibility that came with that was enormous.

I heard the door open in the front room. I called out, "Hello. Who's there?"

Aunt Thea's voice carried up the hall. "I saw your car, so I stopped."

I found her in the kitchen washing her hands.

"How are you, baby?"

"Numb."

"Pastor mentioned your words about your grandmother at church today."

"Did he?"

"Yes. He preached from Ecclesiastes 3, 'To everything there is a season.'" Aunt Thea took some items out of the cabinet and put them on the counter.

"Everything feels empty and different."

"Life will not be the same without her. That's what happens when people leave us. People leave space they once filled up, but love abides. They're never far from our memories."

I understood what Aunt Thea was saying, but I was so hurt. Granna left me without saying goodbye. "The time I had with her was too short."

"You had the time God gave you."

"I should have come here sooner."

Aunt Thea placed a hand on her hip. "Now, Casey, would she want you to be focused on that?"

"No, but I'm not her, Auntie."

"Yes, you are. You are her and her mother, Laura, and Odessa and every other woman whose DNA you have. And that doesn't mean you're Superwoman, but it does mean you can see beauty in what you had. You were born with a lens that looks for the beauty, baby. That's why you take all those pictures. You see beyond what the rest of us see."

My insides churned. My head and heart hurt, but I knew Aunt Thea was right. My grandmother wouldn't want me to cry a single day. "I miss her already."

"You're going to miss her. But God gave you the gift of time that you didn't have with your grandfather." Aunt Thea let out a long plume of air. "Just think, if you had come here this week, all you'd have is me."

I laughed and wrapped my arms around her. "You would be enough." Aunt Thea squeezed back, and all the love I wanted to give my grandmother, I pushed into her.

"Now let's stop all this moping. I—"

Aunt Thea was interrupted when both our phones rang. I took the call from my mother in the front room.

"Hi, sweetheart. I know you had a rough couple of days, but

I have news that can't wait." She paused a few seconds and said, "The team at Now Cosmetics wants to meet with you. They're offering you the job."

"Really?"

"They're behind on the launch, so they need to get you in place right away. The CEO is in town this week. I pushed the meeting as far as I could, but they need to meet Thursday afternoon."

"I'm not ready."

"Casey, you have to be ready. He wants to meet you in person to sign the contract, take some photos."

I was quiet. Thinking about being in New York in four days was too much.

"I'll have Swella book a flight."

"My car is here." I raised a hand to rub my temple. "I'll figure it out."

"But I can tell them yes?"

I looked at my grandmother's empty chair. The empty space Aunt Thea spoke of was suffocating me. "Yes."

Aunt Thea walked in. "That was your grandmother's lawyer. He wants to meet with us tomorrow morning about the will."

I nodded. "I have to be in New York on Thursday."

"Oh," Aunt Thea said, raising a hand to her chest. "I have one more thing to teach you."

I waited, hoping it was what I thought it might be. "The crab and bacon chowder?"

Aunt Thea swirled her neck. "I can't let you leave here without knowing how to make it."

I could taste the bacon and smell the herbs already. Happiness filled my heart. I didn't know how long it would last, but it propelled me into the kitchen. Aunt Thea and I chopped and stirred and talked and laughed until we had the perfect chowder and a little less pain.

35

THE READING OF GRANNA'S WILL WAS A SHORT MEETING, attended by Aunt Thea, Petra, Nigel, and me. It was not lost on me that aside from Aunt Thea, these were the people who were with me on the day I met Granna.

"Ms. Black made changes to her will two months ago to include Casey Black."

"Two months?" I asked.

"It was the day after the seed ceremony," Nigel said. "She told me she was taking care of it."

"She hardly knew me."

Aunt Thea placed her hand on mine. "She didn't have to know you better. You're her only direct heir."

The lawyer cleared his throat and continued. He went down the list of Granna's assets. The land was valued at $890,000 and the farm generated almost $150,000 a year in profit. From her savings, Granna left money to Nigel, Aunt Thea, Petra, and something to every single member of her family. Nigel also inherited 10 percent of the annual farm revenue for as long as he lived. Everything else—the acreage, the equipment, and the house—was left to me.

Even though the farm made a nice profit, Granna lived frugally. She saved and donated heavily to charity.

Granna had climbed into my heart again. "She was an incredible woman. What do I do with a legacy like this?"

"It's her legacy, Casey. You do things your way. She would want you to establish your own legacy," Aunt Thea said.

But I was immediately intimidated. How could I walk in Granna's shoes when I wasn't a tenth of the woman she was? And I missed her so much I could hardly breathe.

The lawyer interrupted, "I just need you to sign some documents so we can take care of the new deed and other legal transfers."

Checks were issued, and copies of everything I signed were given to me. I sat there, stunned, for a long time. Nigel sat across from me.

"I know you're adjusting to all of this, but when you're ready, we can talk about operations," he said.

"What's there to talk about?" I asked, standing. "You said yourself, the farm is a well-oiled machine, and based on these numbers, it's profitable."

He stood too. "Are you still leaving?"

"I'm flying out tomorrow." I'd told him about the Now meeting. I avoided his eyes, preferring to play with my fingers.

"Is that so?" His voice cracked. I'd never heard it do that before. I dropped my hands and looked at him.

"You know, we never finished talking about your work. I still don't really know what you do, and now that you've got this meeting with this company, I want to know."

He was right, and even though the timing was horrible, I was out of time. If I was going to be transparent with him, show him who I'd been at my worst, I had to do it now. I gathered my breath and said, "I'm a social media influencer, Nigel. I have all those followers you saw on my page because I provide content that makes people want to follow me."

He grimaced. "Like a Kardashian."

My stomach dropped. It sounded ugly coming off his tongue. "Not that big, but yes."

He released a long breath. "You said you were in marketing."

"It is marketing. I promote brands."

Nigel raised his hand to cup the back of his neck. "So you're a celebrity." He didn't sound impressed. At all. I didn't need him to be, but the thought that he would be turned off bothered me just like I knew it would, which was why I hadn't told him. "So why were you on a break?"

I reached for my phone to locate the video. The closer I got to finding it, the more my stomach tightened. "Remember I told you Drew left me at the church?" I held the phone out for him to see and clicked the link to the video. "This is how I responded."

Nigel stood there watching the worst ten minutes of my professional career. I would have been more embarrassed if I wasn't dealing with the worst personal situation in my life. At this point, my angst over the video felt silly. When it was done, he pitched an eyebrow.

"So this is what you've been hiding? A video?"

"I was embarrassed."

We were both looking at each other with uncertainty.

"But I thought we were friends, at least that, Casey."

I was expecting him to be angry or disappointed or even turned off, and instead, he was hurt.

"I'm sure that was bad for you and your business, but it's not who you are . . . not all the time anyway."

Did this man ever say the wrong thing? Relief made it hard to speak over the lump in my throat. "I appreciate you saying that, Nigel, I really do. But from a business standpoint, I've lost a lot of money. The beauty and fashion brands that used to sponsor me don't anymore. I'm a trainwreck. And it's not just about the money. It's my reputation. I don't want *that* video to be my legacy, not when I worked so hard for so many years."

Nigel's sigh told his entire story. "That's the problem with social media. Everyone cares what other people think about them."

"This is my name."

"Casey B? She's not a real person. You are Casey Black. She owns a farm."

"Nigel, don't do this to me."

"Do what? Fight for us? I happen to think we have something."

"I've already decided I'm taking this meeting. I'm not a hot commodity anymore. If somebody wants me . . ." My words trailed off. I finished them in my head. *I can't be choosy.*

Nigel moved closer. He placed both his hands on my shoulders. "I want you."

I pressed a palm against his chest. Had he not heard a thing I said about my legacy? I wanted him to understand, but it was obvious he wasn't going to. "When did I promise you I was staying?"

If I had tased him, he wouldn't have looked more shocked. "Okay. Wow. Where did that question come from?"

"I'm asking because you're acting like I made a promise that I was staying."

He hesitated for a few seconds before saying, "You made a promise to me when you kissed me. When you let me hold you all night . . ."

My heart thumped.

"And with every word that came out of your mouth, every smile, look, touch. You had to know that I've been falling in love with you since I met you."

He pressed into me with his eyes. Those beautiful brown eyes I loved to look into were staring through me. He still had his hands on my shoulders. I raised my hand from his chest to his cheek. "We want different things."

Nigel frowned, not following. "What is it you think I want?"

I moved from under his grip. I needed to keep some space between us. "A simple woman."

"'A simple woman.'" He chuckled. "That's a unicorn. I haven't met one of those yet." A thoughtful frown creased his forehead. "You love what I love."

"And what do you think that is?"

"Beauty. I'm talking about nature, food, art, and history. There's a beauty in your curiosity and your spirit, Casey. That's what I want."

Nigel didn't understand the mess I needed to clean up, and he could see that he hadn't convinced me to stay. As always, his face was readable, and that made me feel worse.

"What about your photography?"

Hot tears pushed their way from the back of my eyes. "That's a dream."

"Dreams have to be worked. That farm was somebody's impossible dream. If you haven't learned anything from your grandmother and your ancestors, you should have learned that."

"Don't . . ." My heart filled up. "Don't use Granna that way."

"I'm not using her. I would never do that."

I covered my face with my hands and fought to suck wind through my fingers. He made me feel like I was failing Granna. "I can't stay right now," I cried. The pain in my heart threatened to consume me. "I can't be here without her. It hurts too much."

"I'm here." His strong, determined eyes sank into me. "You don't think I miss her?"

"Of course you do. Everyone will, but this is my grief." I raised a hand to my chest and patted. "I have to handle it my own way."

Nigel closed the space between us. "So don't run away. Feel

it. Feel it here. Feel it with me. Receive comfort and love from people who loved her too."

"I don't know how to do that." I reached across the table and pulled a wad of tissue from the box that was there and wiped my eyes. "It's time for me to go home."

He twisted his mouth and nodded slowly. "You're running back up there the same way you ran down here. Is that what you do when it gets painful, Casey? Run?" Nigel rubbed his hands over his head. He was at maximum frustration. "How are you getting to the airport?"

"Lachelle is taking me."

"Your car?"

"I'll park it at the farm." I knew my having all the answers was hurting him. I could see it. He didn't want me to have thought it all through. He wanted to talk me out of it, but he couldn't.

"Leave a key for the car just in case we need to move it, and you can leave the key for my house"—he paused for a moment—"next to the coffee maker." He turned to leave. "Have a safe trip." He opened the door and stepped out without looking back.

Emptiness and loneliness came over me. I fell into the chair again. Nigel had been my rock. He was the last person on earth I wanted to hurt, but my season here was over.

36

Odessa Black

PEARL HAD FINISHED THE TEACHER PROGRAM AT OBERLIN College. Odessa's children traveled with them to her graduation. Pearl's teaching job was in Chicago, and she was to begin right away with summer classes. She was smitten with a serious young man named Clifford. He was from Chicago too. He had a position as a staff writer with *The Chicago Conservator* waiting for him. Her daughter was living her dream and Odessa's old one. Pearl was living in the North—away from Jim Crow.

Many Negroes moved north to escape the oppression in the South. That had always been Odessa's plan, but she and Elijah owned a farm. They had built a life. Even if she wanted to, Odessa could never leave her father, and he would never leave his church. Life, or rather love, trapped her where she hadn't wanted to be. First it was love for Elijah and now it was love for her father. It didn't always seem fair, but she couldn't complain. She had a good life with few disappointments.

She was no longer teaching because men had taken most of the opportunities in Georgetown, so Odessa's herb garden had become her joy. Growing plants, drying them, crushing them, and making tinctures and salves was her new vocation. It reminded her of her mother, and that was a warm and welcome memory.

Her other joy was her children. Lawrence, Melle, Alphena, and Earl sat at her feet. At fifteen, Lawrence was too old for the floor, but he said his feet hurt from the new brogans he hadn't broken in yet. Beth was a nurse, living in Savannah now. She'd been unable to take time from her job to attend the graduation. Ann, the oldest still living at home, stood with her father, holding her baby brother, Eddie. Ann had no desire to get more schooling, choosing to apprentice under a local seamstress instead. Odessa liked having her at home. She needed Ann's comfort with Pearl and Beth gone. It was unnatural to bear and raise up children just so they could leave you.

Elijah had cornered Pearl's Clifford, literally. He had him alone near a wall at the back of the room. The young man had not asked Elijah for his daughter's hand but had mentioned marriage and family several times at dinner last night. If she knew her husband, he was making sure Clifford understood his daughter was not to be trifled over.

Odessa scanned the crowded room, finding Pearl. Coal-black ringlets framed her daughter's honey-colored face. Curls made of ironed hair, not the coiled hair God gave her, was the first change she'd seen in her daughter when she met them at the train. The other was the look in her eyes—love for Clifford. Elijah wasn't gonna stop that wedding no kind of way. Odessa was hoping for everyone's sake that he didn't want to. Odessa wasn't sure her daughter would require her father's blessing to move forward. Times had changed. These young people were different.

Odessa's heart was swirling in an emotional storm. One minute she wanted her daughters to chart their own paths, have their own journeys, but then she also wanted them home—on the farm where she could love and protect them forever. Her mother would say, "*You betwixt and between.*"

The next morning Odessa's emotions were still not settled. The sun had not yet risen when Odessa opened her eyes. Elijah slept soundly, as did Eddie and Earl in the bed across the small space from their bed. Elijah had rented two hotel rooms, so the girls—Pearl, Ann, Melle, and Phena—shared a room next door.

Odessa slipped out of bed without disturbing Elijah, pulled on a robe, and pushed the door open to access the porch on the other side of it.

The moon was low, but still large enough to own the sky. Odessa took in a deep breath, and when she didn't find it satisfying, she took another. The smell of morning was missing. Every day, she took her tea at dawn on the porch and enjoyed the scent the dew awakened. It was earthy—like the sandy soil and grassy marshlands. It was raw and natural and carried a dampness that promised a humid day. Try as she might, she didn't smell anything this morning. There was nothing here. Not even the fresh coat of paint she observed on the wood railings and posts had a lingering scent.

A door opened and she was delighted to see Pearl come out of her room. She slipped to Odessa's side, and Odessa pulled her close with one arm around her shoulder.

"I knew you'd be up early," Pearl said. "They have coffee in the lobby. I can get you some if you like."

"I'll wait to have tea with breakfast. I brought my own." Odessa noted a piece of paper wrapped with hair underneath the head rag Pearl wore. She supposed that was how she kept the curls. "How long will your hair stay like that?"

Pearl reached up and pushed the stray hair back under her rag. "Not long. It's already getting big. I just wanted it for the graduation."

Odessa could see the puffiness last night. She hoped her daughter wasn't changing herself for a man. "Does Clifford like it like that?"

"Clifford likes me any way I stay."

One less thing to worry about. Odessa returned her attention to the buildings in front of them. Lamps illuminated windows one by one, and the moon was slowly being swallowed by the light of day.

"I didn't think you'd come back to Georgetown, but I never expected Chicago."

"What city would you have preferred? New York, Pittsburgh, Philadelphia?"

"I don't know. Something closer."

"I'm happy about my assignment, Mama. Some of my classmates will be going too. We'll be family to each other."

Odessa smiled. That was a comfort. "And your young man? How far away will he be?"

"He's across the city, so I won't see him every day, but his parents have a telephone, and we have one at the house where I'll be living."

"I guess I'll have to tell your father I want a phone."

"Please do. We can talk every week if you do. Getting letters to post is hard when I'm busy."

Odessa reared back. "I still expect letters. Letters for your brothers and sisters too. And you know to write Papa and Cousin Liz."

Pearl nodded. "Of course, Mama, but it'll be nice to hear your voices."

They were quiet for a moment before Pearl said, "I want to

show you something." She reached into her pocket and removed an envelope. She handed it to Odessa.

Odessa's eyes became wet. She recognized the worn paper. It was a letter she wrote for Pearl in January 1887, after they'd returned from visiting Elijah's mother's grave. Odessa gave the letter to Pearl the day she left for college.

"Oh my," Odessa said, and then she prepared herself mentally for what she was about to read. She opened the envelope and took in her own thoughts, which ended with words she read out loud: "'Please do things I couldn't. The women before you could only dream. But I know they hoped for a better day for their daughters and all the women down their family line. Do me and them the honor of living your dreams so that our sacrifices will be seed that has fallen on good ground. Love, Mama.'"

Heavy tears fell from Odessa's eyes. Pearl took the letter from her hand, repocketed it. "You understand now, right?"

Odessa wiped her eyes and then wiped a tear that spilled down Pearl's cheek. "Thank you for reminding me." She pulled her daughter into her arms and squeezed tight.

37

MAY 23, 2019

THE MORNING AFTER MY PLANE TOUCHED DOWN AT JFK, Swella arrived at my house at eight sharp. Like the days of old, she carried two lattes and a white paper bag. I didn't need X-ray vision to know what was inside the bag—a serving of avocado toast. The smile on her face was infused with a joy I hadn't seen on any of our video chats. It was obvious she was happy to have me back.

We sat at the island in my kitchen and ate while she caught me up on any and everything that was happening in the social media world.

"There's this new app called Flex. It's short videos mostly to music. Like reels."

"*Hmm*," I said, putting the last of my toast in my mouth.

"Right now, there's a challenge running called Sip 'n' Go. It's like you video yourself drinking something. You have to make a loud slurping sound. The sound is an important part of the aesthetic of the video."

"It's like muckbanging with liquid."

Swella cocked her head considering that, then nodded enthusiastically. "Yeah. Anyway, you show your cup or mug or whatever, take a long sip, and say, 'I'm sippin' and goin' to work,' or 'I'm sippin' and goin' to the movies,' or 'I'm sippin' and goin' to the gym,' or—"

"I get the idea." I took a drink of my latte. "It sounds really silly."

Swella threw up a finger. "But it's super popular. It's trending, so . . ."

I looked at my iPad. Now Cosmetics had sent my mother an electronic copy of the deal memo yesterday. It was a decent offer. Less than I would have gotten before the video, but not shameful. Monies to me were guaranteed for three years with stock and bonuses for success at the launch phase. I didn't think the metrics laid out were unachievable. My mother obviously didn't either, or she wouldn't have accepted the terms.

"How are you going to get your car back?"

"I'm either going to go to South Carolina or have someone down there drive it up." I hadn't considered who would do the latter. "If I decide to do it myself, which is a strong possibility, I'll need you to go with me. I'd like company. Maybe Leslie will join us, and we'll make it a girls' road trip." The words made sense, but I didn't feel the enthusiasm. Everything about leaving Georgetown still felt painful and raw.

"Cool," Swella said. "I've never seen a massive farm."

Swella's phone beeped a notification. "It's ten thirty. You should get dressed. I put three changes on the bed. You have to be en route by noon."

"Did you order a car?"

"Yes."

"Cancel it. I want to take a taxi."

Swella scrunched her face. "Why?"

"I just do," I said, hopping down from the barstool and reaching into the fridge for a bottle of water. I went upstairs. Just as I finished getting dressed, my phone pinged a text. It was a message from Drew. It read: I heard you were back in town. I'd like to talk.

I wondered how he'd heard. Maybe he was still following me on social media. Wouldn't that be a trip?

~⚬~

I stepped into the taxi. After greeting the driver, I asked him to take me to the Empire State Building.

"Any way in particular?"

I pushed back into the leather seat. Appreciating that he asked, I said, "Do you think the FDR will be okay?"

I saw him glance at the GPS app on his phone. He tossed a hand up. "It's all about the same right now."

I didn't rebuff, which meant we'd come to an understanding. I reached into my bag for my phone. The smell of a New York City taxi was not something I should have wanted to experience, but I did. I wanted all the unique aspects of the city because nothing felt right. I kept waiting for that feeling to come over me. Even when I had fun, I'd think, *home sweet home*, but that hadn't entered my mind. Not once, which was odd because my house was something I'd treasured since the day I purchased it.

"It's only been twenty-four hours," I whispered to myself. Maybe coming back to New York from a place like Georgetown was akin to culture shock. The adjustment could be just as extreme. I'd read that once in a travel magazine. What had they called it? I googled until I found the words.

Reverse culture shock.

That's what this was, and it would pass.

The taxi took I-278 and made an effortless ride to the Brooklyn Bridge. The tall, familiar buildings in Manhattan came into view. People on foot and bikes traveled the pedestrian walkway. The taxi bumped to the sway of the bridge. Once we reached FDR Drive, we came to a stop. I'd left home early enough, but checking the time on my cell phone was a nervous habit. I hated to be late for a meeting.

The driver reached across the passenger seat and retrieved a half-eaten sub sandwich. Vinegar was what I'd been smelling— that mixed with feet and cigarette smoke.

Georgetown had a smell. It was earthy and grassy. The herb garden was ripe with the aromas of rosemary, thyme, basil, and every other variety planted there. It was distinct and memorable. I looked forward to it every day. With those thoughts came an unbearable tightness in my throat. The garden reminded me of Granna. Her death still hadn't processed. It didn't feel real.

My eyes burned as I fought the wetness creeping into them. I needed a distraction, so I FaceTimed Leslie. The queen of distraction. When she answered I asked, "Why didn't you tell me so many boss clothes came in for me while I was gone?"

"Honestly, I was hoping you'd eat too much corn bread and catfish while you were down there. Then I could take them off your hands."

I laughed. "If you knew how much food I ate, you would for sure think you could have my entire wardrobe. Doctors keep saying it's what you put in your mouth, but that's a lie. Gardening, farming, working in the heat enough to sweat is how you eat and not bump up a clothing size."

"I believe you, but how am I going to do that on a concrete deck?"

"Well, you know what I always say . . ."

"I know. Whatever size you are, it's the right size. You just have to find the right outfit."

I nodded. "Facts."

"So, you're on the way, right?"

I sighed. The distracting part of our conversation hadn't lasted long enough. "I'm in a cab." I pushed the button to let the window down so fresh air could push out the bad air.

"What's going on with you? You look like you need a toilet."

"Gee, thanks."

"Your makeup and hair are pretty, but your face is talking, and it's not happy."

I looked away from the screen and out the window at the city sights we passed. Folks making a mad rush to cross the street when the light changed, food stands, a bodega, steam rising from the sidewalk grates and manholes, tourists taking pictures of everything around them.

"Case?"

"This is a good idea, isn't it? I'd be silly to pass it up."

Leslie was quiet for a moment before saying, "Only you know the answer to that."

I sighed. "I miss Granna."

"I know, honey."

I had to fight to breathe through the tightness gripping my chest. Grief and anxiety mixed in my soul like blood and water. I had no business dealing with this job situation so quickly after I lost Granna. "I left Georgetown too fast. I didn't spend enough time to let it sink in."

Leslie nodded like she understood.

"She's not going to reappear, and the truth is, she wouldn't want to." I chuckled and raised a hand to blot a tear that threatened to ruin my eyeliner.

"That doesn't mean you can't be sad about her being gone." Leslie cleared her throat and took a slow turn in the direction of her next question. "Are you sure she's all you're missing?"

I knew where Leslie was going with her question, and she was right. "I miss Nigel."

Leslie released a long breath. "Have you talked to him?"

"Not yet."

"You should call him."

I nodded. "I will."

"You don't have to take this job."

I sighed. "It's an easy win for me. Three years isn't a big commitment. It's a chance to come back strong."

"Three years is a long time when you're not in your purpose." Leslie twisted her lips. I could see she was thinking through something. Then she asked, "Do you remember that time we went to the Jersey Shore when we were kids? We stayed at that resort called Beach Cabana or something like that."

I frowned. "Barely. What were we, like eleven or twelve?"

"Twelve." Leslie continued. "We entered that diorama building contest thingy that they had in the children's program."

"Go on," I said, interested in where she was going with this.

"We wanted to build the beach house, but we got stuck with the castle, and I didn't really think the castle was that bad once I started working with it, but you hated it. When we were done, you threw yours in the trash."

"Right. There was no room for it in the car."

Leslie shook her head. "It wasn't about the car. You said, 'I don't need to keep it. I didn't want to build it anyway.'"

I was a quick study on my cousin's subtext, so I read between the lines. "Is this where you tell me to explore my commitment issues and stop walking away from things?"

"This is where I tell you to do something *you* want to do. Build something you want to keep forever." Leslie studied me before speaking again. "You are smart and talented, Casey. You don't have to settle. You don't have to do things you don't want to do."

"Doing things you don't want to do is called adulting."

"Not always. Sometimes it's running scared and playing it safe."

I thought about what she said. The words Great-grandma Odessa wrote in the letter to Pearl came to my mind.

"*Do the things I couldn't. The women before you could only dream their dreams.*"

My great-grandmother had given me permission to dream my dreams over a hundred years ago. She'd written those words for every woman in the family who would read them—from Pearl on down to me. I had more choices than many women. The only thing holding me back from a new life was fear of letting go of my old life, but still tension eclipsed all other emotions.

Leslie's phone rang. "I have to get this, but let me know how it goes."

I agreed to, then I tapped out of the call.

I closed my eyes and rolled my head around, attempting to release the tension in my neck.

Do the things I couldn't.

Those words reverberated in my mind. They swirled down to my chest, causing it to get tight. My heart was trying to speak, but this contract was a way for me to rise from the ashes. I could teach my followers that we can come back from mistakes. But was I reaching, and by *reaching*, I mean settling for sharing that message the easy way? I didn't want to be a brand ambassador. It was modeling, and as much as I had loved modeling, it was behind me. I'd already lived that dream and buried it. I wanted to . . .

"Ma'am, which side of the street do you want me to take you to?" The driver's question cut into my thoughts.

I opened my eyes and looked out of the vehicle, then at the driver. He'd turned left onto East Thirty-Fifth Street. "The Fifth Avenue side, please."

He nodded, knowing that was the side where the entrance

was for the offices in the building. Once again, I noted the time. I had thirty minutes to make my meeting. We were about ten minutes away in terms of distance, but I was miles away—seven hundred of them to be exact—in my heart. I squeezed my hands into tight fists. Granna's face entered my mind. That conversation we had when I'd finally told her why I'd come to Georgetown.

"I don't even live here, Granna."

I remembered the way she'd inspected me before she spoke the deep truth she'd been holding.

"You don't really live up there either."

It had kind of jolted me then, but I hadn't given that much thought since. It was time to consider her words. If who I was, was incomplete here, did I belong somewhere else?

I opened my phone and went to Instagram. I visited Casey B, bypassed the evergreen content, and went to the pictures I posted prior to the vow renewal. There were months of images for the ceremony, but interspersed were pictures and videos of my sponsored content, makeup hauls, clothing hauls, and every other thing I did—from asking followers to get dressed or put on makeup with me to just following me during my day-to-day life. It all seemed so distant and unimportant now. What I used to live, breathe, and eat for sixteen hours a day didn't matter. I sighed.

And then there was the farm. Leaving the farm seemed an unbearable, impossible task. How was I going to get through my day without seeing Nigel? Who was gonna take care of the herb garden? Who was going to tie and string the basil, thyme, rosemary, and oregano? Who would give out Granna's tinctures and salves? I had duties that were important and enjoyable. I didn't have to be here.

I tapped until I came to my page, I Am Black Mixed with Black, and scrolled through the pictures, noting how much I loved every single one of them and every single experience—from the food, to Pawleys, the Gullah market, and then there was the farm and the house. There was love there, and these pictures... I smiled to myself. They were quite good. This was my art.

It didn't take long to reach the building. I gathered my things, paid the driver, and hurried into the lobby. The familiar art deco decor that I always admired in this building blurred in the background as I walked to the elevator banks.

Once I reached the twentieth floor, I was greeted warmly by the receptionist. "Ms. Black, we're so glad to have you. Can I get anything for you?"

"Do you have a private office I can use?"

She ushered me into an empty conference room and turned on the light. After she left, I called my mother.

"I'm stuck on the Williamsburg. We've just started moving, I should be there in twenty or so minutes."

Like me, my mother was obsessive about time. Her not being here was meant to be. "I want to take this meeting by myself."

"What? Why?"

Because I don't need you. Not today. I thought it, but said, "I just do. So you should go home."

My mother groaned before speaking. "Casey, this is already a done deal. You're signing papers and taking PR photos."

"I'll call you when I'm finished."

"But—"

"Please," I said firmly, hoping with all my might that this was the bridge of understanding that we would cross together. That my mother would respect my choice and accept the fact that I had agency over my life. "I know what I'm doing."

My mother released a heavy sigh. "Call me when it's over."

I stepped out of the office, and the receptionist escorted me into the conference room. There were seven people sitting around the table. They were undoubtedly the heavies who ran Now Cosmetics.

A well-styled woman bounced to her feet and stuck out her hand as she rushed to greet me. "Casey, so good to see you. I'm Essie Caldwell. I'm the director of new products."

"It's nice to meet you," I said, shaking her hand.

She went around the room introducing me to everyone whose titles and names I didn't register fully due to introduction overload. She offered me a seat and then took a phone call she claimed was urgent. The other people in the room engaged me in short conversations for a few minutes and then my own phone pinged. They backed away when I removed it from my bag.

It was a text from Nigel: I hope everything goes well today. 🙏

I couldn't stop the full-blown smile that inched over my face. He'd remembered the meeting right down to the time. I pressed Like on his message and put my phone on Do Not Disturb. Then I dropped my eyes to the black leather portfolio on the table in front of me. I flipped it open and saw the contract. Dread crawled up my back. I had no enthusiasm for this.

Granna's words came to my memory. *"Time don't always belong to you."* She'd been talking about love, but it applied to everything. I didn't want to waste three years doing something I dreaded starting. My great-grandmother Odessa's words also hovered in the peripheral of my mind.

"The women before you could only dream their dreams. They hoped for a better day for their daughters and all the women down their family line."

I owed it to them to choose my dream. I owed it to myself. And it wasn't this job. It was a life in Georgetown with a vegetable in one hand and a camera in the other. My dream was a place. A place that had crept into my heart and settled there. It called to me from seven hundred miles away. I wasn't experiencing reverse culture shock. My subconscious was rejecting the life I didn't want.

Essie was off the phone. Just as I was about to tell her I had something to say, the door whooshed open, and a man entered bringing big-shot exuberance into the room. I recognized him from the website. He was the CEO. He walked to me and took my hand. I stood.

"Casey, Rick Lassiter. It's a pleasure. I was told you had to delay this meeting. You have my condolences on the loss of your grandmother."

I thanked him. He released my hand, barked an order for water, and took a seat across from me. Smiling, he said, "Let's get this show on the road. I have a plane to catch."

One of the women, I surmised an assistant whom they hadn't even had the courtesy to name during introductions, rushed a bottled water to him. Essie stood. She picked up a remote and clicked it. A white screen slowly inched down. With another click, the first page of a presentation appeared.

"May I say something?" I inched my bottom out of my seat again and stood to my full height. All eyes were on me. "I appreciate this offer, but I've reconsidered."

Rick pitched an eyebrow. "Reconsidered what?"

"The position."

"What about it have you reconsidered?" Essie asked.

"I'm not going to take it."

Every face in the room turned red. Rick cleared his throat. "Not taking it?"

I folded my hands together in front of my waist. "I'm not."

"What is this? Are you looking for more money? The deal memo was sent to her, right?" Rick swung his swivel chair in the direction of Essie and the other executives.

The word *yes* flew out of all their mouths.

"I received the deal memo and the contract."

"You agreed to the terms. The time for negotiation is over," Essie said.

"I'm not trying to negotiate. It's not about money." I pressed my lips together and then opened my mouth again. "I'm not interested in the position. I apologize for wasting everyone's time. I was already en route when I made my final decision."

"You've got to be kidding." The woman who was introduced to me as the director of marketing was visibly livid. "You've got to be." She looked at Essie, her next comment directed to her. "This is why I didn't want her." Then she looked back at me. "Do you not realize how lucky you are to have this? I didn't want you. You got *this* as a favor to an old friend who had to *beg* us to offer it to you."

Blood pumped loud and hard in my ears. My mind raced to thoughts about who could have fought for me, but I knew where the answer to that lay—with my mother. "I didn't know I had friends in such high places," I said. That further enraged them. "I'm sorry about your time."

The marketing director laughed. "Good luck. You're going to need it." She dropped back into her chair and swiveled it around until tufted leather was all I could see.

I turned too. I didn't give them a backward glance. They didn't deserve it, not after screaming about how much they didn't want me anyway. Adrenaline fueled by the conviction and strength I'd gotten from Odessa, Ida, and Victoria Black moved my feet across the floor until I was on the other side of the conference room door. I smiled and thanked the women who had the strength to endure so I could soar.

Within five minutes, I was back on the street and grateful to be breathing air outside the building. This time I ordered a rideshare. While I was waiting, I walked to the street vendor and got me a good ole New York City hot dog with mustard and sauerkraut. I took a selfie near the stand and uploaded it to the message for Nigel with the text: I told you I eat street food.

My car arrived. The driver confirmed I was going to Park Slope and pulled away from the curb. The ride out of the city was just as good as the ride coming in, but even better because I felt better, relieved, free. I decided to make a video. I'd learned a lot about myself over the past months. I could share with my followers. Who knows, maybe they would follow my photography.

I flopped down on a beanbag chair and opened my Instagram account. I turned on the camera. I pressed the button for Live. When I came into focus, I used my free hand to wave and then I said, "Hey, family. It's me, Casey."

I waited ten, twenty, forty, sixty seconds until the hearts and comments welcoming me back flooded in.

@YourGirlCaseyB We miss you!
@YourGirlCaseyB Where have you been?
@YourGirlCaseyB You look beautiful.

People said the same things over and over again.

I appreciated their kindness. I replied, "I miss you all. I took a break. A long one. I was burned out, so I needed it. I'm glad to see so many of you didn't unfollow me." I chuckled and continued. "Part of my message on this page was that all women are beautiful and that we all deserve happiness, but I'm not sure I have always believed it myself.

"After I first made the infamous video, my mother told me to pivot. To be honest and vulnerable. To help my followers see that bad things happen to all of us, even influencers, but I didn't want to do it, and now I know why. I spoke beauty and authenticity, but when push came to shove, I couldn't live it. But the break was a good thing. I learned a lot about myself and found a new fountain of strength."

I paused to smile and read comments. "I can't give you all the details yet because I have a project in the works, but I will say I've been healing and growing and learning. I have the happiness I deserve."

I stayed online for an hour. My message had been only about ten minutes, but I spent the rest of the time chatting with my abandoned followers. I didn't tell them I owned a farm or about Granna. I was saving that for the documentary. But I did tell them I would be publishing a new page where they could keep up with Casey Black. @YourGirlCaseyB was no longer who I was.

I looked at the time on the phone. Nigel hadn't texted me back. He wasn't on his phone all the time like most people— like me—so it was fine. I went to the page I made for him. As expected, it was still private. There was still only the one picture I'd uploaded, the one with the two of us sitting in the water near the edge of the beach. My head was back on his shoulder. My hair smooshed against the side of his face, the sun warming the richness of our skin. And then there was a new caption that he must have recently added: *Looks like love.*

The emotions I'd pushed way down when I left Georgetown came bubbling up. It did look like love. It felt like it too. I imagined him in the hot tub. Relaxed, shirtless, giving enough masculine energy to power every piece of farm equipment I owned. Was he missing me as much? Was he sulking as he soaked?

I hoped so because there was a Black for that problem, and it was me. I was slipping in as soon as I got back to Georgetown. But there was one thing I needed to do first.

38

—

THIS NEW SEASON REQUIRED TURNED SOIL.

I texted Drew and asked him to meet me at a restaurant near his office. I spotted the back of Drew's head before the hostess moved in the direction of his table. Funny, he had his back to the door. Drew never did that. I curiously wondered if he was afraid to face me. The hostess stopped at the table, and Drew raised his eyes to mine. A slight smile tugged at the corner of his lips. Ever the gentleman, he scooted his chair back.

"No, stay," I said, slipping into my chair without his help.

The hostess put menus in front of us. It had been only three months since I'd seen Drew, but it felt like years. I wasn't being mean or critical when I assessed him. He looked tired and older.

"You look great." He told no lies. I had never looked so good in my life.

I thanked him and reached for my menu.

He cleared his throat. "I read about the Now Cosmetics thing. Good for you."

I shrugged as I perused the menu. "I turned it down."

The waitress swooped in and placed two glasses of wine in front of us. I was quick to slide mine aside. "Actually, I'll have . . ."

I hesitated. "Do you have sweet tea?" The stuff had grown on a sistah.

"Sweetened tea." She corrected me, northern style. "Lemon?"

"Yes, plenty of lemon and half the ice." We used too much ice in the North. It froze the flavor out the glass.

"Did you need me to take that?" She pointed her pen in the direction of my glass of wine.

"No, he'll have both." I glanced at Drew, and he reached for his first glass. He always had two—especially at dinner.

"Did you need more time with the menu?"

He closed his menu. "I'm ready." Those words had a double meaning—the look in his eyes clued me into that.

"Nothing for me," I said. My phone pinged, and I reached for it while Drew placed his order.

It was Swella. I silenced the phone and returned it to my bag. "You wanted to talk."

He cleared his throat. "I don't want our last conversation to be the one we had on the street. I want you to know what happened at the end of the marriage wasn't your fault."

The heat of my temper rose, but I contained it. He didn't deserve to see me emotional. "I know that. You couldn't possibly think that I believe I deserved to be humiliated by you that way."

"Of course not." He took a deep breath. "Let me get this out, okay?" He took another sip of his wine. "I treated you poorly, and I'm sorry."

"Drew, I know you're in a relationship with that lawyer from your firm, and I know it started when we were together, so 'sorry' is cliché and tired."

He smiled uncomfortably. "She doesn't have anything to do with us."

Only a coward would say his mistress had nothing to do with his marriage. "I don't want to spend time talking about your girlfriend. What I don't understand is why you couldn't have told me before the ceremony. Why didn't you let me cancel before everyone was there?"

"Because I was going to do the ceremony." He stalled and cleared his throat. Again. It was a nervous habit. Another weakness for him as a lawyer. "My girlfriend gave me an ultimatum. She told me if I went through with the vow renewal, she would leave the country. She's from England. Her family is still there. She was packing."

I fought to keep my voice even and low. "Since when do you respond to ultimatums?"

The waitress interrupted, placing my tea on the table. Once she was gone, Drew continued. "Since she's pregnant."

I blinked rapidly a few times but held on to my nonemotional composure as best I could.

"Six months. I thought you knew. I thought your mother would tell you. She knew before I signed the divorce papers."

He was having a baby without me, seemingly effortlessly. That stung—just a little, but it did. "She didn't tell me."

"I'm shocked. She didn't like me much. I thought she'd revel in telling you that."

I raised my glass and took a sip of my tea. It was nothing like the tea in South Carolina. There was no comfort in it. "Finish your story."

"She thought I was leading her on when I told her . . ."

"That you didn't love me anymore." I nodded. "Otherwise, why would you be renewing your vows?"

"Right. I didn't want her to leave."

I guffawed. "You let your girlfriend manipulate you into embarrassing your wife."

"I wanted the life I could have with her. A simpler life."

I shot him a nasty look before I looked away to ask the next question. "So I was too complicated?" I cut my eyes back to him to see his truth.

Drew didn't respond.

"You were supposed to say no." I laughed bitterly. All efforts to not show emotion were over.

"Case, it's like I said, it was the social media. It was everything, and I should have talked to you about it more. I should have told you I needed our lives to change, but I don't know that I had the faith to believe that it would matter."

"Why wouldn't it have mattered?"

"Because it was bigger than me, Casey. There's a man out there that can get you to put the phone down and pay attention. I'm not that man. You never loved me like that."

"That's ridiculous."

"No, it's not, and you know it. This marriage has been a trio from the beginning."

"You're going to blame my mother now."

"Not your mother. Your fandom."

"And yet, up until today, I haven't posted a single video since we split up." I laughed. "See how you were wrong about me."

"You're right. I guess we were wrong about each other." Drew reached for my hand, but I didn't let him take it. "We grew apart, but I didn't want you to believe a lie. I didn't renew our vows because I was pressured not to and that was my bad. I owed you more than that. I owed you the truth way before that day at the church." Drew took in a deep breath and let it out hard. "You're an amazing woman, Casey. Whoever ends up with you is going to be a lucky man."

Nigel entered my mind. Good, kind, patient, *honest* Nigel.

"Are you okay?" Drew asked.

"Yeah, I was just thinking about the man who's going to end up with me. He's waiting. I need to go." I stood. "Thanks for the closure. I wish you well." This time when my lips parted, my smile was genuine. I turned and strolled out of the restaurant on the same steam I'd used earlier when I left the conference room.

The soil was turned.

39

MY MOTHER WAS ANGRY ABOUT THE NOW COSMETICS DEAL.
We'd gone ten rounds about it already and I didn't care. I'd
stepped out of the spotlight, and I liked my new life. That wasn't
really what the tension was about it. She'd called in a favor, and
I'd made her look bad. But that wasn't my fault. She should have
told me.

We were quiet for a long time. I wasn't looking at her. She
wasn't looking at me. We both sat in dining room chairs with
our legs crossed over our knees and elbows on the table looking
at opposite sides of the room. We'd had more tension in the past
three months than we'd had in years. My social media blowup
had literally blown up my life. As painful and shameful as it had
all been, I wouldn't change it. I needed to inspect the wreckage it
left behind. That wreckage was my life.

"You knew Drew's girlfriend was pregnant." I was expecting
something to enter her eyes, but she was as stoic as if I'd mentioned Drew had an ingrown toenail. "Mother, why didn't you
tell me?"

"I thought it would hurt you, and you were already hurt
enough because he left."

"But, Mom, it's been months. I've been playing the tape of

my marriage over and over in my head, trying to figure out how I missed that Drew had so little love and regard for me. How I got caught out there like that. You could have answered that question."

"I didn't see you as being caught. This is his mess."

"It isn't just Drew's mess. My marriage is a part of my story. It is the story of the ending of my marriage. And I had a right to know. You did the same thing Drew did."

"Casey, when you have . . ." My mother stopped.

I knew what she was going to say. She'd said it a million times when I was growing up: "*Go ahead. When you have a child, you'll understand how hard it is to parent.*"

"I'm not your child. I'm your adult daughter. Those two are not the same thing."

My mother rolled her bottom lip in. Her lashes blinked rapidly a few times like I'd said something that jarred her.

"I had a right to know. I didn't need to be blindsided in some restaurant by him. *That* was hurtful."

My mother's eyes widened. She shrugged and pushed back in her chair. "Okay. I'm sorry."

We were quiet again, and my mother asked, "You're going back to South Carolina, aren't you?"

I nodded.

"Is that why you went looking for your daddy's people? So you could replace me?"

I reached for her hand and squeezed it. "You will always be my mother." I pinned her with my eyes. "Always."

My mother placed her other hand on top of our hands. "Baby, I know that better than you do."

"So you have no reason to think anybody can replace you."

"The Blacks are so lucky. They get to come in for the shiny part of your life. After you've been raised."

My mother was conveniently forgetting that she was the reason they got me after I'd been raised, but there was no point rehashing that. We'd already had that conversation. She did what she did, and she was apparently good with it.

"You keep talking about me having a new family, not me having more family. They are *more* family. More people to care about me and love me and teach me things. No one's ever going to replace you."

My mother took a deep breath and removed her hands from mine. "I was wrong to publish your page. And I see now that I should have talked to you about many things I did over the years, but this Drew thing, that wasn't business, baby. I wanted to protect you."

My mother's eyes got wet. Again, a rare occurrence. She continued, "I knew things changed between you and Drew. Anyone looking from the outside in could see, so I wasn't surprised to find out he had an affair, which is why I hired somebody to confirm it. I was determined he was not going to hurt you that way and then walk away with your hard-earned money so he could spend on his new woman." She shook her head and swiped at her eyes. "I may not be perfect, but let me tell you this . . . I'd fight a lion for you."

My mother had fought for me my whole life. I knew she loved me, but healthy boundaries were long overdue, and I was setting them. We stood and I hugged her, as tight as I could. It was a Granna-and-Aunt-Thea kind of hug. A hug that gave and received the full measure of a person's heart. When we separated, we both had tears to wipe.

"I love you, Mom, but I've fallen in love with Georgetown, and I'm going back to it and everything and everyone there."

My mother nodded. "I guess it's settled. You're going to be a farmer and a photographer."

"It is, but that may not be all. I inherited some money from Granna. I might be investing in a resort on the beach."

My mother's interest was piqued with that statement. "Well, I guess I'll be breaking that vow."

Her words made my heart smile. "Promises made in anger probably should be revaluated at some point."

My mother reached up and touched a stray curl and twirled it a bit. "You know, I really do like your hair like this."

"I look fresh," I teased.

Warmth filled my mother's eyes. "You look happy."

40

SWELLA AND LESLIE COLLAPSED ON MY SOFA.

"I don't know why you two are so tired. All you did was label things."

"A million things." Leslie yawned. "You're a hoarder."

Swella picked up her iPad. She tapped a few times and asked, "What size truck are we going to need?"

"*Hmm*, I don't know. I mean, I'm not taking much, so maybe a ten-foot."

"You need a ten-foot truck for your clothes and makeup. Is that little farmhouse going to hold all your stuff?"

I tossed a pillow at Leslie. "Maybe I won't be staying at the farmhouse. Maybe I'll be staying with my man."

Leslie snatched back her head. "Alrighty now, miss. Go on with your grown self."

"*Gwan*," I laughed. "That's the way the Gullah say it."

Leslie sighed playfully. "Lord, she's going to have a new language."

"I've always wanted to be bilingual." I put the last of the books in a box and taped it shut. "I'm done for the night."

Leslie stood. "So are we. We'll continue this packing for your shacking in the morning."

"My Uber is here," Swella said, popping to her feet.

I walked them to the door and gave both a hug.

"Thank you for not firing me," Swella said.

"You are going to be the best social media manager Black Farm ever had."

"Aren't I the first?"

"Be glad you get to set the standard," Leslie said. "The bar is low. You can't mess the job up."

I watched them leave, Leslie in her car and Swella in her Uber, closed the door, and returned to the living room. This had been my home for seven years, but I was moving on to better.

The doorbell rang. I looked around to see what one of my people might have left behind but didn't see anything.

"Okay, what did you forget?" I yelled, pulling the door open.

It wasn't one of my people. I unlocked the security door.

It was Nigel. I almost fell over. He stepped in and dropped a duffle bag on the floor.

Nigel's warm eyes and slow grin stirred butterflies in my belly. He had a fresh haircut and a new graphic T-shirt that read *I Love New York*. In all the years I'd lived here, I'd never been so happy to see someone at this door.

I practically jumped on him, wrapping my arms around his neck. "What are you doing here?"

He squeezed me tight. "Surprising you." He kissed me and let me go. He reached just outside the door and picked up something I couldn't see and put it behind his back. "Close your eyes."

I happily did.

"You can look now."

I opened them to find a small basket with three full-size Black Beauty tomatoes in his hand, complete with a red bow. "I thought I'd bring the harvest to you."

If I could have melted into a puddle, I would have. I took the basket and brought it close to my chest. "It's beautiful."

Nigel released a long breath, took my basket, and placed it on the foyer table. "Just like you." With one arm, he pulled me to him; with the other, he tilted my chin up. A surge of adrenaline electrified my entire body. My heart stopped right before our lips met. We found our rhythm immediately. We never lost it, even when we were apart—be it miles or across the yard or on opposite sides of the farm. Nigel was always with me, but I savored every second of his taste and his heat right now.

His phone rang, startling us. We laughed and stepped apart.

"I have to check this." He dropped his eyes to it. He crinkled his nose. "It's my mother." He took his call.

I went back to the door, looked outside to see how he'd arrived, and noted my car on the street. After a brief conversation—where he assured his mother he was safe, he'd found me, and he was okay in the big bad city—the call ended.

"You can't let those country mice come to the city unchaperoned," I said, laughing. I hiked a finger over my shoulder toward the door. "You drove."

"I figured you might need it."

I threw my head back a little. "How did you find me?"

"It wasn't easy." His eyes got big. "Not like searching property tax records in Georgetown. I started that way, but it got overwhelming fast, so I used social media, of all things."

"No!"

A satisfied grin drew his dimple out. "I found a comment Leslie made, and I messaged her."

"Seriously?"

"I had a fifteen-year-old tutor."

I laughed at his silliness. "I'm impressed with you."

"Are you now?" He closed the small space between us.

"More impressed than before, and that's not easy."

He took my hand. "I'm in love with you, Casey. I didn't

tell you that in South Carolina, but I'm telling you now." Nigel paused. His eyes said there was a "but" coming. "I know you have a life here and a career, and I would never want you to shrink for me, but I'm proposing that we love each other anyway."

It was a good "but." All I could do was swoon his name. "Nigel."

He smiled warmly. "Whenever we see each other is when we see each other."

"A long-distance relationship?"

His head inclined sideways. "Yes, because you're worth it, and I know I'm worth it. We'll eventually figure out how to be together."

My knees got weaker. "You came all the way to New York to choose me. Do you have any idea how badly I need to be chosen, Nigel Evanston?"

"Yeah, I do, because so do I."

He kissed me again, and happiness filled me. More love made my heart sing.

"I'm glad you're here, because you're a hard worker. I'm going to need some help packing up this house."

His eyes roamed the room. There were empty boxes and full ones waiting to be taped closed and sticky notes with instructions on nearly everything. He looked back at me and pointed. "You're packing."

"I turned down the job with Now Cosmetics. I've decided I'm moving to Georgetown."

Sexy confidence filled his eyes. "Is that so?"

"I miss it. I miss the Blacks, the food, the river, the weather, the beauty."

"That was a whole lot of missing and not a single word about the man who drove twelve hours to get here."

"I miss the farm, and . . ." I teased him with hesitation. "Sir,

I missed you when you were in the Airstream, so you know I've missed you the last couple of days." I smiled. "And by the way, I love you too."

Nigel sat and pulled me onto his lap.

"Oh, wait," I said. "I have a phone call to make."

His forehead furrowed. "Right now?"

"Right now," I said, dialing.

"Hey, baby girl," Aunt Thea greeted me cheerfully.

"Auntie, I need you to do something for me." I looked at Nigel and continued, "I need a shower installed in Granna's house. Do you know anyone?"

"Now you know there's a Black for that. I'll get right on it."

"Thanks, Auntie." I ended the call and tossed my phone on the sofa. "Now that that's out of the way."

I'd managed to excite and amuse the man at the same time. Nigel kissed me until I was silly enough to believe in love again, but this time I understood it. Love wasn't supposed to save me or validate me or prove anything to anyone. Love had one job, and that was to add to the joy I already had. I would never overwork it again.

Epilogue

EIGHTEEN MONTHS LATER . . .

"HURRY UP WITH THE CHAMPAGNE!"

Aunt Thea's voice not only carried through her cell phone but floated on the wind and crashed with the rapidly flowing waves from the river. She fussed at the buffet she set up and slapped the hands of folks who were prematurely attempting to steal a nibble before grace was said. What was supposed to be popcorn and lemonade became a full-on meal with shrimp and oyster perlou, sticky chicken wings, alligator bites, greens, and hush puppies for more than fifty family members.

Nigel finished helping Jay and a few of the others set up the 150-foot viewing screen we'd rented for this occasion—viewing the documentary *Down by Black River: An American Family*. Brooke and I had convinced her boss that this story was a better one than the Casey B story. I was the narrator, so there were still segments of my life and my journey down here, but it focused more on the history of our family, specifically as it pertained to Georgetown and farming. Brooke wanted a serious project, and I gave her one.

We chose to watch it at the river, the place where we gathered under a tent for every special occasion. I only wished my grandmother was here to see it, too, but then I realized she saw everything. Aunt Thea said heaven was generous that way. I don't know how she supposed that, but I believed it. The faith of my ancestors, I did not question.

Nigel walked over to where I was sitting. Seeing him still made my knees go weak.

"Let me take a load off." He reached into my lap and took our three-month-old son from my arms. Elijah Black Evanston squirmed in his father's hands and smiled and cooed. Daddy was his favorite person—that is, when he wasn't breastfeeding.

Nigel settled him with that velvety voice that made everything better. Not only for the baby but for me. Marrying him was one of the best decisions I'd made in my life.

Uncle Roger stood and led the grace. The food was eaten. The sun went down and we were able to see the screen. After a champagne toast, the video began to stream.

I dropped my head on Nigel's shoulder. He wrapped his arm around mine and pulled me close. "You ready?" he asked.

I nodded.

The video opened with me standing in front of the sign for Black Farm.

I said, "This documentary about my family is dedicated to my grandmother, Mrs. Ida Black. My name is Casey Black, and this is the place I call home."

Author's Note

THIS BOOK STRETCHED ME. I'VE ALWAYS LOVED HISTORY, BUT I did not know much about Georgetown prior to doing research for this novel. I chose it simply because of Black River. As it is situated in the heart of the Gullah Geechee Corridor and rose to prominence due not only to its indigo and rice production, but its unique political gains during Reconstruction (every word in my book about the politics/elections is true), I knew I made the right choice.

I sold this book to my editor as a contemporary story about Casey Black. I was halfway through the first draft when Odessa Conway Black spoke to me. She woke me at two o'clock in the morning with the words: "I have something to say." What was a novel about Casey and her grandfather, Eddie Black, became a story about Casey, Ida, and Odessa Black . . . a story about the women. I am glad I'm not a heavy sleeper.

There are some parts of this book that are based on snippets from my own family history. For example, my ancestors' proximity to Black River, the purchase of the land, the tragic disappearance of Earl, and the use of herbs for medicinal purposes. My grandfather, Eddie McKnight, was a local farmer and healer who died shortly after his hundredth birthday. But much of the story is straight from my imagination . . . things that I know could have happened, probably happened, and situations I hope happened for my family and others who look like me. The earthquake of 1886 was a real tragedy and the advertisements seeking lost relatives after Freedom was a hopeful and painful system utilized by many freedpeople for decades.

I am just three generations from Emancipation, with my great-grandfather Elijah McKnight having been born enslaved and great-grandfather George Wilson, probably born enslaved. My ancestors sacrifices are never far from my mind. My family survived. They created legacy. Love, character, and faith endured. Once I started writing the historical chapters, it was my goal to dignify them by rooting this story in truth, while sprinkling it with what could have been possible because they dared to dream of a better day for themselves and me.

Acknowledgments

LORD JESUS, THANK YOU FOR THIS GREAT STORY. I COULDN'T have come up with this on my own if I sat with a pen and paper from now until the end of my days. Every good thing I do, I do because of You. Ephesians 2:10.

My parents, Jimmie and Bessie McKnight, you were there from conception until the last word was typed, listening to every version, change, plot problem, putting up with my moods, and watching all the happy dances when I had something to celebrate. I love you.

My sons, Aaron and Micah, everything I do, I do for you. Hugs from Mom.

My editor, Laura Wheeler, thank you for believing in me enough to buy this book and then embracing Odessa's story too. I appreciate your support and guidance. You are a cheerleader with a heart of gold. Thanks also to everyone on the team at Thomas Nelson for welcoming me and supporting me through the production and promotion of this novel, including my new editor, Lizzie Poteet, and my copy editor, Chandra Sparks-Splond.

Emily Sylvan Kim of the Prospect Agency—we've only just begun, but I know you're a champion for women writers and for that, I'm grateful to have you on my team.

ACKNOWLEDGMENTS

My mentor, Victoria Christopher Murray—thank you for always being available to me. You come through with just what I need to hear. Every single time. You have been a blessing.

Author/writer friends—Unoma Nwankwor, Sherri L. Lewis, Tia McCollors, Michelle Jackson, Vanessa Riley, Vanessa Miller, Pat Simmons, Piper Huguley, Jacquelin Thomas, Michelle Stimpson, Veronica Johnson, Felicia Murrell, Jeida Walker, thank you for it all! Did I say Unoma?!! ☺

Bookish Queens—Angela Anderson and Kenyatta Ingram. Y'all hold a sistah down. Muah!

My siblings Cynthia and Kenneth, my daughter-in-love, Tamaria, Uncle Downing and Aunt Verdica (Nell) Kennedy, Aunt Delores Burgess, Aunt Dorothy and Uncle Dave Plowden, Uncle Frank, Uncle Larry and my other family—you inspire and encourage me.

My cousin and spiritual leader, Ronnie Smiling—thank you for dropping the Word, sharpening this iron, and being more than family. You are my friend.

I extend my deepest gratitude to the following for their assistance:

Mr. Andrew Rodrigues of the Gullah Museum, 3583 King Street, Georgetown, South Carolina, for his informative lecture about Gullah culture and the Michelle Obama Story Quilt.

Mr. Simon Rutledge of Georgetown, whose knowledge of the Georgetown educational system during Reconstruction was invaluable.

The staff at McKnight-Fraser Funeral Home, Georgetown.

Finally, a special thank you to Robin Caldwell (Black culinary historian extraordinaire), one of the most righteous, sharing, intelligent, knowledgeable, and inspiring women I know. Thank you for stepping into my life. Many miles separate us, but God has for real knit our hearts together. Thank you for the prayer for

Reparative Justice that you shared with me and allowed Nigel to share with my readers. I've told you privately and now I'll share it publicly, God used your words to calm the anxiety rolling through me so I could get this story told. Thank you for being a mentor and a friend.

I've written acknowledgments at least twenty times. Someone is always forgotten. If that's you, I apologize. I'm going to say it like they say in the old church, "Charge it to my head and not my heart."

Love, peace, and blessings to my readers!

Discussion Questions

1. Casey's relationship with her mother is fraught with tension. What would be difficult about having Victoria as a mother? Do you think Casey was too hard on her?

2. Victoria's history with the Black family was indeed complicated. How right or wrong was she at the time of Matthew's death? Was she at all justified in keeping Casey away from them? She was estranged from many of her own relatives. Do you think she was selfish or a living example of a hurting person, hurting other people?

3. How might Casey's life have been different if she grew up knowing her grandmother and the other members of the Black family? Do you/have you had someone like Granna in your life? How have they influenced you?

4. The theme of grief was present in many aspects of this story for all the characters. Casey's mother said, "Sometimes we have to grieve the dead thing in the quiet of the night. When we lie on our beds, we can shed our tears because life doesn't allow us to stop moving." How has this thinking played out in your life and the lives of women you know? Do you consider it to be necessary or potentially unhealthy?

5. How did Casey's experience with her family's faith affect her? Do you believe it played a part in her emotional healing and the decisions she made in the final chapters of the book?

6. The freedom to do what we want as opposed to what others expect can be a hinderance to finding our true purpose, particularly for women. Discuss some of the examples of this in the book and share a personal story about how this thinking has benefited or harmed you.

7. There were several parallels between Casey's life and Odessa's. Discuss the similarities and differences. What are some things you can and should do that women before you could not? Have you fully actualized your advantages?

8. Do you think Odessa compromised too much for the men in her life—first for Elijah and then for her father? Do you think she'd make a different decision today?

9. I have no doubt Granna had been praying for a new wife for Nigel when her lovely, albeit wounded, granddaughter showed up in their lives. She did everything she could to push them together. Was this wisdom or overstepping?

10. I enjoy writing about emotionally intelligent men. Nigel was hard not to love, but Casey and Ava were wrong about what he wanted. Why do you suppose that was?

11. Casey and Nigel discuss the fact that neither of them learned very much about Black history in school. Did you learn anything from this story?

12. Casey ultimately got everything she wanted because she made the decision to choose a different life. Her mother advised her to pivot (be honest with her followers) the day after the video, advice she did not take, which

ultimately led her to Georgetown. She eventually
did pivot in many ways and was transparent with her
followers. Why do you think she couldn't do it initially?

13. The use of symbolism for home and farming were
heavily used in the novel. What were some examples that
resonated with you? How do you define home?

From the Publisher

GREAT BOOKS

ARE EVEN BETTER WHEN THEY'RE SHARED!

Help other readers find this one:

- Post a review at your favorite online bookseller

- Post a picture on a social media account and share why you enjoyed it

- Send a note to a friend who would also love it—or better yet, give them a copy

Thanks for reading!

About the Author

Alex Johnson III Photography

RHONDA MCKNIGHT IS THE AUTHOR OF SEVERAL BESTSELL-ing novels, including *An Inconvenient Friend* and *What Kind of Fool*. She is the winner of the 2015 Emma Award for Inspirational Romance of the Year. She loves reading and writing books that touch the heart of women through complex plots and interesting characters in crisis. Themes of faith, forgiveness, and hope are central to her stories. Originally from a small coastal town in New Jersey, Rhonda writes from the comfort of her South Carolina home.

Visit her online at rhondamcknight.com
Instagram: @authorrhondamcknight
Twitter: @rhondamcknight
Facebook: @BooksByRhonda
Pinterest: @rhondamcknight1